Fae Warrior

Book Three: Soulstealer Trilogy

NICOLETTE REED

EPub Edition December 2014 ISBN: 978-0-9856401-7-0
Print Edition ISBN: 978-0-9856401-8-7

PRAISE FOR FAE HUNTER

"Once you start reading Fae Hunter, you won't be able to put it down. The action starts on the first page and never lets up for the entire book. Just when you think you can take a deep breath and maybe even put the book down for the evening, a new twist erupts that makes you keep reading for one more chapter and one more chapter and one more chapter…"
-Romance and Mystery Author and Editor Sally Berneathy

"This book has so many surprises, twists, and turns, I couldn't put it down."
-Paranormal Romance Guild Reviews

"I think it's this love triangle that made the book for me."
-Fantasy and Romance Author J.F. Jenkins

"Great world-building, engaging characters that quickly draw you into the story, and enough twists and turns to keep you flipping the pages."
-Fantasy and Romance Author Crista McHugh

"…if you want a kick-ass heroine who struggles to do her best and save her world then you should definitely check this book – and series – out."
-The Flutterby Room Reviews

TITLES BY NICOLETTE REED

Fae Hunter (The Soulstealer Trilogy, Book #1)
Mane Attraction (A Soulstealer Novella, Book #1.5)
Fae Guardian (The Soulstealer Trilogy, Book #2)
Mane Chance (A Soulstealer Novella, Book #2.5)
Fae Warrior (The Soulstealer Trilogy, Book #3)

"Those who play with the devil's toys will be brought by degrees to wield his sword."
- R. Buckminster Fuller

ACKNOWLEDGMENTS

Though this is the final installment in the Soulstealer Trilogy, it's definitely not my last book. Thank you to all the readers who have taken the time to leave positive reviews and who have loved the characters in my stories as much as I do. You are fuel to my creative fire. I'll keep stoking the flames as long as you are willing to be my audience.

This book would never have been finished without the many hours my critique partner and friend, author Sherri Shaw, put into this manuscript. She toiled as hard as I did on this one. Thank you!

As always I must thank my family. My darling son, I promise that someday soon I will get to writing the "Mister Spill" story you really want me to write for you as long as you will still illustrate it for me.

My loving husband, you are the inspiration for every tender moment I write. You are and will always be my hero.

CHAPTER ONE

"Taking a break already, Valora?" Orris poked his head through the turret of the nearest wall tower, his usual greasy brown locks washed and pulled back into a low ponytail. After the sting of his brother's death dissipated, the stench of poor hygiene worked like smelling salts to snap him back into action. He brought a butterbread to his mouth and took a large bite, letting the slight afternoon breeze blow the crumbs down upon the passersby below.

For the first time, I sat atop the wall walk with no motivation other than to watch over the people of Dell'Aria. To truly be their Guardian whether I was allowed to or not. As a child I played along the tops of the stone battlements to escape the prying eyes of those who viewed me as different and someone who should never have been allowed to live. When I got older, balancing along the narrow ledge proved my agility to the naysayers. Even without the wings of a full fae, I could have served in the King's Guard. Now that I was considered a princess, I couldn't technically be a Guardian. I was not sure what to call myself anymore. Especially with my fate spelled out in the well-worn page tucked deep in my pocket.

"No, Orris, I've been practicing all morning while you've been eating butterbreads, no doubt." I used my copper short sword for leverage to push myself to standing. Having found out the hard way that drawing a sword takes longer than getting hit, I always had my blade at the ready.

Each time a fae fell before me in battle, I felt the sharp pain of their death branded into my skull. I wouldn't forget, I couldn't forget. Any of them. Many had died, some because of me, and the throbbing ache refused to subside—a second pulse beating along with those who survived. Now more than ever, I felt prepared to ready a city and myself for battle.

"This is my first one. I've got a break from my watch if you want to practice your swing." He shoved the remainder of the cake into his mouth and swallowed hard. Orris, once my bitter enemy, now my sworn ally and protector. If his motivations included my newly minted title of princess, I wouldn't accept his loyalties, but Orris' devotion ran deeper. I'd tried to save his brother, and he never reminded me I failed.

"If you lose any more feathers I think my father will take my sword. Another time."

Orris shrugged and disappeared into the castle.

Everyone readies for battle in a different way. Dooley had magic, Aric had wings, and I had a sword. Whatever was happening, the three of us were meant to fight together. We were linked by our amulets and drew power from one another. However, Dooley now spent all his time with Pryn, learning spells and studying any text that might help us defeat Ravanna, the Demon King of Acheron. And then there was Aric.

"All right, ladies, we call this one the Ustrasana." In the

2

courtyard below, Aric led some of the fae women through a series of exercises he called yoga. "Naked yoga." Leave it to Aric to find another excuse to show off his body. And leave it to my wandering eyes to want to linger.

"Really push forward so you can get a deep back bend." Aric modeled the pose, pushing his bare pelvis forward. The memory of tracing each line of muscle cutting across his stomach made my fingers tingle. Once a lover, now a friend, both he and Dooley were untouchable to me now. I set aside my regrets and forced my mind on other, more pressing matters.

Aric had become the center of attention again after the revelation that he had the blessing of the Goddess Varuna. Despite his initial shunning of fame, he soon realized, better they worship at your feet than take your head. And he ingratiated himself deeper into their hearts by providing a welcome diversion from the burbling waters of Lake Mavrovo. The blood-red depths were a constant reminder of the impending apocalypse that threatened our floating fortress. I appreciated his presence as a much-needed distraction to those who couldn't fight. And for some of us who could. I pushed that thought to the back of my mind. My father, the king, might not like Aric's latest endeavor, but our priests, including Pryn, welcomed his silly diversion. Because of him, they didn't need to waste time counseling the panicked masses.

Aric stood, directing his attention to a passing cart loaded down with weapons as the voluptuous hips of one of the older fae pressed toward him. Elderly women, none shy about their bodies, occupied the entire front row. The young girls I was sure he'd hoped would attend were nowhere to be seen. I covered my mouth, biting my lips to hide my smile. The movement caught the attention of his roving eye.

"Valora!" He gestured to his newfound disciples. "You're all dismissed. Go home and prostrate yourself in reverence to the Goddess Varuna. We'll resume tomorrow." The front row stood, covering my view of Aric's naked lower half. Despite my better judgment, I searched through the spaces between the women to get a better look when he slipped his legs into supple white leather pants. My mouth suddenly ran as dry as the Ordos Desert and hotter than the dragons residing there. His eyes locked with mine as he tied the white silken straps of his vest across his sculpted torso.

He spread the soft blue feathers of his wings and shot gracefully into the air. His effortless movement made my heart skip a beat. I caught my breath before he landed beside me.

"Like what you saw?" One eyebrow cocked as he leaned against the parapet. He swept a hand through his hair and flipped the ice-blond locks over his shoulder.

"Are you kidding? You have every old marm in Dell'Aria naked and at your beck and call. I liked what I saw because it's hilarious." I ducked around him to head into the keep. My bed called to me, and my forced celibacy meant avoiding this conversation. The sun signaled midday, not a time for turning in, but sleep had eluded me the night before—a common occurrence these days. He reached out, grabbing me by the wrist, and pulled me a few steps toward him. Talented fingers trailed down my temple, gently tucking a loose auburn curl behind my ear. "Then why are you sweating?"

I swatted at his hand. "Because I've been practicing all morning. Some of us are actually trying to prepare for what's to come." Aric followed close behind, his breath tickling the back of my neck, the silk of his vest cool on my heated wings. He knew all too well how to weaken my resolve. As

4

long as I avoided eye contact, I might make it to my bedroom without having to deflect his advances.

"Don't get angry with me, Valora. It's not my fault Kit and Mane have been gone so long. That is what's really bothering you, right?"

The disappearance of my friends was only one of my worries. Hot tears welled up in the corners of my eyes, and I forced them to stop. Despite the protective bubble I erected around my thoughts, Aric could read me like a book. Showing weakness in front of him would be all the consent he needed to push things even further. And sleeping with him would be suicide because of the tension between the three of us.

The relationship between Dooley, Aric, and I remained unspoken. Reopening old wounds slows down the healing process. *Our success against Ravanna necessitated we work together.* Dooley's voice echoed inside my head, his painful mantra meant to keep me emotionally and physically at a distance. To push me away.

Following the path toward my room, I skirted the practice arena. The rosy scent of a dozen pairs of wings perfumed with naughty thimbleberry blooms blocked my escape route. Before me a hall packed full of hormonal adolescents and lonesome spinsters clamored to see over one another into the arena.

"Your students must have gotten lost." I pressed through the crowd, and the chattering and giggling abruptly stopped. Keen silence, and a particularly full pair of lilac wings, halted my forward progression. Even before I rose on my tiptoes, I knew the local celebrity causing the blockade.

Dooley stood several feet from me in the middle of the dusty practice arena, his once blue jeans now covered in black markings from his practice of the symbol magic. The tops of his hipbones were exposed just enough to remind me of the anatomy below his loose beltline. His tan skin glowed, sparkling in the midday light. Swirls of black sand drifted up lazily from a pile at his feet. His magnetic fingers moved with the purpose of a practiced performer, drawing the audience and the particles of ash dust into the palm of his hand.

The sand formed symbols in the air, something I'd never seen him do. Excitement rippled through the crowd at the sight. A fae girl with pink wings took in a sharp breath, and grabbed her friend's arm in awe.

I felt much the same as I watched his brown eyes blacken, pupils wide and liquid, like the last time he kissed me. The memory made my legs weak, and my body reissued the threat of giving out. The floor tilted. Aric rushed to my side, using the length of his body to brace me before I toppled into the crowd. I wished he were Dooley. The amulet at my neck flared to life—an unmistakable siren signaling my weakened state. I closed my hand around the shining red stone and tried to shove the blazing beacon down the front of my bodice to escape the notice of all those around me. I didn't escape his notice, though.

The sand splashed down to the floor and a plume of dust parted the sea of women who stood aside to let Dooley through. Relief flooded my limbs. If I had known I needed to resort to fainting to get that man's attention, I would have done it earlier.

Aric pulled me to his chest and whispered into my ear, "You're exhausted. Let me take you to your room."

Dooley's concerned stare turned to stone, but his stride lengthened in rigid determination.

I shut my eyes to stop the room from spinning. Aric gathered me up into his arms like a child, my exhaustion winning the war over common sense. I didn't want Dooley to get the wrong idea, but I was tired of trying to figure everything out and wired with unspent adrenaline. I might die before the war even started. There were days I would go without any sleep and times that the fae my father charged with keeping the "princess" tended to could barely pull me out of bed.

"I could use a little nap."

The scent of labdanum resin, with its heady notes of wood, earth, and smoke, caught my nose and heightened my senses, making me aware of Dooley's presence even before he spoke. "I'll take her."

"I can make sure she gets to bed safely." Aric's chest puffed out like some overinflated Sage Grouse. The show was over for the fae women, who I could feel shooting jealous daggers at me for my dilemma.

"I'll take her." Dooley's tone was flat and even—no sign that he cared one way or the other for me, only that he fulfilled his duty. After what happened between the three of us, I understood the reasons behind his anger. Even now, the sight of me in Aric's arms evoked only an uncomfortable silence. How had we drifted this far apart from where we used to be?

Aric let out a long, low sigh and carefully deposited me into another set of arms. "I'll humor you this time. Rest up, Valora."

A second scent clung to Dooley's skin, layered beneath the labdanum. The potent smell of vetiver, both he and Pryn explained, was normal. I never forgot my late uncle's warning. To Artemus, vetiver bespoke of something to come. Something bad. Exhaustion overcame worry. To have just one night of sleep. One night where dreams did not drift toward the two men before me. Focusing on the mission would be much easier if I knew where we stood. But I wasn't going to let my selfish needs take precedence over the safety of the Realms.

Dooley laid me on my bed and covered my shoulders with a light blanket. Seconds later, the click of the latch signaled his departure. No kiss on my forehead, no whisper of soothing words.

Nothing.

Makeshift darkness descended along with the heavy quilt over my head. The fetal position is usually comforting, except when you have a rolled sheaf of paper poking into your gut. I dug into my pocket and pulled out the parchment from the book I found in Mane's apartment. The book, supposedly written by Pryn, was about the wars between Varuna and Ravanna. I unfolded the page again and read for the hundredth time the prophecy, which told me no matter how much I wanted to hide under these covers and cry, I wouldn't be able to hide for long. Pryn's premonition echoed in my ears as I drifted to sleep. *You will save us all.*

⁂

A deep voice curled in and out of me, sending titillating vibrations where they shouldn't be. "Valora. Sweet, sweet Valora. I warned you I would come. I'm getting closer, and there is nothing you can do to stop me. Your weak attempts to keep me trapped in Acheron will fail. There is no greater power than mine, and you are foolish to think you can defeat me. No magic user alive can match me. Not Pryn and definitely not my son."

Eyes open, I found myself running along a familiar path through the woods. Tree limbs whipped at my face, and I pushed past them toward my destination. I didn't stop until I reached the roughhewn cabin tucked amongst the deep green rain forest. Dooley stood tall on the wide porch, a shotgun slung over his shoulder. Relief shot through me. I would be safe here. Safe with him. My hand on the stair rail, I raised my foot to the bottom step, but a distinctive click halted me in mid-motion. Dooley aimed a shotgun at the center of my forehead, his eyes glowing with the demon light of Acheron. Before I could react, a black hand shot up from the mud at my feet and pulled me down—sinking through layers of suffocating earth into pure heat.

I bolted upright and clenched my fists in sweat-soaked sheets. The feathers of my wings were askew and badly in need of a shower. The light of the early morning coming through the open window and last night's dinner setting cold on the table told me I had slept through the day and night. Ravanna showing up in my dreams shouldn't have been a surprise. I tried to prepare myself. But you can't really prepare for a disaster. You can only pretend to be ready, and then when the real time comes, only inner strength and resolve carry you through. An empty pit in my stomach grew in place of resolve. Of course, no matter how many scenarios you have run through your head, the reality is always ten times worse.

A short series of raps sounded at the door before someone opened it an inch. "Are you decent? Better if you're not, but I thought I would show the expected courtesy to a fae princess."

"Mane!" I shoved the crumpled scroll under my pillow and jumped out of bed. Mane pushed the door the rest of the way open.

From the moment I'd met the demon, he wore an air of superiority. He stood tall through the most difficult times, but now a slight slump to his shoulders marred his proud stance. His skin smelled of lilac, Kit's perfume, and his plain linen tunic stretched tight across his muscular chest. My natural inclination was to ask him how he planned to sit in his painted-on pants without splitting himself in two. However, instinct told me this was no time for levity. I glanced around, searching for his other half. He was alone.

"Where is Kit?"

Mane rubbed the back of his neck, and his casual air disappeared. He looked like he'd lived a thousand lifetimes since I'd seen him last. The lines under his eyes were the same ones reflected in my own mirror. "She'll be okay. I wouldn't have come here otherwise."

"No, of course not." I'd go to her myself the second I had a chance. I pressed my hands to my stomach, forcing the upset to settle. Mane's unquestionable devotion to Kit brought an unwelcome spark of jealousy. "What did you two find on your journey into Underworld?"

"A nightmare." Mane dropped down onto one of the two low stools in the sitting area to the left of my four-poster bed. A small stone table was laden with yet another uneaten meal. Dining alone left me without an appetite.

I often went into town to the local alehouse to share a meal amongst people, even though none of them were my friends. I didn't talk to them, but used the time to remind me of my reasons for going into battle. And to remind them they were not alone. These people depended on my strength. Even though sometimes I felt weak.

"Mind if I take that food off your hands?" Mane gestured to the plate of roast beast, baked knotwood corns, and mashed blue slipper seed.

"No, go ahead. I tried to get my father to have the staff quit bringing the food, but he said serving me was their duty, and to deny anyone the thing that kept them busy at a time of impending war would be unwise."

Mane grabbed the meat. He sank his teeth into the flesh and his eyes flared red.

"Are you under control?"

My finger fretted with the worn spot at the pommel of my sword. My new nervous habit. A demon in elf's clothing, Mane often reminded me he wasn't evil, but I never could completely trust him. I supposed that was why Dooley, technically part demon also, found it hard to be around me. If my dreams were any indication, my subconscious mind believed Ravanna still resided somewhere within him. If I couldn't trust him, how could he trust me?

"Control has never been a problem for me. Being in Underworld was not good for either Kit or I. But now that we've returned, we can go back to being our normal, controlled selves." Mane gave me a slightly flirtatious grin. Now *that* was the demon I knew. "Kit needed some extra assistance from Pryn and Dooley, but she'll be fine." His words seemed to be more to convince him then me. He let the stripped bone clatter onto the plate. "Ravanna has already poisoned the land. There are no creatures left, save the dwarves that are not under his control. The elves have retreated somewhere."

"Where do you think they would go?" The elves weren't our greatest allies, but in this battle we were looking for anything to give us an advantage.

"There's no way to tell. I told my elven brother, Torkel, to come here, but no one has heard from them. Their tracks are lost in all the destruction. They may have even been desperate enough to go to the Ordos Desert."

"Dragonlands." My legs wobbled and I sank down into the seat next to Mane. "Then we have already lost." Without the dwarves or the elves, I didn't know how we would overtake Ravanna in Underworld.

Mane surveyed the stack of dishes untouched by myself and the staff. Even the servants were tired of throwing away full plates of food. "You haven't been eating. You need to keep up your strength." He slid the plate toward me and handed me a spoon.

I pushed the vegetables around like I did as a child, in the hope that the dispersal of food would prove I ate at least a few bites.

Mane stole the spoon from my hand and brought the food to my lips. "No, we haven't lost. If I thought that, I would have jumped the next portal and taken Kit with me. Though that would only buy us a little time."

"I don't believe you would leave us all to Ravanna." I opened my mouth and let the demon feed me the flaccid corns. After a few spoonfuls, the churning in my stomach began to die down.

He paused, taking my hands in his. "You have good intuition."

I gave him a gentle squeeze, glad to know that both he and my friend were safe, for now. "What did you mean that if you left you would only be buying a little time?"

Mane pulled a small portion of mirror out of the pocket of his tight jeans and slid it across the table. "Do you recall when we last left Bowen?"

"Of course." I ran my finger lightly along the rough edge of the broken glass. Bowen, my Uncle Artemus' stepson, knew more than most humans did about our world. We gave him a portion of the talking mirror to get through to us if he ever wanted to. Considering the circumstances, I wasn't sure he would ever want anything to do with our world again. It probably would have been a wise choice for him and for Dooley. I should never have changed the course of his life by letting him come to Dell'Aria.

"He contacted me. There are signs. The same thing is beginning on Earth. Ravanna left here without much of a fight because he's busy there."

I swallowed, trying to clear the hard lump of food stuck in my throat. "Have you told Dooley and Aric?"

Mane shook his head. "This is not something they can know right now. You and I need to go there first."

"But why?" I couldn't imagine going to Earth without Dooley or Aric.

Mane stood up fast, knocking his chair to the ground. "Because it involves their mother."

"I know you have some personal experience with possessing the body of another, but their mother had her memory wiped. She doesn't know anything about the Goddess Varuna or Ravanna having possessed her. She doesn't even remember Dooley or Aric. It was the only way to keep her safe." Underneath Kit's perfume, the scent of fear clung to Mane.

He glanced down at the talking mirror used to communicate between long distances. And the message on the other end of this one came from a world as far from the Realms as you could get.

"She's starting to remember."

CHAPTER TWO

"There are those we cannot trust here." Mane repeated the excuse as I continued to prod him with questions. He insisted we leave Dell'Aria before he revealed the details of Bowen's message. His decision wasn't up for debate. No matter how much I prodded, even going so far as to offer him a tour of the sumptuous brothel of the King's Guard, he wouldn't budge. I darted after Mane onto the empty streets of Dell'Aria. The early morning light shone down on stores that were closed and locked, the curtains in the small windows drawn.

"Don't tell me there are more fae here in Dell'Aria working against us. Where are we going?" We passed food carts, which once sold ice fruit creams, spiny sanguinary tarts, and peppery black oak potage, and my stomach growled. The carts only hauled weapons now, and the people of Dell'Aria worked to provide supplies for the upcoming war. Rations came straight from the temple magistrate, who kept a close inventory on our food.

"Who indeed. I won't let anything happen to Kit." Mane ignored my question and raked a hand over his bald head, striking a fist into his open palm. The muscles in his jaw flexed. He wanted to pound more than his own flesh. I wanted to believe his corporeal anger had nothing to do with me or his demon, but I still gripped the hilt of the sword at my side out of habit.

Mane paused before the temple. The large dome atop the marble building now shone brilliant and white, all evidence of the tarnish caused by the Blight disappeared. "Trusting one another is not an option. Even though I know you have found that difficult in the past."

Mane reached a hand out to me, and I accepted it. "I have no reason not to trust you." I tried to inject enthusiasm into my words, but they fell flat. We both knew I didn't trust the demon in him.

"Remember those words if you are ever led to doubt in the future." Mane picked up his pace, leading us through the streets until we came to the old cabin Kali and I used to share.

I stopped short, coming loose from Mane's grip. "We won't be safe from prying ears inside there. I'm sure my father still has eyes here. Did you see her when you were down there? Did you see Kali?"

Kali escaped from me after we all found out she unwittingly gave Ravanna the magic he required to unseal the portal between Acheron and the Realms. At least I still wanted to believe her betrayal was all a misunderstanding. Then again, Kali seemed to make a lot of those "mistakes." How many times had I forgiven her and been made a fool? If nothing else, I had to make sure her actions didn't have any negative effect on this mission. If we messed up this time we might not have a chance to correct our own mistakes.

"She is where she should be and there is nothing any of

us can do about it now." Mane tugged at the door to the cabin, the hinges stiff after so little use.

I didn't realize I was crying until the tear rolled down my cheek. I swiped it away, but Mane noticed, his brusque manner softening. "You must be strong."

I inhaled a deep breath and quickly tightened the laces on my bracers. "I'm fine."

Mane shook his head. "I've got the Edsel through the back. We're going straight to the source. No messages through mirrors. There is no other way to convince you to focus on Earth first."

All the battle plans I laid out in my head, the routes I mapped out as I stared at the stars stitched into the canopy of my bed, were based on the idea that the frontal assault would come straight to me. In Dell'Aria. Now I had to think about a battle in the shadows on Earth, where not only did I have to worry about the actual monsters, but also the humans who might think me a monster as well. I'd always been taught that to the majority of human supernaturals were thought of as freaks, science experiments.

Maybe they had it right.

❧

"Buckle up, Valora. And put this on." Mane handed me a leather jacket to hide my wings. He swiped his hand across the dash and sketched crude-looking symbols in the black dust. Red and white light surrounded the car, coalescing into a pink aura.

"Are you sure you can bring us to Earth all by yourself? I thought you could only get us to the Dragonlands." I would never understand the rules of magic. Potions and poultices made sense. Follow a recipe and get a prescribed result. Abstract magical utterances that could turn a toad into a useful stick of candle wax defied explanation. My mother was probably rolling in her grave.

"Kit and I worked to fix that little glitch." Mane's eyes gleamed. Something transformative had happened on his trip with Kit, but I couldn't get the details now. Kit and Mane had left shortly after we saw the waters of Mavrovo turn red. She told me before they left she had to see if anything remained of the selkie. The two of them seemed the most qualified to go, and the only ones my father believed were safe from Ravanna's magic. They were both alive, but I didn't think they were unaffected.

"Did you learn symbol magic in Acheron?" Dooley used symbol magic to heal me inside and out. Those sessions brought us closer and revealed the truth about Aric, but the more I saw him rely on the guidance of an unseen force, the more he slipped away from me. What if this sorcery brought him closer to Ravanna? What if that had already happened?

"Yes, but I preferred practicing other more pleasurable arts." Mane's voice lowered to a deep purr, and the car roared to life. I eagerly directed the subject away from discussing Mane's interest in the arts, which probably had nothing to do with crafting sonnets or basket weaving.

"Did anything come of your trip to Underworld?" My stomach spun along with the car. I clutched the windowsill, careful to keep my hands off any of the toxic iron fixtures.

"Nothing of value. Rest assured, Ravanna didn't do himself any favors. If he hoped to scare me into submission, he did just the opposite." Mane grasped the steering wheel, his muscles straining to keep the car on a path I couldn't see. "I will do whatever I can to make sure he is defeated."

Mane squinted, struggling to see through the pink mist. I hoped his super demon vision could make out more than I could.

"Hold on!" yelled Mane. He yanked the wheel to the left. The tires struck pavement and slammed me against the door. I clenched my jaw and rubbed at my bruised elbow.

The pink blur of magical light dissolved into the milky atmosphere surrounding the Xanadu, the comic store owned by Bowen. Despite the heavy fog, Mane somehow placed the Edsel between two vehicles, one of which was my uncle's old Vanagon. I felt overwhelmed, in a good way. These circumstances, though urgent, were much better than coming to his store for the first time and having it smell of death.

"He's here." After what had happened, I hoped to keep Bowen clear of any further dealings with the Realms, for his own good. I should have known the curious nature of humans would make that impossible.

"Let's get inside. I don't want to be out in the open for long." Without pausing to take credit for his parking skills, Mane exited and swung around to my side of the car before I could crack open the door.

Mane loomed up, doing his best to shield me with his size and stature. "I didn't ask for a bodyguard. But thanks for volunteering."

"Trust." One word and he made his point. A bell tinkled as we entered the shop, announcing our arrival.

Bowen walked out from the stockroom. I wouldn't willingly go back there again. The location of my uncle's demise held too many raw memories. The waiting room of my psyche was at maximum capacity. Sooner or later I'd deal with all of it. At the moment, later seemed the best plan.

"Mane! Valora! I'm surprised to see you here. I wasn't sure you got my message." Bowen came up and vigorously shook our hands. Although of no blood relation to the fae, the way he lit up a room with his jolly smile made it easy to see how my kin had been attracted to his. Bowen shoved his wire-rimmed glasses up onto his nose and ran his hand through his loose black curls. "I'll make sure we won't be bothered for a while." He secured the deadbolt before flipping the open sign to close. "Not many customers today, anyway."

"We're alone?" Mane asked.

"Yes. So I'm guessing since you're here, things are pretty bad?" Bowen drew the broken bit of mirror from his pocket, and Mane did the same.

"Repeat to Valora what you said in the message. I brought her here so you could explain the situation in person."

I clutched at the pommel of my sword, instincts kicking in. I never went anywhere without my blade anymore. That and my mother's grimoire, which I tried to give to Dooley but he refused to take. Now it was only an heirloom. My instincts with magic were all over the map. No use pretending I could do things I couldn't and get another person killed.

Bowen gripped his chin and then adjusted his glasses. "I would invite you to see the research I've been doing. But I doubt you want to go back there anymore." Bowen gestured to the stockroom.

"You're right, I don't." He was trying, but the family reunion had to wait. "Look, Bowen, at home we're dealing with boiling seas, lands infected with a red dust that kills everything it touches, and so many children without fathers I've lost count. What's happening here?"

"Yes, well, remember how I told you during my studies of demonology I interviewed a woman who called herself Ravanna?" Bowen pulled out a stool, and the sound of the metal legs dragging across the floor made me wince. He sat down next to a glass cabinet filled with booklets displayed like sacred documents, each one encased in plastic. As if to remind me it was there, the scroll shoved into my bodice formed an uncomfortable lump in my side.

"I remember." I adjusted the parchment as best I could.

"She came into the store a few days ago."

"Last I saw her, Irena was in a nursing home, her memory erased for good after Aric tried to restore it and we learned she was a powerful oracle." Once host to the Goddess Varuna and Ravanna, Irena was now simply a nice senile old woman. For good reason, she had no clue as to the amount of power she used to wield. Her mind had the ability to open the portals between worlds.

"She introduced herself as Ravanna. She knew all about you and remembered our conversations from years ago. She had a message for me to give to you."

Mane nodded, encouraging Bowen to continue.

"Ravanna is back in town."

Bile rose up in my mouth. Now I knew why Mane didn't want to include Dooley and Aric on this mission. Their mother was again the host of Ravanna. Wiping out all her memories didn't seal the breach. Dooley and Aric would rather move heaven and hell then destroy their mother.

"I assume you know how to handle this?" I directed my question to Mane, who pushed himself off the wall, arms tightly crossed against his chest.

"Yes. But first, how committed are you to saving this world as well as the Realms? Things will get uglier than they ever have before."

A sinking feeling settled into the pit of my stomach, and suddenly I was studying with great earnestness the recent scratch to the leather in my boots. The answer wasn't obvious to me. There may be no saving Irena. What would

Aric and Dooley do if they found out I had to kill her? "Will what we do here save Dell'Aria?"

"Not necessarily. This is probably a distraction. A way to split our focus. I can't say I know what real benefit meddling in this world will have for him."

"You mean to tell me we've played into his trap?" I asked.

"I don't think it's a trap. But yes, we're playing his game. I think it will be valuable to know what he plans to do. We've banished him more than once. It is possible. If we ignore Earth and let Ravanna run it to ruin, we'll only gain a few more weeks to prepare before he comes for us."

"Valora, you will help us, won't you?" Bowen's mouth slackened, his skin growing paler than normal. I was sure he was unable to understand why I didn't just rush to his defense. His father had been the type to help others selflessly. A trait I was never taught. Spending your life with others putting you down for a physical anomaly you have no control over doesn't really give you a generous nature. And so many of those I trusted had betrayed me.

Betray you? I think Dooley would have a few words to say about that. Aric's voice echoed in my mind. Ravanna's meddling had already split my focus. My mental shields were weakened. *Where have you gotten to, Valora? People are starting to worry.*

People?

Okay, me.

Aric, I have some things to take care of. Don't worry—Mane is here. We'll be back soon.

"Are they talking to you?" Mane asked.

A look of confusion crossed Bowen's face at the unexpected question. "I'm able to communicate to a few of the fae telepathically," I explained.

21

"Wow! Really? My father never said anything about being psychic."

"You can't unless you are burdened with one of these." I lifted the amulet from my bodice and showed him the glowing red stone. "Aric wants to know where I am."

"Cut off communication. It would be very bad if he were to get tangled up in all this." Mane's lips pressed together into a flattened line, his hands clasping until his knuckles went white.

Aric, please don't worry. You'll hear from me again soon. Mane won't let Kit out of his sight for long.

That is the only thing I am certain of.

Mane was right. Aric almost destroyed Dell'Aria when he fought to restore his mother's memory. I bricked up the walls of my mind and tested their strength. It was absolutely necessary the brothers remained ignorant. As of late they didn't speak, but the power of the amulets transcended their conscious thoughts, a fact Aric was all too keen on disclosing to me. If one knew, the other would find out.

"Are we good?" asked Mane.

"Yes. So where is she? Do we check the home?"

Mane shook his head. "No, Ravanna has taken her over. He is likely using her form to complete the necessary rituals to open the portal between here and Acheron and bring his armies through."

"So where do we begin?"

"Bowen, will you assist us in deciding our next move?"

Bowen hopped off his stool and wrapped his arms around Mane, possibly giving him the first real hug Mane ever had, considering his stiff reaction.

"Sorry about that." Bowen haphazardly smoothed the wrinkles from Mane's vest and rushed around the display case to a computer. A picture of woman clad in a tight leather skirted outfit overlaid with metal armor floated across the screen.

"Who is that?"

"Xena," said Bowen. "She's a warrior princess. Basically, she's on a quest to redeem herself from her dark past by using her fighting skills to help people. She always reminded me of Dad. He always said he had penance to pay, though I never quite knew what he meant."

Mane's heavy arm descended on my shoulder. "Sounds like Bowen understands exactly what we need."

"I'll research all night long if I have to." He clacked away at the keys, and the image disappeared.

"Good, we'll return to Dell'Aria to gather supplies."

We said our goodbyes and promised to be in touch soon. This mission was truly going to test my resolve. My mother, always selfless, used her powers to heal others, a true hero. My father lived his life in service to the king, and now he was the king. I was a princess by default who didn't know where my fate lay. Others were putting their trust in me. I owed it to my people and to myself to own up to that trust. All my life I'd wanted this kind of respect, and now that I had it I felt like a fraud.

CHAPTER THREE

I went to the only place I knew I belonged, the training arena. Each swipe of the blade centered my thoughts as Mane's parting words echoed inside my head. *Do what you have to do. We leave in a day. And if you want keep Dooley and Eric safe, you will say nothing.* Keeping them safe meant I must do this alone. My strength had to come from within. Cool tendrils of fog reached out from the night sky. An icy touch caused me to spin around and search the empty space. All alone except for my own personal demons. The wings at my back twitched, an outward sign of all the anxiety building up inside that I couldn't seem to shake.

In the corner of the room sat the whetstone. My weapon would have to be as sharp as my mind. I depressed the pedal to start the wheel spinning, and laid the blade against the surface. Sparks shot into the air. An image appeared, like a black shadow in my vision from looking at the sun too long. Darkness descended, like a leaden weight, which pressed against the backs of my eyelids. My palms moistened as his deep, bellowing laugh stripped away my self-confidence and left me shaking. Ravanna now haunted my waking moments as well as my dreams, and he was going to win. What could I possibly do to stop him?

Footsteps behind me triggered my survival instinct, and I spun around, sword raised. The newly sharpened edge stopped mere inches from Pryn's throat.

His golden eyes went wide and my blade clattered to the floor. I took two steps back, examining my hands as if they had ceased to be under my control, their only good use now to cradle my heated face. I could have killed him. Hot tears rolled between my fingers. How was I going to defeat Ravanna when I couldn't even wield power over my own self? "Oh shit, Pryn. I'm so sorry."

Pryn kept his eyes on me as he dipped down to pick up my blade. "No, it's my fault. I shouldn't have snuck up on you." His eyes regained their inviting sparkle. My mother had trained with Pryn in her youth, and now Dooley studied his lessons. He was in good hands. "Are things okay, Valora? I wanted to talk to you about Dooley, but if you have other things on your mind I think it can wait."

The mention of Dooley's name snapped me back to reality. Something real. Something tangible needed me. Someone I might be able to help. "No, what's wrong with Dooley? Tell me." I quickly slid my sword back into its scabbard, feeling the reassuring weight back at my side.

"It's best if I show you." He gestured for me to follow him.

"Seems like a running theme."

"What?"

"Nothing. Lead and I'll follow." I walked silently behind Pryn. He seemed to sense I didn't have an immediate desire to be chatty. I pressed my hand against my stomach to try and settle my unease, only partially due to skipping meals. The few spoonfuls of food Mane had force-fed me weren't enough to battle the memories. Pryn led the way back to the temple, ascending the same stairs, the same path, Dooley and I had taken to expose Aric's treachery.

Pryn made his ascent with ease. I trudged up the steps, pulling each foot from the previous stair as if it were covered in tar. There were still a few scars left in my heart from the revelation of Aric's betrayal.

After Aric vacated the tower, they fit the door at the top of the stairs with a copper ring. Light reflected off the fixture and I lost my footing, scraping my hands on the stone wall as I stumbled right into the memory of falling at Aric's feet. A gentle breeze came from under the door, bringing with it the scent of a flame-kissed warrior, a sooty, leather-tinged musk.

"Are you okay?" I nodded and Pryn stepped back, motioning for me to proceed. Clutching the large copper ring in my hand, I took a deep breath and pulled. Pryn held the door and dipped down to whisper in my ear as I stood in shock. In the candlelit room, the muscles of Dooley's chest glistened with ritual oils. Sinuous wet leather stretched with his every movement. Dooley's actions were more of a jolt than his appearance. Symbols covered the walls, the same as when he tried to open the portal to Acheron from the Xanadu. I coughed on the thick charcoal dust floating in the air. No blood this time, but no less disturbing.

"I fear he has become somewhat obsessed with the symbols. I've tried telling him they are only a gateway to trouble. But he believes they hold answers." Pryn dipped his finger into the charcoal pot, touching the bottom. "I believe he may harm himself if his obsession grows. Perhaps you can talk to him?" Pryn picked up the pot and tucked it into the front pocket of his robes.

"I thought you and he were working together. That you

were training him like you did my mother?"

Dooley continued the swift strokes of his finger as he sketched the symbols across his makeshift canvas, not at all aware that his sanctuary had been penetrated. His thighs tensed as he practically stood on his tiptoes to reach every last bit of bare wall.

"I'll go and retrieve more charcoal. Better I then have him roam the halls looking like that." Pryn tapped his temple, and my insides suddenly felt like they were quivering. "He has been difficult to reach lately."

Talk to Dooley? Both of us were using this war to avoid discussing things, going to our respective corners and doing what needed to be done. Apparently my belief he was handling this all well was wrong.

I nodded to Pryn, who gave a slight bow and backed out of the room. Aric's Soulstealer, covered in a thin layer of dust, was shoved into the corner of the room. My father had decided not to dismantle the machine that killed his wife. Despite my objections, he felt learning the architecture of the thing may give us an advantage against Ravanna.

Drawings were spread across a table to the right of the device. A postmortem of the machine in artist renditions, as though someone was trying to reverse-engineer it. The extent of Aric's knowledge involved pushing the "on" button. Dooley's father Brokk was the inventor and builder. He couldn't have possibly known how much destruction it would cause, and that it would ultimately bring about his own death.

Brokk's journal was also sitting on the table. My footsteps finally alerted Dooley, who swung around, his hand caked in coal mud. A clump of black muck dropped to the floor.

"Let me help." I reached for a rag and dipped down to

his feet to mop up the sludge. "You're wearing the same…" My voice fell from my mouth. A shredded rag couldn't clean up this mire. Dooley was wearing his brother's boots.

He reached down to help me up, appearing not to notice my observation. "Don't worry about the mess. I'm making enough of my own. Did you sleep okay? You seemed exhausted last I saw you."

His speech came out in a staccato rush, yet Dooley's deep cocoa eyes melted all the worries in my world. His cadence was full of euphoria, and I didn't want to take that from him. Ever.

"Yeah, I'm good. I slept fine." I put a hand to Dooley's vest, the black leather warm against my hand. "Where did you get these clothes?"

Dooley shrugged, completely unaffected. "I found a trunk of things in the room I'm staying in. Felt like maybe I should wear black if I'm going to be working with all this charcoal. Cause less of an obvious mess. Great luck I'm having." He gestured to the floor. "What are you doing up here? I thought you wanted nothing to do with magic practice."

"Is that what this is?" The wall was covered in the Reiki markings now familiar to me. A shiver ran up my spine as I recalled the symbols Dooley marked me with personally.

"I think so. It has to be. I knew my father's Reiki practice was never traditional. I don't think it actually had anything to do with Reiki whatsoever." Dooley paused, dropping the smile from his face and crossing his arms against his chest. "You didn't answer my question."

"Pryn thought I should come talk to you." Before becoming the stage of our worst nightmare, this temple room was a sacred place for the magistrate. The soft yellow glow of the moonlight shone through the open window at the top of the domed ceiling, casting Dooley in an eerie light.

"Of course he did." Dooley's eyes narrowed as he studied his work. "There's something here he doesn't want me to see."

"He has no training with these markings. He has been trying to teach you the same magic he taught my mother. This magic you are doing…"

"…scares him. He can't explain it. But my father taught me for a reason. There's a purpose. If I can get them all out of my head and in one place, maybe I can make sense of it all." Dooley's fae father, Brokk, was responsible for making the machine that killed my mother. Now Ravanna, the father of Dooley's soul, was threatening to take out our entire world. Listening to the advice of either one didn't seem like a good idea.

I reached out to touch his shoulder. "I know what it's like to lose a parent. I know the sorrow that can put in your heart. Maybe you should take a break. It's late. Have you eaten anything?"

Dooley turned, wanton anger briefly flitting across his features. I tensed, awaiting the barrage of vitriol I had been expecting ever since I lay down with Aric, and my stomach growled. His echoed. Instead of venom, I received vivacious laughter. "I guess I can break for some food. But please, tell me my brother is not joining us."

"No reason for him to." I did a quick check to make sure my mental shields were in place and said a silent prayer that one of Aric's naked yoga students would keep him busy tonight.

Dooley wiped his hands on the leather pants before picking Brokk's journal up from the table. "We'll eat and read. Then I can show you what I'm talking about."

"Again with the showing."

"What?"

"Nothing. Lead on."

❧

The warm kitchen still held the scent of the Traveler's Rye baked for the Guardians in preparation for battle. I reached over our shared plate across the narrow bar to wipe the dripping juices from Dooley's mouth. His stories fluctuated between reminiscing about his childhood dog that had a knack for eating inappropriate things and his ideas about the symbols. I almost choked on my food after Dooley's full-body reenactment of the time his dog Spitz got his head stuck in a rabbit hole.

Laughter wasn't a common occurrence between us anymore. Heck, in the middle of this war there was barely any laughter anywhere anymore. Except for, of course, watching Aric and his naked yoga sessions. I tried to push the thought of Aric out of my mind. Dooley was happier than I had seen him in a long time. Excited. I nodded along as he spoke.

"And you see here"—Dooley dropped a bar bone to the plate and pointed to another passage in his father's journal— "he started this back when he was a young fae. All of his ideas. They are somewhat disjointed, but on each page, in the crease, is another one of these symbols."

"What?" I took the book from him and flicked through the pages. The weight of Brokk's journal was familiar to me, but the symbols weren't. I pulled the book open and stretched its spine to see the hidden text I hadn't noticed before. "I wonder what it means." As far as I knew, the symbol magic was never practiced in Dell'Aria. My mother's grimoire was mostly potions and incantations.

"Exactly. Brokk had to know my origins, about

Ravanna—he must have uncovered this in his studies. I'm trying to get all the symbols in one place so I can see if I can make any sense of it. Pryn thinks I'm wasting my time. I don't see why he thought to involve you."

"Well, I'm glad he did." Thick silence fell between us, and I could hear the crackling of the dying coals in the kitchen hearth. I leaned in, waiting for him to say something to reflect what I was feeling, but his voice seemed locked up inside his throat. I pushed my napkin from my lap and stood from my stool. "Do you mind if I study this journal for a night? I promise I'll bring it back to you tomorrow."

"Sure." Dooley rose from his seat, mirroring my actions. I'd almost forgotten he was taller than me. "You don't have to go yet, Valora."

"Yes, I really do." One fingertip was all it took for him to have me within his grasp again. The rough edge of his thumb ran over the top of my hand. The last time we slept together was at Winter Haven, when Dooley was possessed by Ravanna. My body ached for a true moment alone with him. Backward or forward, I needed to know which direction we were going.

"Until tomorrow, then." He placed a hand on my shoulder and dipped down to kiss me on the cheek. A touch that warmed me to my toes, despite being only friendly in nature. If he gave me a chance to start over with him, that was better than nothing.

I gave Dooley a smile and turned to leave with Brokk's journal clutched to my side. If Dooley was obsessed with these writings then I needed to know the source of the obsession. I needed to make sure it was a healthy interest and not something where Ravanna might be involved.

And there was still the matter of going back to Earth and dealing with Ravanna. I rounded the corner and smacked right into the bare chest of Aric. The book dropped from my hands and fell to the floor at my feet.

Aric bent down and retrieved the book, locking his eyes with mine as he placed it back in my hands. "Valora, what are you doing here? I haven't heard from you all day." He tapped his head with his finger. "I was starting to worry you were shutting me out for some nefarious reason. Please, tell me you were up to something nefarious. I just love that word." He pressed forward and I was pushed back, the rough stones in the wall poking into my wings.

"Nothing you need to be concerned with."

He wrapped his hand around my upper back and drew me toward him. "Don't want you to crush your delicate feathers." His fingers found the spot between my wings, which sent shocks of pleasure coursing down my body.

My hands froze inches away from Aric's bare chest. I was afraid if I touched him I might not want to stop. "I don't need your kind of help."

I escaped his embrace and rushed down the torch-lit hall, but his voice rang out in my mind. *I can tell you need assistance of some kind, Valora. Just let me know. No strings attached.*

The floor was either suddenly lined with tar or something inside me didn't want to leave. Aric's intentions were clear. The space between Aric and his brother represented a crossroads. A perfume of dry earth and mosses beckoned me toward the shortest path. One where a shining angel stood at the end with open arms. *Fine, then, what are you waiting for?*

Although I was pointed toward the same destination, something inside me shifted directions. After Mane and I left tomorrow to face Ravanna, I might not see either one of them again. My quarters felt like they were a mile away. Aric stalked me without a word. His breath became more rapid as he jogged to keep up with my pace. I reached out to open my door, and his hand shot over my shoulder and pushed it shut.

"Why won't you let me inside my room?"

"You and he shared that space. There is no reason we need to go there."

I was caught in the storm of his blue eyes. His long white-blond hair fell over his shoulders, the ends tickling the bare flesh on my arm. "And where would you have us go?"

Aric scooped me up into his arms and strutted down the end of the hall to the window. In one fluid motion he unlatched it, spread his wings wide, and jumped from the window. My breath caught in my throat, and I clutched on as tight as I could, since my own wings wouldn't hold me in the sky. Wind pressed against my back, wrapping around me like a hug from a long-lost friend.

Aric shot up higher and tipped sideways as he dodged around one of the castle towers. Brokk's journal broke free from my grip. "No!" I lunged out to grab it and tore out of Aric's protective hold. Suddenly I was free-falling toward Underworld, but I could touch the pages with my fingers. Just a bit to the left and I could reach it.

Aric's arms clamped down hard around my middle, his downy-soft wings blanketing me in a swirling blue cocoon. I pressed my head to his chest and felt the rapid beating of his heart. *You trying to get yourself killed? Your father wouldn't be too happy if I didn't bring you back alive.*

Brokk's journal tumbled out of sight, along with my chance of getting back together with Dooley. He wasn't going to forgive me for this. The last piece left of his father and I lost it because I chose to sleep with his brother. Fate or not, clearly my choice was made. *Where are we going, Aric?*

Ye of so little faith. Aric bent down and spoke slowly into my ear, loud enough so I could hear his voice above the wind whipping past us at an ever increasing speed. The lights dotting the landscape of Dell'Aria flickered as we got farther away, until they looked like nothing more than stars in the sky.

"Charnac."

❧

I kept my eyes shut, refusing to believe that I was going to have to face her.

If I could have escaped from Aric, I would. But since struggling would only cause me to fall to my death, there wasn't much I could do. Of course, I might prefer falling to death over what the queen of Charnac would likely do if she got her hands on me. The last time I saw Calliope, she and her men were chasing Aric and I across the sky as the bottom half of Charnac fell away. But that wasn't the worst part. I was responsible for her son's death. My sword kind of got stuck in his chest. I wished I could say I was sorry, but I was simply defending myself. In war, it was kill or be killed.

I didn't know you hated me so much.

You'll be fine. Calliope realizes there's something happening that is bigger than her quarrel with you or the fae of Dell'Aria. She wants her people to regain their strength, but if Underworld is destroyed then none of the fae will ever be the same.

Some believe we can hide away in our cloud cities and stay under the protection of Varuna.

Is that what you think?

I opened my eyes in time to see Charnac rising up before us. The lights of Dell'Aria twinkled in the distance, but Charnac was blacker than the night sky surrounding its ruination. Aric headed straight for the crumbling castle gates.

He landed gently on the ground before the portcullis, which now served only as a symbolic entrance. The walls of the once-majestic fortress were crumbled on all sides.

Shards of the red mineral glass that once made up the entire underbelly of this isle broke beneath my feet. I jumped on instinct and clutched at Aric's shoulder.

"Don't worry, the ground here is stable. The land is slowly repairing itself." Aric placed his hand at the rise of my hip to steady me, suppressing my desire to suddenly try some flying lessons.

"It still doesn't hurt to be careful." Calliope appeared in the doorway. Her red and orange braids were vibrant even in the dim light. Pale skin as luminous as the first time I saw her. She radiated royalty, and she was fiercely beautiful. It was no wonder her people continued to follow her even after their homes were destroyed, their lives inexplicably changed forever. Their devotion to their queen was nothing short of religious.

"What is she doing here? Aric, I told you there was nothing to say." Calliope's scarlet wings shook, the cords in her neck taut, barely disguising her rage.

Aric stepped between us, blocking my view. I waited for a flurry of hands to come at me from around his chest, except there was nothing but an eerie silence. If I had a son and his murderer had the nerve to stand before me, I would throttle him. I expected nothing less of Calliope.

Aric's voice was calm and even. "I told you what needed to be done."

I dared to look around his shoulder in time to see Calliope sneer before disappearing back into the depths of her asylum, one I had sentenced her to. Aric kept trying to tell me Charnac would have fallen even without my help. I wasn't so sure.

35

The door gave a long screech as it swayed on rusty hinges. Calliope had left an open invitation, and I wasn't about to accept. "We need to go."

"Are you kidding? It went pretty well, I thought. She didn't try to kill you." Aric turned and raised his eyebrows at me, gesturing for me to follow Calliope.

"Yet." I did what my body and my soul told me not too. I went inside. My heart was full of guilt that, unless laid to rest, would hold me back in this upcoming battle. I needed to ask for forgiveness from Calliope, even if I didn't believe she would grant my request.

Aric followed behind me, and I felt his hand on mine, moving my grip away from my sword. "You don't want her to think you have any ill intentions."

The darkness was pierced by candlelight, which grew brighter as we got deeper within the building. A familiar set of stairs leading the way to Calliope's chambers appeared before me. The tattered curtain serving as a door flickered in the breeze.

"You should go up before me. I have no role in Dell'Aria anymore. You are the one she needs to speak to," said Aric.

"Now that seals it, you have gone completely insane." I looked to see where the closest exits were. Calliope's guards were nowhere in sight, but that didn't mean they weren't lurking in the shadows.

"Keep an open mind." Aric tapped his head, reminding me that he and I could speak in a way Calliope could not hear. *Nothing will happen to you.*

The thick scent of incense emanated from Calliope's chambers. I drew back the curtain and searched for the source of the perfume and the queen. I saw neither.

"Calliope?" The last thing I needed to do was to surprise

her and give her another excuse for killing me.

The drapery before the great window—the one that once gave the queen a pulpit to speak to her people, parted—and Calliope appeared with a pipe of beesroot in her hand. "Did you want some?" She offered me the calming herb.

"No, I think I'll be fine."

"Sit, then."

I took my place at the table, glad her temperament would be dampened by the beesroot. "Look, Calliope, I want you to know, I am so sorry that your son...well, that he—"

"That you killed him?" She took another long drag of the beesroot pipe and filled the air with its honey-sweet smoke. Despite not inhaling it, I was starting to feel its effects, a funny buzzing in my head that mimicked the sounds of the animal that produced this strange stuff.

"Yes, I killed him. The situation was complicated. But I never meant to take the one you loved most of all."

Calliope erupted in laughter. My hands, once level with the table, went for my sword. She was either hysterical or I was right where she wanted me.

Calliope placed the pipe onto the table and wiped the tears from her eyes. She looked up, and her eyes went to my sword, which was half drawn from my scabbard. The glint of her own silver sobered her immediately.

"You can put that away. If I wanted you dead, you would already be dead."

The memory of the head of the queen of Dell'Aria rolling across the floor at my feet reminded me how dangerous the woman sitting across from me was. Reluctantly, I clicked my sword back into place. "You'll forgive me if I don't comprehend the humor in what I said."

"Of course. You're a master of not seeing what's directly

in front of you." She went to a small bureau that sat next to her large four-poster bed.

"I see the seas boiling red below us, and I saw a chance for our people to come together as one to stop it. But perhaps I was wrong." I stood to go. Calliope was beyond hope. She was blind to her failings and blind to the needs of the Realms. I didn't understand Aric's reasons for bringing me here. There was nothing for me to convince her of, and my apologies were a waste of time.

She turned, a stack of letters in her hand.

"You always see the physical. Do you ever manage to search beyond to see what lies beneath?" She reached out and lightly touched the ends of my small black wings. "I suppose you've had a lifetime of focusing on the physical."

"I'm learning to let go."

"Learn quicker." She thrust the pile of letters at me and walked back to the table, retrieving her beesroot pipe once more.

It was easy to see the letters were all from one person. Aric. They were his exchanges with Calliope before the tragic events first unfolded in Dell'Aria. There was tenderness in his words, and even in his penmanship. I touched a finger to the page and traced the scrolling twists of the letters he had used to confess his veiled devotion. Even though there was never any direct admission of love, I understood now what Calliope meant.

"What do you want me to take from all this?"

Calliope looked as frustrated as a mother schooling a child on why the sky is blue. She herself, perhaps, didn't know the exact answer to my question.

"Have you ever wondered why Aric continues to chase after you despite your devotion to Dooley?"

"Many times." I knew part of the answer to her

question. Even when I told him to stop pursuing me, I acted in a way that told him to keep trying. Tonight I intended for us to end up in my bed. I never imagined he would bring me here.

"It's guilt, Valora. Guilt, not love, holding him to you. As long as your mother's death weighs heavy on his heart, he will never give himself to the one he really wants. With you he only gets pain, which is all he thinks he deserves." A single tear spilled down Calliope's cheek. A single tear, not for her son, but for a love lost. Her love for Aric.

I handed her the letters, which she returned to the only secure place in the whole rotted-out room. She cherished those letters like I cherished my mother's grimoire, like Dooley cherished his father's journal. A journal that I had lost. Damn. There was already enough drama between Dooley and me. This was just another stab in an already deep wound that wasn't healing quickly enough. I needed to get back to Dell'Aria. And, more importantly, I needed to get back to Earth.

"We're on the same page, Calliope. At least where Aric is concerned. I'll see what I can do." I reached out and squeezed her hand, neglecting to tell her my love for Dooley was not as solid in my mind as she would probably like it to be. A problem for another day.

"My people are at Winter Haven. You can tell your father he has the support of Charnac—though our silver mines are barren, we were able to salvage the last of our stores. I have stayed behind to protect them. We only need a place to craft our weapons, and they are at your disposal."

A surge of hope brought my shoulders straighter. "I'll inform my father at once. There's no reason why your artisans cannot share the armory with our copper workers on Dell'Aria."

39

Calliope took hold of my arm before I turned to leave. "Aric cannot know what we have spoken of." Her chin dipped down and tipped toward her left shoulder before she returned her probing gaze to me, a clear petition marked in her placating tone. "Please."

With great care I took Calliope's words, and with every ounce of concentration I secured them deep within the place in my mind neither Dooley nor Aric could touch. "There is war coming, Calliope. When it's done we'll worry about love. Until then there's nothing we can do about any of it."

"Without love, war has no meaning. Why fight for something you care nothing for?" She dropped her hand from my shoulder and turned her back to me, her bright red wings fluttering like a beating heart. She wasn't the one I was hiding from. I was hiding from myself.

Aric stood near the bottom of the stairs in the very spot I was when Calliope had called on me for help as Aric lay lifeless in her chamber, the chain of the amulet connecting us having been severed by Calliope's son, Henryk. I mindlessly fumbled with the charm at my neck, and it lit up in my hand, producing a brilliant red light that pulsed and beat in time with my heart.

Aric slowly ascended the stairs, careful to avoid the pitfalls and traps of the rotted wood. He took hold of the charm at my neck and tilted his head to the side.

"I find it amusing that I'm your only true link to Ravanna. I'm the one who can keep him from getting through to you." The jewel dimmed at Aric's touch and my rising adrenaline lessened, though didn't fully diminish.

"Seems like there's a lot of inappropriate laughter going on here tonight, which I didn't ask for nor appreciate. I have a job to do." I shrugged off Aric's touch and passed through the castle doors, knowing full well he was the only one who could actually take us from this place. That didn't diminish my stubbornness either.

"I thought this would be good for you." Aric folded his arms around me out of necessity. There was no other intention in his embrace this time. He knew he was out of opportunities with me at the moment.

We traveled in silence back to Dell'Aria. He'd absconded with me tonight under the pretense of making me his lover once more, and I'd agreed. Agreed and gotten to stand face to face with his real love. The one who desperately wanted his affection more than I had in all the years I'd pined for him whilst growing up beside him in the castle. Splitting myself between Dooley and Aric had done none of us any good, and now I didn't have either of them.

࿐

I sprinted through the darkened halls to Dooley's room, the burning tapers stuck in the brick walls lighting my way. It was late and he was probably asleep, but I had to talk to him before I snuck off with Mane. Force him to really listen to me in case I didn't have another chance.

I lifted a heavy hand and knocked on his door. I shifted my feet, anxious to speak with him, yet dreading any questions about my whereabouts for the past few hours. I didn't think I could lie to him. Waiting for his response, I took a deep breath and lowered my head. Rainbow hues of brilliant light spilled out from under the door. Beautiful, but unnatural.

Curious, I pushed at the door, which gave under my touch, opening without a sound as it slowly swung inwards. A chilled air brushed past me. Shivers danced to the tips of my wings.

Odd. Dooley's quarters were usually stifling hot. I

scanned the room, hand on the hilt of my sword. The fireplace in the corner was empty of the dancing golden flames and spastic pops that always kept me on edge. Something was wrong.

Before me, dead center in the room, sat Dooley, a pale slit of moonlight falling on his naked shoulders. Surrounded in mystical light, his profile revealed a slight movement of his lips as he recited some incantation. The lights changed from pale purple to blue and red as it whirled around him, his body the vortex that pulled the energy in different directions.

I tiptoed around the periphery of the room, trying not to disturb him and yet just as attracted to his energy as this light seemed to be. My mother had been a spellweaver, one whose magic manifested physically. Dooley was a natural, and his half-fae nature was completely devoted to magic.

A slight smile appeared at the corner of his mouth, and I wondered if he sensed me nearby. My heart flip-flopped. Longing to be held in his arms, I found myself standing before him, all words of my practiced speech forgotten. Light twinkled around the room like a band of pixies prancing through the constellations. I dropped to my knees, my hands reaching toward the bare muscles of his chest like there was no other option. His eyes flicked open and orbs of red stared back at me.

A horrible smile spread his lips into an evil leer. "Why are you wasting your time, Valora? Tick. Tock."

My core froze solid, a leaden weight in the pit of my soul. I stared past the familiar features and into the devilish face of my enemy, my mind spinning. *How could this be happening?* I tried to stand up, but my legs refused to listen. Back against the wall with nowhere to hide. "You're not allowed to enter Dooley any longer. I expelled you."

He erupted into arrogant laughter that didn't belong to the man I knew. "I was invited, and I accepted the invitation. Although I believe he got more than he bargained for." Dooley hopped onto his feet and strode over to where I lay helpless in a ball on the floor. "I'm certainly glad you happened to drop by."

A dark silhouette loomed above me against the backdrop of even more darkness. My fingers closed around the pommel of my sword, but my soul wouldn't give me the strength to pull the blade from its sheath. Somewhere deep inside, Dooley was still there. I wouldn't kill him. With each footstep he left a trail of electric light, like the heat inside him was burning a path to Acheron. And that was what Ravanna was doing—using Dooley as a bridge into this world. If he took over, his body he wouldn't even need to set foot here. Clever bastard that he was, he knew that not only wouldn't I kill him, I wouldn't let anyone else kill him, either.

Jars rattled on the shelves as he hoisted me by the neck and shoved me into the rough stone wall. My voice was lost behind the manacle at my throat. The only words left were the ones in my head. Hopefully Dooley was listening.

Can you hear me? You need to fight back. I came here tonight for you. Please listen and push Ravanna out of your mind and back where he be—

"Shut up, bitch! Don't you think I can hear every word you try to press into this mind? It's mine now. And I can tell you he is done with your whoring. Though I must admit, I quite enjoyed those intimate moments spent with you while I wore my son's skin. Quite a talented tongue you have." A look of disgust spread across Dooley's face, one that I had been waiting to see.

The fingers at my neck loosened, and I dropped at his

43

feet. Dooley pressed the palms of his hands into his eyes and let out a roar. He backed up, knocking over a bowl on the ground. A viscose substance splashed across the cobblestones, and the weight holding me down lifted. In an instant I was across the floor and at his side.

I reached out and pushed my hand through the magic barrier, catching him by the shoulders.

"Are you okay?" I shook him, partly from annoyance and partly because I wanted to make sure he was conscious before I completely laid it on him.

He blinked a few times and looked around, trying to get his bearings. "Valora. What are you doing here?"

"I came to talk and found you like this. How could you let him possess you again?" I asked, unsure if I wanted to punch him or kiss him senseless.

"I was in no danger. Pryn…" He frowned, his confused gaze scanning the room. "Where is Pryn? He was right here."

Any ounce of anger I had that Dooley may have endangered himself by letting Ravanna into his consciousness was squashed by his upset. "You were alone when I found you."

He looked out the window at the approaching dawn. "I've been here all night." His stance faltered, but he steadied himself on the edge of the table. "I was speaking to Pryn, and he suggested I try and meditate and see if I could use my connection to Ravanna to reveal what his plans are. He was here with me." Dooley searched the room for Pryn as if he were hiding.

"Did he also tell you to invite Ravanna into your mind again? I thought we agreed that was a bad idea?" I helped Dooley to the edge of his bed. As he sat there, a faint red glow pulsated in the amulet at his chest.

"My protection spells were up. Something went wrong. I never thought it would go as far as it did." Dooley gripped me by the wrist. "Whatever he said, you need to know it wasn't me. It was him."

I nodded, swallowing the lump in my throat. I wished I could believe him. Ravanna exploited his victim's weaknesses. Deep down, I sensed Dooley's resentment, and longed to make things right—but was it too late? "I'm just glad you're back. Let me help you clean up."

Dooley bent down to gather up the bowl on the floor as I lit the candle on his nightstand. Even in the dim glow of the candle there was no mistaking what was in the bowl and now spilled across the floor. He dabbed a finger into the remainder of the mixture, bringing a bloody red fingertip into the light.

"This isn't my blood. We need to find Pryn and make sure he's okay."

I would find Pryn, all right, and when I did he'd have a lot of explaining to do. If he'd had anything to do with jeopardizing Dooley's safety, more blood was about to be spilled.

CHAPTER FOUR

I stared at my feet and counted down each stone step between Dooley's quarters and the safety of my bed. It took me a while to talk him down, but I finally got him to agree to get some rest. If we did find Pryn, I was going to throttle him. He had a lot of explaining to do.

Absorbed in my own thoughts, I nearly ran into Mane. His arms tightly cradled Kit as they stood in the hall outside her room.

"Sorry," I stammered, and fell headfirst into her tear-stained eyes. Pools of pain whose mere reflection caused a sting. "What's wrong, Kit?" Something terrible had happened when Mane and Kit were down on the surface. I hoped Kit would confide in me one day. Mane was the better one to soothe her.

She shook her head and buried herself deeper into Mane's arms.

"She'll be fine. She's just not ready to talk yet. Have you seen Pryn? I need to speak to him before we leave."

I slapped my hand over my mouth and spoke through my parted fingers. Anger does make you blind. "You don't think his summoning of Ravanna has anything to do with Pryn's disappearance, do you?"

"He's missing? Let me put Kit to bed and I'll come speak to you in your chambers."

Lying on my bed, I tried to sleep but found myself studying the stars embroidered in the fabric of my bed covering. How many nights had I lain awake staring up at this same ceiling? For whatever reason, I never realized the sky stitched into the fabric was not the sky of the Realms. I reached up and traced the patterns, making careful note of each constellation. A reflection of our actual sky reversed, the same as looking into a still pond.

Strange.

Mane came in, and I waved him over. "Check this out. The stars my mother stitched into this design are mirror images of the constellations."

"As viewed from the Elysium." Mane sat down on the side of my bed.

"How is it you thought of that and I didn't?"

Mane shrugged before lying next to me without invitation and placing his hands behind his head. The man thought he owned everything. "I got Kit to close her eyes, but I'll have to tend to her soon. She's going with us. Have you figured out yet how to control your men while we are on our mission? We can't afford them interfering. Ravanna will take advantage of any weakness."

"Did you just say 'control my men'? You must be joking, except I don't find it funny." I fought to keep my eyes open and my senses alert enough to parry any witty remark Mane threw my way. "Besides, Aric knows where we stand."

"Does he? Do you?" Mane rolled onto his side and propped his hand under his chin. "It seems you have a knack for ignoring the obvious."

The wadded-up paper that had found an uncomfortable spot in my side cut off the epic scowl I tried to give Mane. I fished it out and smoothed the creases. Mane wasn't in any danger from this secret.

"What is that?" The reflection of Mane's demon eyes shone briefly before returning to normal.

"From your apartment. It fell from a book as we left, and I've been trying to figure out if it means anything," I lied. I knew exactly what it meant—only I refused to admit it.

He stole the paper from my hand. Outraged, I tried to snatch it back, but he held me off with one arm. The ease with which he dominated me snapped the precious hold I had on my temper. Before I realized, I had unsheathed my blade and pressed the lethal edge to the pulsing vein in his neck. "Kit will be upset if I return you to her with only one arm."

Mane tilted his head to the side and held the rest of his body still. His voice was slow and deliberate, like he was trying to talk me off a ledge I didn't even know I was on. "Tell me why you want it so badly."

Because I am afraid. But I refused to say the words out loud. "They can't see it. None of them can see it."

Mane pushed the blade from him with one strong finger. I allowed the sword to drop on the bed between us as he read the message on the paper. His lips pressed in a grim line, he rolled off the bed. The paper dropped from his fingers and fluttered to the quilt. "You're right. It will have to wait."

"But we're not waiting to fight Ravanna?" Part of me wished the prophecy meant we should stay put—to face Ravanna on familiar territory. I wished with all my being that everything was where it should be—that everything would

48

be all right.

Mane walked to the doorway and turned before he crossed the threshold. "No, princess. But you must find a way to reign in your suitors. As much as you may think they will fight the same noble fight as you, there are certain things that can distract a man from his duty. And a woman is definitely one of those things."

"So that's it? Where did the fighter I once knew go to?"

A familiar lilt broke the silence of my hard-fought slumber. My heart soared one second and sank the next. Impossible. I didn't want to open my eyes for fear of scaring away the spirits of the dead, but curiosity got the better of me.

Through cracked lids, I saw my mighty warrior friend perched on the edge of the vanity I sat at to brush my hair in the morning. Her short, dwarven legs swung back and forth. The yellow braid I'd cut from her after she had passed onto the Elysium was still missing.

"Please don't tell me I had a heart attack and died in my sleep."

"Even with your eyes closed you should be able to see, Valora. But even awake, you are asleep." Franca hopped off the edge of the desk. I closed my eyes for a second, opening them to find her nose to nose with me. "Your foundation is rotting away."

Her words thrust images of all the recent events in Underworld to the forefront of my mind. I saw the selkie pour forth from Mavrovo, everything they touched dying in their wake. The dwarves trapped inside their mountain home. Franca's mother rocked a small child in her arms while the others lay sick and dying all around her. Bodies floated in the red waters of Mavrovo. The shriek of a dragon sounded over the yellowed trees of the once-lush forest of the Riparian.

I bolted upright and searched the room. Franca had melted back into the ether. My hand pulsed in pain. Ragged cuts littered my palm. Wounds made from me clutching my blade too tightly. I shoved it aside and wrapped my hand in the corner of my sheet to stop the bleeding.

I shifted uncomfortably, trying to find a path to peaceful sleep, but my thoughts centered instead on the impending battle. In a few hours my blade would taste blood, and it wouldn't be my own.

"Your memory will be honored, Franca. I will fight to free your people from their mountain prison. I promise." Franca's spirit allowed me to rest the few hours left until morning fully bloomed.

❧

Learning how to fly would have been easier than explaining our plans to go Earthside to my father. Of course, I didn't expect it to be simple. Mane could probably get us Earthside in the Edsel, but I refused to sneak off. I wouldn't leave him or my people completely unaware and defenseless. Besides, craving my father's approval was a disease I couldn't shake.

"There's a good chance this might be the break we were hoping for."

"I need to sit down a moment." My father's shoulder drooped with the weight of the royal robes. The impossible task of being a king during a time of war belonged to him. He didn't have any of the answers, and resources were running thin for the fae of Dell'Aria. Not even magic could solve everything. He rubbed at the middle of his forehead, eyes closed.

Mane remained a few steps behind me. "Your daughter is right. If we confront Ravanna on Earth, we may be able to stop the war from even reaching the Realms."

"You know it already has." My father directed his next statement to me. "Your demon will not convince me our best warriors should be sent away."

"But Father, your best warriors are doing nothing here. We've been training and waiting." I waved Mane off. My father seemed to listen to only one person these days. "Pryn is missing, but even he encouraged Dooley to try and figure out where to meet Ravanna head-on. He'd advise against you waiting until the battle is raging at our doorstep."

"Pryn has gone missing. But the old man has gone off alone before. I'm sure he'll return soon. If he agrees you should all go, then I'll allow you to go without argument. He's already shown me the temple scrolls. I'm convinced only the king's sacrifice for his people will end this fight."

I caught the edge of my father's robe as he made his exit, the rough edges of the heavy fabric biting into my skin. "Father, you cannot sacrifice yourself. There has to be another way."

My father paused and turned his head slightly, speaking but not looking directly at me. "My sacrifice doesn't necessarily mean my death, Valora. Perhaps it's a sacrifice of my crown. Whatever the resolution is, I am prepared to sacrifice for my people. To follow your mother's example, if I must. *Same as your mother*."

I rubbed at the raw scratches left on my hand from the robe. Every interaction between my father and I seemed to be like a fight with a tall patch of nettle weed. On the surface the meek plant seemed harmless, but once in the middle of it, you realized each leaf was covered in a vexing mix of soft, downy fur coated in a substance so toxic the slightest brush left you tender for weeks. Direct confrontation with my father was worse. Better to wall yourself off from both and give each other space.

Mane examined my hand. "You'll live. It doesn't seem like he gave us his blessing."

"Not exactly."

"Then we'll have to find our own way. I'll get Kit and make sure she's ready to go. We'll meet you at the ship," said Mane.

࿐

Portals can be fickle. There has never been a working portal in any of Overworld, except on Winter Haven. In order to take a portal Earthside, we had to journey down into the Riparian Forest. Every step I'd taken amongst those trees led to bloodshed. I didn't expect this mission to be any different.

Mane and Kit waited at the docks where we used to keep the great airships of Dell'Aria. There were only a few left, only one vessel large enough to take our whole group. I walked onto the deck, and the boards groaned beneath my feet. A vision of Kali—the former captain of the Peixes, and once my dear friend—resting against her gnarled cane brought a brief smile to my face. The once-grand ship was a battered hull now, and lay dormant beneath the swirling red waters of Mavrovo. Strange to think of those as fond memories.

Kit's shoulders were rolled forward, her blue hair hanging in her face. Mane dropped their bags on the deck and held Kit by the arms, placing one finger under her chin and forcing her to look up into his eyes.

Kit shook her head, and Mane cupped her cheeks,

dipping down to whisper into her ear. She nodded as he spoke, her spine straightening. Her voice barely rose above a murmur, but it was more than I'd heard her say for days. "I'm ready," she said.

Mane smiled and drew her in for a quick embrace before taking charge of the helm. He was the logical choice to steer the ship to the portal, since he knew the Riparian better than any of us did.

As we left the docks, the gentle whirring of the magic keeping the ship aloft brought me comfort. Ravanna might be coming, but the magic of the fae of Dell'Aria was restored. We were ready for him and his army. But if I had the power to prevent any more death, here or Earthside, then the benefits of this mission outweighed the risks. I only hoped we weren't falling into a trap.

I sat down next to Kit, who stared out at the floating fae isles that dotted the deep blue skies of Overworld. "Life is never exactly what you think it will be, is it?"

I rubbed Kit's back and steadied myself on the rail of the ship. A difficult journey lay ahead of us. Now wasn't the time to ask what happened on her trip to Underworld. "Not usually."

"Valora, I really appreciate what you've done for me." She placed a hand over mine.

"I brought you here, which I wonder if I did more for myself than for you. I couldn't stand to let you die."

"It's not selfish to want someone to live, Valora." Her shoulders rolled forward again, and she hid herself behind a mask of blue hair.

"Whatever happened down there, I'm sure it happened for a reason. My father told me you and Mane saved many lives."

A choked sob erupted from Kit. Eyes reddened from all

the tears she'd cried. "Mane tells me one day I'll learn to accept the reason behind my actions. He says in war many have to die in order for many more to live. I don't want to get used to death."

Kit stood up on shaky legs and leaned against the railing. She listed slightly with the motion of the deck before immediately throwing up all over it. She fell to her hands and knees.

"Goddess, Kit. Should I get Mane? Are you okay?" I crouched beside her and tried to get her upright. I grabbed one of the deck rags and wiped away the evidence from her trembling chin.

I dipped another rag into a bucket of cool water and pressed the rough fabric against the dark circles under her eyes. So many sleepless nights replacing joy and hope with a vacant stare. "Have you noticed the waters of Mavrovo, Valora?"

"Yes, they're as red as ever."

Kit's voice was a flat monotone. "All the selkie are dead. The cinnabar is no more. We shut the portal. But the waters still run red—with their blood. I'm the last selkie in the Realms."

I embraced Kit, and she let me. Her body became jelly in my arms, and I let her weep. No amount of tears could wash away the blood on her hands. But Mane's premonitions were correct. This war wasn't about to end here.

When she stopped shivering, I pulled her away and stared her dead in the eyes, an uncomfortable activity to engage in with a selkie who can easily mesmerize. This time, however, I needed to weave some magic with my words and convince her she was ready. "Are you certain you'll be okay going to Earth? I'm confident in you. Are you still confident in yourself?"

Kit straightened her shoulders and wiped the tears from her face. Her sadness disappeared under a mask of hatred. "Those are the last tears I will shed. The only way to really stop this is to destroy Ravanna. I intend to be there when that happens. His death is one I want to see."

"How are you with a sword?" I removed my own from my scabbard and handed it to Kit. She gripped the hilt at an awkward angle and pranced about like a child pretending to fight an imaginary foe. Her inherent naiveté made me feel immediately overprotective.

"It's a beautiful weapon. But I prefer another." She handed me my sword and took out a long single-tail whip from the pouch at her side. With the flick of her wrist, she cracked the leather, and a sharp snap penetrated the air. "This delivers quite a punch."

"You'll have to show me how to use that. I might need to keep Valora under control." Aric emerged from the shadows of the cook shed, his arms crossed across his chest and a familiar glint in his eyes.

I whipped about, stunned. "What the hell are you doing here?"

A million thoughts ran through my mind. Being here could mean their death. No matter what I did, I couldn't stop them. And Mane was going to have a field day laughing at me after he finished telling me how bad this was for us.

"I'll gladly let my brother take all the blame for this one." Aric offered a cocky smirk and pointed over his shoulder. Dooley stepped out from behind Aric, a knapsack slung over his shoulder, and tugged on the belt loops of his jeans. The black tattoos covering his shoulders and upper arms were just visible under his white t-shirt. "Your father says the portal will be open to us for forty-eight hours. The more of us who can help dispose of Ravanna, the better. He can't risk having the portal open much longer or it will begin to attract unwanted attention."

"I asked my father not to involve you two."

Aric stepped forward. "I guess he figures you don't listen to him, so he won't listen to you."

"I'll get settled in downstairs." Dooley disappeared below deck.

"I completely agree. Aric deserves your verbal punishment, but we need to be united in this battle," said Mane. He peered down at us from his perch above the main deck, "I told you so" written all over his face.

"Can we talk?" Aric's touch lingered on my shoulder.

"Sure." I tried to contain the tone of annoyance in my voice, as well as my frustration, and followed Aric toward the stern. The large rudders flitted back and forth like the fins of a giant fish, propelling us through the air. Dell'Aria faded into the distance as we set our sights on the Riparian. Despite our rapid pace, it seemed like we were barely progressing through the skies. I ached to do battle against Ravanna. I ached to live a normal life.

Aric directed a probing gaze at me. A storm brewed between those lightning-shaped brows. "Tell me what topic you and Calliope were discussing for so long."

"We talked about her people coming to Dell'Aria." I hoped my quick response veiled my unease. Calliope had sworn me to secrecy, and I wasn't all too sure she was that good for Aric anyway. We didn't need any more heads rolling around here right now.

"No, what did you really talk about?" A strange question coming from Aric. It seemed he'd used his affections for Calliope in the past to try to make me jealous, but now he seemed genuinely interested in what she said to me. There was a first time for everything.

"She made me promise not to tell you. But, suffice it to say, she feels you're underestimating yourself." It was as close as I dared reveal what Calliope had told me, and it was partially true.

"Do you think I underestimate myself?" Aric stepped closer and wrapped his hand around my waist, drawing me toward to him. The familiar butterflies churned within my stomach again, and I clutched onto the amulet at my neck.

"I didn't say I agreed." I nudged at Aric's chest, but my efforts were half-hearted. He didn't release his hold on my waist, instead pressing his chest against mine. Part of me figured Dooley would never forgive me for what I'd done by giving in to Aric's affections.

Aric's embrace I could count on, even if I couldn't return his love. I blinked back the tears in my eyes. All the minutes spent in his arms were adding up, and struggling out of the grasp of his affections was getting harder each day.

"You know whatever feelings I have for you doesn't matter, right? I mean, we'll never be together the way you're thinking."

"Oh, and what am I thinking, little princess?" As he named my title, I was reminded that soon I would be crowned queen of Dell'Aria and would have to pick a king. Perhaps sooner than I liked, considering my father's willing sacrifice of himself. Whatever that meant.

"You're thinking you will be named king again." The realization made my breath hitch. Although the fae of Dell'Aria loved Dooley, he was wingless, and a magic user with an absent tutor. Until the fae of Dell'Aria took their own trip to the Elysium, Aric represented the Goddess Varuna to them. Of course—he was biding his time. Waiting for the people to crown me queen and reappoint him king. My king.

"Perhaps I will. We should learn to love one another, then, don't you think?" The smirk on Aric's face grew bigger. "It would be a shame for us to have a loveless marriage, like my last one. That didn't end well."

"Are you threatening me?" I shoved Aric with more force.

"No. Why do you think I asked you what you spoke to Calliope about? As you may recall, she is the one who thought up the plan to dispose of the last queen. I only want to protect you."

I leaned up against the ship's stern and focused on the motion of the tail. "It was easier to know what you were thinking when our minds were open to one another."

"That could be arranged again."

"No, that's not what I meant." I double-checked my mental shields. There were things neither he nor Dooley could know about right now.

"Actually, Dooley believes these barriers between us will only weaken us in battle." He drew a cool fingertip over my back, sending a chill down my spine.

I hugged my shoulders, trying to contain my accelerated breathing. "Did he give you a reason?"

"I'll let you ask him."

❧❧

Aric led the way below deck and quickly excused himself. The smell of fire was the last thing I expected on the ship. Of course, I wasn't expecting Aric or Dooley, either. This day was already full of surprises. Dooley once told me of an Earthside saying, "Bad things come in threes." I was waiting for the third and hoping it wasn't behind the door I had been standing in front of for the last twenty minutes.

There were four rooms on this ship, big enough to house us all. The walls, however, were thin enough for us to hear each other breathing in the next room. Not much privacy.

Dooley hid himself away in the last room on the right, the only one with the door closed. As I finally got up the courage to enter, I felt the warmth emanating from a small fire in the corner of the room. The same field of light that swirled around him the night before surrounded the flames.

"Did Pryn teach you that?"

Dooley concentrated on the brilliant light show as he spoke. Cascades of pink and purple both awed and scared me. "He has taught me a lot. Much like my father. You don't happen to have his journal with you, do you? I was hoping to use one of the incantations."

The confrontation I'd been avoiding leapt right to the forefront. Any comforting words I'd practiced were gone. "I lost it."

"You what?" The blast of rage from Dooley's voice left my shoulders feeling hot.

"It was an accident. There's nothing I can do." I wrung my hands against one another, wishing I had hold of the heavy comforter on my bed instead. To hide. "It fell from my hand when I was flying and I tried to grab it. I'm so sorry. It just slipped. I understand your anger, but don't you think we need to put our energy into what's important?"

"Important? You have no idea what's important. None at all. I can only assume if you were flying that you weren't alone, or have you learned a new trick?"

I opened my mouth to answer, but nothing came out.

"Don't bother answering. You don't understand anything. That book held the key to the magic we need to defeat Ravanna, a skill only my father knew. Now it's gone,

59

along with the last piece of him I had left. I should have known not to put my trust in you." Dooley pointed an accusatory finger in my direction, and the image of him holding a shaking gun to my head returned. When I first met this man, he'd just lost his father and looked to me for answers. Both then and now, I was the only guilty party in the room. Both then and now, I had nothing to offer him.

It only took a few steps to close the distance between us. I wrapped my arms around him, hoping he wouldn't fling me aside in his fury. The warmth of his velvet skin immediately caught me off guard. There was no dancing around the swollen need that suddenly transformed my thoughts to anything but sympathetic. I rushed to the window and gulped in the cool air, trying to douse the ruthless hunger engulfing my common sense.

"If the fire bothers you, I can put it out." He loosened the tie holding his hair and brushed his fingers through the shoulder-length brown curls. Keeping my mind on task was not going to be easy.

"You and Aric agreed to come together, then?" If the only way to get them to unite was by being upset at me, then so be it.

"Yes, and he told me about what happened last night." Barely contained rage deformed Dooley's features. I tried not to move, fearing anything I did or said might set him off. "I will go on this mission because it's the right thing to do, Valora."

"Of course."

Dooley bent forward and mumbled a few words before pursing his lips together and blowing a jet of cool air, which caused goose bumps to rise along my arms. The magic surrounding the fire dissipated, and the flames extinguished.

"That was quick."

"It doesn't take as long to douse a fire as it does to build it up." All evidence of the fire in the corner of the room vanished. Like it was never there. I couldn't say the same thing about my love for Dooley. No matter how much I tried to hide my feelings, deep down inside me, I couldn't put them out. I thought I had my emotions under control, enough so that when passions flared I was the only one hurt. Apparently I was wrong. "Why don't you get Aric? Unfortunately, his presence is required for this ritual."

Dooley turned his back on me, and I did my best to pick up the pieces of my pride. "Neither of you should be here, but maybe it's best we're going Earthside. If nothing is keeping you in Dell'Aria…"

An awkward silence filled the room before Dooley answered. "I used to think you're best weapon was your sword. Your words cut even deeper."

My heart sank into my toes. When I closed the door to his room, I felt the mental barrier come down as well. Aric rounded the corner. I stepped aside to let him through.

"Looks like he started without us." Lights underneath the door pulsated at a frenetic pace. The stink of burned flesh and death smacked into me, causing me to choke.

"Don't touch that knob, Aric." My warning came too late. I didn't know why I hadn't noticed it before. The doorknob, made of the same cinnabar that kept Aric imprisoned in Mavrovo by Queen Elemi, flared bright red as soon as his fingertips came in contact with it.

Aric yelled out before being swallowed up, the door slamming shut before I could reach him. Yanking on the knob did no good. "Mane! Kit! Help!" I jerked on the knob and pounded on the door until pain shot through my fist. "Open the door. Let me in!"

I took two steps backward, the width of the hallway, and

threw my weight against the door. I only succeeded in giving myself a good bruising.

Kit came flying down the hall. "What's wrong?"

"Dooley and Aric are inside. I can't get to them," I said through labored breaths as I continued to try to batter the door open.

The amulet at my neck pulsed, and the lights from under the door went black. Heat exhaled through the barrier and thinned my weak fae blood. I sank to the floor, the acrid scent of death filling the air.

"Oh my God, what's that smell?" Kit put one hand over her mouth and stared at the thin line of noxious black smoke that crawled out from beneath the door.

I clutched the amulet and tried to open my connection to Aric and Dooley. My mind was a labyrinth of walls I'd erected, and now I was running through the maze trying to find my way out.

"Valora, no!" Mane yelled from the end of the hall.

The connection in my mind immediately cut off. "Who the heck is steering the ship?"

"It's taken care of. Don't open your mind to them right now. Whatever is behind that door is from Acheron, and it means to lure you in, Valora. You must not do what it wants."

"But what about Dooley and Aric?"

Mane nodded. "Stand aside."

Kit and I flattened ourselves against the opposite wall and watched as Mane's eyes glowed deep red. He pressed his hands against the door, and even though the muscles in his forearms flexed, it wouldn't budge. He roared, frustration propelling him forward, as he hurled his shoulder into the door. Splinters of wood exploded into the hall.

I rushed to his side and looked in. Except there was

nothing to see.

CHAPTER FIVE

"Where in the hell are they?" I searched for signs of a struggle. Pages strewn about, bottles tipped over—the utter chaos one might expect when two people are violently sucked out of the world.

Instead, starch-straight sheets were tucked tight around the corners of the bed against the wall. A full glass sat undisturbed on the nightstand, not even the slightest vibration marring the placid surface of the water inside. My mind scrambled to understand—all attempts at reason thwarted by the simple fact Dooley and Aric were missing and I didn't even know where to begin looking.

"Hell, most likely. Where in hell, I'm not sure." Mane ran his finger over the cinnabar doorknob. "Did you take this from Mavrovo?"

"What is he talking about, Valora?" Kit peeked over Mane's shoulder. All eyes were on the crystal Elemi used to keep Aric prisoner. The red rock weakened Aric, making him vulnerable to attack because of the blood of the angels running through his veins. My fear about his reaction to the news of Ravanna's return on Earth completely blinded me to the threat right in front of me.

"When we left Mavrovo, I kept the knob. Anything useful in controlling Aric seemed like a good idea. It should be in my bag." I ran across the hall to my room and emptied the contents of my satchel onto the bed. No big surprise. The knob wasn't there.

"You were the only other one who knew its powers." Desperation set in. I repacked my satchel and slung it over my shoulder. As much as I was ready to bolt the moment anyone devised a plan, I feared the next direction was supposed to come from me.

Mane's stance stiffened, his arms crossing over his chest. "All demons are taught what cinnabar does to those of the Elysium. We are created with the knowledge to defend ourselves." He paused, daring me to retract my quasi-accusation. But what other lead did I have? "And I wasn't aware you had it."

I stalked past him into Dooley's room and suddenly became dizzy. The room tipped. Water rushed over the side of the glass and spilled over the table and onto the floor. "Are we under attack?" I thought we had more time.

"Damn, my autopilot must be restless." The ship listed further to the side. I struggled to follow Mane and Kit up the stairs. At the top I heard a short squeal, followed by a string of yapping.

"You let Pika steer the ship? I always heard it was bad luck to have a demon onboard." The round orange ball of fur rolled across the deck and leapt into my arms. Mane thrust his weight against the helm. Trees, mountains, and clouds all raced by in a blur. We were going too fast. The billowing fins of the airship shrank, like the air fizzling out of a paper bulb.

Maybe this was a sign. I should be the navigator on this

65

mission after all.

"Valora has a point—you haven't been the best with ships lately," said Kit.

"We heard you scream. And I really don't need the both of you ganging up on me right now." Mane clenched his teeth and dropped down to one knee. Kit wrapped her arms around the railing of the upper deck. Wind whipped across the gangway, ramming me into the main mast. The screeching sound of grinding metal fought against Mane's guttural roars as he struggled to right the ship.

"We have to help him." Pika barely tolerated me shoving him into the rigging box, letting out a petulant squeak in protest. Smooth varnish coated the handrail leading to the upper galley. No matter what I did, my sweaty palms slid off the surface. We were going down. Unable to get a solid grip to hoist myself to the top, I straddled the mizzenmast. The muscles in my legs quivered, ready to give out.

"Grab this." Right above me, Kit held out the length of her whip. One hand on the rail, the other stretched out toward me. My fingertips barely brushed the frayed cracker.

"It won't reach. Don't worry about me." We were going to crash, and I refused to watch her lose any chance to save herself.

"I'll do as I please. Now take it." Kit let go of the railing, curling her legs around the post to lengthen her body toward me. I gripped the leather thong, wrapped the strong braid across my palm, and released my hold of the mast.

Fumes of melting copper stung my lungs. We were bursting apart at the seams. Kit wrenched me up onto the deck, both of us tumbling into the helm. There didn't appear to be any way to stop our forward momentum. Kit shoved up against Mane's shoulder. There was no way we were going to lose before we even started. I grabbed one of the thick spokes, channeling all my energy into guiding the massive wooden wheel the other way, but the ship continued to list to the side.

"Hold on, we're headed over," yelled Mane. He grabbed Kit around the waist and wrapped his other arm around the foremast. This wasn't happening. Dooley and Aric had gone, and now the princess of Dell'Aria was about to go down with the last ship. Over my dead body.

"Dammit, Valora. You can't fly. Secure yourself."

"We are going to get out of this." The wings at my back beat a frenetic pace in time with my heart as I continued to struggle with the wheel. Every muscle in my body worked to make everything right again. I realized my efforts had failed when both of my feet came out from under me. The ship raced into a full spin.

My entire world turned upside down, my grip barely holding. I watched all the supplies tumble to the ground below. Horrified, I watched all our supplies tumble to the ground. I wrenched my eyes to Kit and Mane, certain they were soon to follow. Helpless and clinging to the ship with every ounce of strength I had left. Trees gave way to rivers and lakes, all tinged a deep red, like the blood of Ravanna's victims. The scent of coal-soaked earth preceded our view of the side of Mount Elbrus, which was about to become our landing pad.

"Dammit to Acheron, I really liked this body." Mane's arm squeezed tightly around Kit's waist.

"And I don't intend to let you lose it." She unfurled the whip from its holster. I heard it crack before feeling a sharp stab as the end wrapped around my ankle. "Do you trust me, Valora?"

"I do. I'm just not sure right now is a good time to test loyalties." Every hollow pore of the rock came into sharp focus. My ankle throbbed, and I imagined my whole body would soon feel the same as we took a nosedive into Underworld.

Mane and Kit exchanged glances. Even though they didn't communicate telepathically, a nod of their heads told me they had agreed on a plan. I hoped it was a good one. The rush of air running by my ears morphed into a deafening scream.

Suddenly, Mane released his grip on the mast. The weight of both of them attached to my ankle stripped the last of my fingers from the tacky wheel. Plummeting toward the depths of the lake below, I scrambled to recall the spell Pryn had taught me to keep myself tethered to the sky.

Scenery rushed by, blurring into a greenish-red swath of leaves, branches, hillsides, and mountains. The dark water rushed toward me, and I closed my eyes. My body tight as a bowstring, I anticipated the inevitable pain of impact.

Kit's shouts were instantly muted when I hit the surface like a dead stone. A wall of water engulfed me. Every surface of my skin stung, but at least it was still intact. Sound disappeared. I opened my eyes to a cavern of darkness, disoriented and unable to tell which way was up. My lungs ached, desperate for sweet air. The water undulated around me, the strong currents sapping my strength as they dragged me deep into the briny depths. For a moment I thought maybe this was my demise, my death, the end of my life.

Give up, Valora. You'll never make it. Even now you are running out of air. Can you feel your lungs burning? Your vision clouding? Come to me, Valora. I will welcome you in Acheron. Dooley and Aric will be waiting for you. All you have to do is surrender.

I tried to ignore his snide commentary, but he was right. My time had run out. I pictured Dooley's face—wishing I could make peace with him, face to face, to tell him how I really felt. I geared my mind for a mental message and concentrated, praying against all odds that I could break the dam that blocked our minds. *I love you.* The last word broke when my lungs gave out. Water flooded my mouth, and a brief spark of panic soon dimmed into a peaceful stillness. Time slowed down and a hundred bubbles floated by me, one by one.

Darkness edged my vision, and I felt my soul drifting from my near-lifeless body when I tumbled head over heel. I shot out of the water, Kit's whip wrapped around my ankle. Water shot from my lungs, but before I could take another breath, I was submerged again. The immense pressure of the water sat heavy on my chest. Limp limbs refused to obey the simplest of orders.

Another tug, and a wave of blue hair denied me my final resting place amongst the waves. The booming sound of my heart beating frantically in my ears was second only to the massive detonation that sent shockwaves through the rock under my back. My eyes flew open, and I watched the last of our ship strike the side of Mount Elbrus.

"Dooley! Aric!" I curled my fingers into the wet sand and tried to find something solid to hold on to. Shivers coursed through my body, and my damp clothes clung to my skin. None of my physical discomfort matched the despair I felt at this moment.

I stared over my shoulder, past Kit's worried eyes, and locked on the plume of dust rising up from the crash. I don't know how long I had been looking at it before Mane waved his hand in front of me, breaking the spell. "They weren't on the ship, Valora. And this strange ball of fur definitely has a sense of preservation." Out of Mane's vest came Pika, a little shaken, but no worse for wear.

"I figured the water was our last chance. Sorry it took so

long for us to pull you out." Kit sidled up next to me, her bottom half morphing from a brilliant fin into two legs.

"You saved me. You have nothing to be sorry about." I watched Mane survey the area. "Why did the ship crash? The magics should have held us to the sky."

"The magics were hijacked. We were all used up and spat out of the sky." Mane picked a chunk of wood from the outer hull off the ground and chucked it into the lake. Concentric circles rippled out from the point of impact.

"Where are they?" My voice came out barely above a whisper.

"Acheron. I don't know anyone else who could rip open a portal like that." Mane sat down on the rock and mindlessly stroked Pika, who snuggled into his side. A simple creature showed me that you trusted those who laid their life on the line for you. "They won't be there long. You have part of the amulet. You are their tie to this world. As long as you are outside of Acheron, he can't keep them permanently."

"We'll get them back." The wheels of my mind began to turn. "You'll help me get them back."

"No, you can't go into Acheron. Being there changes a person. You wouldn't return the same. And I am forbidden from ever entering Acheron again. Even if I wanted to."

"I'm not leaving them there." My jaw tensed, teeth involuntarily grinding down on the nothingness in my mouth. Nothing. I had no plan. "Then I'll do it alone."

Mane looked up at me. I was standing in front of him, though I didn't recall my feet moving. "They're not like any humans I've ever known. There's no telling what will happen, or why Ravanna has chosen now to take them. Maybe they were out of his reach in Dell'Aria and he took a chance. We must have given him the opportunity when we left there." Small clouds of dust billowed around Mane's feet as he approached the nearest tree and slammed his fist square in the meat of the trunk. It barely groaned before falling to the ground.

"This mission was a trap to lead them away from Dell'Aria, and we played right into it." My thoughts were scrambled. I started my own dust storm treading the barren ground. "Why do my father and Aric pace? It doesn't help anything!"

I plopped down and marveled at the steep slope of blackened rock that was Mount Elbrus.

"We should have known," said Kit. "Ravanna warned us we were stupid to think we were safe."

Kit's hollow eyes stared at the ground in front of her. She was folding into herself again. Hiding from painful memories. Mane dropped to his knees before her. "Stay with us, Kit. It was your mother who said those words."

"But they belonged to him. She died long before I plunged the knife into her gut." Mane gathered her into his arms.

My heart went out to her. No wonder she was so upset. I nodded, as if I wasn't surprised, at the same time tightening my grip on the hilt of my sword. I knew Kit had witnessed many atrocities, but I never imagined she was forced to deliver the final blow to her mother. Her own mother. I couldn't imagine having to do something so drastic. Would I have the strength?

Our emotional burdens would become too heavy to bear if we didn't get moving soon. "Getting to the portal is top priority, but we also need the supplies in the belly of the ship." What we really needed were Aric and Dooley, but Mane was right. They weren't on the ship when it crashed. If they were dead I would know. My mind began to settle, as did the plume of dust that signaled the location of the wreckage. If we waited much longer to get moving, finding whatever remained was going to be impossible.

"Agreed. I think the best plan is to climb out of this ravine and head toward the north face of Elbrus. Our portal isn't far off." Mane helped Kit to her feet. The confession seemed to lift a weight from her shoulders, and she arose, ready for action.

I brushed the sand from my pants. "Lead the way."

We made it to the wreckage of the ship before nightfall. Another one of Dell'Aria's resources destroyed. We searched through what was left of the supplies. Inside the remains of Dooley's room was a parcel affixed with the royal seal. Penny sand cakes sprinkled with a fine dusting of Dell'Aria copper. I'd allow my father's indulgence this time.

Mane and Kit then led the way into the Riparian. Stopping Ravanna now became more important than ever. Problem was, I couldn't kill him—not until I figured out how to get Dooley and Aric back first. I wouldn't leave them to rot in Acheron.

"Why do you think Ravanna took them?" I hopped through the rocky terrain, taking up the rear.

"Probably thought beating Varuna to it. They are both weapons in this battle. As are you."

"We have to worry about Varuna now too?"

"I can't pretend to know what goes on in her mind. But I do know how Ravanna thinks. He likes to be one step ahead of his opponents. Kit and I stole his first line of attack here in the Realms when we shut down the portal in Mavrovo. Now he has another advantage."

"But why take both of them? Why not just Dooley?" The way I said it came out all wrong. "I didn't mean…" My voice faltered.

Mane squeezed my shoulder. "This isn't easy for any of us. And we're not here to judge you. Your question is an honest one. But if we are being honest, I don't have an answer. Nothing he does seems to make much sense. He sees the whole fucking chessboard, and I can't even get my mind wrapped around how each piece moves. I'll keep thinking."

"We're close," said Kit.

Behind us a plume of jet-black smoke poured from the summit of Mount Elbrus. Last we heard from the dwarves, they were sealing themselves inside their mountain to prepare for the upcoming war. Their resources were born of the depths of the Realms. Fire, lava, heat—all tools Ravanna might plunder. They were both guardians and prisoners in their own home until we got rid of the threat.

A pop of yellow burst in my peripheral vision. A flash of color through the trees, and then nothing.

"Are you coming, Valora?" Mane crested the hill, his head swiveling back and forth, one eye on Kit and the other on me. He hadn't noticed our visitor.

'I'll be right there, Mr. Bodyguard." Franca might have answers, but she wouldn't come to me with Mane in tow. "Give me a moment to say goodbye to my home."

The sky of Overworld gleamed in shades of red reflected from Underworld. My blood boiled at the thought of Dooley and Aric being taken by Ravanna. If he was trying to bait me, it worked, and if I didn't figure out what his end game was I would truly be sunk.

"We'll wait. Don't be long." Mane gave me a wary glance. "I don't like leaving you alone. Let Kit go with you."

"I'll be quick." I dashed through the tree line before any further protests sounded, and returned to where I thought I'd seen a familiar head of yellow hair. I parted the dense brush and found her perched at the edge of a fallen log.

"You're making it difficult for me to pay my respects to you. You're visiting so often I'm beginning to wonder if I'm the one already in the ground and I just don't know it yet." A million goose bumps broke out across my skin at once. My own joke hit a little too close to home. I had no intention of trying to dispel the ghost of my friend, but if she remained here, it meant she was delaying her journey to the Elysium. She deserved her final rest. She didn't deserve to continue to suffer because of me.

Franca's sorrowful eyes were cavernous, and from the inky-black depths, a light shone out. A beacon. "You need my counsel. Your lack of focus will make Ravanna's job easy."

"Are you already saying you think we'll lose? If you can help, please tell me. Because I'm tired of entering into these situations only half prepared." Tired of being half prepared and just plain tired.

"You've always had everything you need to defeat Ravanna within you, Valora. There's no special incantation or note. You're the connection. Open yourself to it. Listen."

"The voices in my head are gone. Both of them are gone." I swallowed hard against my grief and unsheathed the blade at my side. "The only thing I have is my sword. Dooley is gone and so is Aric. My only plan is to put myself between Ravanna and the rest of Earth and find a way to get them back."

Franca turned her attention to Elbrus. "I need to watch over my people. Your heart and your head reside in two different places and you live in the extreme of one or the other. Please listen to both. You are great at self-sacrifice, but unless your intent is true, I'm not sure it'll be enough for you to see it through."

Before I could question her further, the image of Franca dissolved into the mist clinging to the riverbanks.

"I'm trying, Franca. I really am." I heaved a big sigh, sheathed my sword, and readjusted my satchel. My old friend loved to talk in riddles in life, and the same happened in her death. I breathed deeply of the stagnant air, pulling into my lungs a last taste of the Realms.

I wasn't entirely sure what Franca meant, but I knew that I would do anything I could to stop Ravanna. It was my duty. And I certainly didn't want my father to sacrifice himself at all. The people needed him. And I wasn't ready to be queen. I wasn't sure if I would ever be ready for that.

I headed over the hill and entered the clearing where Kit was weaving her magic. The edges of the portal were delineated by a circle of light. A quivering mass of air bubbled in the center, waiting for us to enter.

"Grab hold. We want to make sure we end up on the other side together." Kit locked hands with the both of us.

I looked to the side and saw Franca standing in the trees watching my departure. I gave her a silent salute, and she responded with a slight bow. Franca's spirit would not rest until she knew her people were safe. I knew how she felt. Until Dooley, Aric, and the rest of Dell'Aria was out of harm's way, I wouldn't rest either. Before Franca died, we had agreed I owed her a favor. Even debts to the spirit world have to be paid.

The sword at my side was a weight of reassurance as I stepped through with Mane and Kit. The familiar sucking feeling took my body apart while leaving my conscious mind together.

CHAPTER SIX

Heat melted through the layers of my clothing, swelling my fingers into useless marshmallows. Kit's hand went limp in mine and she slipped to the dirt floor beneath our feet, passing out in a curled-up ball. Even with all of her magic, she'd not been prepared for this assault. Heat was one thing neither a fae nor a selkie could overcome. We definitely were not Earthside.

"She'll be okay." Mane searched the walls of the round room unbroken by doors and windows. An oubliette. "Must find a way out."

"Damn these portals. They never take me where I want to go." A flickering pale moonlight shone through the bars of a hatch in the ceiling. Despite being open to the outside, heat sank to the bottom, as if a part of hell partially resided exactly where I stood.

My feet felt tight inside my boots, and I yearned to yank them off. I bent over, and a wave of dizziness washed over me. I tried to call to Mane, but my voice stuck in the arid valleys of my throat. The earth invited me down to join the cool floor. *Same place dead people go.*

Mane surveyed my position on the ground. "Whoever created this trap will know soon they've caught someone. I'll need your help."

"I'm guessing this heat doesn't bother you." Sweat dripped down the sides of my face. I gripped the hilt of my sword, drawing it from the scabbard. Every muscle cried out in pain, wings heavy at my back as I struggled to pull myself up. If whoever put this oubliette here came for us, they would see two standing. I might not have Mane's strength, but I vowed to defend my friends.

"No, but these walls do."

Chains rattled above our head, and a shadow passed across the few slivers of light coming from the night sky. Wind whispered a shivery song. Someone was out there. Our stifling confines were the least of our worries.

Hands encased in thick gloves grasped the metal hatch and flung it aside. A rope ladder dropped down and hit the ground with a thud. A means of escape or a trap? If the heat in this pit didn't kill me, then whatever was up there might. My chances seemed better up top. I made to grab the ladder, but Mane held me off.

A familiar voice echoed from above. "We'll get you right out of there."

"It's Pryn." I wanted to strangle that old priest, but if he could get us out of this, he may get a chance to explain what happened with Dooley. Mane tightened his grip firmly on my wrist, his intent stare telling me without words that the familiar was not always safe.

"Pryn? What happened?" I asked. Mane placed a hand on the rope ladder, giving it a sharp tug to test its strength.

Pryn's wizened face peered down into the low-lit space, darkness hiding the fine details of his features. He jerked at the collar of his robe. "A little defense system I set up. I'll explain once you all get up here." He disappeared from sight.

Mane scooped Kit up into his arms and slung her over his shoulder. "Let me go first. I'll come back down to get you."

I nodded and let myself slide to the floor, saving what little energy remained. My mouth felt like the fires of the Dragonlands, and I pawed through my satchel in search of water. Anything to quench my thirst. I shoved aside Pryn's scroll, grabbing my flask. The lid released with an audible pop, and I leaned back, tipping the container, waiting for refreshment. Nothing. I couldn't believe I was so intent on bringing the damn scroll that I forgot something as important as water. My upset over this whole situation with Dooley was making me careless. Yet another thing Pryn had to answer for.

"Hang in there, Valora, I'm coming right down," called Mane from above. I rolled the scroll into a tight cylinder and forced it into the empty flask. If I died, I didn't want anyone to think all hope died with me. The sweet, cool air was so close, but I couldn't stop myself from lying down. If only for a short moment.

Valora? Valora, is that you?

Dooley?

My God, Valora. What are you doing here? You need to leave. You need to find another door. Bowen can help you. You have to get out of here. You're too close. It's just what he wants.

Dooley's warning acted as the bellows to inflate my lungs and my will. Even so, the air was thin, and Ravanna's offer dangled so close, enticing me to take the easy way out.

The satchel under my head offered a poor pillow. Dawn broke, spreading bright fingers of light from the sky above, enticing me to come hither.

Memories floated in my mind, of another dawn lying in

a soft bed, my ear pressed to Dooley's chest, the steady beat of his heart lulling me into sleep. But he was gone, lost to me. I awoke with a start, and squinted as a figure climbed down from the heavens. *No, that's not right.* Mane's face came into focus, and I fought a hysterical laugh. Demons don't descend from the Elysium.

Mane skipped the last few rungs of the rope ladder. "Here, swallow this." He knelt down and handed me a vial of a chilling liquid.

Strength zapped, I downed the blue potion. I slung my arm around his shoulder and allowed him to get me up on my feet. With my satchel and its contents secured around my neck, I pulled myself up the rungs. Sure, Mane was pushing me up from behind, but I wouldn't let him carry me any longer. He already had Kit to worry about. My body might be weak, but mind was becoming stronger.

I wanted desperately to reach out to Dooley. He had obviously been able to reach out to me, at least temporarily, without harm. But who knew if that door swung both ways. With the lightest effort, I probed the barrier between our minds.

Stay out! The force of Dooley's voice snapped my head back with more force than a shot of dwarven mead. A sucker punch to my psyche.

"Hang in there, Valora."

I bucked slightly, my grip loosening. Mane pushed up harder. The drop in temperature sent shivers shooting uncontrollably throughout my body.

An un-realmly scream made the fine feathers on my wings stand at attention. The cry of the selkie. I forced myself up the rest of the way. Kit was lashed to a Devil's Willow tree, its heavy cerulean branches sweeping up like great horns. Eyes of black and fangs extended, the full selkie stared back at me. She would need to feed before we could move anywhere. Yet another problem in a long list. The first being figuring out where we were.

The sparse forest surrounding us was dotted with the most wicked of vegetation. Devil's Willows, thorny pin hedges, and bitterweed spinies. Plants that thrived in the Ordos Desert, otherwise known as Dragonlands. But this was not the Realms. The skies above the Dragonlands are always hot and unforgiving. Swirling above our heads were clouds of an indeterminable dusk or dawn, lights beating a steady rhythm behind a purplish-blue swirl of stormy clouds that seemed to hold a life of their own. A dense fog shrouded the clearing where we stood. Beneath our feet, a dry grit that threatened to swallow your feet at every step.

"You constructed the demon catcher, Pryn. Why?" Mane glowered down on the old priest, his tall frame dwarfing the frail magician. Pryn sidled up next to me, and shrank back from Mane's questioning. The two had never gotten along, and it looked like things were about to get ugly.

The potion finally worked its way through my body, the fog clearing from my mind and power surging through my limbs. "Cut it out, Mane. Back off. He just saved our lives."

"That should never have been necessary." Mane's eyes briefly flared red before he went to Kit's side.

Pryn fidgeted with the ties on his white robes. Something about him seemed odd. I examined his once-neat beard, now grisly, his golden eyes rimmed black in exhaustion. He looked away and shifted on his feet. Then it hit me. There was no sign of his wings. He must be using a glamour to hide his true nature. And what was he doing here, anyway?

"I can see you want answers, but there is no time. We must get to shelter. Aren't Dooley and Aric with you?"

Pryn's nimble fingers reached out and caressed the red stone at my neck—the same amulet that resisted his every attempt to remove it without causing us physical harm.

"They were both on the ship and then they disappeared. We had to come through the portal without them."

A shrill screech drew my attention to the tree. Kit's features contorted, becoming less human and more selkie. Her nose flattening and turning to slits. All semblance of control disappeared from her carefully constructed façade. I had never seen her so bad. I rubbed at the rough scar on my neck, remembering what happened when her demon was in charge.

"Damn!" Pryn didn't usually swear. Pryn's harried expression deepened, and his upset echoed in the string of curses he mumbled under his breath. A very un-Pryn-like response to a situation. Things must be more dire than I thought. But I didn't have time to question him further. Kit needed help. Now.

"Quit your muttering, old man, and help Kit. Your oubliette stole all her strength. Fix it," Mane said.

I approached the tree, Pryn at my side. "I can get her nourishment back at my shelter, but I'm afraid moving her is impossible as long as she has this." Pryn indicated the amulet at Kit's neck, the one that allowed her to walk outside the waters of Mavrovo for extended periods of time. "She's too powerful with it."

She snarled, her teeth gnashing at his outstretched finger. The rope encasing her arms and legs sparked, the magic straining to keep her bound.

Mane stepped between them. "She keeps the amulet. We find another way."

Removing the amulet might weaken Kit, but it could also kill her if we weren't near any water. I tried to get my bearings. The terrain offered no clues. Flat in all directions and every clear line of sight obscured by a milky haze. Our original plan was to end up near Dooley's cabin, meet Bowen, and scout out the forest where Mane and I once saw a demon circle open up. Time to improvise. "Mane, where are we?"

"Good question." Mane stared at Pryn and crossed his hands over his chest.

Pryn did the same. "I had no idea you would be coming through. You can blame yourself, demon. I don't answer to the likes of you. Your kind is to blame for this."

Mane's demon eyes flared brighter, his fists raised. He was letting his anger get the better of him. Kit was going to suffer if I didn't get between these two men and their pissing match. Her head lolled against her binds, and exhaustion cradled her into submission. She fell silent. Even with all the power of the selkie, she wasn't immune to death.

If I could appeal to the healer, perhaps I could end this squabble. The priest had to have some magics that would help. "Pryn, please, she needs our help."

With a gentle touch I envied, Mane patted her cheek and whispered in her ear. Her eyes seemed to focus, but not on anything any of us could distinguish. If she was already seeing across the veil, we might be too late.

"You don't understand," Pryn said. "We could all be put in danger if I help her."

We were already in danger because of Pryn. All of this was his fault. My frustration with him reached a boiling point, and the time for subtlety was over. I gripped my sword handle, prepared to use it if I had to. "Do it!" Mane and I both shouted at the same time.

Pryn's lips tightened, anger evident in the steely stare he cast me. However, he had the good sense to comply with my demand. He drew from his pocket a small flute with varying lengths of wooden pipe strung together. He placed it to his mouth and blew out a short, high-pitched whistle.

A small buckrabbit hopped out from under the brush near Mane's feet. A creature of the Realms. Mane snatched the rabbit and held the plump neck to her mouth so she could feed.

I loved my friend, but the sight of her eating revolted me. I looked back at Pryn and tried to ignore the violent sounds of tearing flesh. "I thought Kit could work the portals." Every time I tried to travel by portal, I ended up in the wrong place, unless someone else was in the driver's seat. Traveling by portal required strong focus on your destination and, at this moment in my life, I had no idea where I was going.

"She can," Mane cut in. Blood dripped down the sides of Kit's mouth and over his fingers as she made quick work of the buckrabbit.

"This is not a safe place. We should go." Pryn looked around as if he was worried something much more menacing than a buckrabbit was about to pop through the bushes. I tightened my grip on my sword. He was right. It wasn't safe.

"Get ready to catch her." I slashed at the ropes holding Kit to the trunk. The bindings released with an arc of sparks, and she slumped forward. Mane gathered her up in his arms. I brushed aside a curl from Kit's forehead and tucked the blue strands behind her ear. "That was too close. We almost lost her. I—"

The ground beneath my feet began to shake in a steady *thump, thump*, and a dull sound, almost like heavy footfalls, vibrated throughout the forest. I glanced from Mane to Pryn, unsure what was happening, but a fierce roar gave me my answer. "That doesn't sound good."

Clouds of dust erupted through the dense fog bank. Whatever was coming was big and didn't mind announcing its arrival.

Pryn gripped the pipe. "It doesn't just attract the small ones."

Mane hiked Kit higher. "Now you tell us, fool."

"Demon spawn," I heard Pryn murmur before he sprinted with impressive speed in the opposite direction of our unknown pursuer.

Although I was unsure if I could trust him, I was less afraid of him than I was of the unknown creature stalking us. I wasn't about to sit around to wait for it to find us. "Let's go."

In seamless unison, Mane and I raced through the brush after Pryn. His wings had reappeared. He could easily outrun whatever was chasing us if he took to the sky. I chanced a glance and spied Mane on my heels, Kit cradled in his arms. She was no longer violent, but she still had some recovering to do.

I wove through the mist, skirting around the mordant trunks. Hopping over the spinies that scratched at my ankles.

"Through here." Pryn paused near the trunk of a tree and motioned toward the base. A solid wall of bark.

"Go where? It's just a tree."

"Only looks like one. Remember my library?" Mane stepped around me and ducked down, disappearing into some invisible entrance along with Kit.

A noiseless vacuum swallowed every sound in the forest. My heart rattled against my ribcage, but the vibrations beneath my feet had stopped. I exhaled and watched my warm breath turn into a smoky cloud in the cool air. The skin at the back of my neck prickled, and I turned toward the source of my dread.

"You next." Pryn put his hands out and murmured some words as blue light came from his fingertips. I followed his gaze, and my heart leapt in my throat at the unmistakable outline. A giant. The mammoth creature parted the tree line effortlessly, as if the ancient oaks were mere saplings. He pulled one out by the roots to fashion a brute club bigger than our hiding spot. The burst of blue light hit him, and the tree froze above his head in some sort of bizarre holding pattern. The creature struggled against it, his hands glued in place. "Hurry, Valora," Pryn said. "I can't hold him for long."

Kali had once used the same magic to pass through the portal during my first trip Earthside. A holding spell. The same one Pryn taught me to keep me from falling through the air.

I hesitated for an instant, unsure if I should leave him. The blue light flared brighter.

"Please, Valora, I'll be right behind you. I promise," said Pryn.

I dove into the tree where Mane had disappeared and tensed my muscles, ready for the impact. It never came. I tumbled down a slope into the inner sanctum and landed in a graceless slouch against a dirt wall. Dazed, I glanced up to find Mane above me, his head barely clearing the rooted ceiling.

"Where's Pryn? He promised to be right behind me."

At the grim shake of his head, I scrambled to my feet and strode to the entrance. I raised my hand and was met with solid wall. "You can't go back. You can only go forward." Mane gestured to another door at the other side of the room, which looked as if it were made for dwarves. "It should go Earthside if my guess is correct, but we need to let Kit recover before we find out."

I slumped against the wall, frightened and a little lost with the wizard. "What about Pryn?" He was the man with the answers. If the giant killed him, it didn't bear thinking about.

"He can take care of himself." Mane rubbed his chin and the back of his neck before going over to a small cabinet and opening it. He reached inside and pulled out a ration of bread and a piece of dried fish from his vest.

"Are you crazy?" The sight of Mane eating hit me wrong, and I narrowed angry eyes at him. "You can eat at a time like this? Pryn was about to be attacked by a giant. We would be dead if he hadn't helped us."

Mane shook his head. "We would never have been in this situation if he hadn't created a demon catcher."

"Are you sure that is what that was?"

Mane gulped down a piece of the fish. "I've been in one before. And I would like to know why he conjured one."

"He was probably trying to capture Ravanna."

"Maybe." Mane swallowed hard. Kit dozed on a small canvas cot shoved up against the wall. She grunted and sat up slowly, grabbing her head like someone with a massive hangover.

"Did I black out?" She looked around, eyes focusing on Mane and the contents of the intimate dwelling. The veil had been lifted. "I must have. I have no idea where I am. Did I bring us here?"

Mane knelt by the cot and took her hand. "No, you didn't. Unfortunately, we were detoured by one of Pryn's spells."

"Pryn?" Kit gripped Mane's hand as she stared at the floor. Her voice came out in a soft whisper. "Please tell me I didn't hurt anybody."

"No, no. Everyone was fine. We just got separated. But

we're still on our way Earthside. You did nothing wrong." Kit was still suffering so much guilt for everything she'd done, which was totally out of her control. I probably should've been feeling more shameful than I was.

"Look, Valora, whatever you do, don't try and reach out to Dooley or Aric while we're in here. We're closer to where they are, but it would be dangerous to invoke your psychic energy this close to the source. This place is a construct, a dimension between the Realms and Earth. Very similar to the area we found in Bowen's shop. They don't just crop up by themselves. They have to be conjured. Pryn created a demon catcher, and must have been hiding out here until he knew it was filled. But there's no way Ravanna would ever be caught in one of those."

My stomach tightened, and I thought I might be sick when the realization hit. Up until now, I was unsure what Ravanna's plans were. Now I was certain. "He can't travel outside of Acheron. But there is nothing stopping him from dispatching his army through the portals to Earth."

Kit looked up from the place she'd been staring at on the ground. "I think Valora is right. Ravanna's reach has increased. My mother said killing her would fulfill the prophecy. She congratulated me, said she always knew I would bring the selkie into their rightful place. It made no sense at the time, and now I realize it was a trap. I thought I did the right thing. But maybe I was wrong."

Mane stopped pacing, and slumped to the edge of Kit's cot. "We completed the sacrifice. I can't believe I didn't see it before. She must have known we would seek her out and destroy her. She was counting on it. All the powers of the selkie now belong to Ravanna. He may give him enough magics to finally step through the portal."

"But he harnessed the power of the fae through the

amulets before, and it wasn't enough."

"This is blood magic we're talking about. Death. Most of the magic drained through those amulets didn't cause death, only sickness. A temporary thing," said Mane. He strode back over, only a small table between the both of us.

The implication of his words hit me, and betrayal left a bitter taste in my mouth. "So we're going in the wrong direction. Whose side are you on, Mane? Did you lead us all here to make sure no one was left to defend Dell'Aria when Ravanna showed up?" I was face to face with Mane in a small space. He wasn't backing up. I prodded my finger against his hard chest, and he bared his teeth before pressing a fist to his lips. My anger gave me added courage, and I stood toe to toe with him, daring him to answer. He stared at me, his expression a mix of fury and sadness.

"Congratulations, you figured it out." Mane gave a heavy sigh and pounded a fist against the tabletop. "I suppose no matter how many times I've proved myself to you I'll always be a demon in your eyes. I wonder how Dooley feels about your judgment."

I took a step back, needing to distance myself before I did him bodily harm. "Dooley is not like you."

"No, he's worse." Mane dug through my bag and pulled out the flask, rattling the parchment inside. "He is of Ravanna. I am only one of the many creatures from Acheron. Otherwise, he has no claim on me. I wasn't cast out of the Realms by Varuna. I am not banned from leaving Acheron. He is. And your husband is his son." Mane didn't let anything go this time, and it stung.

"He isn't my husband." I clamped my hand down on my mouth, the words spilling forth before I could get a handle on them.

"Lucky for you," said Mane. Kit jumped up between us.

"Valora, your fight is not with Mane. He's never done anything but help us. You're frustrated, and we didn't end up where we set out to be, but it isn't Mane's fault. If anything, it's mine. If you're going to take your anger out on anyone, take it out on me."

I reached up and twisted a lock of Kit's blue hair, letting it fall through my fingers. *Franca would not want this. We are falling behind.*

I suppressed my anger for the sake of peace, burying my underlying irritation as deep as I could in a mock truce of sorts. Later, when things were less volatile, we would hash this out once and for all. "We'll find Bowen and see what he can tell us. Maybe Pryn will still make his way through, but we can't wait."

"I certainly hope we run into Pryn again." Mane tapped a finger on the flask. "This seems like some kind of prophecy. He must know something about it. The document was part of his published works. And it seems to talk all about you, Aric, and Dooley."

One more thing about the paper that I still could not share with anyone. Hell, I didn't even want to admit it to myself. They were a part of this too. "Now more than ever, I wish they were here right now." I hugged myself in an attempt to alleviate the pain of their absence. I'd fought without them before, but over the last several months, I had gotten used to them both being in Dell'Aria. Even though I wasn't sure which one I wanted to be with, they were both there. Now they were in another Realm, most likely Acheron, and I wasn't sure how or if I could ever get them back.

A great fatigue settled over my shoulders, and I read a similar exhaustion in my friend's faces. It was as if the journey already exacted its toll, and it was just beginning.

"We should rest while we can. I have a feeling it'll be a long time before we get the luxury again. When we awaken, we can take the other door and find out where we end up."

∂∞

A sharp cry woke me from a dead sleep. I grabbed my sword and nearly smacked my head on the low ceiling in my haste to rise. I turned my head toward the threat and watched Mane collapse on top of Kit. I slapped my hand over my eyes and groaned in exasperation. "Really, guys? I'm right here."

"She's well enough to take it. Better than having her snack on the first person we meet when we go through the door. Don't you think?"

"You've got a hard job." I rolled out from under the ledge and dusted myself off.

Mane grinned as he finished buckling his belt. "Yes, hard. I certainly don't mind, though." He helped Kit to her feet.

"Sorry, Valora, I thought we could be quiet." Kit's cheeks were rosy with afterglow, and she practically giggled as she hugged Mane's bicep. I wasn't about to deny her any amount of happiness after all she had been through.

Waving it off, however, required great effort. I choked back memories of my first time with Dooley, snuggling close in the low-ceilinged dwarf cavern. But dwelling wouldn't help me get him back. We needed to press forward.

As I helped empty the cabinets of any useful items, I found it hard to believe Pryn made this place his temporary home. There was nothing reflective of him here. No spells, no potion-making kits, nothing. In Dell'Aria, the man was practically a walking apothecary. It was unlike him not to travel with the tools of his trade. The barrenness of his hideout was yet another reason to be suspicious of him. A rush of guilt hit me. He'd risked his life to save us, yet at the same time he was the reason we were in this predicament. At the very least, I owed him the benefit of the doubt.

Mane led the way, pressing against the entrance to an unknown destination. My fingers rested on the hilt of my sword, ready for anything that might try and attack us. Even with his full weight against it, the door wouldn't give more than several inches.

"It won't open any wider. One of us will have to squeeze through to see what's blocking it," said Mane.

I sidled past Mane and peered through the crack into the darkness. Reaching my hand through the tight space, I felt something hard and cold. Metal, thankfully not iron. My fingers touched a piece of paper, and I heard a rip as I pulled it free from where it was wedged. The page was covered in illustrations, boxes of characters fighting evil and wearing outlandish costumes.

I felt Kit looking over my shoulder. "That's Superman."

"Hey, you just destroyed a first edition." Bowen's face appeared in the tiny opening.

"Bowen!" I put my hands on either side of his cheeks and squeezed them, since I couldn't put my arms around him. Bowen was my cousin by marriage, although both of his parents were dead. I released his face and handed him the comic page. "Sorry, I wasn't sure where we were."

Mane, Kit, and I all tumbled out into the same heat-tempered warehouse where we were once held captive, the scene of my Uncle Artemus' death at the hands of my selkie friend. Cool metal shelving units housed row upon row of boxes, much like the morgue Artemus used to work in. I sensed Kit's unease, her frame practically crumpled in on itself, her eyes studying the floor like it held the answer to all our problems.

"It's convenient you're here, although I can say I am a bit surprised to see you so soon. It's only been a week."

I frowned at that. Time passed differently Earthside than in the Realms, and Ravanna didn't need much to cause a lot of damage. Mane remained close by Kit's side. "How do you think we ended up here?" she asked.

Mane shrugged. "Pryn would have the answer. You haven't seen anyone else come through this portal, have you?"

"Until now I only thought it was an old, out-of-use heating vent." Laughing, Bowen gestured to our entry point.

From this side, you couldn't even tell anything was out of the ordinary. Sometimes it's all about perspective. I hoped being on this side of the portal would help me gain some. The bird's-eye view from Dell'Aria provided no answers.

"That sheriff friend of yours, Ralph, I heard he found her wandering around in West Seattle by the home she escaped from and returned her there. Fortunately for us," said Bowen.

"My father is involved?" Kit stepped forward into the light from the single bulb hanging on a cord above our heads. She took a deep, pained breath and closed her eyes. "I'm sorry."

Bowen stumbled back a few steps and caught himself on the lip of a nearby desk. His gaze darted around the room before coming to rest on Kit. A box of tissues rested near his elbow, and he offered it to her. "I don't hold any anger toward you. I understand you were not yourself. I also know my father wouldn't have sacrificed himself without good reason." Bowen stood up and walked stiffly toward Kit, his knees appearing to lock at each step.

No words had passed between them after my uncle's

death. Bowen and I had spoken several times, and Kit was never a topic of conversation. Bowen understood his time with his father was limited because he was not a creature meant to live in this world. He had accepted that.

She drew a tissue from the box and slipped her red cat-eye sunglasses from her pocket. "Thank you. I really appreciate that. I do. And I will forever be sorry."

Bowen rocked back and forth on his heels, a weak smile crossing his face. At least it was a start.

"I think the best thing for us to do is to visit Irena. Bowen, have you found out anything more about what she was doing before she was taken back to the home?" I asked.

Bowen cleared his throat and nodded. "I did my best to follow her, and I think you should see for yourself what she created. I'm not quite sure what to make of it. I was hoping everything was okay since she was back in the home. I'm wrong, aren't I?"

Kit buried her head into Mane's chest. None of this was easy for any of us. Dooley was the one who kept Kit alive until she came to the Realms. "Ravanna has Dooley and Aric and we need to get them back."

"Don't forget we need to make sure he doesn't make it Earthside, Valora." Mane and I differed in our priorities. I only hoped for his sake he wouldn't be the one to make me choose.

"Can we agree then we need to see what Irena was working on before we interrogate her?" If there was a chance she had created a doorway between here and Acheron, I was ready to knock it down.

"Sounds reasonable." Mane narrowed his eyes and lowered his head to stare in my direction. I was glad he couldn't read my mind.

"Damn, well, let's get going," said Bowen.

Bowen gave me a long black trench to cover my wings and the scabbard at my side. There was no way I was going to let it out of my sight this time. It seemed whenever I did, trouble was only moments away.

We exited the shop to the overcast Seattle skies, making it difficult to discern whether it was closer to morning or evening. Kit drew in a deep breath of the cool air. Thank goodness for all of us it wasn't sunny, or we would have other problems to deal with. We all piled into the Vanagon once belonging to my uncle. I stared out the window, watching as the city fell away and smaller suburbs took its place. Despite the sleep we had enjoyed in Pryn's hovel, my reflection showed circles under my eyes. Coupled with the fact that I was uncertain as to whether or not we should be here, I couldn't deny I was worried. Mane warned me against reaching out to Dooley and Aric, but I couldn't think about anything else. I needed to focus or I was going to risk all of our lives.

The amulet at my neck had been nothing more than a bauble in recent months. With Dooley and Aric on the same page, most of our speaking was done out loud. I kept my amulet on from necessity. The just because the last time I took it off, it caused great harm to Dooley and Aric. Once upon a time it was I who relied on the amulet. Now they relied on me keeping it on. I pushed it back into my bodice. The last thing I needed was to lose it. I had to believe that if I wore the amulet, there was still a chance I would see them again.

The trees we passed grew taller. I rolled down the window and breathed in the damp earth and pine needles, reminiscent of the forest floor of the Riparian.

"Are we going to the cabin?" I didn't need to ask the question to know the answer, but I also wasn't sure I was ready to go back there.

"Yes, all the activity is centered there. In fact, I think someone has been living there. I'm not sure who, but I keep seeing shadows inside."

The car jolted from side to side as we pulled up the gravel driveway. I fell against Mane's shoulder and reached out to brace myself against the back of the seat. I also braced my mind for the onslaught of memories so I didn't accidentally reach out to Dooley or Aric. In those woods I had met Dooley for the first time. On the floor of the cabin the three of us bonded, and this was where things became complicated. Difficult to ignore.

Even before we got out of the car, my skin began to crawl. Kit reached for the door handle and Mane brought his arm across her chest, pinning her to the seat. He scanned the trees, a soft red glow in his eyes.

"I feel it too," I said. The wind outside picked up, tossing the tree branches back and forth as if they were trying desperately to warn us away from this place.

"Um, guys? Care to fill me in on the whole 'creepy feeling' thing? Everything looks okay to me. Plus there's no car here this time, so we should be alone," said Bowen.

"Whoever is here didn't leave this cabin unattended," I said. "There's something in those woods, and it's just waiting for us to get out of this car."

Bowen twisted around in his seat and craned his neck in an attempt to view the threat. I didn't see anything, but I certainly felt the weight of strong magics surrounding us.

"Why don't I feel anything?" asked Kit.

"I have no idea," said Mane. "If Valora and I can sense it, then it's not of this world—"

A great shriek sounded, and before any of us could move, a ball of fire shot out from the dense forest. The fireball exploded on the ground in front of the van. A wave of heat invaded the small confines, smoke seeping through the ventilation system. Through the haze, I saw small flames flicker to life in the trees, which revealed a direct path to our attacker's last position. There was no way of telling where it was now.

"Everyone out!" I yelled, and Mane pushed Kit out of the side door and into the trees.

Bowen exited the driver's side and bolted for the safety of the cabin. Another flame shot out, landed on the porch, and blasted Bowen onto his back.

"Bowen," I screamed, and hopped out of the van. *This is my fault. I should have never let a human help.* As I raced to his side, I scanned the area for the threat. I managed to reach Bowen without mishap, all the while praying he was alive. He lay limp on the ground, and my fingers shook as I grabbed his collar and pulled his dead weight into the nearby shrub. We were no longer out in the open, but the foliage would do little to protect us from this assault.

Bowen was conscious, but unable to speak. This kind of thing probably happened in his comic books, but to see it unfolding before his eyes seemed to have put him in a bit of shock.

"Just stay low and out of sight. You're not the target, but it will attack anything that moves," I whispered.

"What is it?" The terror in his voice was palpable, and it should be. We were dealing with a creature that should never ever be allowed Earthside. The destruction would be unimaginable.

"A dragon."

CHAPTER SEVEN

Hooked talons emerged from the trees and struck the edge of the fiery path.

My instincts kicked in, demanding everything from my depleted reserves. Dragons aren't your everyday ordinary beastie. I wasn't new to fighting creatures of the Realms who appeared Earthside—however, our scaly friend was a completely different matter. Fire breathers don't use portals. Only a powerful conjurer can summon them. As much as I dreaded another dragon battle, what worried me more was facing the magic user that brought it here in the first place. That and the kind of attention a ten-ton winged lizard would attract in the skies above this sleepy town.

"A drrrr…drrrrr…" Bowen's vocal cords hadn't yet caught up with the shock to his system.

An electric-blue light radiated from the dragon's plated pelt, growing white at the edges. White hot. Yellow orbs set into a massive skull burned brighter than the beacons that guided the airships of Dell'Aria home when I was Hunter. Thankfully, sight wasn't a dragon's strong suit.

Adrenaline flowed through my veins, but I wasn't too

hopped up to know I couldn't do this alone. Dragon encounters never ended well. "Stay here. I'll get help."

The dragon opened his mouth, revealing jagged rows of lethal teeth before letting out another high-pitched roar that sent chills up my spine. Bowen fastened his hand on my wrist. His eyes bulged wide, unable to blink. His palpable fear reflected my own, but unlike him, I didn't have the luxury of hiding. Nor could I allow him to die. This wasn't his fate—it was mine.

"Bowen." I gave him a quick shake, and forced his focus to me. "Listen to me. As long as you don't move, it won't see you. I have to find Mane and Kit so we can get rid of this thing. Trust me. I won't abandon you."

Some of the panic left his expression, and he released his death grip.

I scooted backward, relying on the gentle breeze through the trees to hide my movement. Bowen had no way to defend himself, and I certainly didn't want to draw attention to him.

A hand clamped down on my ankle, and I barely stifled a scream. With a twist of my hand, my sword swung and landed underneath Mane's strong chin. He raised an eyebrow, carefully pushing my blade away while bringing a finger to his lips. Arrogant ass. If the situation weren't so dire, I'd teach him a lesson on sneaking up on someone like that.

A loud pop distracted me. The fire that began on the porch now engulfed the entire front side. The light would act as a beacon to the locals. There wasn't much time to dispatch this creature before someone called the authorities.

The cabin windows bowed under the stress of the intense heat. I motioned to Bowen to stay where he was, hidden out of sight. "What is the plan?" I whispered to Mane.

Before he could answer, the glass shattered. I winced as debris rained down, giving us yet another obstacle to deal with. Flames devoured the familiar faded orange curtains. A fireball blasted toward me, and I suddenly realized I was standing out in the open. Bad place to be.

"Valora!" Bowen's voice reminded me of my duty. There would be time later for mourning lost memories. Rescue Bowen before he became a fried dragon delicacy was task number one. I hurled myself toward him, trusting the dragon leather covering my body to protect us both.

I slammed into Bowen and knocked him to the ground. He wouldn't die on my watch. Using myself as a human shield, I braced for impact, trying to protect him as best I could. All the muscles in my body tensed, but seconds passed and there was nothing.

"You three are difficult to keep up with," said Pryn. I lifted my head and found him standing next to me, his white robes a little blacker than the last time we met. His hands lifted high, he counteracted the dragon's flames. The powerful spell he cast shot a burst of crystalline light, turning fire to ice. Glittering crystals were left hanging in the air like a frozen rainbow, reflecting the light of the glowing fire. Thwarted, the dragon shrieked in dissatisfaction and backed away, its long tail laying waste to the local vegetation.

"That fire will draw attention. We need to get out of here," I said.

Hands moving with incredible speed, Pryn directed the ice toward the cabin. With a swipe of his fingers, he turned it from solid to liquid. The water splashed to the ground, dousing the flames. Smoke billowed in angry hisses from the blackened cabin, and the acrid smell of burning wood permeated the area. Unfazed by his efforts, Pryn sprinted through the dense cloud and rushed into the forest, his words fading as he ran. "I'm going to go take care of that dragon. Wait here for me."

The trees parted, and Mane and Kit stepped out from their hiding spot. I helped Bowen to his feet. Shock left him silent, and it was just as well. I didn't have an explanation for him.

"Did you see all that?" I asked.

"Yes, we were watching," said Mane. He shot glances toward the place Pryn had vanished into the woods. Mane's suspicions of Pryn were obvious.

I shoved my sword into its scabbard. "I would suggest that we go help him, but he's probably more equipped than any of us to battle that thing."

The smoke from the cabin was starting to dissipate, but we were still far from safe here. Drawn to the place where so many happy memories existed, I picked my way through the rubble. I kicked at the edge of the charred steps, and the blackened timber crumbled. My chest felt heavy, as if the press of the past weighed on my conscience.

Kit pulled me against her shoulder. "I'm sorry, Valora. I know this place meant a lot to you."

The scorched walls were beyond repair, and I wondered. If I ever found Dooley again, were we beyond repair as well? As I stared at the broken building and tried not to cry, a shadow shot from the back of the cabin and into the woods, disappearing in the direction of the portal. I had no idea who it was, but I could guess who set the now-smoldering ruins on fire. No time to discuss a plan. In one fluid motion, I shoved off my coat, drew my sword free of the scabbard, and gave chase. The shadowy figure wasn't going to get away with this, not on my watch.

Ferns slapping at my legs, I tried to avoid the branches that snatched at my hair, but I refused to slow down. The last time a shadow from behind Dooley's cabin, it was Brokk's killer. An enemy that remained nameless and faceless. An enemy I had to catch. My wings helped increase my speed through the trees. I gained ground on the slight figure and noticed he was limping. Despite his injury, he still had the advantage. I sucked in a sharp breath at the sight of the eerie blue light cast by the portal that sprang to life. I expected the figure to dive for its safety, but the creature halted at the edge and stared at me. The hate-filled green eyes of the hooded figure pierced through the darkness. For a breathless moment, we stared at each other, each gauging our chance of victory. I acted first, lunging, but I was too late. He stepped into the portal and, with a mocking laugh, disappeared. The magical circle splashed to the ground. Energy drained from me in a giant wave. I wasn't fast enough. Our visitor had disappeared without a trace, destination unknown.

Hands on my knees, I heard the sound of snapping branches over my own harsh pants. With a crash that rivaled the giant's, Mane and Kit arrived on the scene. Didn't they know there was a dragon on the loose?

Kit clasped my shoulder, and her sheet of blue hair brushed my cheek. "Valora, are you okay?"

My breath came out in short, quick bursts as I tried to get my words out. "Tried to stop, came from the cabin…"

Mane scratched the stubble at his jaw and circled the area where the portal had disappeared. "It was good you didn't stop him. My elven brother is wicked with a bow."

"You have a brother? Is that why you didn't want me to stop him?" I asked, incredulous, wondering why I was the last one to know. One Mane was dangerous enough. Now he

101

was springing a brother on me. One, I suspected, who killed Dooley's father. Suspicion colored my next question. "What else are you keeping from me?"

He cast me an exasperated look. "Nothing sinister. You know I lived with the elves before Ravanna's presence. My elven father was the tribal leader. When he died, I was slotted to take his place, but…" He leaned against the tree trunk, frowning as if the memory was too painful to speak of further.

Kit stepped over to him and slipped her hand into his. "Mane thought Torkel better suited to lead the tribe."

I envied their special connection, one I once had with Dooley in this very forest a long time ago. With leaden feet, I glanced back down the impromptu path in the direction of the cabin.

"And as leader, he should be with his people, not skulking around Earth. His business here must be pressing if he risked exposure like that," Mane said.

I, too, was a leader. Should I have stayed in Dell'Aria and guarded my people, or were they really better served by my absence? So far, my mission had been compromised by unforeseen circumstances. Were the fates telling me something, or was I just being paranoid? Uncertainty dogged my heels, but at this point, weakness wasn't an option. He was right. The elves' involvement here at this place, in this moment, didn't make sense.

"I knew you should have let me kill him." Kit clutched her fists at her sides.

"You know him?" I asked her, stunned she'd kept this from me. Mane's silence I could understand—he wasn't exactly the emoting kind. But Kit was my friend.

When she didn't meet my eye, I directed my frustration and hurt at Mane. "No more secrets. Tell me the real reason you didn't want me to stop him."

I expected him to get angry, counted on it, but he hesitated before speaking, as if he was weighing his words. "Because I wouldn't want to have to carry out the sentence imposed on a leader who abandons his tribe. Death. I take my role with the elves very seriously, and I've seen enough killing." Mane directed his last comment at Kit, who rolled her eyes in response.

My anger deflated. There was enough drama tonight without my hurt feelings adding to it. And a lot left to do before it was over. I began to walk back the way I came. "Now I can see why you didn't want the job." I looked behind Mane and Kit. "Where's Bowen?"

"We told him to stay in the car," said Kit.

"Are you kidding? There's still a dragon loose in these woods." I wasn't really mad at Kit. I was mad at myself for reacting rather than thinking.

In silent unison, we picked up the pace until the van became visible. Just shy of the tall hedge, I stopped and motioned down with my hands. Kit and Mane ducked. A sheriff's car and fire truck were driving up the road.

"Dad!" Mane clamped his hand over Kit's mouth.

The sheriff's car was parked behind the van, and the door swung open. Ralph unsnapped the flashlight from his belt and shined it in our direction. I took an involuntary step back, the light barely breaking through the dense brush. He passed it back and forth a few times before he turned his attention to the man exiting the fire truck. Thankfully, the shrubs shielded us and the twilight hid us from view.

"I tell ya, Ralph, we're getting a lot of fire bugs out here these days. Funding for the summer programs just aren't what they used to be. Lots of bored kids." The fireman walked over to the cabin. "Looks like it's already out, but we'll douse it good to be sure."

"Wait!" Ralph cleared his throat and rubbed at the back of his neck. *That's it, Ralph—for his own safety, you need to get this human out of here.* "I knew the man who lived here. I'll want to see if there's anything inside that I can salvage before it's ruined any further."

The fireman threw up his hands. "Suit yourself. Ain't nothing I can do to stop the sheriff. But those boards on the steps look like trouble. I'd try going in through the back. Looks like it's in better shape."

Ralph swept his flashlight over the area where we hid one last time before heading around the back of the building. The fireman unhooked a large hose from the side of his truck. We were not going to be leaving here in the Vanagon anytime soon. I still didn't know where Bowen or Pryn were. Or the dragon, for that matter.

"He hasn't forgotten you. He just thinks you're dead. And remember, it's for his own good," Mane whispered to Kit, and she sobbed softly into his chest.

"We'll just have to wait him out," I said. I watched the fireman pull the hose past the van toward the remains of the cabin. As if sensing he was being watched, he peered through the car window and paused.

I exchange a silent message with Mane.

Ralph rounded the corner, a brown paper sack in his hands. The fireman gestured to Ralph. "I think you need to take a look at this. Seems there's a squatter here in this van. Wonder if he saw anything."

Bowen had kept his word and stayed hidden in the van while everything was happening. The muscles in my legs twitched, aching to do something. Ralph and Bowen had never met. He might take him away for questioning, and I wasn't sure how Bowen would hold up under interrogation.

It didn't take much for Ralph to get me talking during our first meeting.

"We should have left him at the store. Told him to tell us where to go." Teeth clenched, the words hissed out of my mouth. Ralph tossed the paper sack into his car and approached the van. He rapped on the door with his knuckle a few times, but there was no response.

Ralph's hand traveled to the gun at his holster, and he unlatched the snap holding it in place. "You might want to stand back. I'm not sure what we're going to find in here. I can't see all the way in, and whoever is in there isn't moving."

The fireman retreated, the hose still in his hand. Ralph opened the driver's-side door and led with his gun. He knelt down and then sat up in the driver's seat, looking over to the fireman before scanning the woods again.

"Is he dead?" asked the fireman.

"No, he's very much alive. But I think that I'm going to need to call in a specialist on this one. Do you mind if I send you back to the station? I promise I'll keep an eye on the place tonight. My friend would want to make sure I give this a thorough investigation to see if I can find any clues to who was responsible."

The fireman scratched his head. "You don't need me to take a look at him? I have medical training."

"No." Ralph hopped out of the car and slammed the door of the van shut behind him. He placed a hand on the man's shoulder. "Listen, that guy in there is a friend of mine. Looks like he went on another bender. His wife would kill him if this came over the scanner, if you know what I mean."

The man nodded. "Sure thing."

Mane and Kit both shrugged. Was the person inside of

the van really not Bowen? Or had Ralph recognized me when he swept the bushes? We watched the fire truck back out of the driveway. Ralph stood at the driver's-side door until the truck was out of sight, and then he crawled back into the van.

"I think this would be a good time for you and Kit to leave," I said.

"What do you mean, leave? We don't know if that's Bowen, and my father—"

"Exactly. I can handle whatever it is. If Ralph saw you, then I'm not sure how much of our spell would be unraveled. Besides, if Bowen truly is gone, you will need to visit Irena and question her."

Mane placed his hand on Kit's shoulder. "She's right."

I nodded, appreciating his help. "I'll make sure that everything is okay here. Let's meet back at the comic shop tomorrow morning. That will give me enough time to scout this area and maybe find what we're looking for. Then we can figure out a plan."

I watched them leave, glad because I desperately needed to know who was in that van. It would be quite a coincidence if the person actually was one of Ralph's friends on a bender.

Ralph exited the van and ran over to his car. He reached in and pulled a vial of fae magic out of the paper bag he took from the cabin. *So he remembered some things.* He returned to the van, and seconds later a horrendous scream erupted from inside. Ralph tumbled out of the door onto his backside.

I immediately went to his side. "Ralph, are you okay?"

I helped him to his feet as the sounds of suffering continued. His face was ashen and he looked like he was about to lose his lunch. "I tried to help him, Valora." Ralph stammered over his words. "That was the only vial left. Maybe it would have been better to let him die in peace."

"Who?"

Ralph's gaze jumped from me to the van, eyes wide. His mouth wouldn't form any words. His actions frightened me, setting my heart to pounding and my palms to sweating. He pointed toward the moans that came from the backseat, shadowed in darkness.

The beat of my pulse thrummed in my ears and I swallowed as I slowly approached, my fingers cold at my blade. From the guttural sounds, it was more likely that I would need to use my sword to end its suffering than to defend myself. I got into the van and gathering my courage, peered over the driver's seat, expecting the worse. Nothing could prepare me for the sight of what lay on the grimy floor.

"Oh, Goddess, please. No!"

CHAPTER EIGHT

The sheer horror of the scene sucked all of the air out of my lungs. I scrambled over the back of the seat and dropped to his side. The naked man on the floor, curled up against his own blackened flesh, writhed in pain. I was looking at a dying man. One that had held me in his arms. One that I once believed I would give an eternity to. I touched the skin on his shoulder, and it crumbled under my fingertips. He answered with a scream that ruptured reason and bled my soul. If I could give this man my blood, my life...if I could take his pain, I would do it.

"Oh, dear Goddess." My vision clouded over, out of focus through all the tears. "Dooley, can you hear me?"

"Move over, Valora." Pryn squeezed past me to get to his apprentice. "How long has he been like this?" He examined him with his eyes, somehow knowing well enough not to touch him and make the same mistake I had. Dooley's disturbing moans increased, as if he were being lashed by an invisible force.

Pryn took me by the shoulders and shook me, his less-than-gentle actions bringing me out of the trance I had fallen into. "Has he spoken to you? What has he said?"

His face close to mine, I could see his desperation. I tried to pull myself together for Dooley. "No, he hasn't said a thing. I don't know how he got in here."

"This aftermath usually results from travel between worlds." Pryn drew a finger down the wall and rubbed the soot between his fingers. "I'll have to work fast to heal these wounds." Pryn's hands hovered over the scorch marks and claret stains obscuring the tattoos on Dooley's arms. "If only his cabin hadn't been burned. There were ointments that would at least help him with the pain."

"There might be something inside that's salvageable. What do you need?" I eased up from my place on the floor and put myself closer to the door and the fresh air that I desperately needed. Dooley lay prone, his golden skin marked with angry burns, and the smell…if we survived this, I didn't think I would forget the horrible stench of burning flesh stagnant in the air, or the way my heart ached at the thought of losing him. "On second thought, there is a dragon out there still. Maybe I could try to help him heal."

I pulled the amulet from my bodice, and Pryn clasped his hands over mine. "No. You must not interfere. Dark magic caused this damage. Only true magic can heal him. See if you can find some of those jars of leaf salve that Dooley used to keep in his cabinet. It will help with some of these burns. And I did dispatch the creature. He was only a temporary influx, not actually corporeal."

I hung my head in defeat, feeling helpless and out of control. Of course. The amulets we wore were forged in the demon fires by Ravanna. I had to escape, to clear my head and think. "Don't you think that we're dealing with a high-level conjurer, Pryn? Who else could have summoned that dragon?"

"It takes strong magic to summon a dragon's form and power." I watched Pryn mull this over, never taking his hands from above Dooley. Whatever he was doing calmed Dooley's spastic fits. The rise and fall of his chest fell into a steady rhythm. "Yes, I suppose you're right."

Pryn said nothing more, and I read that as my cue to exit.

Outside, Bowen was standing by a nearby tree and headed toward me. "What's happening in there?"

He almost fell over with the strength of the embrace I gave him. "I'm so glad you're okay. Where did you go to?"

"Honestly, I'm not even sure. I backed into the woods a bit to try to take cover. I ran across that guy in there." He pointed to the van and scratched his head. "I saw him and that dragon and then everything went blank. Next thing I know, I woke up resting against this tree trunk."

"That's Pryn. He is a high-level priest and magic user from Dell'Aria. He handled the dragon, and he must have rescued you too." And he was the only person who could take care of Dooley. "I'm glad you're okay. Just stick here. There's something I need to grab from inside the cabin. Dooley is in the van and he's hurt. We'll need to find a place nearby to stay the night."

"Oh shoot, Dooley?" Bowen raked a hand through his loose black curls, and I noticed a new strand of white hair, making him look much the same as his substitute father, my uncle. "I think I can find us something." He pulled a small device from his pocket and started to press some buttons. "At least I can be a little useful."

Ralph stuck his head out the cruiser's window. "Everything okay in there?"

"We'll be fine for now, Ralph. If you could hang out for a bit to make sure we don't attract any locals that would be great."

"Sure thing."

"You've been very helpful, Bowen," I whispered to him. "Just make sure not to mention…the other members of our group to the sheriff over there. We need to make sure he doesn't know about them."

"Sure thing." Bowen gave me a two-fingered salute. He went back to working his own brand of magic on his little device. One day I would ask him how to use it. Magic at the touch of a button was something even I might be able to learn. I certainly could use some right now.

I eased around the side of the cabin, keeping my guard and my sword up. I turned the corner and caught my breath. Bells hanging from the back door chimed as a gust of wind blew past. A rocking chair set under the window box swayed in the breeze. The walls were barely scorched by flame. I pushed the door, and it swung open with ease. Instantly I was transported back to every memory I ever had in this place. Inside, everything in the kitchen was in its place. Except for a layer of soot, the room looked untouched by the flames that had ravaged the front. I wanted to take time to go through the cabin, but my curiosity would have to wait.

"Only magic could do this." I went to the cabinet and grabbed two jars of the ointment. A white t-shirt and jeans hung on the back of a kitchen chair, and I shoved them into my satchel. "A dragon's flame should have disintegrated this place."

I returned to the van, and tears again stung my eyes at the sight of Dooley sitting up. His eyes locked on mine, and I read the desperation and confusion in the umber depths before he closed them, blocking me out. Something definitely was off.

"Will he be okay?" I asked, my voice notably shaky.

Pryn pulled a jar from my hands and rubbed the green salve into Dooley's damaged skin. With each new application, his mouth parted, a small sigh escaping his lips. I could only imagine the overwhelming pain. Part fae and part human—fire wasn't good for either. "He's been severely compromised. And you have no idea how he came to be here?"

"How could I?" I handed the second jar to Pryn, and he started in on Dooley's back. When Dooley and Aric had disappeared I was right outside their door, and although I had an idea where he went, I had no clue how he returned. I couldn't hold back my pain at seeing him hurting, my anguish, the feeling of hopelessness that he might die. A single hot tear fell down my cheek.

"Don't worry, dear. These wounds are superficial. However, I can't be certain that there are not deeper injuries we can't see." Pryn tapped a finger to his head. His gentle demeanor returned, along with his healer's touch. "Right now, all I can only keep him stabilized. We should leave as soon as possible."

Ralph stuck his head in the door. "Sorry, don't mean to be eavesdropping, but you are welcome to come to my apartment. It isn't much, but it's close."

It didn't seem any amount of salve could erase the trauma. Dooley's eyes were still shut tight, like even he didn't want to see the extent of his injury. The quicker I discovered what Ravanna was planning, the sooner I could return everything to normal. "I wanted to search the woods behind the cabin. There was a summoning circle here once for demons. Pryn, we—that is, I—came here to make sure that Ravanna is not starting the war by trying to enter the Realms through a portal Earthside."

"Yes, I know. It's exactly why I'm here. Why the king

sent me."

My father was never one to tell me the whole truth, but he wouldn't send me on the heels of Pryn if he was the one who ordered the priest to handle things. "He never told me that he sent you. In fact, he seemed puzzled that you were gone."

"It is not up to me to question the king's orders. You will have to make your complaint to him." Pryn stared at the sky, which was starting to darken. "Varuna has taken our light. It would be better for you to hunt for the demon circle in the daytime. It would be too dangerous now. And Dooley needs to get somewhere safe. Are those clothes for him?"

I handed over the garments, eyeing him. The way he avoided my direction question only confirmed what Mane suspected. I hated to admit he might be right about Pryn. Good thing he wasn't here to gloat. On the other hand, Pryn did have a point. My father had sent Dooley and Aric along without my knowledge and conveniently rid me of both of my suitors. And the one of the two he liked better had now returned.

"You all can follow me down the hill into town. It isn't far," Ralph said.

Bowen started up the van and followed Ralph's cruiser down the mountain. I twisted in the passenger seat, not willing to take my eyes off Dooley. I was happy he was back, but what about Aric? They both vanished at the same time. Until Dooley healed, I wouldn't be able to ask him where they went and what happened. I wanted to open the doorway between our minds and pick the information out of his head. I was desperate to. But if doing that caused him to be harmed or lost the very information I sought, I would never forgive myself.

We followed the switchbacks down the familiar

113

mountain path until the trees thinned and the scattered lights of the sleepy town of Issaquah announced our destination. Bowen pulled the van into the parking lot of Ralph's apartment building, where the faint orange glow of the streetlamps barely created a shadow. Pryn opened the back door and ushered Dooley out. The artificial blubs always hurt my eyes, but seeing Dooley stumbling up the stairs to the apartment burned into my mind.

Once Dooley was safely inside, I turned to Bowen. "I need you to return to the shop. Find out anything you can about Irena. You know, or strange sightings of fallen angels. If Dooley came back, maybe Aric has come through somewhere else."

"I got Ralph's phone number." He shoved a slip of paper into his pocket. "I'll call as soon as I find anything, and try to meet back up with you in the morning."

I gave him a hug. "Take care of yourself, and steer clear of Irena if you see her." Leaving the van behind, I climbed the stairs, my legs weighted down with each step until I reached the landing. And there was nothing physically wrong with me. What agony Dooley must be in. My hand on the doorknob, I turned. I held my breath, afraid of what I would find inside, but too terrified to stay away.

"Can I get you something to eat, Valora?" Ralph stood at the tiny bar between his kitchen and the living room. Dooley lay sleeping on the couch. Pryn's satchel was open, an array of potions on the low table beside him.

"Sure, if you have any of those pancakes, that would be great." It was the only human food that I knew by name. Dooley made them for me all the time. Dooley.

"Where am I?"

Dooley was sitting upright, staring open-mouthed in each direction, brow furrowed in concentration. His gaze traveled to each one of us, and didn't show any signs of recognition.

Pryn handed him a cup. "Drink this."

"Thank you." He downed the brew Pryn mixed for him and held on to the empty glass.

"You're in Ralph's apartment. We're Earthside," I said. I slowly walked toward Dooley, fascinated by the way his skin re-knitted itself in front of my eyes. His dark brown hair shone with golden glints, and the black markings etched up and down his arms stood once again in stark contrast with his tan flesh.

"Do I know you?"

The room tipped sideways for a moment, and suddenly Ralph was at my side with his hand under my elbow. I gave him the signal that I was all right, and he backed away.

"I'll be in the kitchen if you need me." Ralph put a hand on my shoulder. "Are you good?"

"I'll be okay. Maybe it's a good idea if you can find us something to eat. I'm sure Dooley must be starving." I squeezed Ralph's arm to reassure him, and he drifted into the other room.

I refocused on Dooley, who was still gazing at me in confusion. "So, you really don't know who I am? Who you are?"

I felt the color drain from my face and swallowed hard. It wasn't that long ago that Dooley and I were supposed to be married. If he didn't know who I was, he probably didn't remember much of anything, including where he and Aric had been—where Aric probably still was now. I told myself all that mattered was finding Aric, but deep inside, I cried. My pain must have shown on my face, because he cocked his head.

"I'm sorry, are we together?" Dooley was still covered in

115

black soot. The whites of his eyes locked on me like I was the only one in the room. He rubbed at his forehead, and I think we were both hoping some genie would pop out and tell us what was inside.

Pryn remained silent. I knew he wouldn't approve, but I couldn't wait any longer. Who knew if Aric was in danger and how much time was left? Despite the warnings, I opened up the link between our minds. *Something like that.*

I can hear you in my mind.

Yes, and I was hoping that if I spoke to you this way it might help you remember.

I'm sorry. It doesn't. He pounded his fist against the coffee table, and one of Ralph's fish figurines bobbled precariously close to the edge.

Pryn shot a hand out and caught the statue as it fell, then placed it back on the table. "Valora, Dooley will need to rest."

Dooley obediently lay back on the couch and pulled a tattered afghan to his chest.

"Is the memory loss normal?" Pryn started to pack away all of his potions, many of which looked unfamiliar to me. Had I taken Dooley's warnings more seriously, I might have learned how to use them properly. If Pryn hadn't been there, Dooley might not have made it. I shook my head. I didn't want to think about it. I vowed to myself that if we ever got out of this, I would take Dooley up on his offer to give me private magic lessons. Pryn paused with the last vial in his hand. Dark red beads of shimmering light swirled inside, mesmerizing me. His fingers flexed on the glass, blocking the vial from view. He shoved the last potion into his satchel before he fastened it shut. As if he was hiding something.

"There's no telling with halflings. But there's a chance he'll regain his memory in time. The best thing would be to get him back to Dell'Aria."

"Is that my home?" Dooley raised his head, and I hoped more than anything that the name would spark some recognition in him.

"It's *our* home." I knelt down in front of him and rubbed the worst of grunge from his cheek. *I won't abandon you.* "Let's get you cleaned up. You're a mess."

"Good idea," said Pryn. "I'll see if I can contact your father and let him know we're all okay."

Dooley followed me into the bathroom. "Hands up." I pulled the shirt over his head and tossed it on the counter. When I reached for his zipper, his eyebrows shot up. I hadn't blushed in a long time, but I felt the flush rise to my cheeks.

"I can still remember how to undress." He pushed his jeans down over his hipbones, and I shielded my eyes. "I was hoping there wasn't anything you haven't seen before. But since I can't remember, maybe you could refresh my memory."

"Get in." I pointed to the tub, my back to him. Even though Dooley and I were once together, it wasn't right to take advantage of him in this state. Was it?

"Are you coming with me?" For a second I thought he had returned to normal, his voice as casual and light as always. Or he was acting on instinct, doing what any naked man would want to do with a woman. Trying to get some. And even though every voice of reason was yelling at me to stop, I couldn't help myself.

"Normally I would say no. But there is a very good reason for me to try to stay close to you." I turned in time to see him pull aside Ralph's *Starsky & Hutch* shower curtain and get his naked backside into the shower. He parted the curtain and showed me his dimple. As long as he was

117

smiling, at least we were moving in the right direction.

I hope the more we speak mind to mind, the faster you'll remember.

I'm willing to try.

I stripped off my jacket. Dooley's eyes widened slightly at the sight of my wings. I dropped my bodice to the floor and stepped toward him. He reached out and brought the feathers between his outstretched fingers, causing a shiver to race down my naked spine.

He undid the clasp of my pants, pulling them to the floor. My hand on his shoulder, I slid my feet out, the mundane chore somehow erotic. Baring my body, baring my soul—naked as our first time together, even though there were many other times since. He studied me like he'd never seen me before. The depth of his need shot across the distance between our minds and filled up a space empty for too long.

I understand that we are fae. I do remember that much. Again he stroked the place between my wings that shot pleasure all the way down to my toes.

Seems like you still remember a few things. I twisted the shower knob and pulled Dooley in with me. Soot washed away from our skin and made the water at our feet turn black. The strong scent of vetiver that always clung to him acted like a stimulant to my senses. I grabbed the hair at his neck and pressed my lips to his. Hungry for the taste I'd been missing.

Dooley ran his hands down the length of my side and slid the bar of soap from the dish. Placing it in my hands, he offered his back to me. *Can you help me?*

The view of his muscled shoulders shocked me. Everything was healed. Pryn had so easily fixed Dooley. Why wasn't he able to fix Kali's wings? So many things would be different if that disaster had never happened. Black magic destroyed Kali's wings, and black magic was what stole Dooley from me and returned him.

I massaged the soapy lather into his shoulders and a moan escaped his mouth.

Are you okay? I didn't hurt you, did I?

You don't need to read my mind to know that. He spun around, and the full length of his arousal teased at my thigh.

I guess I want to make sure that all of you is clean. I gathered the remaining lather in my hands and worked it up and down. My feelings were frenzied. I so wanted him to be whole again. I wanted him to tell me where Aric was. And I wanted him. A desperate, aching need forced my mind open wide to this man.

Dooley let the water wash over him and pulled me up against his bare chest, crushing my lips with his own as if he were searching out his identity. His arms wrapped around my backside and he pushed me against the side of the shower. The warm water washed against both of us as he thrust inside me.

I ached to scream, to lose myself in pure sensation. I missed this—I missed us. Dooley read my desires and placed his hand over my mouth. Face burrowed into my shoulder, his teeth clamped down on the soft flesh at the nape of my neck. The pain only enhanced the pleasure, and with each frantic movement of his lean hips, our bodies spoke to each other, muscle memories taking the intensity to a whole different level. Just when I thought I couldn't take much more, I shuddered, riding out the waves of desire. His release was sudden and his body shuddered. In a slow, sensual move, he let my legs drop to the floor.

Did that seem to help?

Dooley's mouth formed a familiar smile. "Yes, but I

wish I remembered more about us."

I stopped the flow of water. Steam filled the air and tiny droplets clung to his skin. I ran my finger down his chest, recalling the symbols he once drew on me to help me unbury what was locked away in my mind. "You asked if we were together. I didn't answer, because it's complicated."

"What, you slept with my brother or something?" He chuckled.

Great, that was the one thing I didn't want him to remember. I pulled an iron mask over my face, one I hoped would burn away any hint of the truth. "We were going to be married. And then someone took you from me. But I won't let that happen again."

I can feel that we belong to one another. If I can't recall the past then we'll make new memories.

He dropped to his knees and kissed a trail from my inner thigh upwards, his hands clamped around my backside. This was the Dooley I remembered, even if he didn't remember me.

∽⌁

In the dead of the night, the town was deserted. Very few cars were on the road, and even fewer people. Dooley slipped onto the winding road that led up the hill toward the old cabin. We were both lucky he still remembered how to drive. I knew Pryn had warned me not to go after Ravanna at night, but what choice did I have? I had to stop Ravanna. He certainly wasn't going to wait for a convenient time to strike.

When we exited the bathroom, the apartment was empty save for a note. *We went to get food, be back soon.* I seized the opportunity to leave before we could be stopped.

Dooley squeezed my knee. Since we'd left the bathroom, his hands hadn't left my body. A slight touch on my shoulder, a hand at my waist. I craved his affections, but I needed to stay one step ahead of Ravanna, and he was already ahead of us in so many ways.

"Remind me again why we stole a police car?" Dooley asked.

"We didn't steal, we borrowed. Going to your old cabin was too important to wait for Ralph and Pryn to return from the store." I laid my head against his shoulder, feeling the soothing warmth of his skin and the beat of his heart. "By the time the night is over, we'll have broken more than a few of your laws. Can't let that stop us, though. Ravanna won't."

I searched out Dooley's mind for any sign of possession. His mind was empty, with the exception of a few recent images. I couldn't help but blush. *Will you get your mind out of the shower?*

I'd much rather take you back. He tugged me against his side, and part of me wished for the same thing. To live in the moment without any reflection on past failures or self-doubt seemed like a gift from Varuna herself. It was a hard thing for me to do. I envied Dooley his freedom. Our attraction returned to its virgin state, free of complications where Aric was concerned.

"I'll go wherever you go."

"This thing with Ravanna, we're both involved in it pretty deep. And he's bad, probably the reason you can't remember anything. Can you?" All those hours of training under Pryn to hone his magic skills couldn't possibly be gone. If driving a car was embedded as a necessary skill, so should conjuring to a fae, with the gifts Dooley had.

"Internal chaos—it's the only way I can describe it. I've got all the puzzle pieces, but no picture to work off of.

Maybe this old cabin of mine will help straighten things out."

"I hope so." Dooley didn't seem to remember any of his magic skill training, which basically put a big target on his back. Maybe his cabin would hold some more clues as to who was using it as a base. That dragon didn't come from nowhere. Though Mane thought the elves were involved I was having a difficult time believing that. Unless they weren't doing it on their own. If they were helping someone else. "Turn off your lights and slow down."

As we got closer to the turnoff, I could see that we weren't the first to have the idea to come up here. Two vehicles were parked out front.

"Looks like I have visitors." Dooley peered out the window.

"Keep driving straight." I pointed up the road, and we continued past the cabin, topping the rise to the driveway leading to an empty lot. "Pull in there."

Dooley killed the engine, and my hand flew to my sword hilt at the sight of the cabin. Despite its destruction, lights blazed from the scorched windows, and shadows moved inside. "Dooley, whoever was there before must be back. Let's turn around. I think there might be trouble, and neither one of us are in any condition to fight."

"Don't you want to see who it is?" he asked, his voice hushed, as if the person in the cabin could hear him speak. "Maybe it's a friend."

"I do, but whoever is in there might be a powerful magic user." I reached inside my bodice and brought out my mother's grimoire, a treasure I always kept with me. I pressed the small volume in his hands. "You once told me that I shouldn't give this to you in a time of defeat. Well, I'm giving it to you now. You may not remember all that you have learned over the past few years, but in here are some of

122

the spells you used to know. Pryn was also my mother's teacher. You can learn them again. No one has stolen your natural ability, only your memories."

"Thank you. You'll have to remind me one day how we met." Dooley slipped the gift into his pocket and then slid across the seat. With gentle hands, he cupped the back of my neck and pulled me within inches of his lips.

The car door clicked and flew open. Before he could react, Dooley was yanked from behind. I lunged across the seat after him but stopped, covering my mouth to keep from laughing. Dooley was standing there appearing quite helpless as Kit wrapped her arms around his neck and squeezed him for dear life.

"Don't tell me I have another girlfriend," he sputtered. He struggled to get his feet under him.

"Dooley, this is Kit. She is a friend of ours. Kit, Dooley is back, but he doesn't have any of his memories." I eased out of the car and gently shut the door.

"Oh, I'm sorry." Kit released her grip. "Dooley? Are you okay?"

"Valora is trying to help me remember." Dooley smiled and leaned against the car. He laid his head on my shoulder, his hair tickling my cheek. My mind plotted on how to get around the cabin without being noticed, but my fingers couldn't leave his brown curls alone.

Kit bit at her bottom lip and drew her eyebrows together. "Mane is down there. With her. He told me to stay put. But I'm worried about him."

"With who?" I asked. I detached from Dooley and studied the cabin windows. The light made it impossible to see inside.

Kit put her palms up. "Promise me that you won't do anything rash. We trailed her back here. Mane said he needed to handle it—said that she must have something to do with everything and that only he could get it out of her."

My stance widened and my whole body grew tense. I knew exactly who was in that cabin. Kit didn't need to tell me. She seemed to be wherever there was trouble. And she always knew more than she let on. If she knew where Aric and Dooley had disappeared to, anything about Dooley's memories being taken from him, or what Ravanna was planning, I wouldn't sit here and hope that she would tell Mane about it. I would get it from her my own way.

"Kali, I'm coming for you."

Dooley grabbed my arm as I marched down the driveway toward the burned-out cabin. "We should do this carefully. Not go in there with guns blazing."

Dooley's voice of reason rang true. This place had certainly seen enough fire. I didn't want any of them to become collateral damage. And the last time I saw Kali, she was infused with so much fae magic that she could become invisible, a power beyond what most advanced conjurers could manage. She must have created the dragon to protect herself.

Kit stood by Dooley's side, fiddling with the sides of her red glasses. She could likely keep me from going if she compelled me, but she wasn't about to do that. She was a true friend. Not like Kali. My body relaxed. "Okay, I'll circle around and see if we can see them from the woods. I promise, Kit, I won't endanger Mane."

Kit nodded and dropped her hand from her glasses. "And I promise I won't eat her until you're finished with the interrogation."

"Deal."

"She's your...friend?" Dooley had seen my wings, but nothing abnormal stood out about Kit unless she revealed her selkie skin.

"Just stay close and you'll be fine."

The dried leaves on the forest floor made it almost impossible to sneak up on the cabin. Although we were out in the open, our best bet was to stay to the dirt paths surrounding the house. I could only hope that Mane was keeping Kali distracted. If we surprised her, she wouldn't have enough time to set up a trap for us. Pryn wasn't here to dispatch another dragon. A real dragon would go down with my sword, but the other kind required magic. Something we didn't have.

We knelt behind the first car in the driveway. I leaned my hand against the license plate and felt the sizzle before the sharp pain shot up into my shoulder. "Iron." I muffled a scream and hugged my damaged fingers against my chest, biting into the back of my leather bracer to suppress my cry of pain.

Dooley peeled my hand from my protective grip and inspected it.

"Well," I whispered, "you asked me to tell you how we met. It was very similar to this, actually."

"You'll be okay." He pointed to the woodpile that abutted the house. A much better vantage point than these iron deathtraps.

"The two of you stay here." I shook off the pain and crept closer, making sure I didn't touch anything this time.

Dooley and Kit stayed by the car while I moved from the woodpile to the edge of the broken window. Despite the chill of the night, heat emanated from inside. I peered in the corner of the window and was temporarily blinded. I blinked away the shower of spots blurring my vision and looked again. Candles rested on every surface of the upturned furniture, stuck on the remaining windowsills, on top of the

125

stove that Dooley cooked me many a meal on, and in a circle on the floor.

In a circle on the floor. My sight returned.

Dooley, whatever you do, don't let Kit over here.

I'll see what I can do.

Kit tugged at the chain of her amulet and stood. She was getting anxious. I tried not to let my concern show in my face, but I was never good at keeping my emotions in check. Dooley snaked his arm around her waist and whispered into her ear. I didn't have much time. Kit wouldn't stay still for long. And when she saw what Kali was doing to Mane, Kali wouldn't have much longer to live.

On the floor, in the middle of the circle of candles, Mane lay restrained. His body lifted inches off the floor atop a low table made into a platform. Under each wrist, a glass captured droplets of blood as it dripped off Mane's fingers. Thick rope bound him from his wrists to his ankles, an extra length pulled taut around his neck.

Kali was in the corner of the room, watching over Mane. I searched for her accomplice. There was no way she could have kept Mane down all on her own. The bottom half of her face and her hands were hidden in the shadows, but I knew those were the eyes of my former best friend. Kali was just as good with regular weapons as I was, and if she had a sword or a bow, I wanted to know before I went in. Unfortunately, the cups under Mane's fingers were almost full, and that signaled something. Something not good.

I don't know how much longer she will sit still.

I looked back to see Dooley wrapped around Kit, holding her down with force. Even Mane couldn't stop her for long, so there was no way that Dooley would be able to without magic, which he didn't know anymore.

Hang in there.

126

I slid into the forest surrounding the back of the house. A faint light caught my eye through the dense brush. Flickering flame. Fire. The wind kicked up, carrying with it a breeze taut with power. I might not use magic, but I could smell it. A deep boom thundered overhead and a crackle of lightning shot across the sky. Rain fell in fat drops, splashing down through the damaged roof of the cabin. Some of the light inside disappeared. Wisps of smoke rose up from the extinguished candles. A gift from Varuna.

Thank you. I said a silent prayer to the Goddess.

Don't thank me yet. In less than a minute you'll have another problem. Kit appeared around the corner, dragging Dooley, who was still clinging to her leg.

I pulled the sword from my scabbard and kicked the door in, quickly crossing the room and placing the tip of my sword under Kali's chin. It was then that I realized my mistake. Kali's face was strewn with tears and her mouth bound with tape. Her hands were tied behind her back and to her ankles so that she was forced to sit in the corner and watch the blood drip from Mane's wrists.

She's coming. I couldn't hold her.

"I smell blood." Kit froze in the back doorway and stared at Mane. For a second, I spied her shock and hoped I'd be able to use her surprise to talk her out of whatever she was thinking of doing.

I stood slowly. "Kit, you need to stay right where you are. It's some kind of ritual."

"You." Kit directed her furious gaze on Kali. "You did this to him. I will rip your head from your neck. You have never been anything but trouble."

Kit rushed forward, but I blocked her path. My foot hit something solid, and one of the cups fell over. The blood moved with a mind of its own, curving around Mane's body.

"Kit, you need to stop." I pushed against her with my shoulder, my sword in one hand. Whatever was happening was dark magic, but I didn't want to hurt Kit.

Dooley, where are you? I need your help.

He appeared in the doorway and swayed, one hand holding the frame and the other clamped over his neck.

"You bit my boyfriend?"

I shoved a little harder against Kit. She sobered for a second, looking from Dooley to me.

"I smelled the blood." She looked over at Mane, who was still unconscious. The remaining cup was filled to the brim. A few more drops landed and dripped down the side. We all watched as the blood snaked around Mane's body and joined up with the other line, almost closing the circle.

"We can't let that cup spill on the floor. I don't know much about magic, but a circle of blood around a body can't be good."

"What do we do?" asked Kit.

I ripped the tape from Kali's mouth, pausing to enjoy it for just a second. "She'll know. Tell me, who's responsible for all this?"

Kali inhaled deeply. "You wouldn't believe me. Besides, it's too late." She started to sob and rock herself back and forth.

"What do you mean it's too late?"

"I can help." Kit picked up the other cup of blood.

"Kit, what are you doing? You can't be that near to the blood." Too late, Kit's eyes blackened and her selkie nature overtook her. She wasn't supposed to drink demon blood, but that didn't matter. It was blood, it was fresh, and it was in her hands.

"No!" I jumped across Mane's body, and the glass toppled from Kit's hands. The blood drew together, mere inches from completing the circuit. "We need to get Mane out. Kit, Dooley, I need your help."

I clasped Mane's arm and tugged as hard as I could. He wasn't moving. Kit's eyes were still black, but she held on to the other arm. Dooley came in behind me and lifted Mane's shoulders. We backed up but there was nowhere to go. The circle widened around all of us. Kali remained huddled in the corner, free from the magic.

My amulet shot out beams of red light like a beacon. A triangle of light bounced from me to Kit to Dooley, all of our amulets glowing bright and casting the room in hues of red and blue. Pryn appeared, his hands pressed against the window. His lips pursed into the word "No!"

I called out, but no sound escaped my lips. Then the mouth of hell opened and swallowed us whole.

CHAPTER NINE

Growing up, I never imagined a hell. The texts I read all talked about Elysium and Varuna. The priests focused on the reward, not the punishment, and we were never taught what the alternative might be. There was no hell because no one ever told us about it.

After learning about Acheron, Dooley shared the stories he learned growing up. His foster family were staunch Catholics, and he attended church every Sunday. Once, in Bible study, all the children were asked to write about what they thought hell would be like. Control through fear. Dooley explained that most of the children wrote about hell as a hot place covered in fire-breathing lava pits, a red-clad, pitchfork-carrying devil residing over it. Most of what he described sounded more like Mount Elbrus than hell to me. Franca would probably have gotten a good laugh out of it.

I spread my hands across the smooth lined surface beneath me. I opened my eyes, confirming the mattress below my hands belonged to reality and not fantasy. A cool breeze blew across my cheek through an open window—no fire or brimstone. Beyond the iron windowsill, a vast mountainside rose up. Lush terraced steps covered in dry grasses bathed in amber light were muted by gentle shadows from clouds passing overhead. I tried to sit up, and all the muscles in my body screamed out in pain. The beauty masked what the place truly was. A prison. I had to get out of here, to escape while I had a chance.

A delicate hand came up under my head and tilted it slightly, raising a cup to my lips. Startled, I batted it away.

"Drink this, you'll feel better," she encouraged. This woman and Kit could be twins except for her dark brown hair, and she definitely didn't have any fins. In fact, she seemed rather normal. Too normal.

I didn't want to take any food or drink from a stranger, but weakness overcame my refusal of her offering, and the warm liquid dribbled over the side of the cup into my half-open mouth. The brew hit my belly like a shot of adrenaline, and I bolted upright. My heart racing, I clutched my chest, my fingers seeking the familiar amulet. Gone. I confronted her, furious.

"Where's my amulet? What the hell did you give me?"

The woman put down the cup and brushed my knee, her apologetic smile belying the calculation in her eyes. "I didn't mean to startle you. I didn't know how to mix this for a full-blooded fae. You're the first of your kind to ever visit. Your amulet has been taken for safekeeping."

"What about my friends?" A quick scan of the room revealed that this stranger and I were alone. The walls were made of a kind of organic material smelling vaguely of oak moss. The sparse décor included a symbol etched into the doorway—a symbol I remembered. One prominently displayed on another doorway that I recalled seeing in Bowen's shop. A symbol traced in Dooley's blood that supposedly led to Acheron.

"Dooley and his father are together. The rest are recovering like you are. Mane, however, has been transferred to the cells." A note of sadness tinged her voice. "He was never supposed to return."

"I don't know how we got here or who damned us, but it wasn't our choosing. Get my friends and we'll take the first portal out of here and leave you all alone."

"You think leaving Acheron is that easy?" Her sweet smile quickly morphed from innocent into a more sinister grin. "Make yourself comfortable. You'll be here for a while."

The woman got up and walked to the door. Instinct screamed that I couldn't allow her to leave. I rushed her as she opened the door, desperate to stop her. She whirled around and mouthed some words. An unseen force slammed me against the opposite wall. Like the woman, the walls appeared soft and pliable, but they were anything but. Pain radiated along my thigh. My leg wasn't broken, but it would be badly bruised.

"Things aren't what they seem here. You would be wise to follow that advice, Valora. Don't worry, you won't have to wait long to learn your fate." As she shut the door, I noticed that around her ankles were thick metal irons that bit into her skin, angry red welts lacing her calf. She too was being held against her will. I cursed myself for not noticing sooner. Maybe I could have offered her help.

Outside, the scene seemed so peaceful. I found it difficult to believe that the demon who had caused me such strife lived and ruled here, and that Mane was so keen to leave it all behind. Beyond the terraced mountains I could see outlines of more peaks and valleys shadowed in black outline against a large fog bank. Beyond that, nothingness.

Through the window, I gauged my cell to be positioned

high above it all. From my brief inspection, I saw no handholds on the sleek face of the building. No use trying to climb out of my prison. On the hillsides dozens of figures worked the land, gathering crops into baskets that were slung across their bodies. Just another world where people lived their lives. Where were these armies that were supposed to be entering Earth? The legions of terrible demons and beasts that I expected?

A click, followed by the rattle of a doorknob, echoed from behind me. I readied myself as best I could, instinctively reaching for a sword that wasn't there. If everyone here knew magic, I would be in trouble. In strolled a man, a brilliant mop of red hair falling forward into his eyes. He swiped a lock behind his ear and gave me a wink. After quickly shutting the door behind him, he dropped a tray of food on the table next to my small cot.

"Valora! I thought I would never have the chance to see you in the flesh, my dear. You are even more ravishing in person than through that old shaman's eyes. I don't believe we have been properly introduced. My name is Niro."

The demon bent down and left a kiss on the back of my hand.

I knew immediately who he was. The demon that often took up residence in the dwarven shaman's head. Nice or nefarious, I hadn't decided which side he belonged to. "Where are the others?"

"You should eat. You must be starving after traveling all that way." Niro brought a finger to his lips.

We can more formally discuss matters without even speaking. Niro scooped up a spoonful of something resembling a baked root vegetable and brought it to my mouth. *You must eat if you're going to have strength for what's to come.*

Are you on my side, then?

133

Niro shrugged. *I'm on my own side. For now, it happens to align with yours. You'll find that's the way of most demons. I have no interest in any of the conflicts going on. They're really disturbing my normal routine.*

I reached for the amulet at my neck, a nervous habit I had developed, but just like the sword, it was gone as well. Acheron demons didn't appear to need anything extra to poke around inside your head. A fact I would do well to remember.

The food went down easily. *I suppose the shaman isn't as fun to hang out with, since he's been locked up in Mount Elbrus.*

Hardly. So many of the dwarves are dying in there. He spends all his time tending to the sick. No more beesroot pipes for me.

The pain in my stomach returned with a vengeance. The dwarves were trapped in Mount Elbrus. I promised Franca that her death would not be in vain, yet I had failed to protect her family. The longer this conflict lingered, the worse it would be.

How do I find the others and get out of here?

Difficult. Niro rubbed his chin. *They're strewn throughout the confines of these walls. You won't be able to retrieve everyone. If you have any hopes of escaping, you'll need to leave Mane and the selkie behind. Ravanna is particularly glad to have Mane to take his anger out on, and the selkies did not live up to his expectations. He'll probably take the girl as another one of his concubines.*

The food crept up my throat and I choked it down again. "I won't let that happen."

"You don't have a choice." Niro stood and left the tray. "Ravanna will send for you soon. Now that he has all the amulets, your interference doesn't concern him. His next task is to amass an army, which he hopes Dooley will lead."

"What? He doesn't even know who he is."

"Exactly. Ravanna thinks you're responsible for that

trick. He will expect answers. Hopefully you have a good explanation." Niro shut the door, and I could hear his footsteps recede down the hallway.

If there was one thing I hated more than being discounted, it was being ignored. No one considered me a threat. I couldn't fly out of the prison because I didn't have proper wings. And they'd confiscated my sword, so I couldn't fight.

I needed magic. I might not have learned the proper spells, but Dooley had shared what he knew. I had spent hours memorizing every square inch of his body, and all the symbols etched into his skin. I scoured the corners of the room for any bit of dirt I could find, and mixed it with the remains of my breakfast. Or dinner. Who knew in this place? Thank the Goddess for a skulking demon and my lack of appetite.

Magic blocked the door to my cell, and I was going to try my best to break it. I inhaled deeply and thought of when Dooley had painted the symbols on my skin to help me unlock memories buried deep within my psyche. Memories that eventually helped me put the pieces together and discover Aric was the one who terrorized the city of Dell'Aria.

I recalled each of the markings and their individual strokes, and mimicked each one. Taking the tray of leftovers, I dipped a finger into the mealy mash and transferred it to the door like an artist and her paint, giving reverence and attention to each small detail. These symbols were similar enough that one wrong stroke and I might be doing the opposite of what I intended.

Without our amulets, opening my mind to Dooley wasn't possible. The best thing to do would be to free myself from this prison and seek out Dooley and Aric and see if we could find a way out of here together.

The symbols finished, I uttered Dooley's words under my breath. Silence made my heart sink. Then a small *pop*, like a change in air pressure, cracked the seal on the door. I pressed gently against the frame seconds before it swung open. An empty hallway greeted me to the right. To the left, I caught sight of a familiar mass of white-blond hair.

"Were you coming for me? I was wondering what was taking you so long."

CHAPTER TEN

Internal condemnation was a harder pill to swallow than being dragged into Acheron. My arms flew around Aric's neck, and I passed my fingers through the down of his blue feathers, unsoiled despite our dire situation. Relief mingled with guilt at his unspoken accusation. "You're not locked up."

"Not much point. My wings won't carry me beyond the mist. I have no weapons, no amulet, no way to get out, and no clue why I am even here. Except…" Aric crossed his arms and leaned against the stone archway. The grime seemed to deflect from his white garments. Unlike the woman who had tended to me, no special irons imprisoned his ankles. I could see his frustration by the way he glared at the ground and sensed a growing unease about him. "I tried to leave, countless times, obviously with no success. I never realized demon scum could laugh so hard. Assholes."

"You're here because Ravanna used you as bait to lead me here, but for what purpose? I only wished I knew what his intentions were and could prepare for it." It was difficult to believe that anyone thought of me as a threat, especially a demon king. Yet here I stood, the only person with any chance of defeating him, and I was scared to death of failing.

A flash of Dooley raced through my mind, voices echoing inside him, telling him to join the cause. To fight for his father, defeat Varuna, and triumphantly free Ravanna from him prison.

"Our minds are all wide open here. If you think hard enough, you'll find the answers. And Niro likes to talk. Ravanna thinks you pulled Dooley out of here and wiped his memories. Which I know can't be possible, since you wouldn't have forgotten me." Aric blew on his nails and buffed them against his shirt. He strolled into my cell and looked at the remains on my tray. "That's disgusting."

I crossed the threshold behind him and stumbled on my witty retort when a warm languor wrapped itself around my shoulders. My eyes drifted to the curve of his backside, and I could only manage a breathy sigh. Disgustingly sexy and equally as dangerous. "Yeah."

The angelic offspring of a fae and possessed human who had an infinite capacity and hunger for sin. Ravanna would be better served convincing Aric to help him than Dooley. But it didn't matter. Prurience singed the edges of my nerves and left my soul chilled. A craving, an itch. Unwholesome thoughts evoking a sheer, unadulterated carnal lust. The magical workings of an unnatural desire permeated all my thoughts. The sane part of my mind—that tiny voice that rested at the edge of reason—said to run far and run fast. I ignored it, lying back and letting the intensely pleasurable and relaxing wave flow from the tips of my toes into the top of my head.

Aric sat down and patted the cot next to him. "When we arrived there was no convincing Dooley to join his father. Without his memories, who knows now?"

I immediately responded to his silent beckoning, my fingers curled into fists, my body humming with need and a vague sense of unease. "No, he can't possibly be considering it. Look, I have no idea how we got here. If our minds are open, Ravanna must know I didn't have anything to do with it." In a rush, I told Aric all about Mane and the blood magic. "Kali seemed to know who was responsible, but she said I wouldn't believe her."

"Kali." Aric grimaced and pushed a balled fist into his other palm. The strips of fabric that crisscrossed over his chest pulled tightly over his flexed muscles. Muscles that seemed to be calling my name. "And of course she was left on Earth."

"Yes, but so was Pryn. He'll help find a way to get us back through." Pryn didn't trust Mane, and I had to admit, I questioned his actions of late. Would father's trusted adviser leave us all here to rot? Even if he wanted to help them escape, was he powerful enough to do so? And what if he was too late? The ever-present paper still rested against my chest, a constant reminder of my fate. I was the one who was destined to save the world. *And that's why Ravanna fears me.* I needed to get us all out of here before it was too late. The thought hit with such clarity and then faded faster than the winds of Dell'Aria, leaving my mind once again focused where it had no right to be, on bedding Aric.

"I'm told no one leaves Acheron," said Aric. Even here in hell, he seemed to glow a little around the edges, his white-blond hair gleaming despite our contaminated surroundings.

"Dooley did." Like in a dream, the edges of my reality blurred until the only thing that mattered was getting closer to Aric. I ran my fingers through his hair again. To make sure he was real. He tilted his head to the side and gave a soft purr.

"Yes, but at what price?" Aric stretched his arms wide and leaned back into my chest. His wings tickled the bare skin at my shoulders. "You say he was burned and now has no memory. He would have died without Pryn."

"That's true." My hand moved from his hair down to his wings. The urge to touch him, to massage him, to have him touch me, created a strange pull that made me want to jump his bones. There wasn't anything I wouldn't do to make that happen right now.

Niro and his bright mass of red hair appeared in the doorway. He cleared his throat, an amused grin on his face. "I see Ravanna's distraction spells seem to be working. Sorry to interrupt, but he wants to see you. Come." Niro gestured me to follow him, and when I didn't immediately obey, he clamped down hard on my wrist.

"Dammit!" The demon king's influence on my love life was becoming a nuisance. My attempt to pull back provoked an amused grin from Niro. "You're hurting me. I thought you said that you were on your own side."

"Yes, and right now I don't feel like getting my ass burned by the boss. So come with me." Niro's eyes lit with a familiar red glow. I wasn't getting out of this meeting.

"Don't worry, I'll come with you." Aric jumped off the bed and adjusted the slight bulge in his pants. If Niro hadn't come by, I wasn't sure I would've been able to control myself. That wasn't a good sign. Not a good sign for my current mental stability and for future decisions I would have to make. But not now. Right now we needed to get out of here. All of us.

"I don't think Ravanna would like that angel boy."

"Ravanna can bite me. I won't leave Valora to him alone." Aric slid a hand around my waist. Niro released his grip on my wrist.

"He does bite you know, and so do I, hard. I would be careful what you wished for."

Aric and I followed Niro into a serpentine labyrinth of roughhewn stone passageways. We passed many chambers or prison cells, depending on how you looked at it. Lantern lights bobbed up and down at the far ends of the passageways, directed by unseen creatures. Afraid of getting lost, I edged closer to Niro and practically bumped into his backside.

"Be careful how close you get, darling. That little distraction spell of Ravanna's is powerful enough to affect even me." The light in his hands cast a sickly glow on his face. The demon less hidden. I wondered if Mane's true visage was as frightful. I backed off a few feet and made sure I kept my eyes on him. Every so often we passed under another gateway, each becoming more ornate as we delved deeper. There was symbol magic on every wall. A weight descended onto my shoulders, one I couldn't shake. I started to panic, afraid I would fall to my knees and sink into the dark earth itself.

"It'll get worse. Don't fight it too much. Easier to kneel before the bastard, since that's what he wants." Aric trudged forward, jaw clenched, his body pitched forward at a slight angle.

The air was thick with incense, clay, stone, a hint of decay, and a heavy, dolorous vapor that almost evoked sympathy. Breathing became difficult, and the suffocating feeling increased until my heart was thudding in my chest and my head ached from the pressure. Trapped deep beneath the Underworld, the hollow scent of a vast subterranean civilization, now buried, was smothered by an impenetrable barrier of magic

"Give me a second." Aric bowed forward and stopped. He braced himself on his knees and clutched at his chest. "He wanted his amulets back. Now that you're here, he has all of them."

Ravanna's distraction spell had worked so well that I hadn't even noticed. "Are you okay without it?" The rules of these amulets were never defined by anything other than our trial and error. But our errors showed us multiple times that if anything seemed certain, it was that keeping them on was the best course of action.

"Better than ever, actually—except for this particular moment, of course."

I had to laugh, considering we were in hell. Aric took in a labored breath. He pushed up, and the cords in his neck went taut.

"The easiest way for Ravanna to get the amulets was to bring us here," I said. Ravanna needed the demon stones for something. I reached over and squeezed Aric's hand. He had to trust me. I was about to try something really stupid. Something I couldn't tell him about or even think much about. I needed some distraction, a way to draw attention away from me. "Mane claimed he saw one of the elves running from the cabin. Maybe he was aligned with Ravanna and helped him get us here."

"You have a plan?" Aric stared at me, eyebrow raised. "Because if you do, I'm all ears."

So is everything else around here. Will you two shut up? Niro's voice rang through my head. The look on Aric's face said he'd heard the message.

"The Gate of Divine Might. This is as far as I go," said Niro. He stopped before a set of immense red doors that were opened wide. He gestured us through, and as I passed, I noticed adornment etched deep into the inset panels. A symbol, like a knot, which repeated itself three times. A triad.

The pressure intensified, and my back screamed for relief from the unrelenting pain.

"I don't know why I always agree to do things your way…the hard way," mumbled Aric. A bead of sweat formed on his brow as he fought the unseen force. "Which, don't get me wrong, I sometimes like."

From my twisted position, I scanned the room. The expanse reminded me of the tombs of Dell'Aria, ominous and unwelcoming. In the center of the daunting room sat a lone piece of furniture piled high with maps and scrolls. I resisted the urge to shudder when I realized the rectangular wooden table and chair were stained crimson red. A loud *pop* from a log in the massive fireplace made me jump, but my stunned reaction was eclipsed by the sight before me. Amongst the scent of dusty tombs and polished oak wood, Dooley sat at a chair studying the papers. Opposite him stood the demon that haunted my dreams. Like in my nightmares, he stared at me, arms crossed over his massive chest. The deep eggplant shade of his skin made the whites of his eyes even more menacing

I cried out, "Dooley!" Relief mingled with dread and an overwhelming horror of what he might have become.

Ravanna spread his hand wide, his long fingers flexing, and then slowly brought his thumb and forefinger together. The words I ached to voice were cut off, and my throat felt as if it were in a vise. Helplessly, I clawed at my neck, but there was nothing there to fight against. Aric dropped to one knee beside me, the sight of his struggle pulling me further out of my panic. My friends depended on me to save their lives—weakness wasn't an option. I inhaled sharply through my nose and redirected my focus even as my body was pulled down by the invisible strings. My voice might not work, but I was betting my thoughts still did. *You must have paid a fortune for this tile work.*

"You're very stubborn." Ravanna unleashed a roar, the sharpened points of each of his sharp incisors revealing the depth of his predatory nature. He either wanted to eat me or rip me into tiny pieces—then eat me.

My legs buckled under me and my face slammed into the granite floor. I stifled my cry of pain, determined to cover up any weakness. Aric dropped down next to me.

With every bit of strength I possessed, I craned my neck, anxious to get a glimpse of Dooley, to beg him for help. He didn't even seem to notice we were there. Then his image flickered and my stomach dropped. Where was the real Dooley? And did I have any hope of finding him?

"You can see my son, but he can't see you."

Ravanna knelt and leveled his gaze at me. Except for the color of his skin, he appeared mostly human. "This will all go much faster if you told the truth. How did you take his memories?" He flicked my head with his finger and grinned at his own cruelty. He knew I couldn't talk and was torturing me regardless of my cooperation, or lack thereof.

"How you have been pulling him back and forth?" He plucked a feather from my wings and pain shot through my back, which arched despite my greatest efforts. I gained strength from my forced silence.

"How did you managed to escape my spell to pull you down here?" He grabbed the back of my hair and yanked hard, his fetid breath bearing down on my senses. "On one hand, it's very useful. All of those emotions were really getting in the way. However, I've expended a lot of power to get you both back here." He tapped the amulets hanging from his neck, all three pieces of the stone that was once one.

I spat at Ravanna's feet. I couldn't move or talk, but I could still show my disgust. He grabbed me by the throat and lifted me. I gasped for breath, and suddenly the air whooshed into my lungs even as he continued to hold me aloft. "You can talk now. I suggest you start doing so."

I swallowed deep and tried to check my emotions, to channel the thoughts of my mother, and keep myself from trying to pry the viselike fingers from my throat. "Send us all back through the portal and I'll return Dooley's memories to him as soon as we're on the other side."

A self-satisfied smirk cracked his hardened visage. "Dooley and the others were trying to convince me that you are powerless. But they were wrong, weren't they? Of course, I can't agree to your arrangement. No, if necessary I'll work harder to pull the information out of your head. I have all the amulets now, and they can be used for this purpose. Use a little of their power to crack through that wall in your head."

Once Ravanna figured out I had no powers then time would be up for me and for my friends. I felt like all the sands were at the bottom of the hourglass. But this was my game, and I had the power to turn it over. "Then let me help you convince Dooley to lead your army. I'm guessing you haven't had any luck convincing him so far. That dragon you managed to conjure didn't work so well."

Ravanna tilted his head. Shadows from the fire played upon his profile, bringing attention to the devious glint in his eye. His finger slithered up my arm, and he drew me forward to whisper into my ear. "I've no idea what you mean by dragon, but if you like I can definitely make that happen. But really, you would abandon your goddess? Your people? I'm not stupid."

I held in the shudder that raked through my spine. Many

lives rested on my performance. "You want entrance to the Elysium and to do that you need to come through the Realms. What if we help you? Your fight isn't with the Realms, it's with Varuna. We're not her army. We are our own people."

"You believe that?" Ravanna looked to Aric, and with a flick of his wrist the spell holding him down was lifted. Aric scrambled to his feet. "Tell her, angel boy. Tell her how much you and those of the Realms are your own people."

"How am I to believe anything you've told me? If you want to spout lies, tell them to her yourself." Aric dusted himself off.

"You're lucky to still be alive." The heat roiling off Ravanna's skin made it obvious we were in hell. All the fancy scenery couldn't change that. "The Realms are dependent on Elysium. To crack that door, I'll crush anyone that gets in my way, including you. Varuna will bow to me as you have, sweet Valora." Ravanna ground his fist into his open palm. It all seemed so simple to him.

"She banished you here. You are no match for her." A headache started to form at my temples, and my wings twitched, unable to hide the visible signs of my hatred for this demon who had valiantly proclaimed my world's destruction. I was running out of options to get us all out of here and to save our worlds. A sacrifice was necessary.

"We have an agreement." Ravanna took one of the amulets and placed it over my neck, leaving the rest around his own. "You will restore Dooley's memory and convince him to go to Earth to lead my army. He is my eyes and ears until I can make an appearance on my own. Once we have sucked all of Earthside dry, I will have the power I need to open the portal to the Realms, and I will be one step closer. I won't be stopped this time. This amulet will let me keep a close eye on you. In exchange, I won't kill all three of you. Deal?"

I almost regretted my next question. "Why do you still need Aric?"

"Insurance. His mother and I don't see eye to eye. But I am willing to bet she would be willing to sacrifice something for this son of hers." Ravanna stepped forward and punched Aric in the gut. He doubled over in silence, obviously in pain but unwilling to give the demon king the satisfaction of any of the sounds of his suffering.

"What about my friends?"

"Friends are the last thing you need to worry about right now, Valora. Soak in this power I have given you and do what you need to do. My patience runs thin."

∂∘⬠

Niro brought us to another section of the compound and left with a cryptic send-off. "I'll check on you guys later." Of all the demons I'd encountered, he gave me the worst feeling. With Mane and Ravanna I knew what I was getting. You couldn't be too sure with a demon, or with anyone whose loyalties shifted with the prevailing wind.

The doors to our cells had no locks. Aric shuffled into a room without a word. I wanted to explain to him why I'd said what I did, but it wasn't clear to me how much Ravanna could detect through the walls I'd erected in my mind. Just in case, I lifted the amulet from my neck and did my best to project a thought he would appreciate. *Ravanna is so fucking sexy. Maybe I could do a little of what he wants, if it will get me closer to his luscious bod.* I quickly replaced the amulet to cover the uncontrollable and repulsive thoughts that followed. This game of constantly altering plans in my mind, sometimes aligning with Ravanna's wishes and sometimes my own, made me worried that when the time came I might not know the difference. The amulet safely around my neck felt like a shot of adrenaline. If I truly did know magic, I could find a way to get us all home. I needed to find Dooley.

"Where would a demon keep a library in this place?" I said aloud to myself, relishing the sound of voice as opposed to thought as a means for communication.

"Valora, is that you?"

I followed the sound of a familiar voice down the hall. Kit pressed her tear-stained face against the bars covering the observation window to her cell.

"Are you okay?" My hand passed between the bars to touch Kit's cheeks, and the familiar tingle of iron stung my skin. Aric and I were free to roam, but the selkie with powers was not, and I couldn't help her. I tugged on the door handle, even though I knew it would be locked.

"Yes, but he won't let us go. He definitely won't let us go. And she won't leave him alone. Valora, you need to help Mane," begged Kit. She gripped the bars and her knuckles went white.

"We can get you out of here. We'll all make it back to the surface." I placed my hand over Kit's fingers and stroked them until she relaxed.

"My life was sacrificed long before we ended up here. At least don't let it be in vain. Mane can help you. I know he can. You need to get him out and get that woman away from him." Kit clawed at her face, dragging her fingers down her cheeks and sinking to the ground.

Her feverish, over-bright eyes spoke to me, and I knew what she was going to say. "Catherine." Kit once told me the story about Mane and Catherine, the human he was connected to many years before he and Ravanna parted ways. She was the reason the two demons were at odds with one another. Ravanna wanted her, and took her to Acheron. And once a human is in Acheron, they are never the same. Mane was never supposed to come back either. There were many good reasons for that, but I couldn't imagine him ever abandoning his true love unless he had no other choice. I didn't know why I hadn't seen it when I first met her.

"We'll do what we can," I said.

Aric suddenly appeared, reaching out from behind me and gripping the bars, iron doing nothing to his skin. Aric carried with him the clean scent of hope, fresh grasses, and lightning-charged rain. A renewed life surged through our bond, along with another surge of power. He leaned in and whispered to Kit, "And we will come back for you."

"He's close by. We're blood bonded." Kit pressed her palms together and closed her eyes. They flicked open with a start, laced with anguish. "I can sense his pain."

"Aric, you've got more charm than any fae I've ever known," I said. "Any chance you can track her down and see what she'll tell you?"

He slicked back his hair and stood a little straighter. "I can try."

"Good, you do that. Remembering some more symbol magic is top on my list. There must be a way to reach Pryn. Maybe he knows how we can get out of this."

Aric disappeared down the hall, and I reassured Kit before returning to my room and closing the door behind me. The amulet at my neck glowed a faint red. Keeping the walls in my mind up and strong while I tried to reach Pryn might be my biggest challenge yet.

I drew my finger through the congealed food. My focus on Pryn, I channeled Dooley and drew the same symbols on the wall. The ones that had helped us locate Aric in the past. I closed my eyes and felt a burst shove my mind forward.

Before me stood the remains of the cabin. Pryn bolted up from his resting place. "Valora, is that you?"

I tried to contain my excitement, keep the connection stable, and get out as much information as possible. Who knew how long this would last? "Yes—we're trapped in Acheron and trying to find a way out. I have my amulet, but Ravanna still has the other two. He's trying to get me to convince Dooley to lead his army out of Acheron and through the gates Earthside to the Realms. I'm not sure how I can avoid doing that."

"Don't."

The image before me flickered, my concentration broken at the divide between what I felt was right and what Pryn was now suggesting I do. "What do you mean? Let Ravanna lay waste to Earth? I can't do that."

"No, Valora, you can defeat Ravanna, just not in Acheron. Ravanna will be vulnerable to attack when he is first brought through the portal, before he can draw any power of his own. If you have one of the amulets in your possession as you enter the portal to Earth, I think we can destroy Ravanna on Earth before he enters the Realms. It's the only way."

"But Mane and Kit are stuck here. And Aric. How do I get all of them through?"

"Once the gates are opened, they will remain open until Ravanna closes them. Pray he has no reason to do so, and then, once he dies, they'll remain open. We can get them after we destroy Ravanna."

"It seems like you have this all planned." And it did seem that way. It was too easy. Coming to Acheron was the only way to execute the plan. "Pryn, did you have something to do with creating that spell which brought us here?"

"Valora, there was no other way. I've always known that

you are the prophecy. You must understand. I had good reason."

All the secrecy, escaping, and creating his demon catcher—unexplained reasons for everything he had done as of late. It all made sense now, and made me sick to my stomach. "We can talk about your good reasons later, Pryn. Stay at the ready for us. I don't think I can do this all on my own."

I broke the bond between us. Pryn may have good reasons, but I wouldn't leave my friends here. No matter how self-sacrificing they wanted to be. It wasn't going to happen. The only guarantee for their safety was if they came out with me. Not after me.

I dialed up another number and hoped I would get an answer. The picture in my mind formed, and a chuckle escaped my lips. In front of me were dozens of people dressed up in various costumes. Either Bowen was at some kind of party or he was visiting another world I wasn't familiar with.

"Sorry if I'm interrupting something."

"Valora? Oh my gosh. Hold on a second." Bowen ducked into a men's bathroom and closed the door. He searched around to find the source of my disembodied voice. "I'm not in a very good place right now."

"Exactly where are you? Besides the bathroom. And don't worry, I'm not about to appear from thin air. This communication is strictly mind to mind." And one I hoped was long distance enough to escape Ravanna's notice. If he couldn't appear Earthside right now, logic seemed to dictate he couldn't hear my conversations there either. At least I hoped so.

"I'm at the ComicCon. You know, we all dress up as our favorite fantasy characters. It's fun." Bowen talked to the stall door. Outside I could see the line forming to use his stall. An orc, a dragon slayer, and a large yellow dog with black-tipped ears jostled from side to side, patiently waiting their turn. Except for the dog, it made me miss the Realms.

"And who did you choose? A fae, right?" Blue wings sprouted from his back and orange horns from his forehead. It was my best guess.

"Valora, here on Earth, if I wore fairy wings I'd be sending mixed signals. I'm Charizard, a legendary Pokémon. Anyway, where are you guys?"

I filled Bowen in on our predicament. If anyone could help me find a way to pull the others out of Acheron at the same time as me, it would be Bowen.

"I'll see what I can do. I picked up several boxes of Artemus's things. And I have all that research I did on the demon portals. I'm sure I could find something." Bowen pulled out a pad of paper from the cream-colored belly of his costume and jotted down a few notes.

A voice sounded in the background. "Hey, dude, stop talking on your walkie. There are others that need to use the bathroom."

"I've got to go, Valora. I'll get what you need and go out to the cabin."

"Wait, Bowen. I…there is something strange about Pryn. I don't know what it is, but he seems to have his own agenda. If you need any help, ask Ralph, but keep Pryn out of it. The less he knows the better."

Bowen gave me a thumb up before our connection faded. My consciousness slammed back into my body as the door to my cell flew open.

Aric burst in, slightly out of breath. "Chasing Catherine wasn't easy, but I found Mane. And believe me, it wasn't pretty." He quickly explained what he'd seen.

My legs weakened at the thought of Mane being tortured. I had to rescue him, to rescue us all. We had to get out of here. I looked outside at the mist surrounding the castle, and a thought occurred. "You say you have been in the mist?" It seemed to have a life of its own, swirling around the air as if it lived and breathed.

"Yes. I flew into it the first day I was here. I thought I could find a way out. It didn't happen. I only ended up right back here. There's no end to it. This world is finite, small. It's no wonder that Ravanna wants to break free."

"We need a bargaining chip. Perhaps a quick pass through the portal to Dell'Aria might prove the perfect distraction."

"What? Are you mad? There's no way that would work." Aric set to pacing the stone floor, something he did when he felt overwhelmed. I didn't need to read his mind to know that. "None of us can open the damn thing except that traitorous wench, and don't even think about involving her, Valora. She'll only mess things up."

Every strategy to solve our problem thus far had encountered a roadblock, and we were running out of resources at our disposal. This was the answer. My new problem was convincing Aric. "You were given a chance to redeem yourself. Why shouldn't she be able to do the same?"

"Kali is not like me." Aric turned, his lightning-shaped eyebrows drawing to a pinch above his nose.

"Yes, she doesn't have an ego the size of the Realms." I scrubbed at the symbols on the wall, meshing my makeshift paint into the grime that coated everything else. I didn't need to leave any more breadcrumbs for Ravanna. Aric would have to learn to follow.

"No, she doesn't have any true regrets."

His words hit me harder than they should have. My

regret was standing right before me, and he knew it. My relationship with Dooley wouldn't be as complicated if I could sort out my feelings about Aric. He paused for a moment before continuing, looking out the window instead of at me.

"You think she was sorry that your mother or any others died because of what she did? No, she only wanted to get her wings. She goes where the reward is, Valora. I think you're making a big mistake."

I came up behind him and wrapped my arms around his waist. His intentions were always good, just not his actions. I needed to keep that in mind. I drew him away from view of the encroaching mist, and we sat side by side on the cot. "The only way to kill Ravanna is to get him out of here. And the only way I can do that is to do it this way. It's the best shot we have."

"I don't like it. I don't like it at all." Aric lay back on the bed with his arms behind his neck, and studied the ceiling. He seemed to have a lot less energy than he once did. He was either pouting or everything was starting to take a toll on him. "But I don't have any other plans. So I suppose we'll have to go with yours."

"You did what you thought was right at the time. I know you didn't mean for harm to come to so many. You don't need to feel guilty about that anymore." I thought I'd given Aric my forgiveness many times before, but sometimes the guilt-ridden don't hear you.

Aric looked at me, a storm brewing behind those eyes. I couldn't read his thoughts or his mind this time, and although his body was probably up for grabs, whatever was truly bothering him was locked up tight. He slid his hand onto my upper thigh. "So, is this your way of telling me you want to sleep with me tonight?"

I shoved his hand away. "Damn it, Aric. Just when I want to think that you're a decent person."

"You're wasting your time with that one." He rolled over and faced the wall.

"I'm going to find Dooley and try talking to him." Even though he couldn't help us escape, I needed to keep up the pretense that I was following Ravanna's plan. "It shouldn't be a problem if you stay here."

Aric waved his arm dismissively without turning to look at me. "Be back by sunup—we'll need to contact Pryn and Bowen one last time."

❧

The passage of time had ceased to exist since Mane, Kit, and I entered the portal. I stood in the hallway outside Aric's room, closing my heavy eyelids for a brief moment, and let my mind open up to Dooley. A picture of him sitting at the same desk entered my mind. He looked as tired as I probably did. Letting go of control of my physical body was easy, but it wasn't easy to stay standing once I entered the passages heavy with Ravanna's enchantments. When I arrived at the door to Dooley's room, I could barely stand.

I grabbed the large knocker on his door and pain shot up my arm, knocking me on my ass. I could almost hear Ravanna laughing in my head. A demon who loved to play practical jokes. Great. "Damn the Goddess." I jumped up and kicked the door with my foot while holding my damaged hand to my chest. "Open up, Dooley. Open up."

The door swung inwards and Dooley stood before me, his tan, muscled chest glistening with sweat. The throbbing pain in my hand was replaced with a throbbing ache in my heart. Beyond, his room was not unlike the library Mane kept in his small apartment Earthside. Books spanned

155

shelves that were two stories high. Long ladders reached up to the ceiling, and in the corner, a blazing fireplace kept the room a bit warmer than I would have liked. Besides the books, there was a small cot and the same wooden desk I'd seen him seated at before. It was covered in scrolls and papers and large volumes of leather bound books.

Dooley's dark brown hair hung in his face, and a pair of reading glasses was propped on his nose. He looked absolutely edible. Between the pain, the heat, and the effect he was having on me, I pitched forward into his arms, feeling faint. He caught me and brought me inside to sit down.

"Your hand. You're hurt." He pried my hand from my body and assessed the damage. He hurried over to one of the books open on the desk, running his finger down the text. "I can fix this. I've studied the symbols for healing. I have everything I need. Give me a second and I'll have you feeling better."

Even without his memories, he couldn't suppress the healer inside him. "You've done this before for me."

"I have?" Dooley continued to mix the ingredients he needed in a pot he discovered in one of the darkened corners of the room. "Sorry, I don't have all my memories yet."

"Not all? You mean you've been remembering things?" I wanted Dooley to remember us, but I also enjoyed us without the complications of our checkered past.

Dooley set the pot over the fire and hesitated before facing me. "Yes, I remember a time between you, Aric, and I."

I slapped my ruined hand on my forehead and immediately regretted it as pain shot through my arm again. "Of course you would remember the one thing I was hoping you wouldn't."

Dooley turned back and stirred the pot in a slow and deliberate motion, focusing on the spoon instead of me. "As far as I can recall, I was a willing participant."

My mouth opened and closed. There was nothing I could say that would make things better. Yes, Dooley willingly participated, but we later found out that he was under the influence of his father, who was trying to pull our energies together. It was questionable how "willing" Dooley was. His behavior after the fact led me to believe he wasn't all too happy about it.

"It's complicated."

He unhooked the pot from over the stove, and placed it on the ground before he sat next to me. He clasped my hand, his large hand dwarfing my own. He dipped a finger into the pot and started to rub the black ointment into one of the deep red welts forming on my palm. Dooley once healed an iron burn with only his own energy. No potions or symbols. He was becoming a powerful magician. One who, in the wrong hands, could destroy the world.

"Things like that usually do complicate things. I don't have to have my memories restored to know that much." He folded my hand closed and put his other hand on top of mine. "I can't dwell on what I can't clearly remember. And I don't want to rely on what others tell me is truth. Ravanna has told me many stories. I can't possibly believe all of what he says is true."

He stood up, bending down to take the pot back to the fire. I caught his arm with my good hand. I knew he wanted the truth, but giving it to him now would not help any of us. "We need to go Earthside, Dooley. We need to open the portals."

He nodded and returned to his desk, putting a palpable

buffer of space between us. "I've been reviewing all the texts in this library. It's a lot, but I think that I can learn enough to prevent us from being destroyed by Varuna's army."

"Varuna's army?" In all the time I contemplated not letting Ravanna through the portals, I had never anticipated that we would have to fight an army of angels. "Is this something Ravanna told you?"

"It makes sense, doesn't it?" He walked over to the table and brought one of the scrolls to me. "This is the story of when Ravanna was banished to Acheron. It tells of a great battle that laid waste to many species before Varuna was able to confine Ravanna here. It also makes it clear that the death toll for the innocents was due to armies from both sides."

If I wasn't already sitting, I would have fallen on my ass.

"We are in the middle of a war of the gods."

And then it hit me. Pryn had always said our world was on my shoulders, and here I was, the one with the choice to open the portal to another war or keep it shut. Dooley, Aric, Mane, Kit, and I would be stuck here, but if it would prevent a war that would destroy hundreds of thousands of innocent lives, wouldn't that be the better choice?

"I need to talk to someone. I'll be right back." I knew that Ravanna was keeping tabs on Dooley and everything he did. I wanted to confide in him, see him look at me the way he used to, and for us to walk down the aisle at Winter Haven. It was everything I desired, yet I was never further from any of it. And I couldn't confide in him as long as we were here.

Dooley motioned around the room. "I'll be here. Rumor is there isn't much scenery to take in."

This man could always make me smile, even in the darkest of depths. Proof was that we were here. "I won't be long."

The amulet pulsed at my neck. Ravanna was trying to pry into my thoughts. I could feel it. I pulled up the walls around me. As I rounded the corner to the block of cells we were kept in, Niro stepped out of the shadows. On instinct, I reached for the sword no longer at my side.

"You need to get out of here. Whatever you do, don't decide to stay." Niro's direction conveniently echoed my fears. He had been listening in to my thoughts as well.

"Is that what your boss told you to tell me?" I shoved a finger into Niro's chest. "Look, I'm starting to figure out what's happening here, and I'll tell you one thing, I won't let you or anyone else tell me what's best. If that portal opens then all hell will literally break loose. Varuna's army will swarm down and kill innocent people along with anything coming out of this portal."

"If you don't open those portals then Ravanna will live on. One way or the other, he will get what he needs. You think these cells are all empty because Ravanna wanted large living quarters?" Niro became agitated, and pressed his forehead. "Not now, old man, I'm busy."

"Is that the dwarf shaman talking to you? Is everything okay?"

"No, it's not. And it will get worse. If he stays here, eventually he will amass enough power to open the damn portal himself. It's all in the balance of souls. Elysium has always had more." Niro pulled me to the window and pointed into the blanket of mist in the distance. "You see the mist growing each day. You see it growing thicker, and less of the mountains show than ever before."

"Isn't that the natural cycle of days here?"

Niro laughed. "When you're dealing with eternity, there is no night and day, Valora, Who told you that? Aric? He tries to make himself feel as if he has some control over this situation when he doesn't. But you do. That out there is what will bring Ravanna power. Those are the souls he's stolen. Soon you and the others will be out there too. As soon as you have lived out your usefulness."

"Then why does he bother with this mission Earthside? Why not keep me here and wait it out?"

"I can't be too sure. He's agitated. I think he feels time is not on his side, and there have always been others who have tried to claim the throne at Elysium. He thinks he needs to act now. But in reality, it won't be long before we're all his to do with what he wants. I was born of this world, as was Mane. We belong here. You and the others don't."

"Mane does not belong here." Mane had proven again and again that he deserved to be valued as much as anyone else—perhaps even more, considering what we'd been through.

"You're fooling yourself. But it shouldn't matter what happens to him. You need to make sure that Ravanna does not win, and you can't kill him here. I'm rather fond of your little world the way it is." Niro's unfocused gaze penetrated nothing and everything at the same time, as if he were seeing something that wasn't visible to me. His eyes glistened with the threat of tears that would never spill. "I need to speak to the shaman. He doesn't have long for your world."

Before I could ask anything else, he left. But there was one other whom I needed to seek counsel from. Pryn seemed to know everything from the very beginning. I might not listen to him, but I needed to know his advice. Niro was the only one giving me a good reason to open the portals. Every choice was a risk, and I wasn't willing to risk anyone else's lives.

I checked in on Aric and Kit, who were both asleep. It seemed like nighttime to everyone but me. I wasn't sure I would ever be able to relax in this place now that I knew the mist was a living and breathing thing. Souls of those trapped down here. But were they not supposed to be down here? If they were banished to Acheron, like Ravanna, perhaps they deserved to be here. But then there was Mane.

His father once told him that when he reached the Elysium he would beg entrance for his demon-possessed son to come with him, because he'd earned his place. And yet Mane was stuck here as Ravanna's prisoner. Where was his justice? It seemed the only way justice would happen would be to make change. And the only way you made change was sometimes through an act of war.

Pryn was quick to respond when I contacted him. "I hope that you aren't upset by what I did."

"I understand I must open the portals. But there is a chance that lives will be lost. Even if we can defeat his army, his presence may cause Varuna to send down an army of warriors to defeat him. Many lives may be lost in the battle."

"We will dispatch him quickly. Don't worry, Valora. Your act will save us all, but I will be ready to assist you. You don't have to do this alone."

Bowen was harder to reach, but when I did, he was in a frenzied state. "Valora, thank God you contacted me. I don't know what's happening, but we have a slight problem."

"You have a problem? I am stuck in hell and *you* have a problem?"

"Well, yes, Irena broke out of her home again and, well, she kidnapped Kali. Ralph left for a moment and I stood guard. I couldn't stop her. She was spouting some nonsense about portals and treachery and who knows. But she disappeared. Ralph is out searching. Valora, there's one other thing. I've been reading my father's journals, and I came upon something he wrote about the selkie queen amulet. He was saying that it acted kind of like a USB drive for magic."

"You're speaking gibberish, Bowen."

"Oh, right. I mean it stores magic. I wonder if the amulets you and the guys have do the same thing."

It made sense. I knew that at one point it kept me alive by stealing magic from others. No doubt it would be able to store it somehow. But now it was broken into three pieces. Three pieces that were now all down here in Acheron at the same time. We needed to change that.

"You can't open the portal to the Realms without Kali, can you?" asked Bowen.

"It's been done before, but not by me." Perhaps I had found Kit and Mane's ticket out of here after all.

Although I didn't want to open my mind up to the demon king, I also wasn't in the mood to trudge down to his quarters and kneel at his feet. I took the amulet from my neck. *Listen up, Ravanna. I have a proposal.*

CHAPTER ELEVEN

The longer I spent in Acheron, the more the glamours covering up what this place really was started to fade. The beautiful scenes I saw when I'd first arrived were jaded by hopelessness and despair. The floors were rutted by misery, and I fought the oppression that weighted down everyone as I followed the narrow hallway, one that had become too familiar of late. My marker, a patch of what appeared to be a particularly nasty piece of bog moss, told me there was one more passageway before I came to my intended destination. I couldn't wait to tell Kit about my escape plan.

I peered through the bars of her cell and found her asleep. She curled in a tight ball in the center of the narrow cot, her legs tucked tight to her chest, her arms wrapped around her shins, and her face a study of anguish. My heart ached to see her that way. With caution, I touched the handle to her cell. Ravanna had agreed to my plan, but I still didn't trust him. The demon was fond of playing with his victims, and I wouldn't put it past him to pull some cruel joke on me. Innocuous steel turned to burning iron just to see me squirm. I was sure he could do it if he wanted. I bit my lip in anticipation of the pain of the iron, and turned. A click echoed in response and the door swung open. I'd barely taken a step when a figure lunged from the shadows. I cursed my stupidity. I knew I shouldn't have trusted Ravanna. Kit's blue hair caught the light as she nearly knocked me over.

"Valora, I didn't think I would see you again." She loosened her grip and stood back, weaving from side to side as if she was going to faint.

"Kit, are you okay?" The dark circles under her eyes made her look as sick as the first day I met her. The only difference was then she was full of happiness despite her condition, but now she gave me the glazed-over look of someone who could see through the veil to whatever lay beyond death. "What did they do to you?"

Kit clawed at her throat. The sharpened incisors of her selkie teeth pressed into her bottom lip. "I'm so hungry. But there's nothing here I can eat. I think I might be dying."

Dammit! Kit wasn't allowed to feed from demon or angel blood. This was truly hell to her. She would starve and die soon if we stayed her much longer. "I'm working on a plan, but I need your help."

I explained the full details of my plan, and a touch of the old spark I was used to seeing from her briefly flared in her eyes. When I was finished, she took her time before she spoke, like she was afraid of the answer I would give. "I can see Mane again?"

"Yes, but he's been…he might not be the same as when you saw him last." I could only hope that Mane still clung to whatever soul he had left. Being in Acheron couldn't have been good for him. If I was wrong, and Mane was once again Ravanna's lackey, then I might be doing the demon king a favor in taking him with us.

Kit dusted off the scales that formed a delicate skirt around her bottom half. Shadows, like ripples across the surface of the water, passed over her skin. Even her cerulean-blue hair shimmered in the darkness. "He helped me remember who I was. I can do the same for him."

Her admission made me realize how parallel our lives were. Kit and I now found ourselves in the same predicament. We both hoped our love could bring back the men we loved to their former selves. Were we deluding ourselves by wishing for the impossible? The odds had been stacked against us before. Kit had the advantage of actual magic. The selkie amulet, a magic Ravanna likely didn't want to tangle with, still hung around her neck. I had only my sword and my wits. *And that damn prophecy.* I wasn't a spellweaver like my mother. My only option was to get rid of Ravanna and any lasting hold he had over Dooley.

Although Ravanna agreed to allow me and Kit Earthside to open the portal, Mane was a hard sell. His pet Catherine enjoyed torturing her ex-lover, the man that had damned her here to serve under the demon king. Convincing him that I needed Mane to help control Kit required acting skills I didn't know I possessed. In a way, it was an easy story to sell, because at times it was completely true. I knew from experience what Kit's hunger could lead to.

"Finish sleeping. You'll need whatever rest you can manage. Tomorrow we go to war." I tucked her back into bed and managed to find my cell. Exhaustion finally took over, and I fell onto the cot.

Nightmares quickly descended on my fitful sleep. The scent of a cold, moonless night, lost deep within the darkest wood. Thick, viscous pine branches whipping at my face as I push through some half-remembered image of tragedy that visited me much too often.

You may need to kill me, Valora. It might be the only way.

Dooley's voice in my mind, like a shot of iron, jolted me awake. Niro stood before me, my sword in his hands. He set my blade into my outstretched fingers. The weight of it reminded me of what I was supposed to do. I was a warrior now. Time to start a war.

"I can't believe you listened to me."

The sound of the sword sliding into the scabbard reverberated in the small confines of my cell. "Don't flatter yourself too much. There are others I need to take care of outside of Acheron. My being here won't help them. Opening the portals and starting a war is my only chance to change things."

A smug smile crossed Niro's face, reminding me of another particularly difficult man in my life.

"Excuse me. I need to visit Aric before I leave."

"Sullen angel hasn't left his room for quite some time. Shouldn't be hard to find him."

When I entered his room, Aric's gaze was out the window, his eyes on the mist, which continued to grow. The outlines of the figures on the mountainside were barely visible through the dense fog, yet they appeared to hold his interest, and not in a good way. "You look like you did when you would look out over Dell'Aria during the Blight—troubled."

Aric half turned, his face as white as his leather pants. "I controlled the Blight. Now, I have no control and no idea how to escape this mess."

I didn't have time for his pity party. Aric needed to come to terms with his own past, but now was not the time. "I do. But I need time, time away from here. I hate to do this to you, but I have to leave you and Dooley behind."

"It's what you should have done from the start."

I closed the distance between us and placed my hand on his shoulder. He still wouldn't look at me. I was trying to save the world and Aric was pouting. But there was no use being heavy-handed with him. I just needed him to keep it together and not do anything stupid. "I will come back. For the both of you. Despite everything, I still care for you, Aric. You can deny that all you want, but it's true."

Aric dipped his head down and leaned forward out the open window, the slight breeze from the mist ruffling the strands of hair hanging in his face. "Yes, I know."

I gave his shoulder one last squeeze and walked down the hall to say goodbye to Dooley. Instead I got a face full of Ravanna. He blocked the entrance to Dooley's room, his beefy arms crossed and his eyes direct, piercing.

My heart pounded like rain in a storm, and my fingers tingled with nerves. I forced my shoulders back and mimicked his aggressive stance. "You're in my way."

"Not a good idea." Ravanna stepped forward, coming inches from my face. I tilted my head back, expecting to be repulsed, but I felt oddly compelled. And equally determined not to be. The way his muscles flexed, the unexpected desire in his eyes, and the aura of authority he carried—he knew how to shape his image to get what he wanted. The both of us could play that game.

"Your mind-control tricks won't do anything to me." I scouted for an exit, but his broad shoulders blocked my view. He filled the hallway and my thoughts at the same time. In a bid for self-preservation, I took a half-step back. He followed. "You might hear my thoughts, but I won't let you manipulate them."

A deep, gratified sigh spilled from his parted lips. His hand languished on my cheek. "You think I'm compelling you? So naïve. Why do you think you find my son so attractive? Have you never thought that it was because of the little piece of me inside him? You have a distinct knack for falling for the bad boy."

"That's not true. Aric and I aren't together anymore." I squeezed my fists tight, letting my fingernails bite into my palms. I couldn't believe Ravanna was actually making me defend my taste in men. Time to wake up from this nightmare.

"But you know now that he isn't bad. You're not too sure about Dooley, are you? Think he still needs saving. Then what? The portal is open now, but not for long, and your friends are waiting." He opened the door to Dooley's room and paused before disappearing inside. "Don't keep me waiting."

☙❧

I clutched my sword, confident with its reassuring weight at my side. Niro guided me through the mouth of a large cavern, where a shimmering barrier enshrouded the other side of a low archway. He placed his hand to the light, and it dispersed into thick steam that shot through my parted legs and out the way we came. "Ravanna sure has a taste for theatrics."

Just inside, a great round room opened. Shadowy figures lurked in the corner, and cut into the center of the floor, a gaping maw spewed forth a swirl of red. The blinding light snaked around the room and hissed by my ears. The entrance to this hellhole. Mane stood, barely, slumped against Kit, his arm draped around her shoulder for support. They perched at the edge of the portal. Mane's focus hadn't left the swirling light since I stepped inside.

This was my "army." A half-selkie who was crazed with bloodlust and her demon boyfriend. I tried not to think of

168

the obvious problems we might encounter. The one thing I was certain of was that they were on my side, the most loyal friends I'd ever known.

I circled around the portal on the floor and moved to Kit's side. "Is he going to be okay?"

"All my parts still work, if that's what you're asking." Mane lifted his head and gave me a wink. The faint glow in his eyes, combined with the sneer he was giving me, made him look even more menacing than usual.

"Your eyes are a little red there, Mane. Are you sure?"

He pulled a pair of sunglasses out of some pocket on the inside of his vest. "Looks like both Kit and I will be wearing these for a while." He reached over and tipped the pair on her head to cover her eyes.

"Aren't you two quite the fashionable couple? Do you have a plan for when we get through? Kit hasn't eaten in days." I loved my friend, but I didn't relish being her dinner.

"Oh, we have plans. You may or may not want to stick around for the show. Depends on what you're into."

Relief at having the old Mane back pushed through the dread that rested just shy of the surface. "Yep, you're fine. Let's go."

I drew my sword before stepping through the portal. I had to find a way to save the world. No problem. Right? Whatever was going to be thrown at me on the other side, I was going to be ready.

∂∾∾

I tumbled out of the portal first and landed on the mossy forest surrounding Dooley's burned-out cabin. Light filtered through the trees and the touch of cool air made me mistake, for a moment, this place for home. Tension eased from my muscles and my stomach growled. Safety found, if even only temporary, my body was reminding me that I needed real nourishment soon. Mane and Kit crashed in a heap on the ground next to me. Mane wasted no time in making sure that Kit was satiated. I couldn't say the same for myself.

"I'm going search for Bowen and Pryn. You guys stay here. Don't go too far."

Mane waved me off as he pulled Kit's top over her shoulders. Something told me I wouldn't have to worry about them taking off for a while. I crept around the side of the cabin and could see Bowen fast asleep in the driver's seat of his van parked in the driveway.

I tapped on the window. He startled, and slammed down on the horn, then quickly rolled down the window when he saw who it was. "Valora, you're back! I was so worried."

"Has there been any luck finding Varuna?"

"Well, yeah. It's kind of a standoff situation. She's been holed up in this old clinic for a day, and Ralph has been keeping an eye on her to make sure she doesn't get out. He didn't call in any backup, trying to keep it on the hush-hush. But he can't do it for long."

"Did you say she was at an old clinic?" If Varuna was controlling the portal entrance at the clinic, our whole plan could be ruined. Stopping her was the only way to make sure everyone I loved got out of Acheron alive.

"Yeah, I've never been there before, but I think I can find it," said Bowen.

"Move over, I'm driving." I grabbed the cup of cold coffee resting between the seats and downed it, retching slightly at the taste of the wicked brew. Horrible stuff, but I needed the energy.

Minutes later, we were stuck in what Bowen called

"rush-hour traffic."

"How the hell do you guys get anywhere? I have never wanted wings more than I do now." I pounded my hands on the steering wheel in vain. Ralph was stuck outside the clinic again, and here I was unable to get to him because there were too many people in this world.

I stuck my head out the door. "Hey, would you all move? I am trying to save your world here."

My only response was the honking of horns.

"Yeah, it can get a little annoying."

When we finally got to the exit, I raced through the side streets, swerving around the occasional car and nearly hitting a man that looked like a dwarf in tattered clothes that stumbled off the sidewalk. With a screeching of tires, I slammed on the brakes, and the van skittered to a halt only inches from the bumper of Ralph's squad car. Bowen and I clambered out of the van. It broke my heart see Ralph staking out the same clinic he'd cased years earlier in a desperate attempt to get medicine for Kit. Now he was here because Varuna kidnapped Kali.

Ralph got out of his car and clapped a hand on my back. "I have never been so glad to see someone in my life."

"Anything since they went in there?" The windows of the clinic were boarded up and the open sign was off for good.

"Nothing. But I figure they have to come out at some point."

I shoved my hand through my hair. "That's the problem, Ralph."

"What?"

"There is a portal in that clinic. Kali knows how to open portals. She probably isn't even there anymore."

Ralph started across the street before I could stop him.

171

It surprised me how fast a portly, unwinged man could move. He flung open the door and drew his gun from its holster. "Anyone in here? This is the police!"

Silence greeted us. I peered over Ralph's shoulder into the darkened clinic. "Ralph, you really should let me handle this."

"Yeah, Ralph, we shouldn't be messing around with portals," said Bowen. He hovered in the doorway, keeping a quick exit in sight.

"You think I haven't messed around with magic, boy? I've had it flowing through my veins. Lived underwater with a selkie queen and visited a cloud city. What have you done?"

"My mistake." Bowen retreated a few steps.

"Bowen, why don't you head back to the car? If we're not out soon, hunt down Pryn. I thought he would be with you." He was supposed to be. Another lie from the priest.

"He said he had a few things to do and would meet back with us at the other portal," answered Bowen.

It appeared that Pryn snuck off a lot these days. The prophecy weighed heavy on my mind. Although it still seemed rather clear to me what it meant.

"I think I see something moving back there," said Ralph. He stepped into the clinic.

"I'll go wait in the car," said Bowen.

I followed Ralph into the shop and closed the door as best I could behind us. The bell at the top of the door tinkled as I did so.

"Shhhh," said Ralph.

"Sorry," I whispered.

I looked down the hallway in search of movement. I could barely see anything in the inky shadows that seemed to have a life of their own. Straining to get a better view, I flinched when a flash of blue light flared. The air around me constricted, and then imploded in an otherworldly brilliance. The impact swept me off my feet, and I landed hard on the cracked linoleum next to Ralph.

CHAPTER TWELVE

A cascade of mauve sparks showered down the hall and created an opaque curtain. Someone had just blown their magical wad to keep us away. I was never too good at following the rules. Fortunately for our attacker, I wouldn't disregard the safety of others to immediately chase after him. Or, as I suspected, her.

The choking and coughing to my right signaled Ralph's location. I kept myself flattened to the ground and tried to suck in a clean breath through the smoky barrier. Something smelled burned, and I hoped it wasn't Ralph. "Are you okay?"

He pushed himself up on one knee, gun drawn, aiming through the haze, and held a finger to his lips. *Right, Valora, probably not a good idea to shout out when you were hoping to keep yourself hidden.* I rolled onto my side toward the wall. The culprit remained hidden. I was hoping it was because he hadn't seen us, not because he was gone. My father had shut this portal down, but I was betting that a goddess could open it again if she really wanted to.

The haze that draped the hallway faded. The charm had

dissipated. Relief shot through me. I was able to see down the hall. It was empty. The sight lessened my earlier comfort. There were still a lot of rooms to inspect, and a thousand different sabotages I couldn't anticipate. I could only be vigilant and pray we got out alive. "We'll go room by room. You follow close behind me," I said.

"I'm the one with the metal." Ralph brandished his weapon. Being this close to that much iron made the wound on my palm ache. I rubbed my hand on the side of my pants and remembered the last time I saw Dooley. My only chance at saving him and Aric was to shut down whatever Varuna was planning and get the portal to the Realms open. I never thought that I would be warring against the Goddess. But how was I supposed to make her understand?

"That will do nothing against whatever caused that explosion." Ralph nodded and fell in step behind me. No need to tell him I hadn't exactly earned my degree in Magic 101.

I kicked down each door as we stalked down the hall. Ralph peered in after I moved forward, and scanned the rooms with his gun drawn. "Clear," he said as he holstered his weapon. The only one left was the large wooden door at the end of the hall.

"Uh, Valora? I think that blast might have singed you a little."

The burning smell was coming from me. Asshole burned some of my feathers off.

"I think you better stand back."

Behind this door pulsed a portal to the Realms and whatever remained of Aric's experiments. I went for the knob and froze. A polished, crystalline cut of pure cinnabar, the same as the one that once held Aric captive in the selkie domain, the same as the knob that appeared on the ship before Dooley and Aric disappeared. *How did it get here?*

I checked behind me to make sure Ralph listened to my direction. The knob turned easily in my hand. Ralph and I gasped at the same time. The man standing over a hog-tied Irena startled. I suspected he thought his wave of magic had killed us.

"Surprise."

In an instant my sword jabbed at the tender flesh under his chin. He swallowed heavily, and the rope in his hands fell to the floor. Defiant eyes met mine, and then flickered to the corner of the room. My feathers stood on end, and I saw another figure rushed the portal. "Ralph…" I began, trying to warn him, but the portal shimmered, and whoever it was disappeared before it went dark again. Surprise gave way to irritation. Thwarted again by some mysterious stranger that was too cowardly to show his face. All was not lost, however. I still had one of them.

I pressed the blade harder to his throat until my eyes adjusted to the dimness. "Who was here with you?" By the soft green glow leftover from the portal magic, I could tell that the man was not a normal human. Upon inspection, his ears confirmed my suspicions. "You were there. You must have been the one who conjured the dragon spell that almost killed me and burned down my friend's cabin."

"Friend? You keep interesting friends, Valora Delos. You should be more loyal to those of the Realms and not these other halflings who are bringing about the destruction of our world."

I was done being shocked that people seemed to know who I was. After being named the next in line to rule Dell'Aria, it seemed like everyone knew. I was at a serious disadvantage. "You know who I am, that's nice. I can tell you're an elf. But why are you working against us? We're trying to save the Realms and the Elysium."

"She is your goddess, not ours. As far as I'm concerned, she's part of the problem." The elf pointed to Irena. Her mouth was gagged and her hands and feet bound, but still her whole body trembled. Whoever possessed her, be it Ravanna or Varuna, was probably long gone by now. All that was left was a scared old woman who didn't know who she was.

"She gives a home to your kind in the Elysium after they've passed—how can you say she is not yours?" There was someone else I was working against, and I didn't know who it was. The only way I could find out was to get this elf talking.

"Because she has abandoned us. The elves have no place to live. We are wanderers in our own land. There is no food. She is trying to kill us before our time so she can claim our souls forever in the Elysium. Elves live longer than the fae. We're more powerful. Can't you see? She wants that power."

Niro was right. Ravanna did have something to worry about when it came to others wanting to get to the Elysium before he did. The deep ache in my hand returned as Ralph shuffled closer to the portal opening, his gun drawn. "No, it's Ravanna that wants all the power. He is the one who infected the land with cinnabar. He is the one who made you have to abandon your home."

The laughter that came from the elf was ugly, his smile cold. He leaned forward, ignoring the tip of my blade. "Do you not see what's right in front of you?"

The portal sprang to life again. As it did, Ralph gathered up Irena and threw her over his shoulder, running out the open door.

"No!" shouted the elf. I pushed him back with the flat of my blade. He tumbled to the ground near the edge of the portal. "You will regret this, Valora. You will. And when all those you care about are dead, you will wish you had seen the real truth."

A hand shot out from the portal entrance and grabbed the collar of the elf, pulling him in before it closed down once more.

Bitter tears clogged my throat. My only lead had disappeared. How was I going to save Dooley now? I walked out of the room, and Ralph and Irena were in the first examining room. She was seated on the table, her head buried in her knees, which were drawn up to her chest. Ralph was pacing back and forth, his gun still in his hand. "She says that Kali girl isn't here anymore."

"What? Where did she go?"

Irena lifted her eyes to me, and they were just as deep and blue as Aric's. Her voice echoed as if from a great distance. "She does not belong here, Valora. Neither do you."

"You don't either." I was giving the Goddess lip. Yes, that just about summed up my day.

"I was forced to reinhabit this body so that I could make sure Ravanna does not harm these people."

The Goddess didn't want the portal open, but I needed it open. "How will I get Dooley and Aric back if I don't open the portal?" Irena hung her head, and I thought for a moment that perhaps Dooley and Aric's real mother was in there somewhere and remembered them. Remembered her sons. "Don't you want them to be safe?"

The Goddess looked at me, looked through me. "They know their sacrifice. They know it's meant to be this way. They would never ask to be saved."

Never asked to be saved? Was my wish to rescue them a selfish act? I knew the answer deep in my heart. No, saving them was the right thing to do. "There has to be a way. They were not meant to be down there. Both of them have done so much for the Realms. For Dell'Aria." I couldn't stifle my tears. "Dooley was supposed to marry me at Winter Haven. I am supposed to save them all. All of them. Including Dooley and Aric."

Irena stood up and walked over to me. With a gentle hand, she wiped a tear from my cheek. "Dear Valora, you must know in your heart that I'm right."

"No." Ralph got up and stood next to my side. "I don't know about Aric, but Dooley is all right. What I hear you saying is that you need that Ravanna character to stay down there so he doesn't bug you. Our kind has been fighting off evils for a long time. Let all hell break loose, we'll be ready."

"I'm sorry, Irena, but Ralph is right." I took the amulet from around my neck and placed it over Irena's before she could flinch. Our recent trip to Acheron had powered it up. She fell forward, and Ralph caught her in his arms.

She looked up at Ralph, confused. "Where am I?"

"Ralph, I think I dispelled the Goddess. Take her back to the home. If Kali isn't here then I just hope that she doesn't get in the way."

Bowen didn't mind my idea of going back to the cabin. I think being my escort was starting to freak him out a little. "If Ravanna is going to enter through any of the portals, it will be there. He doesn't have any others that are quite as established as that one." Bowen thumbed through a notebook that he had taken out of his pocket.

❧

Traffic was lighter as we left the city. I was grateful that all the occupants of the vehicles were off the road. Our drive to the cabin was worse than the darkest hell of Acheron.

"Seems like you've been busy studying."

Bowen flipped the notebook shut and placed it back in his jacket. "Yeah, since my dad died I really want to make sure that I know all I can about what's out there, you know? Better to be prepared than to be caught off guard. I always relied on him to tell me if anything weird was going on. Now I have to figure it out on my own."

"I know what you mean." Both Aric and Dooley were stuck in Acheron. It was usually one of them that guided me in the right direction. Gut instinct was all that was left. All it told me was that I wasn't leaving them there.

"Since you seem to be up on your studies, tell me what you think of this situation." I pulled the crumpled parchment from my coat and handed it to him.

His eyes widened, and he turned it over a few times before smoothing it out on his leg. "This is amazing. So you brought this back from Acheron with you?"

"No, actually I found it in one of Pryn's books, but I haven't been able to pin him down yet to ask him about it." The last time I'd spoken to Pryn, he'd promised to help lure Ravanna through the portal and kill him before he could get anywhere near the Realms. Hopefully he kept his word and his plan was already in place. "This prophecy and Franca's words are too convoluted. I still have no idea how to save everyone."

"How?" Bowen turned it over again and then held the paper up to the light. "It's strange that Pryn would have something like this."

"Like what, a prophecy?"

"Well, that seems to be what it is. More important, the paper itself isn't like any normal paper. It has to be from Acheron."

My fingers tensed on the steering wheel at his assured

comment. How would Bowen know something like that? Unless…

He raised his head and stared at me through red eyes. "Come now, Valora. Bowen is smart, but not that smart."

I slammed the brakes on the van and heard horns honking from all around me. I was able to pull off to the side of the road as we fishtailed back and forth. Cars whizzed by, and the occupants all seemed to be giving me a finger gesture that I guessed didn't indicate a friendly greeting.

Bowen stared down into the paper in his lap. "Bowen, look at me."

He was watching me. A familiar smirk twisted his face. "You are wasting time, Valora. Dooley I need. Aric is expendable. I could easily start plucking the feathers from his wings for my amusement. And I could make it last for what seemed an eternity to him." The smirk turned into a vicious sneer, and Bowen seized me around the throat. "Open the portal now. We're waiting."

I pulled at Bowen's hand, but was losing the battle with inhuman strength. "Bowen, let go. It's not you." Spots began to form in front of my eyes. Both words and air were failing me.

"You have until nightfall."

The red light faded from Bowen's eyes, and he immediately released his hold. I drew in a deep breath and pressed my hand to my chest, which ached from the lack of oxygen.

Pale and sweaty, Bowen looked at his hand and then back to me, incredulous. "I'm so sorry. I don't know what happened."

"It wasn't you." I snatched the paper from him and shoved it into my coat. "It was my fault. The paper I handed you is from Acheron. Ravanna was able to use it to possess you."

"Why would Pryn have a paper from Acheron?" Bowen asked, still shaking.

Pryn was the key to all of this. I needed to find him, and fast, before Aric was killed and Ravanna forced me to do what I never intended to do again—fail the people of Del Aria. "Exactly what I intend to ask him."

❧

Bowen's van struggled to keep the pace I demanded of it. Uncaring of the damage I inflicted, I gunned the engine, and it bucked down the rutted driveway to Dooley's cabin. The ever-present rain of the Pacific Northwest created spectacular mud puddles. Each one I hit splattered the windshield and incited a squeal of fear from Bowen. Relentless rain pelted the van, making it impossible to see past the hood of the car. Rain was normal around here, but this sort of deluge wasn't natural.

Bowen couldn't get out fast enough. The second he placed his hand on the door latch, I pulled him back inside. I didn't trust what waited for us outside. "Not yet."

"It's a little rain. We'll be okay. Happens around here all the time—" His voice ended on a high squeak as the van shifted.

The back door was pulled open. I turned and slipped a short knife from a sheath at my hip. My hand fell when Mane and Kit flung themselves into the car. Steam rose from their bodies and each groaned in pain.

"Are you two okay? What happened out there?"

"Damn." Mane grimaced and rubbed at his eyes. "Do you have a towel or something?"

Bowen pulled a small blanket out of his backpack and handed it to Mane.

Mane wiped down his face and opened his eyes enough to help Kit do the same. "That's no regular rain. More like a cleansing. Stings like a bitch. If I didn't have this elf body, I would have been singed."

Kit scratched at her skin, causing long red welts to form on her legs and arms. "I feel itchy all over."

Once again, it was my fault my friends were in such pain. But I couldn't let that bother me. Not now. I had to find Pryn and get some answers. Time was running out.

"Babe, you need to stop or you'll scratch your skin off." Mane rubbed Kit down with the towel.

Varuna must already be on her way. The deluge suddenly stopped. Water fell down the windshield, and as I looked out, I saw Pryn standing on the porch of Dooley's burned-out cabin. Finally. "We are going to get things straight once and for all."

"Valora, you shouldn't go out there alone." Mane put his hand on my shoulder. He winced as a drop of water fell from his earlobe down onto his neck.

I shook my head. The time for hesitation was over. "You're in no position to help me. I need to do this alone. You three stay here."

As I exited the car, the air seemed thick. Being in the demon realm may have made me overly suspicious, but the stuff falling from the sky didn't seem to be holy water. I surely wasn't feeling blessed.

I stayed next to the van, afraid to be out in the open. "Where have you been, Pryn?"

Pryn looked up to the sky and held his arms aloft as if he were wishing for another rainstorm. "I've been waiting for you. Did you see that blessing that Varuna bestowed on us? She wants us to win here today. I know it."

"Yeah, well, that 'blessing' almost toasted the one

183

person who can open the portal back to the Realms."

Pryn was shaken from his reverie. "Is she okay?"

"Yeah, fine." The hair at the back of my neck lifted, and I moved a few steps closer. From this distance I couldn't judge the color of his eyes. I wondered if, by possessing the prophecy, he was hiding other secrets. "Are you okay, Pryn?"

"Yes, doing well. But the time is growing near. I'm afraid we must prepare ourselves for battle."

"Pryn, before we start, there's been something I have wanted to ask you about." I pulled the prophecy from my pocket, and as I did, I could see the smile on Pryn's face melting.

He pointed at me like I was holding something awful, his stricken expression causing me concern. Was I right? Had the prophecy affect him in some way?

"Where did you get that?"

"Does it matter? You know what it is, don't you? Why don't you explain it to me?"

Pryn hopped down off the porch and started to walk toward me.

Instinctively I drew my sword. "You can stay there and tell me."

The car door opened, and Mane got out. "Is there a problem?"

"One you would know all about, demon. When did you take to stealing my possessions?" Pryn turned his attention to Mane.

I tamped down my irritation. When I had more time, he and I would talk, and the conversation wouldn't be nice. Usurping my orders, especially at such a critical phase, didn't bode well. "I said stay in the car, Mane. I don't need you in the middle of this."

My command, issued through gritted teeth, made him hesitate. He fixed me with a probing gaze. "I'll be watching." Kit pulled him by the arm, and the door clicked shut.

I faced my other adversary. "So you've known all along that this was going to happen? When were you planning on telling the king?"

"Your father knows everything he needs to know, Valora. My job is to act as his advisor, and I have. Yes, I have known longer than that, but did you really expect me to tell Aric when he was making deals with the demon king himself?"

I shook the paper in my hand, refusing to be discouraged. "But this came from Acheron. How did you come upon it?"

"The same as you, tucked within a book. I added it to a volume I was working on that chronicled Acheron and everything about it. I needed to know what was happening, so I could prepare. And it has worked. You are here. Kit is here. Everything is as it should be. And when that portal opens, we will destroy Ravanna and the threat to our world."

"But what about the portal? Won't it remain open once Ravanna is cast back into Acheron? Who is to stop everything pouring out of it and causing a path of destruction?"

Pryn approached me, and I dropped my sword to my side. "Once Ravanna is dead, we can leave here. The portal between our world and this one can be closed. Forever. This place is of no concern to us."

"Are you serious?" I retreated a few steps, disgusted that he would even think that. "You would let this whole world die to save ours? Is that what you think Varuna would do?"

The maniacal gleam in his eye disturbed me as much as his words. "You think she really cares about this world,

Valora? She possessed Dooley and Aric's mother. She used them repeatedly to protect herself. You think she would deny you entrance to the Elysium for saving your own people?"

"I don't care about the Elysium, Pryn. I care about here and now, and, yes, I care about these people. What about Dooley? Bowen?" I looked to the car and could see Bowen staring at me nervously. He could probably hear what we were saying, which made me more determined to save his life. "And Kit is also from this world, don't forget, and her father Ralph. You're telling me that you would sacrifice it all?"

"In a second." He reached out and tried to snatch the paper from my hand. I kept it out of his reach. "We need to complete the ritual. We have no choice. Unless you want Dooley and Aric to remain in Acheron."

"No." I didn't want them abandon them. But I knew that they would sacrifice themselves rather than let this world die. "It's not about what I want or what you want. It's about what's best for everyone. And I think maybe it might be best to leave the portal closed."

The weight of my own words caused me to stumble back a few steps and connect with the car. The amulet at my neck flared red, and I felt a scream welling up from inside me that wasn't *of* me. It poured forth through my mind and formed into a pulse that rocked me to my knees.

"You think he will let you get off that easily, Valora? As long as he has you bound by that amulet, you're his servant. And until he is dead, you will always be his servant."

I looked up into Pryn's eyes. The only person it seemed I was serving was him. But I couldn't deny that I'd been brought to my knees by a very different command. "Where do we begin?"

Pryn fell back into his usual mannerisms as soon as I agreed. "Get Kit and Mane and have them stand by at the portal to the Realms. You and I will go to the demon circle. We will be ready for Ravanna when he comes through."

I rifled through my mind, trying to find anything I could that might help me prevent the death of Ravanna and close the portals once I knew that Aric and Dooley were safe.

That's right, Valora. Let that fae kill me and I can guarantee you that Aric and Dooley will be trapped here. And they will die a slow and gruesome death, which will take a thousand lifetimes to end.

No need to convince me. But I have other problems. Our deal is that you bring them with you. You need to show me that they are safe.

Don't make demands of me. Open the portals and we can be done with all of this.

Mane and Kit agreed to go to the portal to the Realms. Kit had fed on something in the forest—I didn't bother asking what, but at least she looked like she was gaining some of her strength. "Valora, if I do this, please tell me that everyone will be okay. I don't want to be responsible for the death of my father too." Kit choked on her last words.

"He is far from here, Kit. Don't worry. He'll be fine."

Just as the words exited my mouth, I heard a siren in the distance. An engine revved, and a car that looked like it had taken a drive through the acid baths of Ordos pulled into the driveway, spitting dirt and rocks. It came to a quick stop behind Bowen's van. The sheriff's car close on its heels, lights flashing.

Ralph got out, his gun drawn. "Everyone get down."

Kit looked at me, her mouth opening and closing. I pushed her behind me and whispered into Mane's ear, "Get her out of here. Now. We're going to have a problem, which will get worse if we don't get that portal open."

Mane nodded and escaped into the brush. It would take

a lot of Kit's strength to get it open and keep it open. Our time was already running out.

As soon as Mane and Kit disappeared, the figure from inside the first car opened the door and stepped out. The last person I expected. Kali.

"Valora, you can't do this. You can't open the portals. She told me it would end in disaster." She approached me without a weapon. The wings she'd abandoned everything for looked like they were coming apart. The magic gave her the illusion of wings, but it didn't really restore them. It was all a lie.

Ralph stepped forward. "I knew she was a problem for you, Valora. She came around the home after I dropped Irena off. As soon as I saw her I tried to stop her, but she hijacked this car and headed here." He kept his gun trained on her head.

"Kali, my child, you are misguided," said Pryn. "We must draw Ravanna to the surface. Opening both portals is the only way. How else do you expect us to kill the demon king and save the Realms?"

"It's not that simple, Valora," she said. "Don't listen to him."

"Why am I supposed to trust you?"

"We don't have time for your foolishness, Kali Mirch." Wind swirled around Pryn's feet, tossing us all off balance. The aim of Ralph's gun shifted toward Pryn, and with another flick of his hand Pryn tossed the weapon into the woods.

Kali grabbed the edge of the car as she tried to shout above the sudden storm appearing before us. "I told the Goddess that you wouldn't listen to me. I told her that I betrayed you."

A viselike grip wrapped around my throat, and closed

down my ability to move on my own. I turned, and Pryn held his hand out. As he closed his fingers tighter, the invisible fingers at my throat got tighter.

"I thought you said I would save us all."

"You will, but it would seem I need to help you realize your role in all this." With the other hand, Pryn gave a broad sweeping motion, and Kali was thrown hard against a tree trunk. Something cracked, and the look of shock on Kali's face was frozen as her body slumped to the ground.

"You and the other human should probably find a place to hide. Come, Valora."

"Ralph, take Bowen home. You need to get back to Irena and make sure she stays where she is. We must handle this." The last thing I needed was to worry about Bowen and Ralph. They were defenseless out here.

"Will do. You take care. I consider you my daughter."

Bowen and Ralph hopped into the cruiser and left. A knot formed in my throat at their departure.

Pryn pulled me on an invisible leash through the woods behind him. I looked to the left and saw the pulse of purplish light as the portal to the Realms sprang to life. No more stalling—the wheels had been set in motion. Whether or not it was the right thing to do, the war started now.

Branches struck at my face as Pryn pulled me deeper into the forest. I felt as much a rag doll as Pryn was when I'd hauled him from the dragon's lair. This was planned from the start, but why? It didn't make sense. Did Pryn really think he was doing the best thing?

As we approached the clearing, the amulet at my neck flared red. I glanced up and saw Franca's image, standing on the edge of the clearing. She peered at me with sadness, her head hanging low. This was not what was supposed to happen. That much was clear to me now. What wasn't clear was how I was going to get out of it.

CHAPTER THIRTEEN

Deafening wind roared through the trees, sweeping us toward victory. We entered the clearing, and Pryn released his hold on me. I couldn't abandon him even if I wanted to. We had come too far. The portal to Acheron was about to open wide, and who knew how many legions of Ravanna's lackeys would pour through? From behind us, a ray of purplish light emanated from the portal Kit struggled to keep open. Our window of opportunity was small. Ravanna wanted the Elysium and, once liberated, wouldn't stick around here any longer than necessary. Finger-like tendrils threaded through the trees and brushed over the edge of the demon circle. It flared to life. A red beam burst into the sky and the clouds parted. A new dawn formed on the horizon. *Dear Goddess, what have I done?*

A dark hand snaked out of the portal. I brandished my sword, embracing my destiny, a fight until the inevitable death. My gaze darted between the portal and Pryn. Even though I didn't stand a chance against the demon king, I'd take my chances on the front line and give Pryn the upper hand.

My step faltered as a head and upper half of a body appeared, shadowed in the portal's opaque energy. Time was running out. The figure fully emerged and stumbled, landing at my feet. I took a step back, the breath leaving my lips in small, sharp gasps.

"Nice to see you again, beautiful." Aric wiped at the thin layer of black soot that dusted his face, pale skin stark against the grime. My knees weakened and I sent a silent prayer to the Goddess, joy shifting the fear from my heart. Ravanna had kept his end of the bargain.

From the cocky half-grin Aric flashed me, he was unharmed. The good feeling evaporated as I searched for Dooley. "Where is he?"

"He was right behind me." Eyes scanning the area, Aric braced himself on solid ground, legs taut, his magnificent wings fluttering in the wind caused by the maelstrom.

"Pryn, Dooley is coming through there. Don't blast him." I shot a look at Pryn, whose arms were extended toward the night sky. Light danced across his fingertips. "I didn't know you were a spellweaver too."

"Who do you think taught your mother?" I had always assumed my mother's abilities were natural, like Dooley. Sure, Pryn had been her teacher, but even he hadn't been able to teach me. Or had he neglected to teach me on purpose?

Aric tilted his head to the side. "You plan on killing the Demon King?" There was an edge to his voice that shouldn't have been there. He curved a finger at his lips, silently commanding me to keep quiet.

Before I could react, another figure emerged from the portal. Dooley. He was dressed head to toe in blood-red plated armor, his movements unnatural. Suddenly a blast came from Pryn and struck Dooley straight in the chest, throwing him sideways and down to the ground.

"Dooley!" Without any concern for my own safety, I raced to his side. He rolled over, a burn mark on the armor, but seemingly unharmed elsewhere. Lucky for Pryn. "I told you not to shoot."

"I'm okay. I'm okay." He sat up and tried to free himself from the heavy plating.

"Keep that on," I ordered. He would need it for the fight to come. Gravel crunched under Pryn's shoes as he got closer. He stood somewhere behind us, commanding attention. I refused to turn. My hands shook with rage.

"If he were who I thought he was, he'd be dead, regardless of the armor," Pryn said. "Where's your father? I thought if we opened the portal to the Realms it would force him through."

Dooley winced and tried to stand, pressing his hand into the spot where Pryn's spell made contact. "He's not my father. And he wanted to send us first to make sure it wasn't a trap."

"What? You mean he's not coming?" shouted Pryn, completely disregarding the fact that he had both insulted and assaulted Dooley in less than a minute.

Dooley slumped to the ground, dragging me down. "What is it?" I asked.

"Have to rest a second." He closed his eyes. I removed the rest of the plating. The force of the spell had scorched his chest, leaving a black mark.

"He'll be fine. The spell only stunned him a little," said Pryn.

I glanced sideways at Aric. He was focused on Pryn, his movements slow as he crept toward him. If I warned Pryn, then he might kill him. But if Ravanna were disguised as Aric that meant the real Aric remained in Acheron. Ravanna couldn't die until both Dooley and Aric were safe. And Pryn was trigger-happy.

"I'm sure he'll come after he amasses an army to go before him. He doesn't do anything in a small way," said Aric. His eyes flashed red but quickly dimmed before Pryn noticed.

"We must form a new strategy," Pryn said to me, ignoring Aric. "Can you contact him through the amulet?"

"She sure can." Mane entered the clearing.

The light of the demon circle burned brighter, matching my temper. Mane could jeopardize our mission.

Ravanna's disguise decomposed. He thrust out his chest and stared down at Mane from his greater height. "Making trouble again, Mane? Given the last time you crossed me, I thought you'd think twice before interfering in my business. Pity you cared so little for Catherine. Looks like you have already forgotten about her. Probably a good thing. She is getting on in years, and I'm in need of an upgrade. A Kit for a Cat."

Mane's fingers retracted, becoming claw-like as a visible vein throbbed in his neck. "You will die before I see you take Kit anywhere."

I crouched down, maneuvering myself into a better position. Dooley was passed out, but out of harm's way. The best place to be during a fight between two demons was probably on the other side of the open portal, but I had a job to do.

"If I die, you will take my place. I know you've always longed to sit on the throne at Acheron. You and Catherine, broken toy that she is, can be together forever. You madly in love with her, and she just plain mad." The last traces of Aric's smooth voice blended into Ravanna's coarser laughter.

Against my will, I shuddered at the sound, and horrible

memories of Acheron flooded my consciousness. It was as if every sad thing I had ever witnessed, every regret, settled on my chest. Acheron had that effect on me, and I had spent little time there. If Mane were banished there for a lifetime, what would become of his soul? Would the lightness leave, and the blackness seize him for all eternity? It required every bit of inner strength I possessed to pull my mind from that horrible place. I had to stay focused if I ever hoped to extricate my friends from this nightmare.

I watched Pryn's jaw slacken as Aric's face molded into Ravanna, his shoulders widening, arms lengthening to embrace his freedom. In Acheron, he was frightening—on Earth he was terrifying.

Stunned, the meaning of his words creeping over me, slowly I realized that if I allowed Pryn to kill Ravanna, I would lose Mane to Acheron. Thoughts scrambled through my mind. Where before I wanted to hurry things along, now I ached for more time. As I stood, indecisive, Pryn crept closer to the demon king. Thankfully, Ravanna remained focused on torturing Mane.

I noticed the light from the portal to the Realms was fading. There was no way Kit could keep the doorway open this long. "Is that true, Mane?" I asked, knowing the answer before he uttered the words, but I had to hear it from his lips.

Mane refused to meet my eyes, his voice monotone. "You can't save everyone, Valora. Do what you must and I will do what I must." He glared at Ravanna.

My hands shaking, I straightened my spine. How could I kill Ravanna if it meant banishing Mane to Acheron? As a friend, he may help to unite Acheron and the Realms. But if he spent too much time there, the soul he had worked so hard to cultivate could wither and die. Being torn from Kit, he may become an even greater threat than Ravanna. Revenge is a powerful motivator.

The cinder-burned rattle of Ravanna's otherworldly laughter jarred my nerves. "He hates me, but he can't kill me. Tragic. And he can't stop me from taking Kit. She's mine now. See for yourself," Ravanna said. The brush parted and Kit appeared. Her eyes were glazed over. She was obviously no longer the one in control of her actions.

A blur of movement from Pryn startled me. He lunged, yanking the amulet from around Ravanna's neck, the chain snapping off in his hand. Ravanna charged for him, and light shot forth from Pryn's fingers.

Ravanna spun around, voice rough and bubbling with pure hatred. "Who the hell are you?"

I stepped in front of Pryn to block any further attack from both of them. "Pryn, you can't kill him. We have to return him to Acheron."

Pryn kept his hands raised toward Ravanna, bafflement intermingling with caution at my rash behavior. "Finish this, Valora. You have the other amulet. If you hold both, you will hold power over Ravanna and he can be killed. This has been your destiny from the beginning. Can't you see it, Valora? You were meant to save us all. Mane is a demon, the same as Ravanna. You would only be delivering him to his rightful home."

A tilt of his head, and Ravanna summoned Kit forward. He smiled and stared at Mane. "Bring me that amulet there, little one. At any cost." He motioned to Pryn.

Kit shot past us and seized the amulet. She bent down to set it in Ravanna's outstretched hand.

Mane rushed me. I sidestepped the attack, but too late. He yanked the amulet from my neck, knocking Pryn over in the process. I dropped to one knee, a wave of dizziness hitting me as the magical connection shattered. He pounced on Kit, and they fell to the ground. He bit down on the chain of the amulet, holding it in his mouth as he snatched at the one in her hand.

Kit let out an inhuman cry that seemed to come from her and Ravanna simultaneously. Her fangs extended and she sank her teeth into Mane's neck. My amulet dropped from Mane's mouth and tumbled to the ground. "Kit, no!" he yelled.

I ran to her side, dropped my sword, and worked to free him from her grasp. Her eyes met mine, and I saw nothing of my friend, just a tortured soul. Tears threatened to fall, but I held them back. "Kit, please. Listen to me. This isn't you. Fight it, fight him." Although I was sure she couldn't comprehend all my pleading, her struggles waned. Using all my strength, I held fast until her mouth slackened and she collapsed. Relief shot through me until I felt her body convulse, her eyes rolling up into her head. Her two legs reformed into a selkie tail and she flopped onto the ground like a fish out of water.

Through my blurry vision, I saw Mane holding his hand to his throat. Blood ran in rivulets down his hand, through his fingers, as he tried to stanch the flow.

"Kill him, Valora. Kill Ravanna—it's the only way," yelled Pryn. Everything inside me screamed *no*. I had made a pact before I set out on this mission that I would bring all my friends back alive. But Mane couldn't die. Sending him back to Acheron would be a fate worse than death. I would lose the good friend I had to his demon side. A short-term solution that would create an even bigger problem. I couldn't take the chance—no matter how foolish everyone thought my decision. I knew it was the right one.

"I'll do it. I have wanted to do this a long time." Mane

collected both amulets and grabbed my sword from the ground. He reared up and plunged the sword forward, targeting the center of Ravanna's chest.

Don't let him do it. A voice ran through my head. I lurched forward and seized Mane's leg, sending his aim off. The sword plunged into Ravanna's shoulder.

Pryn shot a spell, and Ravanna tumbled backward from the force of the blow. The demon circle was right behind him. A hand snaked up from inside and caught his ankle, dragging him in. An explosion of light coated the field. I was forced to hide my eyes from the blast.

As the light died down, night became day. Mane rocked Kit in his arms, her complexion far too pale. I heard her gasping for air, her limp body unresponsive to Mane's pleas. Dooley lay on the ground not far from them, rolled onto his side, his face hidden from me. Pryn remained where he was, as if nothing had happened. In the middle of the dormant demon circle was Aric. The real Aric.

"What the hell?" asked Aric. "Or I guess I'm not there anymore, am I?"

Pryn rushed over and put his arm around Aric's shoulder, eyeing myself and Mane with a nervous twitch. "You've been involved in a demon portal crossing. It will certainly shock your system. Come lie down over here."

I stood to let them pass. When I looked back, Mane was glaring at me. "You did this," yelled Mane, his grip on Kit tightening. "I almost killed him. And you sent him to Acheron, where he will heal and begin again. You think I don't know how Acheron works? You should have listened to what I told you. I have lived ten more lifetimes than you and I know all about it. You made a mistake today, Valora. One you might never recover from."

"Look, Mane, it's more complicated than all that." Again

I had saved someone who didn't want to be saved. The whispering in my head was more than a gut feeling. It made sense. Ravanna denied any involvement with summoning the dragon, and it wasn't like him to deny any display of power. Then there were the elves that were somehow wrapped up in this. It didn't seem possible they were the cause of it all. They were working with someone. There was more to this, and it was not a time for rash decisions.

Pryn approached Mane. "Would you mind handing those amulets over to me?"

Mane complied, his face still a mask of fury. "I don't have any use for them anymore. You might as well try and keep your world safe, because he doesn't give up."

Had I done the wrong thing, as he accused? Inside it felt right. Regardless, I had to stick to my decision. "Pryn, is the threat here gone?" I asked.

Pryn clutched the stones, a distant expression on his face. "It seems as if Varuna has not decided to retaliate. Of course, things could be very different in the Realms. Mane, I can help Kit if we bring her to Dell'Aria."

Mane scooped up Kit and hugged her to his chest. He continued to scowl. "I'll follow. You stay here. If you are so keen on saving Earth at all costs, protect it." He brushed past Pryn, heading into the forest toward the portal to the Realms.

"Pryn, I…did I do the wrong thing?"

"I'm not certain." He drew in a deep breath and traced the intricate border lacing the edge of one of the amulets. "You need protection here. I can make these amulets do what they did before for you, Dooley, and Aric. I think it is best that the three of you be joined again. Keep the balance between those two, Valora. I will return as soon as Kit is settled and we can make another plan."

"Yes, whatever you think is best." I slid to the ground, defeated.

Smoke rose from the charred remains of the demon circle. Dooley sat up and looked over at Pryn and I. "Is it over? Oh, he's still here." He jabbed his finger at Aric.

"You remember?"

"My memories of Acheron are fuzzy. But I do remember everything else." He grimaced at Aric, who smiled and held up his hands. For whatever reason, I was pleased by their adversity. I was glad to see some things never changed.

Pryn cradled the three amulets. "You three once wore these thinking that they were a burden. Wear them now to strengthen all of you. This battle is not over. I fear the days to come will hold even greater challenges."

He placed the amulet over my neck and then Dooley, and the last on Aric. As soon as we were all connected again, a surge of energy pulsed through my body.

"Wow, too bad the bed burned in the fire," said Aric, breaking the tension.

"In your dreams," said Dooley.

"Quite often, in fact."

I bit back an unexpected grin at the banter. "You two stop it."

"They're feeling better. I must leave," said Pryn.

The short burst of amusement faded, and I snatched the edge of Pryn's robe. "Tell me. Will she be okay?"

Pryn's golden eyes sparkled. "I will do everything in my power to help her." Pryn closed his hand over my wrist. "Find Irena and make sure that there's no further intrusion here. If so, I'm not sure how to stop the Goddess."

Pryn disappeared into the woods, leaving me alone with Dooley and Aric. I stared after him, wondering how my actions would affect the outcome in this war. If I had killed

Ravanna, Mane would have been king. Would his new role have taken him to the dark side, or would he have been a different kind of ruler? Now I would never know.

CHAPTER FOURTEEN

The sun was at its highest point in the sky, shining a light on all we were and all we weren't. I had saved my friends, but at a cost. Mane hated me now. Love or hate, I didn't regret my decision. Especially watching Dooley survey the damage to the front of his cabin. The only real home he knew was gone. His face was a mask of pain, blue bruises marring his cheek and standing out in stark relief. Aric disappeared into the forest, saying there was something he "had to take care of." I had no desire to discover what.

Dooley flinched when I touched him. Was he in pain or did my touch repel him? "Are you hurt?" I asked, the question running more deeply than the physical.

"No, you startled me." He crossed his arms over his chest and hugged himself tightly, shutting me off. I should have expected this. The old resentments were still sitting under the surface, and we needed to talk. "I was thinking of another time."

"Are you ever going to forgive me, Dooley?" The words came out raw and needy, and I felt the tips of my ears pulsing.

Dooley passed his hand through his hair and inhaled deeply. "Depends. Can you forgive yourself?"

"I—I don't know." Hard to forgive yourself when you keep making the same mistake. Aric and Dooley were combined into one man inside my mind, and I was having trouble separating them. Both of them had stolen a little part of my soul, which was proven to me the moment the amulets joined us again. I finally felt whole.

Dooley clasped my hands in his and faced me, much like on the day of our wedding, when I'd gazed into his eyes and thought we'd be joined forever. "I never blamed you for what happened. And I can't even blame myself, even though I tried. We're caught up in a master plan a lot bigger than we are, Valora."

"What does that mean for us?" I choked on my words, hoping he wouldn't say we were doomed, because it certainly seemed like everything was telling me we were.

"It means we better figure out who is responsible and stop them so we don't have to keep putting out fires."

"It has been a little crazy. But in Dell'Aria, when we were preparing for battle, you barely spoke to me."

"I barely spoke to you or you barely spoke to me? I was always around. Weapons training kept you busy." Dooley drew me close to him, my nose brushing against his. "I missed you."

His fingers slowly trailed down my arm and rested on my hip. The intimacy of his touch sent shivers along my spine. A fluttery emptiness pooled at my core, craving to be filled. The anticipation of our time together was killing me. And from the feeling I was getting from his nether regions, he was having a similar reaction.

"We could send Aric on an errand."

"What errand? I already got us a bunch of food." Aric's

arms were full of ice fruits.

A vision of Franca flashed in my mind. "Franca said the ice fruit plants here would die unless they were tended to by a fae. Yet they're alive and not one of us has been here in months."

"Someone certainly has." Dooley gestured to the remains of the cabin.

"We're sure the elves are involved, but not other fae." I broke contact with Dooley and headed toward the cabin.

"There are probably others around here besides us." Aric handed me a fruit, and I inspected it before taking a bite. He was right. Kali's whereabouts were in question. She could have decided to make this her home. But that would also mean she and the elves assisted Ravanna together. Or maybe not. The true intentions of the elf remained a mystery I hadn't solved. Ravanna's comment still triggered something visceral in my mind. I was sure that if my thoughts weren't bogged down from exhaustion, I could put the pieces together.

"Hey, guys, I'm going to borrow Bowen's van to stop at my apartment and grab a few things. Don't leave without me." Aric tossed an ice fruit to Dooley and slung a jacket over his wings. "Take care of Valora."

But not too well. Save a little for me.

I hadn't got used to the fact that our thoughts were no longer our own. "Dammit, Aric. I heard that."

"Whoops. I forgot." Aric covered his mouth in mock surprise. Nothing about what he did was ever an accident.

"Are we alone?" Dooley rubbed at the base of his neck, tilting his head slightly. He managed to keep his old jeans intact through this whole ordeal, but he wasn't wearing anything beneath the plated armor. Through the dirt staining his skin, his sinewy arms gleamed golden in the sun. I wanted to touch the tantalizing vein that ran across his biceps. "Let's check out what's left of my home."

My stomach dropped and then rebounded when his suggestion was something other than *being alone together*. "Sure. I started to go through things before, but we didn't have much time."

"Being under attack by a dragon will do that to you. Come on." Dooley held my hand and we stepped up onto the old porch. The wood was burned through for the most part, and it crackled beneath us. A board snapped under my foot, and I tensed, expecting the damn thing to split any moment. Dooley's hand tightened on mine. His arm brushed my bare shoulder, and I looked at him, about to apologize, but my eyes didn't want to leave lips that were close enough to kiss. "Be careful," he said.

Too late, I've already fallen. I forced myself to move. "Do you think it's safe? There is less damage to the back."

"Actually, I was hoping if we were closer to where the fire broke out it would be easier to access the memories." He jammed his heel into the burned wood and kicked at it a few times, gathering the charred bits in his hand.

"Which memories? There's nothing else in this head you haven't already seen." Even though I wasn't sure it would help, it was nice to see Dooley using his magic again. He settled onto a low stool by the remains of the fireplace.

I sat next to Dooley on the floor, being careful to balance my weight evenly on the scorched timber as I crossed the room. He poured water from a broken piece of crockery into his palm, combining it with the ash to create a salve. Raindrops from the night before clung to leaves. I stretched out my wings and enjoyed a deep breath. It seemed the first time in a while that everything was calm.

"I have to return to the library. Ravanna's library. I'm

certain I saw something important while I was there. But now I'm blocked."

The softness that was there a moment before disappeared, and his haggard features spoke of frustration. This was hard for him, and I wished I could help, but only he could find the answers.

It didn't take long to shatter the illusion. "How will you access that?"

Dooley's mouth opened and shut, yet another answer evading his brilliant mind. He knew enough to cover his fingers in black paint, which was a start. I had to help him any way I could.

You are the connection. Open yourself up. Franca's words. *We are caught up in something bigger than we are.* Dooley's words about a master plan. A variable in this equation was missing, and I had a feeling Aric was the answer.

I grabbed Dooley's hand. "When I was in Acheron, there was a symbol. A triad painted above the doorway to Ravanna's throne room. It's the symbols for the Realms, Earthside, and another one I've never seen before. I'm guessing it's Acheron. They were woven altogether. I made sure to memorize each stroke. I think I can replicate it."

My excitement was contagious.

Dooley slid paint from his hand to mine. "Draw the symbol on my chest and then I will copy it onto yours."

My knees shook at the thought of his hands moist and warm smoothing the paint across my breasts, the slickness of his palms gliding over the tips. The look he gave me spoke of his own need, a dance of seduction my body answered. Sensation burned a path along my thighs, sending a riot of need coursing through my blood. But the triad spoke of three. The two of us alone wouldn't work.

"Aric must be a part of this."

A half-hearted shrug was all I got in response. "Unfortunately, I agree."

Aric, we need your help.

The door to Dooley's cabin flung open, almost sending it flying off its hinges. "Ready and waiting."

"I thought you were running an errand." The way Dooley could speak through clenched teeth was quite impressive.

Aric plopped next to me on the burned log and slung his arm over my shoulder. "You wouldn't have approved of me taking a shortcut. Didn't want to tell you I planned to fly."

"How did you do that without anyone seeing you?"

"Why don't you ask your boyfriend here why he has a case of magic sitting in his house?" Aric tossed an empty glass vial over to Dooley, who caught it in midair. A familiar hum buzzed through my body, which was reacting to the copper magic from Dell'Aria.

"I thought that was all gone." He held the glass up to the sun, shimmering opalescent swirls reflecting the light. Aric and Dooley had been in Dell'Aria for so long, it didn't seem possible either one of them was responsible for this. Magic needed to stay in the Realms, lest an unsuspecting mortal find it and wreak havoc, or a renegade fae overdose on the power it provided.

"It is now. There wasn't much left, but it did make my errand go by quicker." Aric playfully tugged on the feathers of my wings. An intuitive feeling told me this wasn't right. Even with an injection of magic, Aric was far less affected by the trip to Acheron than he should have been. I wasn't entirely sure Ravanna had completely released his hold on Aric. Dooley was of Ravanna, and even he lost his memories and suffered considerably when he returned the first time.

"Didn't you say your father shut down the clinic and

that portal?" asked Dooley.

"Yes, but he probably didn't do it himself. He would have sent someone else." Again, the answer was right in front of my face and I wasn't seeing it. Every time I tried to put all the pieces together, my thoughts blurred out of focus.

"What was it you two wanted me for? I honestly only came because I thought I would get to see a little action."

Dooley glared at his brother and made a gesture with his hand, the same one the drivers gave me on the freeway that I was sure was unflattering. "*Want* is a strong word. Valora thinks we require your assistance in order to help access my memories of Acheron. I'm not quite sure why."

Aric jerked his hand from me and hopped up to his feet, pacing the short length of the burned-out room. "Why remember that place?"

"You remember it?" asked Dooley.

"Of course I do. The beds were hard, the food sucked, the wait staff was psychotic, and let's not forget the mist of souls." He shuddered. Perhaps Aric had been affected, only I couldn't see it. Erecting the walls in my mind came naturally after I'd discovered how vulnerable my thoughts were to these two. It would take effort to remember how to let them go again.

"Aric didn't see what you saw, Dooley. That's probably why you weren't allowed to remember. Let's see if this will work."

I finally coaxed Aric into his place beside me. Aric and Dooley could have won a glaring contest any day, but right now we had to work together and I had to make that happen.

I drew the symbol onto Dooley's bare chest. My fingertips tingled, but not only from desire—there was magic here. It was working. Aric got the same treatment, although his false sighs of pleasure made it difficult.

The fight over who was to draw the symbol on me was solved by the fact Dooley possessed the paint and Aric didn't. Joining hands was easy. Opening our minds was less so.

Why can't we fall into the memories? A white noise filled the space between their words in my head, blocking a deeper connection.

Try taking off the amulets. Aric's suggestion came as a shock. The amulets once ruled our lives, and he was suggesting we remove them. *Trust me on this.*

We each placed the amulets into the center and reconnected. Pictures flooded forth, knocking me back a step. There was so much information that I was drowning in it.

Aric's words rose above the din. *Focus on my voice. I'll take us to Acheron.* Suddenly we were in the library seeing Dooley sitting at the table. Next to him was a sheaf of paper that he was taking notes on.

Can you remember what you were writing? Time was short, and there wasn't a lot of time to go thumbing through his memories of every text he studied.

I was taking notes on the stone. The stone forged by Ravanna and made into the amulets we have now. It was never meant to be split. The stone, it stores magic…

Bowen told me that. He said it was like a "USB drive." Any clue what he meant?

Dooley's voice gathered all his thoughts together, and suddenly two words appeared on the page. *Destroy it.*

An arc of pain shot through my spine, and it felt as if my eyes were on fire. *I didn't invite you here. Leave, unless you desire to become part of my mist of souls.*

The picture dissolved and the three of us materialized in

a place I was certain didn't reside inside any of our memories.

꼬∽꼬

For a moment gravity seemed to suspend itself. I was floating in darkness. Beneath me, a pinpoint of white light grew larger. I didn't feel like I was falling, but it was certainly getting closer and closer.

As the white light replaced the darkness, my feet hit the ground and I tumbled to a stop. I squinted against the bright light and crushed the blades of grass under my fingers. The smell of flowers and sunshine surrounded me, bringing an overwhelming sense of peace and wellbeing.

"You can open your eyes now." Dooley's voice came from my right. I tilted my head toward him before opening my eyes a crack. If I was in hell again, I'd prefer to keep them shut tight.

Behind Dooley, a large castle sparkled in brilliant whites and blues. The walls of a deep valley rose up on both sides, and there was nothing more we could see from our vantage point except the tall castle set atop a lush green hill.

"You don't seem to be at all disturbed that we are in a fairytale land, and not one I've ever seen before." I stood and dusted off my pants. Then I noticed something else. Dooley had wings.

"What the heck?"

"There are worse places to end up. I know. I've been there." Dooley stretched his wings out. Raven-black feathers glinted electric blue as they caught the light.

"Dooley, your wings are so beautiful." They were soft under my touch. It seemed unreal we would be here and he would have wings. Certainly we were dead. There couldn't be any other explanation.

"Yours aren't bad either."

I stretched out what used to be my short span of wings and realized they were heavier. With great concentration I brought my wings up and down sharply. I lifted off the ground several feet before dropping.

Dooley snapped his fingers in front of my face, but I couldn't respond. I finally had what I thought I was missing. The physical disadvantage of being wingless was nothing compared to what it really cost me. My identity as a true fae.

"Where do you think we are?" I asked.

"Haven't you guessed?" answered Aric. He was sitting on a rock dipping his toes in a stream that seemed to form out of nowhere at his feet. "Mom can't bear it when I ignore her."

The Elysium. I was at the gates to the Elysium, where all fae longed to go in the afterlife. But rather than feel comfort, I felt fear. We weren't supposed to be here now.

"Can she hear us? Can Varuna hear us?"

"Yes, I'm usually better at blocking out her signal. The amulet usually does that for me, but we removed them. She brings me here from time to time to try and remind me where I came from—who really owns me." Aric spat on the ground and kicked his foot through the stream. "Let's leave. She won't help you."

"Wait, I want to speak to her." Funny thing about speaking to the Goddess. I had done it a million times over in private. Staring up into the stars my mother stitched into the canopy of my bed, I asked so many times for guidance. I never received an answer, but then I never expected to. This time would be different. "Varuna, if you can hear me, please listen. Ravanna is alive and sealed in Acheron. It's what needed to be done. I couldn't sacrifice my friends."

Sound was a mystery here, none of it coming from

where the source appeared to be. I supposed that was why I wasn't surprised when I heard a voice answer right next to me even though there was nothing to see.

"There is one whose heart's desire will harm those of the Realms." The premonition hit me like a mean left hook. Pryn said I was the one who was supposed to save us all. What if I became the destroyer?

"Who?" Dooley stepped forward. I couldn't get my eyes off his new wings. He truly looked like a dark angel.

"Like vibrations pulsating through a spider's web, I can feel the pull. A direction, but from whom I am uncertain. If you don't find out, I fear this magic will cause the destruction of the Realms."

Dooley and I were the only ones who searched the skies for the source of the disconnected voice. Aric appeared thoroughly bored.

"Why do we have wings?" Varuna's words were kind, but an alternative motive stirred under the surface. I remembered Mane's words about the gods having their own agendas. At least I knew what Ravanna had planned. Varuna's reasoning wasn't clear.

"Here in the Elysium, you live the life you were meant to. Both of you should have had the wings of the fae, but your world changed you. You had to learn to live with the burden of this cruel twist of nature. Once you are in the Elysium, you will suffer no more. The two of you and my son have to work together to figure out what is happening. It's critical."

"Speaking of your son, why didn't you tell him this rather than bring us all here?" Every second that passed, I could feel my hold on the physical world slipping away. They say when you pass into the Elysium you accept a whole new order. That you no longer care for the physical trappings of the world you left behind. Time being infinite, you no longer miss your loved because one day they will join you. I didn't like the degree of comfort the idea brought to me.

Varuna's voice faded into the distance. "I can speak to Aric at any time, much to his dismay. I tried to get him to relay this information to you, but he suggested I tell you myself. He can be difficult at times."

"You think?" said Dooley.

"She talks like I'm not here. Touché, Mother. Touché. Are you all ready to go now? I told you she wouldn't help."

I wanted to laugh and cry. I was speaking to the Goddess Varuna and I was in the Elysium. A place I hoped to be one day, but I wasn't ready to surrender my life yet.

"Yes, let's get back," I said. "Dooley, those amulets must be destroyed. Any idea how?"

"None."

"I'm sure Pryn can help." Aric stood and walked over to us. He absolutely glowed. "He's the one who initially led me to the amulet. He should have the power to get rid of it."

That didn't surprise me. Pryn was researching the stone, and he was once very attracted to my mother. No doubt he would have wanted to help Aric keep me alive and not draw attention to himself. He couldn't have identified the depths of vengeance that boiled beneath Aric's steady countenance. "But he wants to destroy Ravanna, and possessing those amulets is the only way. He won't agree."

"He will once he learns the truth. Without them, Ravanna will never be able to leave Acheron. It's time they were destroyed." Dooley's declaration defined our next mission. Get to the Realms and find a way to destroy the amulets. It was the only way to keep the Realms safe.

Aric nodded and retreated a few steps. White light surrounded us. I covered my eyes, and my body was

213

buoyant. Nothing tethered me to this place anymore. The air thickened, and I was thrust against solid ground, the weight of gravity feeling ten times heavier than normal. We had been returned to the cabin. Stars twinkled above our heads, a full moon casting a dim glow on our surroundings.

A tingling energy washed through my body, stimulating my hypertensive nerves. Dooley rolled over onto his side, his wings no more.

"That was interesting," said Dooley. "I guess we found our way. With the power we share, I'm betting we can open the portal to the Realms ourselves." He slipped his amulet over his neck, and I did the same.

Aric replaced the one thing that seemed to block the Goddess' signal. "I understand you both would like to destroy these as soon as possible, but please let me enjoy the peace and quiet for a little bit longer."

"Why is it you can block out the Goddess, but Dooley has trouble controlling Ravanna?"

Dooley's eyes widened, and his brow furrowed. "You haven't a clue what it's like having a demon inside your head. You have no idea." Dooley jumped up and stalked off into the woods. He was wrong. I had an idea. Ravanna had been in my mind more times than I cared to remember while in Acheron, but he never brainwashed me. I was aware of my identity the whole time. Dooley still wasn't the master of his own mind.

"Don't blame my baby brother, Valora. He hasn't had as much practice." Aric came from behind me and put his arms around my waist. "I, on the other hand, have a great range of experience."

Oftentimes I'm thrown into battle situations where my opponent is right in front of me and I can do nothing but react. In this moment there was far too much time, and I could see what was coming a mile away. All the muscles in Dooley's back stiffened. Aric's obvious attempt to pick a fight had succeeded. The testosterone was getting out of control.

Leave him alone, Aric.

This has been a long time coming. The statement seemed to come from both Aric and Dooley at the same time.

"Don't think I'm going to sit and watch you have a go at one another." I put myself between the two of them like the force that keeps two magnets apart. As long as I was here, they wouldn't kill each other. I hoped.

"Sorry, I have to do this," said Dooley.

"What?" I whipped my head around in time to see the sparks shoot out from his fingertips. The magic hit me and every muscle froze me to the spot, arm outstretched, mouth open to protest. Temper shot through my consciousness, and I screamed at them to stop this childish behavior before someone got hurt for real. We had a mission to accomplish, and I didn't have time for useless posturing. But it wasn't just my body—the fevered stare on Dooley's face froze my heart. His teeth were bared and he appeared more the monster than Aric ever was.

And then Aric said the one thing guaranteed to make this a fight that wouldn't stop until one of them won. "How does it make you feel that I have pleasured Valora more completely then you ever have? I don't have to prove it. You can see it in your mind."

Aric possessed his own talents in the bedroom, as did Dooley, but lacked command of fae magic, and Dooley's memory—as well as all his training—was at his disposal. Magic wins over charm. A blue-green fog striped with a dark red vein writhed up from the ground at his feet and collected into a ball of energy in his palm. "I can focus my magic. I

215

doubt you've kept up your lessons." A roar erupted from Dooley's chest as he sent the orb sailing over my head toward Aric.

I squeezed my eyes tight, ready to brace myself against my impending impact with the ground. I couldn't move, but that much magic was bound to send a shock wave that would help me along. Face, meet dirt. Only silence met my ears. I cracked open my eyelids and saw Dooley standing tall, heaving in great breaths of air as he stared behind me.

Prostate and weaponless, I forced myself to listen to my surroundings, and followed Dooley's gaze. Aric stood, orb in hand. He gave me a wink before pinching a section off the ball, and then another, until he had three equal spheres, which he then juggled like a court jester. "Wrong, little brother. I don't need to study magic. But I am better entertainer." The orbs flashed, creating a brilliant light show. "I've extra fae magic stored up in my veins. I won't have a problem deflecting yours."

The three orbs landed in his hand and he molded them together, launching them at Dooley with a force so great he stumbled to his knees. Dooley cried out, and the spell holding me released. Aric, his eyes as cold and dark as the halls of Acheron, advanced toward Dooley, who still fought to catch his breath from the force of the magic that hit him hard in the chest. The look of hatred twisting Aric's face set my body moving before my mind could process what he intended. I scissored my legs around Aric's waist, throwing him to the ground beside me with a muffled *thump* before he could reach Dooley, giving him time to recover.

Aric untangled himself from my grip and bolted toward Dooley. Adrenaline impaired my hearing, every thunderous explosion of fists between them registering as only a faint whisper. I'd bitten through my tongue, and the tang of blood stained my mouth. I looked up in time to see Aric swing his leg and strike a solid kick to Dooley's gut, bringing him down again.

Stop! Both of you stop! I can't take it! It was good I could still project my thoughts, because I hadn't worked all the dirt out of my mouth yet.

Aric froze mid-swing. "Valora, I'm sorry—I…" His voice lost its power, and the once-maddened expression grew pained.

I spat the rest of the dirt onto the ground. "What the hell where you thinking, Aric? You could have killed him pulling a stupid stunt like that. Return to the Realms. I know you have your ways. The real fight is there, not here."

Aric shot upward into the night sky. There was no telling how much magic he'd consumed. Hopefully he could work it out of his system soon. I'd had enough machismo for one night.

❧

"If he hadn't of been hopped up on fae magic, he'd have lost." Dooley stayed on his side the next morning, his pride more wounded than anything else. The roof of the cabin had suffered significant damage. A patchwork of rough-edged holes let in a view of the indigo horizon. A welcome scene compared to the crimson haze. Earth may not realize it, but we had saved it from a demon invasion. At least I could claim success here. I wasn't so sure about my own world.

When he flipped over, there was blood still oozing from a cut on his lip, small drops of it dotting his chest. We'd fallen into separate cots the night before, exhausted from so many revelations. I retrieved a cloth from my pocket and crossed the room. I sidled in next to him and dabbed at his wound. Dooley stared at me, a dazed look in his eyes. Aric's fireball had knocked more than the wind from him. I hoped he wasn't seriously hurt.

"His actions worry me." My eyes locked on his bare skin. "He's being reckless."

Dooley rolled his eyes and slid off the bed, taking his blanket and pillow and lying on the floor next to his cot, inviting me to stay where I was while he separated himself. He settled into his makeshift bed on the floor. It was stupid of me to bring up Aric. He was gone now and we were finally alone. And we didn't need Aric for anything.

"What are you doing?"

Dooley smiled and shook his head. "I thought you wanted to actually sleep. If I lie next to you we may not be getting much rest."

"Okay by me."

Dooley sat next to me, his hands on either side of my hips. He leaned in to my neck and whispered into my ear, "If you mean it, I don't want this to be about anything other than you and me."

An ultimatum tinged his voice, but even he was smart enough to make me choose right now. We needed each other too much. "It won't." I snaked my arms around his muscled back and tried to urge him closer, but he withdrew an inch. Despite the strain on the front of his pants, the man possessed an infinite amount of patience.

"I wish I could savor each second." His finger trailed down the front of my bodice and stopped at the leather lacings, which he slowly untied. "But I don't trust Aric to actually stay away." He tapped his head, and with one quick snap, the lace was tossed across the room and my bodice fell open. Dooley's warm hands were immediately on me. He thrust me onto the cot and our bodies melded in an instant.

I struggled with the waistband of his jeans. I had to

make sure the man in front of me was Dooley. Not Ravanna. Dooley. Even an iron burn wasn't as hot as his touch, but the pain was so good.

He filled me up and a cry left my lips, echoing through the silent forest.

"Are you okay?" I wrapped a length of his damp brown hair around my finger. This was the tenderness I knew him for. Aric was wrong. Dooley could control Ravanna. When we returned to Dell'Aria, he would see. They all would.

More than okay. My thighs caught him around the waist. He rolled us over, putting me on top.

The residual magic curled through me, making me quiver as Dooley cupped my breasts. *Wouldn't want your wings to get crushed.*

Each caress stoked the fires of our love, inside our minds as much as it was our bodies. Our mind-body connection complete on all levels, each caress stoked a fire within our hearts and our minds. Just like when we first kissed and I tasted Winter Haven bathed in our shared energies. Hand in hand we were showered by glistening waterfalls as we danced through the velvet blooms at their peak.

A mental paradise. Our own personal playground where nothing evil lived. Protected behind the walls in our mind. Confident we were alone. For now.

CHAPTER FIFTEEN

The day turned to night and back to day again, and we spent the entire time in each other's arms. The honeymoon we never had. Love nourishing our bodies enough to stave off hunger. Warm rays of sunshine covered our nakedness, legs entwined. Dooley dug his hands into the hair at the nape of my neck and drew me into his embrace. All forgiven and forgotten. My rightful place was in the arms of this man. I may be the one who was supposed to save us all, but this man had saved me a million times. Saved me from myself without even trying. I was better with him.

"That cut won't ever heal if you keep using your lips." I put my finger to his mouth, and he ran his tongue along the length, his heat setting my finger ablaze.

"I'll just have to use my tongue instead." He pressed against my thighs, which parted for him willingly, and nuzzled the soft flesh of my belly. Muscled arms gripped my waist and tugged me to the edge of the bed. His velvet lips bathed the swollen need radiating from my center. I tipped my head back, closing my eyes and relishing his tender touch.

A long screech, which didn't come from me, ripped through the air. I looked up as the broken front door collided with the floor. Pryn stood, his mouth open in shock, before plastering a hand over his eyes. Dooley's head whipped up and bumped a small table next to the cot. A glass of water teetered dangerously at the edge, and he caught it before it hit the ground.

I rolled to my side and drew a thin blanket over my body. Dooley stood, giving me a view of his chiseled backside. "Didn't expect a visit from the Realms so soon."

Pryn peered through two fingers and let out a heavy sigh. He tugged a scarf from around his neck and tossed it in Dooley's direction. "For the sake of Elysium, boy, clothe yourself."

Dooley laughed and wrapped the makeshift skirt around his waist, enough to cover up the show. He waggled his hips at me, bringing on a fit of the giggles.

"If the two of you are quite through, I've come on serious business. You were never meant to stay so long. Your father sent me to fetch you, Valora. And Dooley is welcome too, of course. There are events which require your attendance, and you'll be happy to know that Kit is doing much better. Physically."

There was a nervous beat between his last words, as if he weren't quite confident in his proclamation. The oppressive weight of responsibility came crashing onto my shoulders. Time moved at a different pace in the Realms. What seemed like only a few days here was probably a week or more in Dell'Aria. I knew I'd have to return eventually. "I'm glad to hear that."

"I'll put on some pants. If the king needs us, we will embrace our destiny." Dooley rose up his fist in mock grandeur. Although I wasn't certain what was in store for us, at least Dooley would be by my side. Though Pryn clearly said I was required, not Dooley.

Pryn stepped forward, and thrust a bag he had across his shoulder in my direction. "Your father asked that I have you arrive in this."

Dooley buckled his belt and pulled a white t-shirt over his head. He sat on the edge of the bed and thrust his feet into some work boots that had survived the damage to his cabin. "Well, what is it?"

I undid the knot on the canvas bag and ivory tulle burst from the opening. The full-length gown had a fitted bodice and a wide skirt woven with flowers and lace up the back. The top of the strapless number was made of hundreds of the stiff indigo petals of the Water Yarrow flower delicately sewn together. I ran my hand over the intricate stitches. Dooley had no idea what this meant, and I didn't want to ruin what was between us now by explaining it to him.

"I'll get dressed and we can get going." Better to face my fate now and let my father know I had no intention of agreeing to his plans.

Pryn guided us through the trees toward the open portal. Dooley grasped my hand, sensing my hesitation. "Don't worry—I'll hold on to you, and wherever we end up it will be together."

A cold pit formed in my stomach, and although my shoulders wished to collapse in on themselves, the corseted confines of my bodice kept me upright. We came through the other side and were greeted by a contingent of the King's Guard. They flanked us on all sides as they ushered us through the Riparian toward a waiting airship, which quickly took to the sky.

"That dress is beautiful on you." Dooley pressed the length of his body against me as I stared over the railing and surveyed our approach to Dell'Aria. No one on board the ship had said anything to me, and for once I was glad. I wasn't looking forward to this homecoming at all.

I spun around and laid my hands on his chest. "Whatever happens when we get back, know that I wish we could have stayed Earthside, right there in that burned-out cabin, for eternity. You have to know that."

He brushed a tear from my cheek. "You're acting as if this is the end of us. It's only the beginning."

The low humming sound that filled the air surrounding the ship was drowned out by shouts and cheers as we neared the dock.

"Wow, I've never seen so many of your people gathered in one place." Dooley stepped away from me and brought a hand up to shield his eyes from the sun.

I spun around and a wave of guards flew by my side, grasping me under the arms and pulling me into the air. Mane and Kit stood in the midst of the crowd. Kit jumped up and down, waving excitedly in my direction, while Mane's hands remained crossed over his chest. Apparently not enough time had passed to cool his temper.

"Morning, Princess Valora. We're happy to see you again." Orris smirked. At least he might be able to tell me exactly what I was getting into.

"How many days have passed? What's gone on since I've been away?"

The four guards landed on the path before the docks, and Orris set me down gently. "It's been fourteen sun cycles, or days as you would refer to them Earthside." The crowd before me parted, but their eyes weren't focused on me— they were turned toward a brilliant carriage that had rolled to a stop about twenty feet in front of me. "I can't really explain everything, but you'll find out in a second." Orris gestured to the carriage.

Behind me, the shout of the captain signaled the ship's docking. The guards worked to tie the floating fortress. Dooley leaned against the railing and waved at me. I waved back, and gasps rose up from the crowd. I turned to see the carriage door open, Aric standing proud at the top step, clad in the formal vestments of a future king. And I wore the dress of his bride.

❧

Weeks had passed since our trip home, and I should have been happy. The threat for now was gone. Ravanna was locked away, and Pryn confirmed there were no signs of his return, and the amulets were no longer connected to Acheron. However, there was the fact that Aric had been appointed king again. Initially it came as a shock, and I argued fiercely with my father. I refused to talk to him now, but in a way he was right. The people's renewed faith would bring them strength under Aric's lead. They all fell at his feet, and being directly connected to the Goddess certainly would have its perks. And I'm sure my father was really hoping it would put an end to Aric's naked yoga sessions in the courtyard. If it did, it would only be because he was too busy.

The problem with Aric being the king is I was expected to be his queen. The role itself would not prevent Dooley and me being together. A fae queen was allowed anyone she desired. But Dooley meant more to me, and he held fast to his traditional human notions of devotion. He would never agree to put himself in that position.

A knock sounded at the door before it opened slowly. Dooley. I startled, shocked to see him. *Speak of the devil.* He

224

had thrown himself into his training from the moment we returned, and everything appeared on the surface like when we were all still preparing for battle. I hardly saw him. My days were full of meaningless ceremonies and meetings meant to keep me occupied. I'd had no time to visit with Mane or Kit, and although I wanted to question Pryn further about the elf and what more he knew of the dragon conjured at the cabin, I was only able to communicate with him through messages from Orris.

I was able to make Pryn agree to research a way to destroy the amulets. I wasn't willing to risk their power or Ravanna returning. I'd looked forward to seeing Dooley this evening at the ceremony, and hadn't expected him to visit me sooner.

"Do you have a minute to talk?" He poised at the threshold, waiting for permission to enter.

"Of course." The ache in my chest increased the closer he moved. The best thing for the people of Dell'Aria would be to have Aric as their king and I as their queen, but that didn't leave much room for Dooley. He had come back with me expecting we could continue where we left off, and now here we were again.

Dooley paced the length of the red runner, motioning for me to sit on the bed. He paused, and I could see the tension in his jaw as he forced himself to speak. "There's no easy way to put this." He went down on one knee and grasped my hands. "I've decided to return Earthside. After Pryn's finished the ritual to separate us from the amulets tonight, he'll open the portal for me in the morning. I think it's best."

Kit had once explained to me the whole human ritual for proposing marriage, so when Dooley went down on one knee I hardly expected him to dump me. My lungs tightened, not allowing me to take in a full breath. Desperation clawed at my gut. I struggled to find something to say that would keep him here. "But there's nothing for you on Earth anymore. You're more fae than human."

Dooley dropped my hands, repeating what I said, devoid of all emotion. "More fae than human. Your uncle was able to survive, and he was full fae." He crossed his arms and planted his legs wide, speaking slowly to emphasize his hurtful words. "There's nothing more for me here, and I don't intend to be a third wheel. Your people are what matter most, and that's the way it should be. I've already contacted Bowen. He's agreed to put me up and give me a job in his shop until I can get the cabin rebuilt."

I didn't know why I thought things might be different. I'd accepted my role by Aric's side for the good of the people, and now I faced the possibility of losing Dooley. If he stayed, he wouldn't have a full life, and I could never forgive myself for making him miserable. "I understand. You know I never intended things to end this way, Dooley."

The corner of Dooley's mouth tilted in a half-smile. There was nothing left to say. The door clicked shut behind him as he exited the room.

My childhood dream of marrying Aric, the king of Dell'Aria, was about to become true. But this dream was all wrong. I clasped my hand around the amulet at my neck, once a burden, now the last thing connecting me to Dooley. I didn't want to let it go.

Hot, salty tears fell down my cheek onto my hand, and the amulet beneath my palm grew warm, but there was no amount of magic that would be able to heal a broken heart.

The old wood protested as I pounded on Pryn's door.

Before Dooley left, I wanted him to have my mother's grimoire. His father's journal was lost and there was nothing left for me in the grimoire anyway, never had been. Just like Dooley and I never stood a chance, no matter how much we wished. At least Dooley might be able to put it to good use. Plus, it was an excuse to see him again.

A glass shattered and the floorboards creaked under heavy footfalls. Pryn answered my call, a pinched, tension-filled expression making him appear years older.

His sour mug became genial the moment he saw who I was. Being the princess did have a few perks. "Sorry if I disturbed you. I must speak to Dooley."

Pryn shuffled from one foot to the other in the doorway, politely denying me entrance. "He's not here. If you'll excuse me, I have to continue my work so I can perform the ceremony."

His mannerisms struck me as odd. His normally pristine priest's robe was soiled, and his golden eyes lacked the luster that usually shone out over those that came to hear him preach. He must have sensed my surprise, because he wiped at the stain on the front of his robe.

"You'll have to excuse my appearance—your presence here surprised me and I dropped what I was working on. Quite a mess I made."

Despite his posturing, I was drawn inside the room. I popped onto my tiptoes, and on the floor was a puddle. A copper puddle.

"How did you get that?" I didn't need him to tell me what it was. How had he gotten it and at what cost? The copper magic of Dell'Aria, which was only supposed to exist inside the veins of the fae, lay in a pool on Pryn's floor.

"Now, Valora…" Pryn stumbled and stuttered over his words. He backed up, and I followed him into the room. "I know how this looks, and what with your mother—please hear me out before you jump to any conclusions."

Sometimes what was wrong was wrong, and that was it. I was done being sold on others ideas of morality.

"Your father instructed me."

So much for standing up for my ideals. I motioned for him to continue. Whatever he said, I would ask my father to confirm, and intuition told me his entire story would be valuable.

"Your father sent me Earthside after we found out what Aric was doing. I closed the portal and brought the magic stolen by Aric."

"But the portal wasn't closed. And not all of the magic made it here. I was at the clinic. There was an elf there who'd kidnapped Irena. And Aric found at least one vial in Dooley's cabin."

Pryn rapidly paled—considering his white wings and white robe, not an easy task. He leaned against a nearby chair, teetering dangerously to the side before he was able to sit down. I hurried to his side and helped him into the chair. He became unnaturally motionless in my arms. I waved a hand in front of his face. "I didn't know. You must believe me. I didn't know."

He clutched to my arm and looked past me to the box on the floor. "I—I brought what I could find, and it has sat here ever since. When you came to me to ask about destroying the demon stone, I did research. I haven't found a way yet, but I can free Dooley of the connection using the magic."

"I see." That was what Dooley had meant when he said *separate*. He knew Pryn hadn't found a way yet. The same adrenaline I had as a Hunter flowed through my veins. Dell'Aria wasn't safe as long as the stones within the amulets existed. Ravanna could make a play to come again. The Realms wouldn't survive another attack. The dwarves had lost half their people while they were trapped inside Elbrus, and the elves hadn't answered our calls. Mavrovo was barren, and Dell'Aria appeared to be the only isle in Overworld functioning at full capacity. Refugees arrived daily.

"I'm certain I'm getting close to finding a way to destroy them." Pryn regained his balance and stumbled over to a table set against the open window. The breeze blew in, churning the scent of the copper magic in the air, an irresistible perfume.

"If we don't get that cleaned up, I'm afraid I'll start licking the floor."

"Right away." Magic spun from Pryn's fingers with ease. His skills were greater than before. It twirled around the puddle on the floor. The reddish-brown pool rose through the air and collected into an empty vial in his hand. He corked it and returned it to the rack on his desk.

"That magic you used. I saw Dooley do that. You must have taught him. Tell me why he would leave when you are his only teacher."

Pryn closed his eyes and inhaled a calming breath. His short, jerky movements belied his nervousness. "We spoke about it. Since I can't destroy the stone, the best way to guarantee that Ravanna does not interfere here is to break the connection and return him. At least with Dooley disconnected from the stone, he has a better chance of keeping his father out of his head. I thought you would be happy."

Hope continued to push for answers in my heart. "If he stays here…"

He finished my sentence: "…he could reconnect with

the stone unknowingly. It's too risky."

"Thanks. I'll find him." I made to exit the room, but something caught my attention. In the corner were Pryn's sleeping quarters. Normally my vision wasn't this acute, but there was no mistaking that face. The golden eyes gleamed out of the photograph like a living, breathing person.

But of course she wasn't. My mother was dead. The memory still stung my eyes with tears. Pryn followed my gaze. "You have a picture of my mother." I sped across the room and picked up the frame, cradling it like you would a prized treasure. In his grief, my father destroyed had all her photographs, and the images in my mind faded long ago.

"Yes, she was my best student. Better than all the rest. She should not have been taken so soon."

My mother smiled into the camera like someone who was smitten. "Aric said you were the one who told him about the amulet—the demon stone. Is that true?"

I laid the photograph into Pryn's outstretched hands, and he held it close. "I only wished to save you. I didn't know it would cause you so much misery. I cared deeply for your mother." He traced his finger down the side of the glass frame. "If I could bring her back, I would do it in an instant. I'm sure she would know how to destroy these amulets."

The tears in Pryn's eyes were evident. He curled in on himself before I could say anything more. I was young when my mother died. There was a lot I didn't know about her, except for the warmth I felt at night when I stared up at the curtains she made for me and traced the stars. I certainly never knew that Pryn's feelings ran so deep.

"You should go to your father. He may know where Dooley is. I sent him to get permission for the portal crossing once the ceremony is complete."

Exactly the fae I intended to visit. My father once did his

best to keep me away from Aric. Now he was the one to suggest I marry him. We needed to have another talk.

"Thank you." I placed a hand on Pryn's shoulder and gave it a squeeze before leaving him to his mourning.

My walk to the king's chambers was the easy part. Talking to my father was next on the list. Orris stepped aside as I approached. "Good afternoon, Valora. Are you coming to force your father to eat? He's worse than you these days."

This was news to me. What could my father possibly have to fret about that would make him not eat? "Yes, thanks. He's in there, then?"

"Been in there all morning. Only other person come by was Dooley, but he's gone now."

Can't seem to catch him. "I won't be long." I bowed slightly, as was custom before entering. Father drilled it into me that we must keep up our pretenses even though things were tough. It was the job of the monarchy to stay the course and set an example. All I desired in this moment was to do was sling my leg over my motorcycle and ride through Underworld again. Go fast enough that no one could put a microscope on my movements.

My father sat at his paper-strewn desk, hands in his head, apparently napping. A soft snore emanated from between his closed palms. I picked up the nearest paper, which contained lots of numbers—inventories, people coming into Dell'Aria, calculations of how long our supplies would last. We weren't going to be able to operate like this for long. No wonder my father's appetite was gone—given that there wasn't much food left, we'd all have to tighten our belts. I cleared my throat.

My father raised his head and smiled as he saw me

leaning on the edge of his desk. "Thank goodness it's you. I thought it was Orris again trying to get me to eat my breakfast." He gestured to a small bowl of wild rye shoots, which weren't usually good even when you were hungry.

"Of course you don't want to eat that. Why haven't they brought you a proper meal? Does it have to do with this?" I waved the paper in my hand.

"I can't ask my people to ration if I don't do the same." My father thrust his shoulders back, his chin high. In the weeks since I'd avoided his company after his unfair pronouncement, he'd gotten thin, his face drawn. He looked old and frail, a state I wasn't used to seeing him in since my mother's death. I averted my gaze, guilt thickening in my throat. He was a proud man, and I wondered why he and my mother were ever married. She was nothing like him, from all accounts. A talented magic weaver who served as the king's healer, she thrived on being simple and fair. She never insisted on the pomp and circumstance that my father reveled in.

"Might I remind you that rationing does not equal starving? What can we do?"

Again my father's head fell into his hands. "Pryn said to give refuge to these fae. He sent messages far and wide, and they are all responding. The fae of Overworld have all been suffering, and now they are all traveling here. We are supposed to provide for them."

"Won't that be Aric's job soon?" Aric never relished actual work. Hard to believe he had transformed from destroyer of Dell'Aria to its savior.

"You really think he has any interest in this?" When Aric was king, this room was a stage—now shelves were stuffed full of ledgers and papers and probably all the things that my father always managed.

"It's his duty as king, is it not?" I cringed internally at the formal alteration of my speech in this place. Formality would actually demand the queen regnant control the city. "Unless you mean for me to take it on."

"No, no, no. It's best that he be king as the symbol of Dell'Aria. I don't suspect my role will change much, and neither will yours."

A king in name only—the very thing Aric always hated about his arranged marriage to the queen. And now I was in the same position. "Then why am I supposed to marry him? Explain this to me again so it makes sense."

"Because you are the princess." He crammed the papers into a pile. I think I had found my father's limits of conversation. "It is expected. Don't worry. I can handle all of this. And I gave Dooley his permission to travel through the portal, so that should make things less complicated for you."

There was no point in arguing with a man who may have once been part of a love triangle himself. "Did you know of Pryn's feelings for Mother?"

The shuffling stopped. His wings lifted and fell, hands limp at his side. "I've never been good at expressing my feelings. I can't blame your mother if she found comfort in another when I could not provide that for her. That was my mistake."

Before I knew it, I tripped over the threshold of the door. I was right. Dear Goddess, I was right. My mother and I had more in common then I knew. Both torn between two men. "Well, I won't let Dooley get away before I tell him how I feel."

"Please. I love you and I'm proud of you. I always have been. Situations arise that get in the way of me expressing that. But I mean that." He rubbed a hand against his heart.

"When you were born, I was the one who petitioned for your life to be spared."

A sudden coldness hit my core. It was a lie. There was no way he could have been the one. "Yes, but on Mother's request, right?"

"I don't wish to speak ill of your mother. Please."

At this point, none of it mattered. I could let my father think it was his idea for the petition. Mother was dead and she would have wanted us to mend our relationship. This was the first time my father hadn't danced around his feelings, and I didn't want to break the connection. Finally one of the men in my life was happy. I couldn't help but smile.

He bowed his head and returned to his papers. "You can probably catch Dooley out on the grounds. Last I saw him, he was taking little Pika for a stroll."

Orris gave me a goofy grin as I skipped past him. I wasn't sure what to say to Dooley, but before he left he would hear that I loved him. Whatever else was happening with the politics in this city, I knew I loved him.

Dooley's location was marked by the sound of sharp yapping. Rounding the corner, I could see him petting Pika on the head.

"What is all that barking about, boy? What did you find?" He knelt down to search in the tall cat grass below my window. He lowered his head, lips pressed tight, and drew out Brokk's journal. The one I had lost.

A gasp escaped my lips, and Dooley turned, fire in his eyes as he clutched the book. "So you lost this? Just below your window, you lost it? And you wonder why I don't stay. You can't just toss me aside, like an old book." He was shaking it at me now, Pika bounding around his ankles, completely unaware of our conflict. "I'll see you at the ceremony."

Dooley tucked the journal under his arm and brushed past me. No words came out of my mouth. Maybe I was more like my father after all.

‹❦›

I awoke suddenly. Night blanketed the room. I squinted to see what had ripped me from my quiet slumber. After Dooley had stormed off, I retreated to my bed, seeking comfort. I hadn't meant to fall asleep, but my exhaustion had finally gotten the better of me.

"I said, Valora, are you in there?"

I flipped my covers off and stumbled toward the door. Orris brought up his torch, and I squinted at the light from the candle. "Pryn was getting anxious, so he sent me over for you."

"Give me a second." I shucked off in the coat I'd dozed off in, being careful to transfer my mother's grimoire to my pocket, and adjusted the amulet at my neck. "I must have fallen asleep."

We rushed out the door toward the temple. The dome shone brightly as the moonlight reflected off its white surface. A blank slate and a new start for me. I might love Dooley, but I loved my home equally. Yes, this was the best decision for Dell'Aria. No more threats, all of our people living in harmony, the Realms repairing themselves after battle. It was the right thing to do. It wasn't as if I didn't have feelings for Aric.

Orris pushed open the door to the temple and led the way to Aric and Dooley, who were both seated at the steps of the pulpit. They both rose as I entered, Aric continuing toward me. Dooley put one foot on the inlaid floor at the center of the sanctuary then retreated.

"Good morning, sleepy head." Aric tussled my locks and wrapped his arm around my waist. "Pryn, we're ready."

Pryn, his back to us, was busy preparing something on the altar. He swiveled around and smoothed his hands down the front of his robes before pasting a false smile across his face.

"Pryn, I'm so sorry I was late. I hope I haven't ruined anything. I know Dooley is hoping to get home soon." Dooley's head snapped to the side, as if my words were a slap to his face. "I mean, I know he would like to be released from these amulets before he leaves. We can still do this, right?"

Pryn wiped away the sheen on his brow, his bottom lip trembling. "Yes, we can." He beckoned us all forward and pointed to a vase of red liquid set atop the altar. "This is an elixir made from the cinnabar."

"The demon's blood?" Aric loosened his grip on my waist, the muscles in his jaw tightening. "Do you mean to kill me?"

"It's not enough to do any such thing, your grace. Think of it like a vaccine you were given as a child. Enough to cause your body to react and break the spell of the amulets so you can all be free of your connection to them."

"Why four glasses?" asked Dooley.

"In order for the incantation to be successful, all four of us must connect, but only briefly."

"Good, because I'm not looking to add another bunch of thoughts to my head." I rubbed at the ache forming at my temples. My breath caught in my chest and my stomach tensed, uncertainty brewing inside me.

Pryn poured the liquid into each of the four glasses. I couldn't help but notice that his hand shook slightly as he did. Maybe he wasn't confident this would work. I wasn't sure I *wanted* it to work.

We each selected a glass. "Form a circle around me. I will say the words, and then we will all drink together. The sensation you feel may not be pleasant. You are having your connections severed. Your connections to each other and to the magic bound within these amulets. It may be shocking. You may feel ill, but you'll recover."

Pryn closed his eyes and tilted his head upward, murmuring words under his breath that I couldn't make out. Dooley studied him, his eyebrows slightly knitted together, as if he were reading the old priest's lips.

I leaned in to him and whispered, "After this is done, you can stay. I'm sure there is much that Pryn could teach you. He isn't your father, but I'm sure he would be happy to help." It wasn't what was in my heart, but it was all that would come out. As I moved close, I slipped my mother's grimoire into his satchel. He would never take it from me, but I wanted him to have it.

Aric drew me closer. "He'd be trapped here in Dell'Aria, Valora. The ships haven't been repaired yet. There isn't anything here for my brother. He presents as a human. It's best for him on Earth."

Best for Dooley to be on Earth. Best for the people of Dell'Aria for me to be their queen. "He's right," said Dooley.

Pryn stopped mumbling, and his eyes shot open, pupils dilated into black orbs. "Drink the elixir." His voice came out so deep that it rattled the floor beneath my feet.

I rested my lips on the edge of the glass and watched the others over the rim. We tipped our glasses simultaneously. The red liquid, which I thought would warm my insides, chilled me to the bone. The fae usually didn't mind the cold, but it overwhelmed me in an instant.

I was vaguely aware of hitting the floor. The images in

front of me spun, and when they stopped, I was staring at Dooley convulsing on the floor in front of me. I couldn't move. Pryn knelt before him and detached the amulet from his neck, fastening it around his own. He did the same with Aric and then knelt in front of me.

"Soon you will be as you were before any of this happened. Welcome back, Valora. You have done your part and saved us all." He slipped the amulet from my neck. All three stones rested against the intricate design of knots along the front of his robes. A triad. I welcomed the deliverance of sweet oblivion.

CHAPTER SIXTEEN

The excited voices outside my bedroom drew me to the window against my will. I had to give it to Aric. He made a charismatic figure in his purple cloak shot through with threads of silver, standing on the pulpit and addressing the people. The guard surrounding him had resumed their old duties protecting Aric, son of the Goddess. Even though a queen had always ruled over Dell'Aria, Aric commanded the attention. I had just saved the world, and now I was right back where I was when it all started. Watching him speak to the people, I couldn't help but feel like everyone was where they belonged. Everyone, that is, but me.

I scanned the crowd. The people had returned to a comfortable rhythm and their usual tasks, except instead of the shops being full of copper sheeting to protect us from the Blight, they were full of the fresh bounty of fruits from the ice fields, the creamy smell of butterbreads, and the sound of laughing children. The sight should have thrilled me, but I was too stuck in my own misery to raise any enthusiasm. I plopped down on my bed and realized my mistake immediately. Breathing was difficult in the stiff bodice of the dress I'd been forced to wear as the future queen. An empty title.

Father had stepped down into his role as hand to the king, and I was left to wander the castle. No purpose, reminiscent of when I was a child. The day after he'd removed the amulets from us, Pryn opened the portal and Dooley stepped through it. He barely said goodbye. That was several weeks ago, and I'd heard nothing from him since. I rubbed my fingers against the edges of the piece of magic mirror I always kept in my pocket in case he decided to try and contact me. I flopped onto my bed and quickly realized I was stuck on my back like a turtle. Some queen I was. I tried to roll onto my side, but a lack of oxygen translated to a lack of strength.

If Aric had his way, I'd likely stay in this position. Being stuck with Aric didn't seem as horrendous as it once did. At least he wanted to be with me. Pryn visited me several times, and each time I asked if Dooley had contacted him, he had shaken his head.

"Time to snap out of your funk."

I pulled the covers further over my head at the sound of Kit's voice. "I'm not ready."

"This time we're going to do this wedding thing right. My job is to make sure you get there in time, and I'm going to do my job." The covers were ripped from my fingers, and I pulled my arm over my eyes to shield the blast of light.

"You look like crap. Have you even left this bed in the last three weeks?"

My mouth opened and then shut again, the words stuck in my throat. When Dooley left, they didn't come out, and they weren't going to come out now. Kit balled up the blanket in her hand and sat down next to me on the bed. The amulet at her neck gleamed brightly, infusing her with the magic she needed to continue her stay outside the deadened waters of Mavrovo. She brushed a strand of my hair from my forehead. She wore her amulet with pride, whilst I'd always seen it as a burden. Until now.

"Hasn't Aric even come to visit you?"

I nodded, trying to shield my face from her as best I could. Shame colored my cheeks. I hated to admit to the pleasure I felt each time he checked in on me. Dooley's rejection hit me hard. As much as I wanted to be unwavering in my devotion, he'd left me even though I asked him to stay. "He has, but he's letting me have my space. And my father and Pryn have made sure he keeps busy. Between rebuilding Dell'Aria and reopening talks with the dwarves, we haven't had a lot of time to talk."

"Well, clean yourself up. I have a surprise in store for you." Now it was Kit's turn to avoid my questioning stare. She fiddled with the azure stone at her neck.

"Please tell me it's not another naked elf ritual, because I don't think I'm up for it."

"Not everything is about you." Kit pushed her hands into her hips, and for a second, I saw the young girl I met so long ago. "I have a dilemma and I need your help sorting it out. It'll require you coming with me and trusting me."

"You've got me interested." Kit had persuaded me to participate in a bachelorette party before my last wedding, and the wedding didn't happen. Part of me was hoping that we could repeat history. No matter my desperate attempts to see Aric's good side, or my acceptance of Dell'Aria's need for him, I wasn't in love with him. Not like I loved Dooley. It wasn't the same. Distance didn't lessen my love for Dooley. Though it seemed his thoughts weren't on me.

It's best to close that door, Valora. There is no good to come from you hoping for what can never be. Pryn's pronouncement had

241

driven me to my room, more depressed because of the truth of his words.

"Good. Get showered and we'll meet you at the docks."

"We? I thought Mane was tracking his tribe." It was disturbing that even after the threat of Ravanna was gone, the elves hadn't yet made an appearance—even more so, considering our encounter Earthside. If they weren't on our side, they at least should know their side had lost. Mane had volunteered to find out what he could. I was sure he wasn't just avoiding me.

"He's back." Kit clasped her hands together and glanced at them before returning them to her sides. "For good."

"I'm happy for you both." And deep down, I was. I wished my life had turned out so well.

Kit smiled and skipped toward the door. "Make sure to wear an outfit you don't mind getting wet. I'll meet you at the docks. We might be going where there's water, but…you smell. So scrub up."

"Kit, wait! Help me out of this bed." It was true I'd ignored personal hygiene lately, a subconscious effort to put a wall between myself and Aric. My lack of perfumed skin didn't deter him, though.

After she removed my ridiculous outfit, I was left to freshen up and redress myself in water-resistant attire. Her puzzling warning was enough to get me moving. When Kali and I had lived in the small hut on the outskirts of town, we were only able to bathe when our shift as Hunters was over, and then in the communal pools that dotted the outskirts of town. The benefit to being an "almost queen" was the private bath chambers.

The stone beneath my feet was cool, but the water that poured from the fountain above my head was warm, enchanted by the magic of our people and fed by the massive network of copper piping throughout the city. Aric's first action had been to make sure more fae were able to have all the luxuries of the royalty. His actions made him quite popular, and provided busy work for the many fae now living in Dell'Aria.

I closed my eyes as the warm water poured over my body, removing days of sweat and grime built up from my own neglect. I passed my hands over the soap and lathered it into every space I could find. Suddenly another pair of hands were on my wings. My eyes flew open, but they were covered in soap that stung my eyes.

"Ah, dammit. Who the hell is it?" I tried to wipe the soap away and managed to make it worse.

"It's okay, Valora. It's me." Aric put his hands on my shoulders and whispered into my ear, "Let me take care of you." He gently pushed my down into the basin of the tub and dabbed a warm washcloth over my face. "I think I rinsed most of the soap out."

I blinked and opened my eyes. Aric sat on the edge of the tub, the king's cloak unclasped and set on the ground, leaving him in his white pants, white-blond hair falling forward across his chest. It had grown a lot in the last year. I reached out to touch the silky strands. There was not a fae woman in Dell'Aria who would not trade me positions at this moment. And I felt sorry for him. Any one of them would probably be better than me.

"How did you get in here?" I looked around at the door to the bathroom, which remained closed and locked. "I didn't hear the door open."

"You'll find out soon enough that this castle is full of passageways. How do you think I was able to visit you at your mother's tomb the night before you left for Earth without alerting the guard?" He leaned over and felt along the edges of one of bricks in the wall opposite the door to the bathroom. He pressed inward, and a narrow passageway opened into darkness.

I peered into the blackened space. "You came through there?"

He nodded and glanced around uneasily. A hard, obvious swallow preceded his words. "To speak to you privately. I'm glad to see you're up and about again."

I laid my head on the side of the tub, holding on for dear life. The warm water was rapidly making me sleepy, and even though I had spent several days in bed, my worries interfered with my sleep. I dreamt, and the thoughts in my head were not friendly. I closed my eyes before he read the uncertainty within. My actions probably confused him, but I wasn't in a place to think about anyone else.

"Let me wash your wings. You can barely reach them." Aric grabbed the soap and rubbed it down my back and into the upper arches of my wings before I could protest. A small groan escaped my lips. "That's what I like to hear."

"Oh, Aric, why?" I lifted my head up and looked him square in the face. It was unfair—he was standing before me and Dooley was gone. "Why do you have to ruin everything?"

He leaned away, putting distance between us. "My mother likes to ask me the same thing. Again and again. Really, she won't shut up about it. But I didn't come here to force myself on you."

"I know you wouldn't do that." The amount of space he'd given me in the last several weeks had made me wonder if his obsession was over. The thought of losing both of them was unbearable.

"The choice is yours. You think that you have to marry me for the good of the people. But I've been working to convince your father and Pryn to change things so that you don't have to. We both know that you would rather pursue other interests. I'll stay here and lead the people of Dell'Aria. I have no intention of abandoning them. But I won't force you to do anything."

He looked more vulnerable than I had ever seen him in that moment. I couldn't refuse him when his whole life was devoted to winning my affections. I was the one who'd agreed to marry him. And he was the one who'd stood by me at every step and was still by me now. I'd denied happiness to the both of us long enough. "Shut the passageway, take off those pants, and get in here."

The level of the bathwater rose up several inches as he lowered his naked body into the tub, facing me. "I can't tell you how long I have waited for you to say that."

Aric caught me around my waist and pulled me closer, our legs wrapping around one another. He clutched my bare thigh and slid his hand between my legs, easily pinpointing my most sensitive spot. I brought my lips to taste the sweet, honeyed flavor that was him. A heavenly embrace from an angel. A familiar ache engulfed me, and I arched forward, thrusting myself in time with the thundering rhythm of his strokes. I crumpled forward, useless at the ends of his fingers as the pleasure radiated through my body. He pulled me into his arms and held me.

The tears quickly followed, and he held me tighter, allowing me to ride the wave of my sorrow. The floodgates of emotion were open, and I felt the ache in every muscle, every bone in my body. The pain cleared my mind and I had a moment of clarity. What I most yearned for wasn't my fate.

ॐ○ॐ

Love would have to wait. That's what I kept telling

myself as I rushed to the docks. I could truly and deeply love Aric one day. I would love him. Wouldn't I? I'd loved him once before. Time would pass and I would forget about Dooley and move on. My body was taking the lead, and it was a matter of time before my mind followed.

"Come on up." Kit waved from the deck of the ship, dragging me out of my own shell. I rushed up the steps to a ship greater than the Peixes ever was, and spied her standing next to Mane.

"Where exactly did you two get the funds to afford this ship?" I crossed my arms and watched Mane hand a fae on the dock a small sack in exchange for a barrel. Mane heaved it over his shoulder and headed up the gangplank, skipping our reunion.

"We've been doing odd jobs around town, like bringing in local delicacies. I swear I haven't been using my powers on anyone."

Those last words came out fast. I looked over at Kit, who brought her fingers up, indicating that perhaps she had used her powers a small bit. "But they were all well compensated. Besides, people around here could use more to do, and the queen required a ship. They were all too happy to oblige." Kit waved her hand across the deck.

"It's yours. This is your new ship so that you can travel to Underworld anytime you like. You won't be trapped here like you were before. You'll be free." Her words came out a little too singsong.

Freedom. After a few steps onto the gangplank, I realized how I'd missed it. During my days as a Hunter I'd often escaped to explore Underworld on my motorcycle. It was on those rides that I discovered the most about myself. Now my motorcycle was under a tarp Earthside. My future didn't hold any more visits there.

The fae on the docks detached the tethers from the moorings. The ship was enormous and foreboding. Its large black sails rose high into the sky, reminding me of the coal dragons who belched smoke and created a path that you could easily follow to their lair if you dared to seek one out.

The fae waved to me, and I did the same. I would be expected to do a lot of that in the future. I wanted to be the best for my people, but I wasn't sure I was the best even if it was what was expected of me.

The ship was built to operate on a skeleton crew. Orris had agreed to come along in his position as captain of the Queen's Guard. He was probably getting tired of watching my closed door. I often noticed him dragging his heels when he thought I wasn't looking.

Orris perched at the edge of the railing and peered out as we got further and further from Dell'Aria and descended into Underworld. I approached him from behind and put my hand on his shoulder.

"We've never really spoken about what happened."

He didn't flinch, his shoulders back, respect radiating from his simple nod in my direction. "Not necessary. You tried to save my brother. He believed in you. Nothing more to say."

The ship quickly descended to the banks of Lake Mavrovo, its red hue now faded. Crystallized remains of cinnabar belched up from the depths of Acheron lined the shores. "I appreciate you sticking by me. Queen or not." He used to be the first to offend me, and now he was the first to defend me. An enemy destroyed, he was now a loyal friend who'd help bring the rest down.

"My pleasure." Orris looked at me and then out to Dell'Aria again. "I never thought I would see us rebuilding like this again. I'm glad we don't have to fight amongst ourselves anymore."

I followed Kit down the gangplank to the edge of the shoreline, and surveyed the surface.

"Is there anything left?" I asked under my breath, more to myself than anyone else. The stench of death rolled off the water. Kit and I never spoke about her and Mane's mission here. When our conversations came to that topic, her countenance paled.

Kit looked to Mane. "Will you stand watch?"

"Sure." Mane leaned over and gave her a kiss on the forehead. Their connection was so pure and real that their words were solely for the benefit of those around them. They read each other's body language fluently. With Dooley and Aric all I did was talk, out loud and in our heads, and I definitely wasn't getting through to them.

Kit slipped the amulet from her neck. Her voice went soft, almost tentative. "If you place this over your head, you'll be able to breathe underwater. I want to show you something."

"Valora, are you sure that's a good idea?" Orris was quickly by my side.

I stepped forward and the warm water enveloped me. "I'll be fine. Why don't you stick by Mane and help him keep watch?"

I sank down and water flooded my lungs, sending my heartbeat racing. Anxiety ratcheted up my senses. Every molecule of Lake Mavrovo weighed ten times more underwater, and I felt the pressure. I relaxed my muscles and reined in the panic that threatened to undo me.

Despite the opaque surface, I could easily see Kit swimming down in front of me. We dove deeper and deeper until we came to the familiar spires of Queen Elemi's kingdom. Kit and Mane had assured me that everyone died when Ravanna flooded Mavrovo, so we were coming upon a ghost town. Eerie lights around the perimeter of the castle and the detritus we disturbed as we moved through the water signaled there was once life here.

Kit and I descended to the steel entrance gates, which lay open, no longer guarded by the selkie. Kit was the only one left. She swam in further to where her mother's chambers once were. Inside, the selkie queen lay on her bed, arms crossed over her chest. Her diaphanous gown floated about her like a living thing, even though she was obviously dead.

"How is it she's still here? Where are the others?"

"Their bodies disintegrated. She's here so she can be the seed for the next generation." Kit inspected her mother's nightstand and brought over a volume of magic similar to my mother's grimoire. She indicated the page it was opened to. A ritual restoration of the selkie race using the dead queen's body as the seed. Millions of dormant cells floating in these depths were waiting for the spark of life. "She wanted me to find her and perform this ritual. If I awaken the lake again, it will lead to more of the same. The selkie would be monsters. Why bring them into this world?"

Kit handed me the book, delivering it to me between pressed palms, as if one wrong move might break it apart. Weight again settled into my shoulders. She was entrusting me with a whole race of people. "But you aren't a monster, Kit. Mane isn't a monster." I couldn't help but dart glances at the queen's body. Her presence was disturbing, and I half expected her to sit up and attack us at any moment.

"No, but she was, and all the others were just like her." She swept her arms through the waters and cradled her forehead. Undulating ripples agitated the surface tension, peppering my skin with her internal struggle. I understood the difficulty in answering the call to lead.

I reviewed the spell again, sweeping my finger down the words and trying to remember what Dooley had taught me. Some of the symbols were familiar. "You're the spell caster. Control over these selkie belongs to you. You can make sure they don't do anything foolish."

"So I'd spend the rest of my life babysitting a bunch of monsters."

"You could teach them not to be. You can teach them control, like Mane has taught you."

Kit nodded. "I know you're right. It's why I came to you. Will you help me perform the ritual?"

A knot formed in my chest. I missed Dooley. He'd be able to tell me what to do, but then again, he would probably tell me the power was mine all along.

"Let's both do what has to be done." I cupped Kit's hands before pulling her into my embrace. "Let's do this."

Kit sat on the side of her mother's bed and clasped her dead hands in her own. "Tell me the words."

She repeated each word I said, and suddenly a sharp glow erupted from the amulet at my neck. Selkie magic, selkie amulet. And I wasn't a selkie. "The amulet! You were supposed to be wearing it!"

The waters surrounding us became like a tornado, and we were at the vortex. Queen Elemi's body slowly began to disintegrate. Kit touched her mother's cheek, and it melted under her hand, giving way to the waters, which captured each piece and spun it out wards. A flash of light lit up the center, causing each particle to shimmer like diamond dust.

The door to the room blasted open and the swirling energy was carried out. The amulet at my neck dragged me forward. There was nothing to dig my heels into. I grabbed Kit's hand as we were thrust out the front gates. The swirling cloud of shimmering energy dispersed in the water and continued to pulsate, gathering together slowly into dozens of balls of light that began forming into—I wasn't quite sure.

"What did we do?" Kit came up beside me and held on to my shoulder. We both stared in amazement as the energy formed into arms and fins and looked distinctly selkie, except they had wings.

"I think we've created a new race."

❧

Swimming to the surface of Lake Mavrovo, I could already see Mane in the water, his head dipping down and searching around for us as we got closer. We surfaced, and I removed the amulet from my neck, handing it to Kit. "This belongs to you."

"What happened down there?" asked Mane. Orris was quick to repeat the question using his pointed gaze and hands on hips.

"The waters of Mavrovo are alive. Part selkie and part fae. I'm not sure exactly how it happened, but I'm not alone anymore." Kit was clearly happy. Her people were spared and would be better off under her reign.

Mane wrapped his arms around her. "That's good. Very good." He brushed an errant hair from her forehead. "You see, all your sacrifice was worth it. All the pain. You have to believe in yourself now."

Kit nodded and buried her face into Mane's chest.

"Are we about ready to wrap this up? Valora barely has time to prepare for the ceremony," said Orris.

"Are you ready to go, Valora?" Kit's eyes sparkled. She tipped her glasses onto her face and practically bounced on her toes.

For weeks, I'd asked myself if I was ready to marry Aric.

Now I knew I was. My sacrifice would bring about a better life for my people, and I was confident it was the right decision. "Yes, I'm ready."

CHAPTER SEVENTEEN

Bells rang throughout Dell'Aria, and ice wine flowed freely amongst the merry fae celebrating my upcoming wedding. Sitting at my dressing table, I allowed what felt like a whole army of servants to tug, fluff, fuss, sweep, curl, and generally transform me into the bride I was reluctant to be. Not too long ago, I was being readied for my wedding with Dooley. That had been a relatively simple affair. Kit had been the one to tame my tresses. Even though we were at Winter Haven, it was not a royal wedding. Countless tears swelled at the corners of my eyes and threatened to ruin my carefully made-up face. I stared up at the ceiling, blinking them away.

More merriment sounded from outside, followed by cries of "Gods save the queen!" I sucked in a deep breath and adjusted the sheer, stiff silk over my knees. Nervous moisture dampened my palms, and I flapped them in the air, the motion reflecting my growing unrest. I was scheduled to marry Aric in little over an hour and accept my responsibility as queen of Dell'Aria. I waved off the staff while I stood, unable sit any longer. The anticipation was getting the best of me, and I had to move or I might scream. Although resigned to my fate, I wished things were different. And not just with Dooley. The first time Aric had proposed to me and how I had refused him. This time it had been my father's doing. Aric didn't even get down on his knee.

Kit burst through the door. "Valora, it's time. Is she ready?" Without waiting for an answer, she shouldered her way through the handmaidens surrounding me, and they all parted easily for the new selkie queen. My father had been made aware of the new developments in Mavrovo, and was happy to have Kit at the helm of this new breed of selkie fae.

The rigid corsetry of my dress tossed me off balance. I steadied myself on the mirror of my vanity, and as I did, I saw a reflection on the wall behind me—symbol magic.

"Can you all leave us alone for a moment?" The fae attendant closest to me pursed her lips in dismay. I couldn't blame her. I didn't have a great reputation for being where I was supposed to be. And while I'd wanted to escape earlier, what I'd just seen froze me in my tracks. "I promise I won't be more than five minutes."

The entourage all shuffled out, and I quickly closed the door behind them. My heart pounded.

"You look like you've seen a ghost." Kit followed my gaze to the writing on the wall. "What's that?"

I walked slowly toward symbols, which had been hidden by one of the many tapestries lining the wall of my room. The furniture and wall dressings had been moved during the deep cleaning of my chambers. It wasn't until I saw it reflected in the mirror that I noticed it. I traced the symbols, and a shiver ran up my spine. A delightful sensation evoked by only one man in my life. Dooley.

"He's saying goodbye to me." A month had passed since Dooley had left. Each night my dreams of him grew in strength, and the urgency always felt the same, like he was trying to tell me something. Those deep brown eyes of his invaded my thoughts and spoke of something important. Did he miss me? Did he love me? Did he forgive me? Maybe this was the message all along—a final farewell. Symbols I didn't quite understand but were definitely left by him. After my marriage to Aric today, hopefully my mind would let me rest. There was no going back. I would have to leave this lingering hope behind.

I traced the thick black scrawls one last time, willing my hand to remain steady. The inky writing vibrated like a living entity under my fingertips. His essence reached out to me, and my heart squeezed tight, making it difficult to breathe. A shock coursed through my spine and sent a tingling sensation into the top of my head. *It's not a dream, Valora. Do you hear me?*

I stumbled backward and tripped on my skirt, dazed by the jolt and his voice in my head. Kit righted me before I fell. "What happened?"

I pushed out of her grasp and went back to the wall, drawn by the lure of the mystery. My voce shook, heart beating too fast. "I opened the door between our minds. I heard Dooley."

I ran my fingers over the symbols, hoping to get through to him. The cryptic communication haunted my memory, and I knew there was a vital message here, if only I could think. If indeed all my dreams were really of him.

My concentration shattered as my father burst through the door, my dismissed entourage trailing close behind. "Valora, we cannot delay the ceremony any longer. The dwarves and the elves have a schedule, and we should return them to their homes as soon as possible."

Ignoring him, I continued to study the symbols on the

255

wall, Dooley's voice in my head whispering, *Listen to me*.

"Valora!" My father settled his hands on my wrist and pulled me out of my trance. "Stop this foolishness. It's no use. Think of your people and not of this man who left you. Aric is at the altar."

The excitement that had gathered in my throat at the sight of Dooley's words, his voice echoing in my head, plummeted into my gut. My father might be right, but the knowledge still hurt. Dooley had left voluntarily and without any protest. All the tension left my hand, and my father loosened his grip. The last bit of hope I had that Dooley cared had dissolved. Dooley had abandoned me when I needed him most. How could I still love him? Aric was waiting for me. The people of Dell'Aria were waiting.

Kit put her hand around my shoulder. "I'll escort her myself, King Delos."

"I'm sorry, Kit, I must insist. We have no room for error." My father clapped his hand, and the Queen's Guard came into the room. Orris made his way inside and trailed behind me.

"I promise not to knock you off any ledges this time, but do us a favor and don't take too long," said Orris.

I straightened my shoulders, stifling the urge to glance back at the message. Dooley was in the past. Aric was my future.

❧❦

With my father in the lead, Kit at my side, and Orris in the rear, I was escorted through the streets of Dell'Aria. The handmaidens had done their best to weave my hair into the traditional style of a royal princess awaiting her crown. Feathers of white fabric were woven into my tresses, and billowed out behind me as they caught the breeze. Orris wouldn't have been able to bump into me even if he wanted to. He had to stay ten feet behind to avoid being caught up in my plumage. The weight of my position pressed itself into the set of my shoulders.

The fae of Dell'Aria lined the streets. It was the first time I could recall their gazes so full of hope and admiration—such a far cry from the days where people averted their eyes because of my wings. Perhaps the reminder I had been allowed to live when maybe one of their own had been sentenced to death was too much. Maybe they thought I'd end that practice. I had always wished to. But now I was here, in this position, and things had changed. I always thought I would be happy if I was ever queen, but I wasn't.

If those like me were allowed to live, the fae would have to consider abandoning their homes in Overworld. It wouldn't make much sense for us to have any great number of our people who were dependent on the other fae to become transports for them. Resentment breeds war. It was smart for the royalty of the past to get rid of all those like me. Aric's father had let my father keep me, and that, amongst other things, was his weakness.

A small child broke free from his mother and ran through the throngs of guards surrounding me. His bright green wings shimmered like emeralds in the bright sun, and he came to a stop in front of me, bringing the entire procession to a halt.

"My mother asked me to bring this to you." He handed up a note and quickly disappeared again.

I unrolled the scroll and read the two words. I scanned it again, as if by rereading it the meaning would become clear.

I'm sorry.

Kit peeked over my shoulder. "Guards. Formation.

Keep your eyes out. Where did the child go to?" She called out orders like a proper queen.

The familiar emerald wings dashed through the crowd. I should have known. I crumpled the note in my hand. I had never seen the likes of them before, and I thought I would never see them again. The problem was, whenever I did see them, destruction usually followed.

Orris sent a few of his men to search the crowd, but there was no sign of the child. Of course not—it had been Kali all along, infused with enough magic to transform herself. No doubt her wings carried her into the sky as soon as she crossed the border. A mixture of emotion stirred inside me. Aric and I had received our forgiveness. Should she be forgiven as well? Did she deserve as much?

The procession reformed, and we made it to the gates of the temple. The sound of the music inside gradually got louder until the gates could no longer contain it. My nerves strained in equal chaos. Orris swung wide the tall doors, and a wash of sound poured over us, strident and regal. The attendants filed in, the gates closing behind us all. Father stood proud beside me, dressed in his formal robes, while Kit flitted about, adjusting the train of my dress. I tried to suppress the residual panic and enjoy the moment.

"This is the way it should have always been." My father removed his crown, the copper metal reflecting the light. Orris held it aloft in front of him, to be presented to Aric. Then it would be my turn. He would receive his crown, and then his new queen.

At the head of the temple, Pryn leaned against an ornate copper pulpit adorned by massive arrangements of dremoraburst blooms. Aric stood to his left, rocking back and forth on his heels and occasionally pawing at the stiff collar of his robe. The best man, or rather demon, locked his eyes on Kit. I heard her giggle behind me. Franca's mother sat in the front row, as my mother would have on a day like today. The audience was full of fae, dwarves, and even those of Mane's clan he'd been able to locate. I never remembered another day in history, in all the books I studied as a child, which had brought together so many from so many different parts of the Realms. My chest expanded, pride of my land, pride of my people, filling the empty place left by Dooley. Whenever I felt an ounce of regret, I would think back to this moment and believe in my decision.

I approached the end of the aisle, my father by my side, and noticed two things. A flash of red to my right told me Calliope had decided to attend. And Aric was staring at her, not me. I recalled the love she'd expressed, and a flash of guilt hit me. All this time, I'd thought only of myself, my sacrifice, my grief. I read my misery in her face. I was willing to marry Aric because it was what I thought he wanted, what was expected of him. Yet he seemed as miserable as me.

Mane nudged him as my father approached, crown in hand. "To the rightful owner, King Aric, I hereby relinquish the crown and wish you a long and fruitful union with my daughter, Valora Delos."

Aric tipped his head to receive the crown, and I noticed a thin chain at his neck. Oddly similar to the chain that bore the amulets he, Dooley, and I once wore.

"Aric and Valora, I invite you both to come forward so we can begin." Pryn's speech began, and I could see the same chain poking out from beneath his clothing. Whatever it was, the explanation for it would to have to wait.

Aric grimaced, perhaps tortured to have to pry his attention away from the audience. When he finally looked at me, he stared through me. That small gesture confirmed my suspicions. Both of us in love with another, yet here we were, doing our duty for the good people surrounding us.

Pryn led me through the repetition of the vows, a mixture of pride and sadness choking my speech. I hoped no one noticed. Pryn brought up his hands to address the audience. "King Aric and Queen Valora have said the words and are soon to become your faithful rulers. At this moment, are there any here who would take issue with either of them taking the throne? Speak now, or any act against these two in the future will be considered an act of treason."

The words were traditional pledges spoken by those in the royal family. Utilitarian and devoid of emotion, but full of duty. Original words weren't even allowed in this type of ceremony. Nostalgia hit me again when I recalled that Dooley and I had written our own vows. So it was quite a surprise to me when someone actually rose up and answered this ritual refrain in the affirmative. A collective gasp rippled across the crowd when a voice shouted, "I object."

I whipped my head around and spied Calliope's fiery red hair. Her wings shook, her obvious rage barely contained. "Yes, I object. It's not the will of the king to marry this fae. It should be known by all that he does not wish her to be your queen."

"No!" Pryn shouted, and all eyes shifted from Calliope to him. I watched him clutch at the string of the amulet at his neck. Why was he wearing that? He'd sworn to destroy them all. Had he tried and not succeeded? Before I could think to question him, Aric's voice cut through my shock.

"I'm sorry," Aric whispered to me before escaping through the side of the rectory. Calliope dashed toward the front and was stopped by Orris and his guards.

And then the first wave hit.

The air shimmered, and I knew exactly what it was. The Blight. Horror filled my consciousness as fae dropped down to their knees. Their screams tore through me, and my gaze flew to where Aric had escaped. I trusted him and he'd betrayed me—betrayed all of us.

I ripped at the bodice of my dress, trying to rid myself of the weight. I had to get to Aric and find out what he'd done. Dizziness struck me, and I tumbled to my knees, numb to the pavement beneath me.

"Valora!" Kit slid the chain of her amulet over my head.

Mane propped me up. "Let's get you out of here."

"Help me find…Aric." The words barely came out of my mouth, and I realized if I didn't get out, the Blight would make sure I wasn't around to find Aric anyway.

☙❧

The initial blast of the wave knocked most of the fae off of their feet. Some died on impact, their lifeless bodies crumpled into a heap on the floor. Wailing howls of the grief-stricken echoed through the hall. Those who were left rose up, faces twisted in panic. A wave of bodies surrounded us as the masses tried to make it out of the temple and into the open. The Blight could strike anyone, anytime, anywhere in Dell'Aria. The panicked crowd rushed to escape the immediate scene of death and destruction.

Mane shielded Kit and I as best he could, and helped her carry me outside. Although I had been knocked off my feet, Kit's amulet helped give me strength to stand on my own.

"I have the ship ready. We can get out of here," said Mane. Once we were outside, he slung Kit onto his back and collected me into his arms.

"We can't leave until we know who turned on the machine again," I said.

"Don't you know, Valora?" Mane focused on weaving through the crowd.

"Aric has no reason." His unspoken blame resonated in me. The logical choice was Aric, but why? His goals were different now, his head in a better place. I had been inside his head. I knew of his regret for the past. No, I might be naïve, but my heart told me Aric wasn't guilty.

As we approached the docks, fae were scattered all about, most packing up their belongings and their families—whatever was left of them.

Orris ran past us, and I called out to him, "Where's everyone going?"

He swiveled around. "Valora! I'm so glad you're safe. They're leaving. They'd rather take their chances in Underworld than stay here. Get as far away from that machine as possible. We have enemies here." His jaw was set firm. I knew he'd always preferred Dooley to Aric.

"It wasn't Aric. He was right in front of us when it happened."

"He could've had an accomplice." His flushed face brightened even more, and he avoided my direct stare. "He had one before. Sorry, Valora, I'm on the first barge out of here. The dwarves have agreed to grant us safe passage to their mountain. Maybe we'll see one another again."

I squeezed his shoulder as he turned to go. Amidst all the terror the fae had been through, they had always stayed together. They believed the one in power, their king, would help them. Now they would rather cast their fate and attempt to survive in what was left of Underworld. Aric hadn't helped matters by running away without explanation. He might have acted like a coward, but I wouldn't. I was queen, and I would lead my people.

We got closer to the docks, and Mane paused, letting Kit slide off him. "Give me a second to catch my breath." The sweat slid down his brow. This demon had sacrificed his life many times for Kit and me. I only hoped to repay the favor.

"We don't have time to rest, our ship is leaving." Kit pointed to the black beauty as it drifted away from the port. At the helm, a shock of unmistakable red hair and wings spread wide.

"Calliope! Wait!" Kit and I hobbled toward the ship. Mane ran ahead and grabbed one of the ropes, jerking it tight and digging his heels into the dirt. The ship continued its ascent. His muscles strained and his eyes lit up bright red, but even his demon powers were no match for the weight of the mighty ship that dragged him mercilessly across the sand.

"Mane, let go of it." Kit ran toward him. My legs threatened to give out, but I stayed on my feet. She grasped Mane's waist as he strained to keep hold of the ship.

"Let go of the rope." Calliope leaned over and shook her fist at Mane. "Don't make me drive an arrow through your heart."

"Calliope, let us on that ship," I yelled.

"Get your house in order. I don't know what's happening here, but I want nothing of it." She jerked the wheel to the left, steering the ship farther away. She claimed innocence, but maybe this marriage had been the last straw.

The rope dragged Mane over the side, and he lost his hold of the rough hemp. He grabbed the edge of the dock, his legs dangling above the ground far below.

"Mane, hold on!" Kit clutched his hands and tried to help him up. "Valora! Help!"

My weakened legs refused to respond to my pleas for them to save my friends. But I wouldn't stand here and watch them go over the edge. I was inches from Kit's ankle and reached out to grab it, but my hands clutched a shimmering tail instead of legs, the magic she needed to sustain her human form hanging around my neck.

Kit gasped in horror, and her grip loosened on Mane. My own heart nearly jumped out of my chest. No, this couldn't be happening. Not now. He yelled out, and I could see his fingertips on the edge of the dock. I gathered more strength and lunged.

"No!" Kit grabbed at Mane and clutched his fingers as he lost his grip, sending them both plunging over the edge.

A scream escaped my lips. Tears streamed down my face, and I searched frantically for any sign of them. Only murky blackness met my quest. Sinking to the ground, I realized it was giving away beneath me, as if a portal was opening at my feet. I said a silent prayer to the Goddess Varuna. *Save my people. Help them, please.*

☙❧

I awoke under the cover of darkness. The chill in the air signaled nighttime, that much I knew. When I finally dared to open my eyes, my surroundings were familiar—only it was not a place I ever expected to be in again. The cabin Kali and I had shared as Hunters.

The moonlight filtered through the window, and my senses adjusted to the lack of light. The contents of the cabin had shifted around haphazardly. A long wooden table that once served as our dining area blocked the door, and the cot I slept on was shoved from its spot along the wall to the center of the room. It was impossible to know what lurked in the shadows around the periphery of the room. But I could tell I wasn't alone.

"Who's there?" I called out, the tremble in my voice betraying me in an instant. I wasn't too eager to face whoever brought me here. I tried to shake off the quaking in my hands and felt for Kit's amulet at my throat.

Kit. Mane. They'd both died trying to save me. Anger

quickly replaced my fear. Adrenaline shot through my body. "Who are you and what do you want?" I forced myself into a sitting position and grasped for my sword, which was, of course, not by my side. Not many bridal gowns allow for weapons. A design flaw I would remedy if I ever got the chance to walk down the aisle again. I managed to rip off the heavy bodice, leaving me clad in only simple slip. Not much in terms of armor.

"Please remain calm. The Blight drained a lot of your energy. Your strength hasn't returned. Let the amulet do its job." Through the darkness came a familiar voice, but I couldn't put my finger on who it belonged to.

"Who are you and why did you bring me here?"

A figure emerged from the shadows and shocked me to the core.

"I'm here because you needed me." My mother stepped from the shadows. She was wearing the same robes she had when she was a healer for the king, Aric's father. Her bright white wings pierced the darkness, and I wasn't sure how I hadn't seen them before.

"You're not real. You're an illusion. My mother is dead. I don't appreciate the mindfuckery." I squeezed my eyes tight and tried to focus on what I knew as reality, but all my hopes, dreams, and little-girl wishes rushed to the surface, drowning out the voice of reason.

Valora.

My eyes flashed open at the sound of Dooley's voice. But it was only in my mind.

She spoke gently. "He's trying to connect to you. I think the demon child knows."

I hung my legs over the side of the bed. This creature who purported to be my mother and I were alone in this cabin. The wheels of my mind turned, trying to plan an escape. I had no idea how much time had passed, how many more had died. And no one knew I was here. "So you can read my mind?"

"Obviously not too well." The illusion vanished, and Kali appeared before me. I had never seen her so radiant. The sharp outline of her body was softened by beams of magical energy. Her green eyes glowed in the dim light.

"What are you doing here?" I faced Kali, a friend whose multiple betrayals had always made things worse for me and better for her. "You're particularly vibrant today. Let me see, would that be in any way related to the most recent wave of the Blight that decimated the city?"

Before I knew it, my hands were around Kali's throat, anger propelling me across the room. Rather than put her hands up to stop me, she choked under my grip. Tears formed at her eyes and rolled down her cheeks.

"Why aren't you stopping me?" I thrust her away, and she stumbled only a step back, despite the force of my blow. She had enough magic to bring a lot of pain down on me. Yet she made no move to harm me.

"Because I deserve whatever punishment you think I should have. Not only as my friend, but as my queen."

"In case you forgot, you kind of interrupted the ceremony. I'm not actually your queen. In fact, I don't even know where our king ended up." I shivered, all of a sudden remembering Kit and Mane falling over the edge of the docks. "I don't have time for any of your nonsense, Kali. I must find my father."

I brushed past Kali. She grabbed my arm. "I was instructed to activate the machine. He said it would be the best for all the fae of Dell'Aria. The Goddess was supposed to finally take notice and come down to make us whole again."

"You've done nothing but lie to me, Kali. I have no interest in any more of your stories." I wouldn't be surprised if Ravanna got through to Kali, but it didn't matter. The damage was done. I shook free of her grip and exited the cabin.

Night and an eerie silence fell over Dell'Aria. I ran as fast as I could toward the castle. I needed to find my father and regroup. As I got closer, I stopped dead in my tracks. The flag of Dell'Aria, which always flew at full mast, was lowered to half-staff. That meant only one thing. A chill of dread sent my body into uncontrollable spasms, and stars dotted my vision. A king had died. The only question was. Which king was it? My father or Aric?

CHAPTER EIGHTEEN

I sprinted down the corridors to the King's Chamber, the heavy reverberation of my breath bouncing off the stone walls, the pounding of my feet matching the erratic rhythm of my pulse. Around the last turn, I smacked square into Orris' rotund belly. The force of our impact sent both of us tumbling to the floor.

"What the hell? Would you watch…" Orris moved from rubbing the knot on his head to helping me to my feet. "Valora, we've been looking for you."

"What are you doing here? I thought you were on your way out of here. You shouldn't be here." I was bargaining with him, knowing full well that the deal wouldn't work out in my favor. If he was still here, it meant he'd been deterred. "I need to get to my father," I said.

Orris stepped to the side, mirroring my actions and blocking my path.

Fear made me short-tempered. I had to get to my father, to see for myself that he was alive. "Get out of my way."

He rested his hands on my shoulders, the same as my father had when he confirmed my mother died. This wasn't happening again. I tore at his fingers. His pained stare was reflected in his emotion-choked voice. "Pryn did all he could."

A sour taste rose up in my mouth. Despite the trembling in my limbs, I jostled past Orris and shouldered open the large door to the King's Chambers. Dooley sat on the side of the bed, holding my father's limp hand. Shock waves of grief rippled through me—my lost father and my lost love side by side. I gripped the beveled archway to steady myself.

Pryn skittered toward me, each tap of his foot on the marble floor echoing through the immense space. "Valora, you're alive. We're so relieved."

The look of pity on Dooley's face told me all I needed to know. The lifeless form on the bed was my father.

"No!" I dove forward and Dooley caught me in his arms, holding me close. I beat against his chest, screaming for release from this nightmare. I wanted my father to hold me in his arms like he had when I was a child. It was all I'd wanted over these past years, to know he loved me. Each choice in life I made to please him, and now he was dead. I was supposed to save us all, and he was dead.

"He's gone. He didn't survive the blast."

I crumpled in on myself, my cheek pressed tight to Dooley. My tears soaked through his white cotton t-shirt. I inhaled deeply, smelling the sweet pine from his Earthside home, gaining comfort from the familiar scents. Anything to suspend the spinning of my world.

"What are you doing here?" I wiped away the tears from my eyes as I searched out the emotion in Dooley's face—the face of the man who had decided to leave me and return Earthside when I choose to become Aric's queen. He wore my slack expression, dull eyes wishing comfort and turning in on his own sadness. He had lost his father as well.

269

"It's a long story." He tucked an errant curl behind my ear, and I snuggled deeper into his embrace. All I wanted was to hear his voice tell me he came back for me and that he wouldn't leave me.

"Long stories aren't for those at war." Pryn snatched my wrist and tugged. Dooley wouldn't let go. A protective wave pulsed from his consciousness to mine, and his arms flexed to keep me in his grip. Somehow our link was as strong as when we had the amulets, though it was a different kind of connection that had nothing to do with the magic that bound us together. Love. "I need to make sure she's not been infected. You wouldn't want the same thing to happen to Valora, would you?"

"I can protect her." Dooley loosened his hold. "I'll go with you."

"You need to report to Orris. I'm sure he wants to know all about your long story and how you arrived here unannounced," said Pryn.

He rubbed the amulet at his neck. I eyed it for a moment, unsure what had changed—but *something* was different. His fingers tilted the stone, and a rush of recognition hit. The broken demon stone had been fused together in the elaborate setting. "You rejoined the stones. Not a good idea."

A rush of color dotted his cheeks, and he avoided my further inspection by tucking the amulet into his robes. "Your father requested that I harness the power in order to protect Dell'Aria."

While my father and had lacked the closeness I craved, I knew deep down that he would never condone using such dark magic. Pryn had been tending to my father before his death. Had he truly tried to save his life or did he expedite his death? With my father out of the way and Dell'Aria in a state of chaos, he'd be free to control what was left. He was hiding something. I tried to funnel my pain into the tool that would help me unlock this mystery.

"Didn't help much, did it," growled Dooley.

"No, I must admit I don't have much practice with *demon* magic," said Pryn.

Dooley clenched his fists, rising up slowly from his place on the bed. He'd never been comfortable with that side of himself, seeing it as an infection rather than a part of who he was. I expected banter like this from Aric, but not from a priest. Not Pryn.

Pryn continued, a malefic drop to his voice, and unleashed the full weight of his feelings on the matter. "And when there are devils in our midst, it seems their nature to disrupt our peace. I haven't been able to locate Mane either."

"He's dead. So is Kit." The horror reflected in Kit's face—the fear in her eyes as she was pulled over the edge. I was helpless to save her, like I was helpless to save my father. Desperation made me push the image deep down and focus. My grieving period would come. To prevent any further deaths, I needed to act. If perhaps I could bring the three of us together—the triad. "I'll go with Pryn. Help Orris find Aric. He ran off before the Blight hit." I knew he wasn't guilty, but I needed him. I was certain now that Pryn had something to do with this.

I don't want you alone with him. Dooley stared into my eyes as his words flooded through my mind. I could sense that he'd already imagined the worst-case scenario.

I have a plan. It was a bluff, but Pryn wouldn't lead me to the source with Dooley by my side. I needed to be alone with him to find out the truth before anyone else got hurt. As hesitant as I was to leave my father's body, I knew that we needed to find out what kind of damage had been done.

"I'll find Aric." He paused briefly as he swept past Pryn, exchanging a strong-arm stare instead of any further words.

"Come, Valora. Let's go to my chambers." Pryn tipped his head to the side, speaking to me as we walked down the barren halls. "Usually when the king and his hand are both disabled, it is the role of the church to oversee. I have no interest in taking the reins from you. It's a technicality. However, the people may want to respect tradition. First, we must find out who activated the machine again."

My mind raced, searching for answers. If Pryn was behind all of this, why pretend he didn't know? With his magic, he could easily strike me down. The old priest's face was shrouded by the lengths of his gray hair, hiding any facial twitches I might be able to discern. I had to press him for the truth. "I can answer that. It was Kali."

"You saw her?" Pryn faced me, his mask of emotion faltering. He drew his eyebrows together. "Stupid girl," he muttered under his breath.

I suppressed the triumph from my voice. I'd opened the door a crack. I didn't want him to realize I was sneaking inside. "Don't worry. I don't trust her in the slightest. She's completely drunk on magic. I'm sure she did it to keep her precious wings intact."

His face drained of all color. I'd reached the heart of his actions. He wanted the fae magic—the question was why. "We need to go straight to the machine."

Pryn clamped down on my wrist. With a swift flick, he swung me in front of him, urging me forward. I broke free of his grip. His hands twitched at his sides, like he was trying to prevent himself from clocking me over the head. I tamped down my temper, reminding myself that I needed answers before I kicked his ass.

"I didn't get to say a proper goodbye." I crossed my

arms over my chest, testing him, waiting to see if his fist would fly. A smoky breeze billowed through the corridor, wafting past the both of us.

Pryn sniffed at the air and straightened his robes. "It will have to wait. Lead the way to the machine. We must see how much destruction it's caused."

We reached the crossroads of the underground passages and arrived in the main chamber, still decorated for my wedding, which now seemed like it had happened days ago instead of hours. I bent down, commandeering a sword from one of the King's Guard who had fallen. A surge of bitterness at the injustice of it all rekindled the anger inside me. The man, like countless others, had died for no reason other than greed.

I crept up the spiral staircase to the topmost tower of the temple, the stone wall at my back and Pryn close behind. A powerful magic user trusted me to go before him. The weight of the sword was reassuring, a tangible reminder that I wasn't helpless.

I wasn't sure Aric was alive. Perhaps Calliope didn't leave without him. He could very well have been on her ship. It was clear to me now that she'd come here for him. She really did love him with all of her heart. She was passionate about him. Could I really say the same thing? Would I ever be able to say the same thing? No. The truth came to me without a touch of regret. While I was no longer in love with him, I never wished him harm. I owed it to myself and him to clear his name.

I motioned Pryn to be quiet as I leaned my head against the closed door. There was nothing but silence from the other side.

"You're wasting precious time." Pryn nudged the door, and it creaked open, unlocked. A metallic tang laced with a yellow-bright and smoky brown-black scent, horned, pronged, and strange, drifted out in an amorphous cloud, stinging my lungs. Pryn shoved me inside, and I scanned the copper piping that snaked from a large cylinder, wrapping around an arm aimed outside the open dome above our heads. The machine thrummed a steady cadence, reminiscent of another event too horrible to remember. Despite the assurance my father gave me that it had been dismantled, it remained. My father. Pain struck hotter than a fist into my heart. He was gone. *No, not now, Valora.* If Pryn had his wish, my body would be interred next to my father's in the tombs. Either way, I would go down fighting. I forced myself to concentrate on my surroundings, a new determination riding my heels.

Below the large cylinder, drips of copper essence fell into a floating glass vial, the blood-red tinge a reminder of the destruction it caused. I moved my attention further into the room, taking in the furnishings and any means of escape. As a warrior, it was imperative I check out the battleground, to be aware of my surroundings. I stepped out from behind the blindness caused by my sorrow, and the sight sent a flush of adrenaline tingling through my body.

Perched in a glowing cage sat a being of magnificence, a fiery aura that transcended mortality. My eyes misted over at the gloriousness before me, the white-blond hair, so much like her son's, threatening to blind me to her faults. Almost. There was no doubt in my mind. This was the golden Goddess Varuna. The moment our eyes locked, she shot forth a blast of psychic energy past me at our captor. Hopefully that meant we were on the same side.

Pryn retaliated, a red flare jetting past my face and knocking me to the floor. "We'll have none of that," he demanded.

Pain, pain, pain was the refrain throbbing through my head. He stepped over my legs and walked to the machine. I fought to bring the multiple images before my eyes into one clear picture of Pryn taking a vial of the copper magic. He inspected the contents, holding it to the light, and quickly drank it down. He had known all along.

Darkness blocked my vision, and I was falling into a pit. The last thing I heard before sinking into unconsciousness was Pryn. "Bitch took too much. I should have known. But it will be enough to keep you in place, Goddess."

തso

I fought to waken myself from this nightmare. The aching in my wrists was the first thing I felt as I regained consciousness, followed by a pounding in my head. I lay still, afraid of a beat down by a souped-up Pryn.

"Are you awake? He's gone." With blurred vision, I followed the sound of the voice, and gradually a figure came into focus. The Goddess paced the small confines of her cage. There was no sign of Pryn. "So sorry about that. I don't seem to have much control over my aim in this form."

My head pounded like the morning after too much dwarven mead. I crawled to my feet and tugged on the locked cage. Hopeless. I slumped against the bars, dizziness from my efforts making me weak. Some soldier I was. It was going to require more than a hungover fae who didn't know much magic to make it budge. I glared at the glowing bars. They weren't of iron, but they might as well have been for all I was able to do. I was still seeing double and had difficulty concentrating.

"How did he bring you here?" I stumbled to the door and tested it. Locked as well. We were both trapped in here.

"I am not really here, not yet. My consciousness is

tethered here. My corporeal self cannot leave Elysium unless the portal between our worlds is opened."

I studied her. With the bright light gone, I could see right through her. Even though her image was faint, her voice was as clear as if she were standing right next to me.

"But now he has the demon stone. Soon he will be able to open the portal. He wants to control the Elysium. He is not the first one to try."

I surveyed the room for a means of escape. Pryn hadn't completed his ritual, because he didn't have all the talismans he needed. And he wouldn't get that far, not on my watch. Bastard said I was going to save us all, and damned if he wasn't right. "Who was the last to try?"

Her image flickered, rattling from one edge of the cage to the other. She was testing her confines too. "Ravanna."

The demon king. What a coincidence. *Dooley. Can you hear me?*

"It is no use reaching out to him. I have already tried to contact Aric and had no luck."

The fact Varuna could pluck the thoughts out of my head was significantly less disturbing then her inability to connect with her son. "Aric might not be alive anymore."

The Goddess took a moment to consider my words before she spoke. "I would be deeply saddened if my son did not survive."

There was no good explanation for why Pryn had decided he needed to dethrone Varuna. No reason to kill so many fae for the chance to get to the Elysium a little ahead of schedule. If he hadn't done this, he would have received a fast pass to the front of the line. Now he was probably scheduled to become a part of the mist of souls. "Pryn is a priest. He isn't supposed to be doing this. He's been in charge of worshiping you. Of teaching about you."

"I never asked for worship. I think your priest, and those before him, made up this idea of a goddess because they wanted to study how they could invade our Realm. We have been trying to prevent that, and have been successful thus far. In fact, I believe we grew complacent because there had been no signs of attack."

"What possible benefit could Pryn have by opening the door to your world?" And then it struck me before she could answer. I had thought by his actions that Pryn welcomed death. The state I found him in when I encountered him in the dragon's cave, his despondence over my mother. But it was the exact opposite.

"Immortality. True immortality."

"In case you were wondering, there is a war happening down there, princess, and your attendance is requested." Mane appeared in the doorway. I hadn't even heard it open. Alive. Mane stood before me alive. How was that possible? I saw him fall, but here he was.

Joy swallowed my voice and I flung myself into his arms. "I thought you were dead. Does that mean…"

"Kit is fine. We both are, thanks to Aric. He was sky-borne when the first alarm sounded and was scouting the area for potential threats when we fell."

"That pleases me," said Varuna. Mane didn't seem to notice her.

"Have you seen the others? We need to regroup," I said.

"I need to get you to the airship. Dooley and Orris are already aboard and ready to leave." He held the door open, obviously anxious for me to follow him. But I wasn't going to be following anymore. I was going to lead.

"We have to find Pryn. He has the demon stone, and we think he's going to open the portal to the Elysium." I gestured toward Varuna. Mane looked at the cage, but didn't acknowledge the beaming light of the Goddess. Although it seemed difficult to deny, Mane didn't see Varuna, and I didn't see any reason to explain. If we succeeded in stopping Pryn, she would be returned to her rightful place.

"The demon stone gets its power from Acheron. That, combined with the fae magic he has collected, will be like a nuclear bomb if he opens the portal to the Elysium," said Mane.

"That's all I needed to know. Find the others and tell them to get the rest of the fae to safety." I rushed past Mane, following the twisted passages toward the outer walls of the temple. I had to find that crazy priest before he destroyed everything.

I burst out into a barren alley. Silence blanketed the streets, eerily similar to the day my mother died, in the seconds after the first shock wave of the Blight struck the city. Now the fae of Dell'Aria had abandoned their homes. I hoped they could shelter with the dwarves. Deep inside the mountain passageways of Mavrovo may be the only safe place if Pryn was successful.

A familiar shock of yellow hair disappeared around the bakery. I dashed through the scent of butterbreads and steamed pudding that clung stubbornly to the air, rounding the corner at the moment whomever it was circled back toward the front of the temple, disappearing again.

I clutched my stomach and doubled over. Out of breath. Out of answers. Legs jutted out from behind two upturned food carts, tan boots relaxed at the ankles. The owner was either dead or not a threat to me. A gasp escaped my lips when I reached the open space between the carts. On the ground lay Dooley, grabbing his arm in pain. His eyes squeezed tight, chin tilted back, he didn't even notice me. If he was here, then what had happened to the airship?

"Dooley, what are you doing here?" I knelt down, and his eyes flicked open, pupils struggling to recognize me. I tried to pry his hand away to check his wound, but he grimaced. "Mane said you were on the ship."

"I was." Blood dripped between his fingers. It was hard to tell if he was holding it in or squeezing it out. "Then I saw Pryn running toward the temple, so I followed him. I fell right into his trap. He overpowered me with his magic. I didn't see the blast coming. When I came to, I found this."

Dooley revealed his ruined arm. The markings once etched along his upper arm had been carved away. "He needed it to complete the incantation," said Dooley.

The missing talisman—which raised the question: what did he need from me? Or Aric? My eyes darted toward the shadows. I wondered if I too had fallen into Pryn's trap. A warble bat tottered out from behind a barrel, dragging its long mane of dark purplish-gray fur. My heart dropped into my stomach, each nerve on edge. The creature squawked and spread its leathery wings, taking to the sky. Even the animals were abandoning Dell'Aria. "If he needed that from you, then he needs something from Aric too. Was he on the ship with you?"

Dooley shook his head. "He was going to fly around and see if he could find Calliope. He didn't come back before I left."

I reached into Dooley's satchel, hoping he still had my mother's grimoire. He wouldn't survive his wounds if I couldn't stanch the bleeding. My hands closed around the familiar binding, and he offered a weak smile. Whatever his reasons for returning, he hadn't totally abandoned the thought of me. My stomach did a somersault, and if the situation hadn't been so dire, I might have shouted with happiness at the revelation. I thumbed through the pages and found the spell I sought.

"This should help." Beneath my breath, I murmured the words to the healing spell, drawing not from the power set within my genetic makeup as a healer's daughter, but from my love for the man under my hands. The desperate urge to knit together his severed flesh centered my mind into the tool it needed to be, to fix all the wounds inflicted by Pryn, and also the deeper cuts I'd left on his heart. White-hot heat emanated from my fingers, but didn't burn, stanching the bleeding. Dooley cried out. I removed my hands from him, and the glowing light faded as the wounds closed. There would be scars, but he wouldn't die. I bent down and pressed my lips to his stubbled cheek. Even if he never saw me again as his lover, I knew I would always care for him. I just wished it didn't have to end this way.

Dooley and Aric were too much a part of this. Now I knew. Pryn had stolen what he needed from Dooley. All he needed was the missing piece from Aric and it would all be over. For all of us.

"Find Mane. I've sent him to the docks to check on the evacuation. I have something I need to do." The moment of retribution had arrived, and empowerment seeped through my bones.

"I'm going to help you." Dooley rolled to his side and let out a groan. Painful pink flesh replaced the tan skin of his strong arm. But he was weak from the loss of blood. "He'll bring you down in two seconds. You can't overpower his magic."

"Something tells me I can." I rubbed the amulet at my neck. Forged by the selkie to allow the queen to carry the magic of Mavrovo with her, it was meant to store power. Being in the same room as the Goddess would give it quite a charge. But Dooley would need a bigger mission than heading to the docks. "I need you to find Aric and make sure he stays away from here. If Pryn gets hold of him, it will be too late."

"It goes against everything inside me to let you go against him alone." Dooley reached out as I helped him to his feet and trailed his fingers across my cheek.

I grabbed his hand and pressed my cheek into the warmth of his palm, burning the familiar touch in my mind. If I lost him, I would remember this moment. "You have to trust me. I think this is what I have always been meant to do."

"Then Pryn was right. You will save us all." Dooley dropped his hand and took a few steps back. "I'll find Aric."

I opened the secret doorway at the side of the temple. As it shut, I half expected Dooley's foot to appear, like he had done once before. It closed with a thud, and the stillness of the corridor surrounded me. I knew I was truly alone in this endeavor.

Pryn's selfish teachings were meant to help him achieve his own goals of entering the Elysium. But if he knew that his actions would actually destroy us all, would he go through with it?

I raced through the empty tunnels, once full of priests, guards, and the people of Dell'Aria. My town had become empty, sucked dry of life. Even when the Blight was at its worst, the people had breathed hope into this place. Much like Calliope's people had never given up, not until the ground was physically pulled out from under them. Yet the docks had flooded with refugees desperate to leave. I couldn't let that happen.

A short tremor vibrated through my toes, pulsing up my spine into the tips of my wings. The shaking settled into a gentle rocking motion, like the idle sway of the deck of the

Peixes, and I pressed forward.

Valora, did you feel that? He is powering up the machine again. I think he means to suck every last ounce of magic from the copper foundation of the city.

The ground shook again, and pieces of the ceiling fell at my feet. So much for hope. The amulet at my neck radiated a deep blue light, and a chill entered my body. The weakness that usually came with the Blight didn't come. I glanced down at my chest, expecting to feel pain, but nothing happened. My theory had proven true. The amulet protected me.

I'm okay, Dooley. Have you found Aric?

No, but I found Mane and Kit and the others. We're searching the skies now.

It is imperative that you find him, Dooley. I broke our connection and focused in on the light path me.

For Pryn's plan to be a success, he had to use all the magic and possibly even sacrifice Varuna. I had to trust that Dooley and the others would find Aric.

My footsteps echoed against the dank stones of the narrow passageway. Stealth didn't matter anymore. I wanted Pryn to see me coming. I reached the end and shoved open the heavy door. A tremor hit the city, and my foot slipped on something wet. I toppled over, knee connecting painfully to the floor, hands searching for something to break my fall. My fingers settled on a familiar white-clad thigh, and the blood drained from my cheeks. I gulped in a heavy breath at the prone figure spread out before me, a pool of blood surrounding his broad back. Aric.

҈

Pristine fabric flecked with bright spots of fresh blood swam before my eyes. I didn't want to see what the remainder of him looked like, but I had no choice.

I held back the scream that threatened to erupt when I reached his torso. Aric's beautiful blue wings were gone, cleaved down to the roots, which wept tears of blood. Aric's head lay back against the stone wall, his arms and ankles shackled, but it didn't matter because he had no fight left in him. I stared at him, and while he didn't speak, I read the despair in his thoughts.

A shuffling from across the room reminded me that I came here for someone. For Pryn. I turned and saw Kali cowering in the corner.

I drew my sword and she rose up, her green wings glittering in the remainder of the sunlight that shone through the plate glass at her back. The room was empty except for her and Aric.

"Was this your plan from the start?" I shook my sword at her, willing it to stay in my hand instead of forcing it through her gut. Before I killed her, I had to know. "Get your wings and then grab a little immortality while you were at it?"

Kali held up her hands, her eyes wide with fright. "No, you're wrong. It was all Pryn. He made me do everything, I swear. It started with the ice wine. He said he would let me keep my family's fields. That he wouldn't confiscate it all in the name of the temple if I did a few things for him. But he kept demanding more."

"And your wings, the magic you stole, all of that was because of Pryn?" Disgust sent cold prickles across my flesh, like the legs of a hundred skitters crawling over my skin. The strands of his deception wove through every part of Dell'Aria, stretching out to clutch at those Earthside, to bring down Elysium and to foil the plans of the demon king himself. And to think, had I killed him when our paths crossed in the dragon's cave, this would never have happened.

"I knew that once you found out what I did you wouldn't forgive me. Why would you? So I did those things to protect myself." She wanted my forgiveness for killing my father, my people, and doing this to Aric? How dare she ask me for forgiveness? My hand settled heavily on my hilt, the blade goading me to end her miserable life as easily as she wasted those poor fae lying dead on the ground.

"When has Valora ever not given someone a chance?" Aric rasped. I spun around, dropping to his side to cradle his pale hand in mine. His eyes, watery and rimmed with red, stared into my own as he spoke his words meant for Kali. "I can say that she has forgiven me repeatedly. I doubt you really ever wanted her to forgive you. If she did, then it would make what you did less awful."

Aric was right. No matter how angry I was, it was in my nature to forgive. Hate was easy to hold on to, but it destroyed more than it repaired. As much as I wanted immediate justice, she would stand trial for her sins. Aric needed my sympathy, and I offered it willingly. Though nothing I said would erase the damage done to him. "It's not all that bad, believe me. You can live without them."

"None of us will live if Pryn succeeds." He erupted in spastic coughs, and blood appeared on his lips. The damage was deep.

I wheeled around to face Kali. "If you truly care about repentance, than you will tell me where he went."

"It's better if he goes to the Elysium. If he leaves us all alone. Can't you see that, Valora?" Her eyes darted to the window. I wouldn't put it past her to crash through and leave this entire mess behind her.

I took two steps forward and pressed the edge of my

blade under her chin. "If he opens the door between our worlds, we will all be destroyed, as will all our kin who reside in the Elysium."

Aric pushed himself up, and swayed a moment before bracing himself against the stone wall.

"Our kin in the Elysium?" Kali's normal demeanor wavered. I'd finally hit a sore spot with her. She might not care about herself or anyone else anymore, but she did care about the family that had been taken from her.

"Yes, your parents and your sisters will have all died for nothing. What's left of their souls will be destroyed when the gates are opened. All this destruction so that Pryn can get his immortality, and who knows what he will do from there. He has access to the Underworld and Earthside. He could bring it all under his control if he were truly immortal."

"But Varuna is immortal. Look how much control she has. He has her caught up in that tower like a caged animal. Being immortal doesn't make you all-powerful. I don't think it's all as bad as you think it is. You are always blowing things out of proportion." She crossed her arms over her chest, staring at me in defiance. Willing me to give her a quick death, but I wouldn't let her off so easy.

"Thank you, Kali." I pasted on a smile, letting my sword dangle at my fingertips as I held out my arms in embrace.

Hesitantly she raised her arms, palms up, a silent plea for surrender. "Thank you for what?"

My hand behind her head, I gripped the hilt and brought it down on the crown of her skull. Dazed, she fell back, striking her head on the plate glass. I felt a rush at the power exchange. A jagged crack formed, but the panes held. She slumped to the floor, out cold.

"Thank you for proving that I should have done that I the first place."

"You should have killed her," said Aric.

I stared at the prone figure, a sneer settling on my lips. I would deal with her later. "Not my style. Let's get to the tower. He has to have Varuna to complete the ritual, so he'll be where she is."

❧❦

I lifted my hands from Aric's back and watched the color return to his face. The blood crusted at the corners of his mouth, but no longer flowed. A dizzy spell struck me, and I wavered slightly, but he caught me around the waist.

"Are you okay?" His deep blue eyes pierced into my soul, asking so much more than if I was physically well.

"Yes. I mean, I will be." I did nothing to further the distance between us. "I hate to see you this way."

"My mother would laugh. I never wanted to be a fae, and here I am with my wings cut off. I got what I asked for."

"You didn't deserve it." I caressed the wounded skin of his back. "You were ready to lead the people of Dell'Aria again."

"And marry you." His voice was barely above a whisper, and he bowed his head, refusing to look at me.

"But that's something you didn't really want to do."

"It would have been the right thing to do."

I shook my head in admonishment. "The right thing would have been for you to stand up to my father and tell him that you love Calliope. I think she would think that would be the right thing to do."

Aric's pained stare encompassed his soul and mirrored my own shame. Neither of us had been truthful to the other—or to ourselves, for that matter. "Was it that obvious?"

"That and she pretty much gave me the speech about

how you like to punish yourself. I get it. I do it a lot. We both need change."

"Does that mean you and Dooley are back together?" Aric lifted an eyebrow.

"I suppose if you get the speech then I deserve it too. When this mess is all over, I'll talk to him. But he probably doesn't want me anymore. He left. Remember?"

"But he also came back."

The thought crossed my mind again. He had come back, but I never knew why. After this was all over, I was going to have to find out.

"You'll always be my first love," I said. He gave me the smirk I was all too familiar with.

"And you'll always be mine." He tipped forward, and I welcomed the contact of our lips. It needed to be done. One last kiss, not as lovers, but as a final goodbye. We were now free to live our lives without the weight of guilt. Well, almost free. We certainly wouldn't be free until Pryn was caught.

CHAPTER NINETEEN

I ascended the crumbling stairs, Aric by my side, and entered the main chamber of the temple through the open doors. Not long ago music had filled the white marble dome, but now it was stone silent, echoing with despair. Dooley surveyed the space from just inside. He'd come to the same conclusion as I. Pryn must be here. Where else would he go? Mane and Kit stood by him.

"You found him." Dooley stared at his brother, pain reflected in his eyes as he absorbed the extent of his injuries. It was the first time I'd sensed something other than hate or mere tolerance where Aric was concerned. I hoped we'd live long enough to see them be able to be real brothers one day. His hopeful tone darkened. "Pryn has what he came for."

Aric closed the temple doors behind us, but there was no lock. This was a place of worship, not a fortress.

"We can stop him," I said. "He's hiding the Goddess in the tower above."

"You think he has Varuna here in Dell'Aria?" Mane said in disbelief. "Only the magic of Acheron can make that possible."

"He has all of the parts of the demon stone. It's been his plan all along." I lifted my burden, a rolled-up piece of parchment, from amongst the contents of the soft leather satchel at my side. It didn't feel as heavy anymore. I laid the prophecy on one of the offering tables, carvings of the Goddess etched into the side and inlaid with copper. Magic hummed through the surface under my fingers. Hope remained. I had to tell myself that as I accepted this final revelation. Next to it I set my mother's grimoire, resting them side by side. My eyes watered at the familiar hand and the evidence of the betrayal she'd perpetrated against me. Throat tight, I began to read the words, not sure if I read them or recited them from memory.

"One made from above." I saw understanding dawn in Aric's face. His mouth slackened, eyes widened. His thoughts more fractured then his body.

"One made from below." Dooley slipped his arm around my waist, supporting my weakened knees, his strong presence a welcome crutch to the agony of what I had to face.

"A third to tie them together." I had been searching for a reason, anything to clear her name, but I could no longer deny it. The handwriting in the grimoire matched that of the prophecy. Both belonged to one person. My mother.

Aric froze, our thoughts connected. He understood the conclusion I had come to. He now knew he wasn't the only one whose parent had betrayed him. My voice broke, and Dooley tightened his fingers along my side. I tried to read, but my mouth was too dry. Dooley sensed my distress, and picked up where I'd left off.

"A child of Acheron.
A child of Elysium.
With a child of the Realms."

How could the one person I had always thought loved

me unconditionally use me like this? My father had been the one who'd made the initial request to the queen to spare my life. I knew that before, but now I felt it in my bones. My friends always pointed out that I could not see the truth. More like I couldn't accept it. They were right, and there was no more time to mourn. I placed my hand on Dooley's shoulder. This was my burden to bear. I continued where he left off.

"Between them is the answer.
The key that will open the door."

Dooley's eyes narrowed, as if he were trying to focus on the meaning but couldn't quite grasp it.

"He intends to open the doors and give himself eternal life, and he thinks he can bring my mother back from the Elysium. And I'm the key. I'm the one who he thinks will 'save us all,' but it was never about the fae of Dell'Aria. It was about him. It was about my mother. Their own selfish needs above everyone else."

My tone gained strength, and I ground out the rest between clenched teeth.

"And finally put everything
Back in its place
Back where it needs to be for balance."

Mane stepped forward. "What do you need from us?"

What I needed was a battle plan. I knew deep down what I should be doing, but I hadn't taken action yet. If I could get them all behind me, working together, then maybe we had a shot. "He loved her once, and this was her idea, but then she died. He has Dooley's markings and Aric's wings—the symbols of their magic. But for this truly to work he will need me—all of me—to trade places with my mother."

I recited the last line of the prophecy. *"A final sacrifice.* Me. I'm the final sacrifice."

Dooley held out his hand, and I gave him the paper. His fingers trembled as he quickly reviewed it and then tried to pass it to Aric, who waved it away. "I won't let you do that. How will we stop him?"

Asking Dooley to let me die was too much. I knew that. Besides, I wasn't entirely convinced it was the right thing to do. But I certainly wouldn't let him sacrifice himself.

"There's got to be a way to convince him I'm going to give him what he wants."

"If he has the demon stone, I think I can help," said Mane.

"Every one of us is a part of this now. Kit, you'll need your amulet." I unclasped the chain and handed it to Kit. A shimmer passed over her skin, glowing iridescently, much like the scales of her selkie tail. Renewed vigor visibly coursed through her.

"I can feel the air changing." She approached the temple doors, and they flung open wide, revealing an angry sky. Bolts of lightning shot across the clouds. Without our magic to shield Dell'Aria, we were about to have another problem on our hands.

Kit thrust her shoulders back, head held high against the onslaught of wind whipping her blue hair into a frenzy. A charge electrified the air, predicting the impending magic storm. Of everyone standing here, I was worried most about Kit. She had been my responsibility. I had told Ralph I would take care of her.

"Are you sure you're ready for this?" I asked.

She tilted her head back, breathing in deeply. There was a gleam in her eye, an inner light that spoke of confidence. "It's the path my life was meant to take. If anyone is to blame, it is my dead mother," said Kit. Her light-hearted teasing gave me strength. "And besides, you can't do this alone."

Kit raised her hands and murmured words under her breath. The amulet at her neck glowed blue, and in the sky appeared the newborn selkie fae. One became hundreds of beautiful and fearsome creatures. They grew in numbers so great they appeared to fill all of Overworld. Streaks of multicolored wings brightened the sky. They circled their new mother, parting when a large airship descended through clouds.

There was no mistaking the captain at the helm of the ship, her brilliant red wings blazing a trail through the tempest. We all exited the temple.

"Calliope!" Aric leapt to his feet, gaze fixed on the ship. Calliope ignored the swarm of flying creatures in the sky. She yelled out commands, and the airship descended into the open area in front of the temple. She had spotted Aric—and his injuries.

Before it could land, Calliope flew from the deck and landed at our feet. She ran to Aric, tears in her eyes. "What happened to you?"

I saw Aric struggling to reply. I answered for him, hoping to ease the pain of his confession. "A prophecy happened to him. More specifically, Pryn."

"Where is he?" Calliope drew a small blade from the harness at her thigh. "I'll slit him a new opening in his throat."

Dooley put his hands up. "You won't get past his magic. We're trying to come up with a plan of attack."

"Is that why you summoned the selkie fae?" asked Calliope.

"You know of them?" Kit came forward.

Calliope sheathed her blade. "I've been around for a long time. They used to be quite common, then the fae separated and our ancestors wiped them out." She rubbed at her exposed forearms. Aric pressed a hand to the small of her back, and the tension visibly released from her shoulders. "My own mother participated in the slaughter. The ability to belong to either the skies or the waters threatened their power. Their prejudice thinly veiled their fear."

"I'm not trying to take any power," said Kit.

"We're all on the same team here," said Calliope.

"Do you have any weapons?" Mane motioned to the massive ship being anchored down.

"Better. I have reinforcements." Calliope put her fingers to her mouth and let out a loud whistle. The side of the ship opened and formed a ramp to the ground. Hundreds of fae equipped with all manner of weapons alighted. The portly dwarves brought up the rear.

"We've been working with the dwarves to excavate the minerals hidden deep within their mountain. By working together, we managed to harvest quite a bit of material— what was left after the poachers, anyway."

The troops lined up, their heads forward, all attention focused on Calliope, whose arm remained around Aric. She stepped aside and made a gesture, effectively handing over their command. The weight of their stares settled on me.

"These people belong to you," I said. Guilt weighed heavily on me. These remaining fae's homes and families had been destroyed because of what my mother had done. The dwarves—so many of whom died of starvation inside Elbrus before they could be released—stood proud.

"Dell'Aria is our home now too. You are their queen," said Calliope.

"But I'm not. Aric and I didn't—"

"She's right," said Mane. "Your father was the ruler and king, and when he passed away that title went to you. Aric may not be king, but you are queen."

My father once told me I'd make a great queen. If I could believe in myself, the people would follow. How could I believe in myself when I was so unsure? I was queen by right of ritual, not by rite of passage. Could I ever match up to my father's expectations?

Aric clasped my hand. "When Pryn said you would save us all, he may have meant for his own agenda, but what he didn't realize is that you truly have. You are the one who has united all our people together. You are the one who befriended the dwarves."

"And the elves and a certain demon," said Mane.

"And the selkie," said Kit.

"You have brought all of the creatures of the Realms together. I don't think Pryn or your mother ever expected or anticipated your strength when they wrote this little prophecy." Dooley balled up the paper in his hand, voice tinged with a surge of purpose. "Mane, mind doing the honors?"

Mane stepped forward and touched a finger to the paper, setting it on fire. The ashes spun into the wailing winds and spiraled up into the coming storm.

As the final ashes dispersed, the selkie fae settled into the crowd. They were all waiting for me to speak. I swallowed, nervous and afraid but utterly embracing the solidarity that vibrated amongst those gathered.

"We are united together for one singular purpose. To save the Realms. I promise you, once this is all over I will do my best to make sure we stay together, even if we have no more battles to fight."

A series of chuckles arose, and Aric leaned in to whisper into my ear. "You're killing it. But really you should leave the speeches to me, or we might all actually be killed." The sky grew even darker. Clouds formed around the central spire of the temple and swirled around angrily. Bolts of blue and purple lightning erupted from the heavens, pouring over the white marble dome.

"Let's get in there," I yelled.

"He has some backup," said Mane, pointing to the sky.

A screech echoed across the sky, announcing the arrival of a golden-bellied beast, an ebony dragon whose wings spanned the width of the temple. I remembered all too well this most fierce creature of the Realms, likely brother to the dragon Aric ordered to die. My stomach tied in knots at the sight. I pushed back my shoulder and tried to appear confident. Everyone here depended on me, and I couldn't let my old terrors stop me from my quest. Every animal has a weak spot, and my sword had already tasted dragon's blood.

"Why is it here?" asked Kit.

Growing up, we'd been told the dragons belonged to the Goddess. They were sacred creatures that protected her. If they were here, it meant only one thing. "Varuna. If Pryn overpowers her, he will have power over them as well. It's started. There is no time."

In the center of the courtyard, a cart that once sold ice fruits and butterbreads to the local children was tilted on the axis of a busted wheel. A testament to the many battles we had been through. Our children would never survive if we didn't win this battle. I ran up to the cart and climbed to the top of the wreck, placing one foot on the spinning wheel. All eyes were on me, and I, in turn, met the eyes of each person before me willing to give their life for the Realms. I felt overwhelmed, but in a positive way. I wanted to drink in the moment and remember this feeling of gratitude forever.

"Send the selkie fae up to keep them at bay. If they're busy, we can make it into the temple. Ground crews, fan out and try the south openings to the temple. Are there any magic users amongst you?"

A slight woman with graying yellow hair stepped forward from the crowd. I recognized her immediately.

"I can't have you risk your life," I said.

"You won't be risking it. I will. And I won't sit by while our world is destroyed, not while I can prevent it. Some of the dwarves will remain. Our iron can help you," said Franca's mother.

She shoved her fists to her hips, and for just a breath, the image of Franca melded with her mother and I recalled my promise. Stopping Franca or her mother was out of the question.

"Take Calliope's people and go around the south side." Calliope had handed over command of her people to me, but they would always belong to her in her heart. I wouldn't forget that.

The dwarves answered her orders by raising their war hammers into the air. The fae around them shirked from the debilitating iron ore. I stepped between them to defuse their fears. Good thing we weren't fighting one another. But Pryn, although a magic user, was fae. A little iron might be what we need.

Franca's mother stepped forward and handed me an item wrapped in a fragile cloth of woven grass. "This is a gift. A special weapon forged by our ancestors during a time as dark as now. A time when we all once betrayed one another."

I carefully unfolded the cloth, revealing a blade that shimmered in copper from pommel to point, the tip coated in pure iron. I lifted the weapon, surprised by its weight. It was a fae killer. Shining copper to laugh in the face of the one you were about to bring down with iron venom.

"Thank you. Hopefully after today, it will become a relic."

I gave Franca's mother one last embrace before she left, a contingent of our army close behind.

A scream rent the air, drawing my attention skyward. One dragon became four, and then I stopped counting. The selkie fae did their best to keep the dragons occupied, ducking and dodging as their flames lit up the sky.

My hand closed around the handle of the temple door as a bolt of lightning struck the spire. It traveled down the side and into my body before I could react. A sudden sting in my fingers gradually spread, like the feeling of hot, thick water rippling under the surface of my skin, gluing me to the spot. My copper blood threatened to boil out of my veins if my heart didn't explode first.

Hands clamped down on my arms and ripped me backward. I met the ground with all the grace of a flightless fae, every breath clear and cool, though the rapid pulse continued. A slight tapping on my shoulder alerted me to the presence of something beneath me that wasn't my wings.

"Kit—what, are you okay?" I rolled off her and tried in vain to rub away the feeling I had been sacked with a dwarven sledgehammer.

"Of course. I'm kind of used to the lightning thing."

Mane hoisted her to her feet. Dooley stepped toward the door and held his hand near it. As he did, the lightning struck a second time, the powerful force causing him to retreat a few steps. This wasn't a natural phenomenon we were dealing with.

"He has other defenses in place." Dooley lifted his hands and closed his eyes, concentrating on the field of magic in front of him and trying to break the spell. Beads of sweat formed at his brow, and he dropped his hands, defeated. "Without my markings, I can't focus my magic. He's cut out the one weapon I could have used against him."

Dooley wavered, his battle wounds and the efforts to push his magic to the limits draining him. Mane caught Dooley before he sank to the ground, tugging him to his feet by his shoulders. "This battle is not over."

Kit flung her arms around Mane. Behind them, explosions of fire raced across the sky. Shrieks of deadly beasts pierced through the overture of chaos threatening to consume us all. My heart was drawn to the one-inch space between their eyes, a pinpoint of hope giving me tunnel vision amidst the wreckage. The cries of the dragons overhead increased. Fire erupted from one of their gaping maws and struck a selkie fae. Its smoldering body fell to the ground at our feet.

"Hurry," whispered Kit. Mane tucked a lock of her hair behind her ear.

Some unheard conversation had passed between them. Suddenly he clasped her hand and they both reached out to the door. A dagger of lightning ripped across the sky. It made contact, and blinding light covered the temple.

"No!" I surged forward, trying to get to Kit and Mane before the curtain could come down on them. Aric caught me around the waist, his wing coming up to act as a visual barrier. Dooley came to my other side and tucked my head under his chin, laying my cheek against his chest. Heat radiated from his skin.

"Don't watch, Valora," he whispered into my ear.

But I wasn't going to hide. Through my tears I saw the light hit Mane and Kit. As it did, beams of energy burst from the amulet at Kit's throat. Mane's eyes went bright red, and the combination of their two magics weakened the spell, sealing the temple. The shimmering field solidified and fissures appeared in the glassy dome. Deep cracks shot up from the ground, tearing down the wall.

A final blast threw us to the ground. Shards pierced my exposed flesh, biting into my skin before scattering to the winds. Dust settled at the base of the temple steps, and I wiped the dirt from my eyes. Mane and Kit were lying on the ground, their arms around one another. They weren't moving.

Dooley rose to his feet, each of his steps seeming to encompass a full minute as he trod toward our fallen friends, like the weight of the world was on his shoulders. Before he could reach them, Kit began to cough then rolled on her side, and Mane sat up straight, clutching his head and moaning.

"Damn, that hurt."

Aric helped me to my feet. For a moment my heart had been ripped out. But instead of sorrow, flights of violent fantasy had flashed through my mind. My blood boiled. Two more of my friends might have died because of Pryn's treachery. No more lives would be lost.

I bent before Kit, wiping the soot from her brow. "You gave me quite a scare. Are you up for more?"

"Fuck yes!" She hopped to her feet. Mane accepted Dooley's arm.

"I need to two of you to lead the selkie fae. Make sure you're keeping the dragons busy out here." A sense of renewed purpose flooded my body and propelled me up the temple steps. "I will save the Realms."

I kicked the door, and it swung in easily, echoing against the hollow rise of the temple as it slammed into the wall. Never before had the silence of this space been so welcoming and foreboding at the same time. The calm before the real storm.

The size of the dwarves, and what was left of their army, was further diminished by the transverse arches spanning the main dome. We moved with caution in the shadow of the oculus, like the solitary eye of the massive Cyclops I once read about as a child. We were completely out in the open, with little place to hide. I stepped forward, and Dooley yanked me aside as an arrow went whizzing by. The only sound was the thud as the colorless, but brilliant, rod of diamond sparkled in the rock wall by my head. Few used this type of weapon.

"Arrows!" I yelled. As I ducked behind one of the monolithic shafts that supported the dome, my gaze traveled up the marbled surface to the elevated platform of the tribune above. Another arrow came within inches of my head.

Dooley peered out from another pillar next to me. "Magic isn't his only weapon."

Aric grunted as he snatched the arrow from the wall. "This arrow is iron-tipped. They mean these for the fae. But Pryn didn't count on our other friends."

One of the dwarves encased in black kettle mail, a helmet drawn tight across his brow, snuck a glance from his hiding spot. Another arrow flew from the upper walkway of the temple dome, striking him on the head. His helmet gave off a thud and the arrow fell to the ground. The dwarf picked it up, shaking it in the air and letting out a fierce battle cry.

"I guess not. But who is helping them?"

Aric studied the weapon. Calliope looked over his shoulder at the glittering sheath of the arrow. "These are of the elves."

I remembered the figure I saw in the woods after we had been attacked by the dragon, its eyes glittering bright green, like the many facets of this most exquisite and fiery of gems. I had seen an elf. There was no doubt in my mind they must be helping Pryn and stealing from the dwarves. Most diamonds come from the volcanic rock of Mount Elbrus, and elves are not known for getting their hands dirty.

"The elves helping Pryn? What could they possibly have to gain?" asked Dooley.

"He probably lied to them," said Aric. "They are almost as close to immortality as the Goddess is. Maybe he promised them they could finally have it."

I tossed the arrow to the ground. For a moment, the onslaught stopped. "They don't have to die. The power of Pryn's deception ends here."

"There is another way to get closer to Pryn's chambers," said Aric. "The passageway is through the catacombs."

"We'll get lost down there," I said. The final realization of my destiny dawned on me. And I knew what I needed to do. "Wait here. I have a better idea."

If I detailed my plan, they'd either try and talk me out of it or come with me. Neither was an option. I ducked out from behind my column and into Dooley's arms.

I hugged him close and buried my face into the curve of his neck to take in one last breath of his scent. There were no guarantees I'd ever be this close to him again. "Cover me. Keep them busy. Keep them here."

Dooley nodded and opened his mouth to speak, but before any words spilled out, I pressed my lips to his and any words he was thinking of saying translated instead into his embrace. He gripped both of my arms and squeezed me tightly. He clung to me, wrinkles creasing his forehead. I knew he was worried. I turned from him before I convinced myself I shouldn't do this. If I didn't, then he and all the others would disappear in a blast that would utterly annihilate the Realms. I wouldn't allow that to happen.

I ducked out from the column and ran toward the entrance. An arrow embedded itself into the wall in front of me. I didn't slow.

Dooley came out from behind his column and waved his arms. "Hey, over here."

He retreated behind the pillar as a volley of arrows sailed toward him. The others caught on, and the dwarves made themselves into moving targets, darting from one pillar to the next, shouting and hollering as each arrow thudded off their impregnable armor. They gladly retrieved their stolen property. The elves appeared on the walkway and, by their triumphant stance, knew they were the only ones who had flying weapons.

I tried to shove the door open, but it stuck. I pressed my eye to the slit, and a deep, boiling anger surged from my gut, giving me the strength to force my way outside. The bodies of the selkie fae littered the ground. There were still many in the sky, but they were outnumbered by the dragons that had come to Varuna's aid, failing to understand they were actually aiding Pryn. More of Pryn's treachery.

Kit pressed her fingers to one's temples, speaking to the selkie fae with the power of the amulet around her neck. Tears streamed down her face. Mane flanked her, a sword in his hand to protect her from attack while she directed her people.

I raced to their side and placed a hand on Kit's arm. She looked into my eyes. She was strong, but I knew the pain a leader felt when those fighting for her were dying. "They've done enough. Send them home. We don't need to lose them forever. There is something else I need to ask you."

Kit pressed her fingers to her temples once more. The skies emptied as the brilliantly colored selkie fae raced toward their home. They were safe for now, but if I didn't do what was necessary, no creature of the Realm would have a home much longer.

"Where do you need us?" she asked.

"I have a plan, which I can't exactly spell out to you. But it will require your amulet, which will mean you and Mane need to find a safe place to hide. You won't be able to fight." I knew asking Kit to give me the one thing that would defend her was asking a lot, but I couldn't be afraid to ask for help anymore. I had to trust that if she was going to make this sacrifice that she would be doing it for more than just me.

She removed the amulet and placed it around my neck. "Do what you need to do. We'll be okay."

The amulet at my neck flared blue. I set off on my path, trusting they would find shelter. There was only one way to find out if my idea would work. The streets leading to the castle presented their own challenge. An obstacle course of a world Pryn hoped would be forgotten. Aric had given me an idea, which I took one step further. I rushed toward my family's crypt, taking the steps two at a time. I might not have another chance.

Gingerly I approached my mother's grave, remembering Aric's half-naked torso clad in his purple robe leaning against her tomb. His passageways weren't the only way to move between places here on Dell'Aria. Thank the Goddess for giving that bastard unforgettable abs, since he gave me the idea.

I fell forward to the edge of the pool and gazed at my reflection. The eyes staring back at me this time were my own. None of them would be able to get to Pryn. I was the only one capable of doing this.

I patted the dwarven blade at my side. I might be alone,

but I wasn't unprepared. I inhaled deeply, filling my lungs out of force of habit before clutching the glowing blue amulet at my neck and plunging into the fountain.

CHAPTER TWENTY

A burst of bubbles exited my lungs, but when I breathed in I didn't drown. The amulet at my neck glowed brightly, and I swam forward, remembering what Kit once told me about travel between the various pools of water controlled by the selkie. Like portal travel, I needed to concentrate on a location and have the key to opening the door. The amulet was that key. Now I must focus on my destination. Unfortunately, the thing uppermost in my mind was that I'd never been too good at portal travel.

I clutched at the amulet and focused on the wellspring that fed the priests' chambers, where the fae of Dell'Aria partook of their sacrament and where the children were blessed. It was a large pool, but accessible only to the priests when there were no ceremonies being held, and was otherwise behind a locked door. It was the closest I dared get to Pryn's chambers and not have to face an elf's arrow. And I was hoping it was Pryn would not be expecting me.

The magic of the amulet swirled around me, and I had the same feeling as when I was being torn through a portal, like my entire body was being forced through a three-inch iron ring. My skin burned, and the scene before my eyes changed from a peaceful sight of swirling bubbles to a painful bright light.

I squeezed my eyes tight until the pain subsided and my breath returned. Apparently I was wrong about a few things. Wrong that I had any idea what I was doing, and wrong Pryn would not have thought to protect the fountain.

Through the shimmering water I saw a figure pacing back and forth. He hadn't yet seen me, but he was about to. His ears were pointed, and I could tell it was one of the elves.

It would be easy for me to fly out and possibly slit his throat. The harder task was not killing him and convincing him not to kill me.

I tucked the dwarven blade into the sheath at the small of my back. Easily accessible, but not in plain view. I hoped I wouldn't have to use it.

Keeping my hands out in front of me, I slowly rose up above the waterline. But I wasn't selkie, and moving silently through water wasn't my strong suit. At the first splash, the elf swiveled around. I wasn't even halfway up and I had an arrow aimed at my head.

"He told us you might be coming through this way. I didn't believe him, but I suppose he hasn't been wrong about anything so far." His glittering green eyes glowed brightly in the dimly lit alcove. This was the elf that had tended to Dooley's cabin, making sure Pryn and his lies were hidden. We had all been fooled.

"You're wrong. Pryn didn't tell you the truth. We don't have to fight. We should be on the same side. He hasn't told you that what he means to do will destroy all of the Realms, and perhaps the Elysium as well. Whatever you think you are fighting for won't matter if we don't stop him." I continued to move as I spoke. My only weapon was the knife at my back, and if I wasn't close enough to use it then I would die with it.

The elf dropped his sight an inch and spoke to me, his bow still at full draw. "Who told you these things?"

"Mane. He was an elf, like one of you."

He relaxed the string of the bow and put the arrow into his quiver. "Where is he? Is he here?"

"Many have died helping me get here." I fought the overwhelming urge to arm myself. I wasn't going to lie to him, but if he thought Mane was dead maybe he would sympathize with me. "Don't you see? The dying and the killing must stop."

Shadows shifted as the elf nodded in agreement. "My name is Torkel. Mane was my brother."

He drew a short blade from his belt and grabbed me by the arm. The flat of the blade pressed into the small of my back, and he urged me forward. "Come. I can take you to Pryn."

At this point I would take anything to avoid more bloodshed. He followed close behind, directing me down the hallway. The doors on either side of the upper gallery became more ornate as we delved deeper into the inner sanctum. Inside the markings of symbol magic coated the doorway and surrounding wall. My throat burned as a sour, bitter taste filled my mouth, and I was glad I had skipped breakfast.

The skin Pryn cut from Dooley's arm nailed to the center of the door. Black paint continued the symbols that had been on his arm and covered the entire door.

"Why?" I ran my fingers over the door as my mind worked overtime imagining the horrors these symbols might contain.

Torkel shoved the door open, and I realized why the symbols were here.

"But I thought—no!"

Torkel's hand was casually anchored on his hip. His smile was distant, unfocused. There was a history here I never could have read before he decided to reveal it to me. And now it was too late. "I told you I would bring you to Pryn. I never liked Mane. My father did, and all it got him was death. He accepted Mane as a part of our family, but I always knew what he truly was. A demon. If he was trying to stop this, it goes to prove it was meant to happen. Here she is."

He shoved me forward and slammed the door shut. Pain shot through my kneecaps and settled in my clenched jaw. I would not cry out in pain. Before me was the last person I wanted to be alone with in such close quarters. After tucking the amulet into my bodice, I slid my hand to the small of my back to draw the dwarven blade from the sheath. Before I could bring it forward, the blade ripped from my hand and flung against the wall, clattering to the ground.

"You brought the wrong weapon to this fight, Valora. Lucky for me," said Pryn. "You were never as clever as your mother. What a disappointment you are in so many ways."

Pryn held his hand out and squeezed his fingers together. My ribcage compressed as I was again in the grip of a dragon's claw. His hand out, he strode over to a cage, and I saw her. My mother. It could be no one other than her. Her figure was a glowing yellow light, but there was no mistaking her silhouette. Her features were slowly coming into focus. He was using the magic to bring her here. Both worlds would be destroyed.

All around the edges of the cage were the parts of Aric's wings, which had been hacked from his body. Pryn flicked his wrist, and I was thrust against the wall. He quickly clamped iron lashing rope over my wrists and secured me to the rings above my head. The iron burned into my skin and I went boneless, my footing faltering as I struggled to fight against the pain.

Struggling was useless. There was nothing I could do to undo the ties, and they were quickly draining any strength I had left. I was supposed to save the Realms, and I had already failed.

My head fell forward, and I stared at the amulet tucked into my bodice. *How will I get out of this one?*

You can begin by telling us how you got in there so we can help you.

You can't get to me. It's impossible.

As impossible as us being able to speak to you even though we no longer have the amulets?

I remembered what Mane had said to me. I was the conduit. I was the connection between Aric and Dooley. Pryn's plan would cause a massive break between worlds. Maybe if I could channel the energies through the selkie amulet then I could diffuse the blast and truly save us all. But that would mean replacing the demon stone in the machine with the amulet around my neck.

On a center stone, Pryn laid out a parchment and traced his finger down the page as he added different ingredients to a bubbling pot.

"You'll destroy everything, Pryn. What you are trying to do won't work. You can't bring her back." I could barely recognize my own voice. I was much weaker than I thought.

Pryn had repurposed the device Aric had used to steal all the magic from the fae of Dell'Aria. He patted the machine. "Oh, I don't intend to try and suck any more magic from Dell'Aria. I've harvested all I require. But this little device isn't used solely to extract magic from the fae—it can be used to focus magic. Through this amulet and the power of the Soulstealer, I will open the door to the Elysium."

Pryn removed the gleaming red demon stone from his neck. He inserted it into the device, an air of sacrament in his every move.

"We will be ready shortly. There is only one more step to complete." He raised his hand, and a polished dagger gleamed. "The blood of the one who will save us all."

"Dooley and Aric will stop you. They're alive, you know." He stalked toward me, and I struggled to get the words out. I needed time to think of a real solution to this problem.

"You mean he survived?"

"So did Aric. I healed them."

Pryn seemed actually taken aback. "You? No, you have always been horrible at spell-casting."

"I knew enough to stop the bleeding."

"Even if they are alive, they will never get through that door. Dooley and his father stumbled upon quite powerful binding spells. So powerful, in fact, that I cut them off him. Easier that way."

Dooley had been so angry when I lost his father's journal. Was this why? He had been dabbling in powerful binding spells, dangerous spells he should never use. In my mind, I could feel Aric and Dooley getting closer. If they couldn't get in the room, they wouldn't do me much good. Getting Pryn to talk was crucial.

"So tell me how you're controlling the dragons. I thought they were creatures of the sky and they only served Varuna."

"Soon they will serve me. They're learning. It's all starting to happen, the change." The beam of light from the sky intensified, and his gold eyes glittered as the stone glowed blood red. We were running out of time.

Pryn renewed his march toward his prey. I struggled against the binds. Aric and Dooley were getting closer, I could feel them. A thud sounded against the door.

Pryn pressed the tip of the knife to the soft flesh in the inside of my arm, cutting into me. I bit back a cry of pain as my skin gave under the sharp steel. "I bet you wish you'd stabbed your sword through my back in that dragon's cave so long ago."

"The day's not over," I growled. He lifted the blade, and blood ran as hot as my desire to stop him.

The wood door exploded in a shower of splinters before Pryn could touch the stone. Vials shattered as they hit the ground. Blood dripped from the knife as Torkel's head came rolling across the floor through the dust and stopped at Pryn's feet.

"Blood magic isn't as strong as you might think," said Dooley. Aric raised his sword, slick with blood. I imagined he'd delighted in beheading the elf.

Pryn's eyes teared, his face reddening to suppress a maniacal laugh. He was drunk with power. His hand rose, and the sword sailed out of Aric's hand and was flung across the room, coming to rest next to mine. "You must know those weapons can't hurt me."

Dooley murmured indiscernible words under his breath. His eyes flashed red and a quirk in the set of his mouth bothered me. Something wasn't right.

Aric took advantage of the distraction and made his way over to me, easily undoing my binds. "Is that…?" he whispered into my ear as he pointed to the transparent form coalescing into the image of my mother. Her mouth was moving, repeating a word over and over.

"She's saying your name." Aric wandered toward her, and I reached out to stop him.

"My mother died long ago. Long before your Blight ever stole her from me. A soulstealing machine can't steal from someone with no soul." Words he had to hear, words I was glad I could still speak. Finally he could be free of the guilt of my mother's death and take his own path in life. If we made it through this. And I could be free of living in my mother's shadow.

He nodded, and the tears glistening in his eyes were reflected in his heart.

Dooley rose to his feet, a sheen of red covering him from top to bottom, like he had been sprayed with a fine mist of blood or cinnabar. "Oh Goddess, no. Dooley." The words left my mouth, and the corner of his own curled into the familiar grin of someone I thought I had banished. One I thought was gone forever.

Pryn let go of the malevolent laugh he'd been holding in, his focus remaining on Dooley. "You trying magic your father taught you? It didn't help him stay alive when I stabbed him in the back. I doubt it will help you now."

"Actually, you did me a great favor getting rid of Brokk." The voice that came forth was certainly no longer Dooley. "It's funny you were working for me this entire time and you had no idea. *I* had no idea. What a treat!" Dooley clapped his hands together and paraded toward the machine. The demon stone pulsed brighter as he moved closer.

"Yes, yes. This was the one thing I was missing. I thought perhaps I could use these three. The triad of power to open the gates to the Elysium. But it is difficult to get people to actually do what you want. Much more efficient to use a machine. And what's this?" Ravanna gestured to the cage that held the vision of my mother.

Pryn jumped up and situated himself in front of the entrance. "No, you won't harm her."

"Sorry to say, appears she's already dead."

"She'll return. I'm sending that one to Varuna, where she is supposed to be, and I will bring her back to me." The last shred of the man I knew as Pryn dissolved before my eyes. Aric held me closer.

Ravanna waved a hand, and Pryn was thrown facedown. His eyes glittered brightly as he got closer to the demon stone.

"Don't let him touch it." Pryn flipped over, the front of his white robe marred by a stain of burgundy. The coin-sized blotch spread from the center of his chest, from the place the dwarven blade was embedded to the hilt. His fingertips brushed across the pommel of the sword, shock spreading over his face as the blood spread over the knots in his robe, before he fell to the ground.

Aric rushed toward Ravanna, catching him around the middle and throwing him into the wall. The demon acted slightly perturbed as he grabbed Aric by the neck and held him high in the air. "Stop causing me trouble and perhaps I will have mercy on your mother when I am ruling the Elysium."

The demon stone glowed brighter, and the floor beneath my feet rocked as a thunderous roar came from outside. The talons of one of the great dragons grasped the window, and it fought to get its way into the tower. The beast sensed the magic of the Elysium within. It had no idea it was a trick.

I grabbed on to the machine before I was knocked to the ground, and the stone dropped into my hand.

Ravanna flung Aric to the ground and stalked toward me, easily picking me up by the shoulders and setting me on my feet. "I told you I would win, Valora." He snatched the stone from me and put the amulet around his neck.

I loved this man. The caress of my lover's lips. A soft, sensual touch with a wicked bite that poisoned me. It was a part of me now. I was infected, and there was no salvation. Thoroughly corrupted and better for it. Logic didn't have a purpose here, and he would never listen. I would never get through to Dooley again. Behind those red eyes he was lost forever. To win I'd have to fulfill the prophecy. Bring this war to an end.

"Give a girl her dying wish? One last kiss?" I stumbled toward Ravanna and set my hand on his heart, hoping to feel nothing, but the definition of sacrifice is to give up something important for the sake of other considerations. In this case, the fae of Dell'Aria and every inhabitant of the Realms. His heart beat fast and furious. I pressed the demon stone hard against his chest and leaned in to him. Dooley was fighting, but it was too late. I was meant to sacrifice to save us all. But it wasn't myself I was meant to sacrifice. It was my love.

Ravanna gripped my wrist and forced my body against his, pressing his mouth to mine. The raw, untamable power of chaos flooded my senses, but not before I placed the selkie stone where the demon stone once was.

The light pouring from the sky morphed from red to blue. Ravanna's face contorted in anger. The dragon shrieked, almost untangled. It was the last chance I would have. I thrust the demon stone against his chest as hard as I could, and he stumbled back, his hand over top of it. The sky roared again as the dragon tried to free itself from the window, his talon now stuck inside—in Ravanna's chest.

His body slumped to the ground and his red eyes dimmed, bringing back Dooley for one last breath, a jagged tear where his heart once was. The dragon flew into the sky, the demon stone in his clutches.

"What's happening?" Dooley stared down at his chest, confused.

I knelt down and tucked one of his chocolate-brown curls behind his ear for the last time. "Everything will be okay." The light in the sky brightened. The image of my mother faded even as she continued to mouth my name.

"So you really did save us all?" Dooley's words came out choked as the blood filled up his lungs, filling up his mouth.

Bending forward, I kissed his bloodstained lips. "Not everyone, my love."

He circled his arms around me and held me tightly, putting his mouth to my ear. "Yes, you did," he whispered. Tears ran hot and fast down my face, and I stayed there in his embrace until the muscles in his arms went slack.

Aric stirred, and I could feel him behind me, but he didn't disturb me.

The magic designed to steal all the power from the Elysium and give Pryn the ability to open the doorway had now been reversed. The selkie stone and the infusion of Pryn's binding magic knitted the magic of the Elysium together again, sealing the rift between our worlds. But my world, my very existence, was fractured forever. I lay next to him, numbness encompassing my soul. Coldness settled into my limbs, but I couldn't move.

I watched Calliope appear and throw her arms around Aric. "Don't ever disappear on me again. Promise."

He gazed into her eyes, holding her tight in his embrace, and tucked a red curl over her ear. "If you'll have me, I won't have any reason to leave you ever again."

Watching their love blossom before me was too much to bear. I'd spent all my time waiting for a second chance with Dooley. Memories seeped from my veins, leaving me hollow.

Empty. I crumpled down upon my weakened shell, collapsing over his body. Silent prayers sent up to the Goddess to take mercy on the soul of this beautiful man born of the fire who'd given his life to save so many.

I reached up to close his eyes, clinging to his body. I did not know how I would ever be able to leave his side and accept the reality of his death. Inside I felt just as dead. I pressed my hand to the wound on his chest, wishing I knew enough magic to bring him back.

"I'm so sorry. Valora, we need to get to the others. Please come with us," said Aric. Through a blurry haze, I stared up at him and Calliope. They both held out their hands, encouraging me to take their support, to give them part of my burden. "Dooley's finally able to rest. I think we all can now."

CHAPTER TWENTY-ONE

I reached my hand toward Aric. As I stretched away from my core, the shaking started until my entire soul quaked. Adrenaline crashed and receded in waves over my body, leaving me gasping for breath on the shoreline. I wanted to drag myself back to those waters, to drown in a sea of despair.

A beacon of cerulean-blue light rose before me. Its brilliance was blinding, and I shut my eyes. Through closed lids, I felt the soothing, blissful heat infuse me with buoyant energy, a welcoming numbness to my overwhelming pain. With little effort, I floated to my feet

Looking down, I saw the selkie amulet had been slipped around my neck once more by my dear friend. She stepped from the doorway, and her arms wrapped around me, her warmth contrasting with my cold skin. I buried my face into her shoulder, and she stumbled. Her feebleness cut through my grief when I truly looked at her for the first time. I studied her battle-weary face and traced the physical pain she'd endured without the power of the amulet. Panicked by her obvious weakness, I pressed the stone into her hand.

She anticipated my move and refused to take it. "I'm fine. I'll just have to get back to Mavrovo soon."

I forced it into her palm and wrapped her heated fingers around the smooth surface. "Take it, Kit. I've already lost so many. Don't let me lose you too."

I dared not allow my attention to stray to the body lying a few feet from me, but focused on fastening the necklace around Kit's neck.

"They've gone. The dragons have retreated," Mane shouted as he stormed through doorway, a long sword slick with a fiery red substance that could belong to only one being. A dragon. He swept the area, and his attention settled on Dooley's prone body, still in death. The sword went lax in his fingers.

I fixated on the molten gleam of dragon's blood that coated the metal, and hope surged. The waves returned to the shores of my heart, but I dared not let the idea weigh anchor. Not until I knew I was right. I reached for the sword handle, my hands shaking. "Please, I need your blade."

Mane cast me a curious glance, but complied with my request.

I crouched down by Dooley's side and wiped my finger over the blade.

"What is she doing?" Kit asked, and I could hear the concern in her voice.

"The dragons are followers of Varuna. They are said to carry her power in their blood," Mane said.

"And if a dragon killed Dooley, then a dragon's blood can return him to life," I said. Gathering as much as possible, I brought it to his lips. Droplets fell from my hand into his open mouth. A collective tension constricted the air. Were the healing properties of the dragon enough to bring him back? I felt the weight of the four at my back pressing into me, hoping, as I did, that this would work.

Seconds stretched into long, agonizing minutes before Dooley's right hand twitched. The anchor dropped, filling my limbs with strength, filling the void within. I tore open his shirt, and tears dripped from my lashes as I watched the gaping wound over his heart began to knit itself closed. His eyelids fluttered, mouth opening and closing.

Through the last few weeks, I had tried to remember what my life was like before Dooley. There was an unending stream of things to keep me busy, but never enough to occupy my thoughts—never enough to keep me from thinking about him. A tingling sensation blossomed inside my chest, spreading into my fingers. A gasp escaped my lips. The man of my dreams was awakening.

A sweet melody filtered in through the window that had been ripped free by Varuna's dragon. A soft sound that grew louder as the voices of the fae and dwarves rose as one, singing a song of victory known by all the creatures of the Realms. Proud and triumphant. My people had survived and were celebrating. Dooley was alive. I felt like I could fly.

A finger brushed my cheek. I grasped Dooley's palm and kissed it, squeezed it, like I wanted to hold him, but didn't dare for fear of hurting him. "A guy comes back from the dead and all he gets is a kiss on the hand?"

He wrapped his hand around my neck and pulled me close, pressing his lips to mine. There was no prophecy that defined what was between us. Our connection was tangible and undeniable.

"Princess, I think the people would like to hear from you," said Aric. He crooked a finger, calling me over.

I turned to Dooley and my chest tightened. Just because we loved one another, didn't mean his life was best served by staying in Dell'Aria.

"We'll talk," he said with a sad smile.

I swallowed every bit of heartache that wrenched at my soul and did as Aric bid. Dooley's place was Earthside and mine was here. I walked to the window, and Aric took a step back, giving me the stage. For the first time, I stood before my people with no motivation other than to watch over them. As a child I had played along the tops of the stone battlements to escape the prying eyes of those who viewed me as different, someone who should never have been allowed to live. When I got older, balancing along the narrow ledge proved my agility to the naysayers. Even without the wings of a full fae, I could have served in the King's Guard. Then I was considered a princess. Now I knew what to call myself—their queen.

⇛⇘

A sweet, sugary smell preceded Orris, and I turned to see him standing behind me.

"Everything okay down there?"

I had sent Orris down to begin talks with the selkie fae, and all appeared to be going well. Little by little, things had returned to a normal rhythm. The relations between the fae of Dell'Aria and the rest of Overworld were restored. Kali worked the ice fruit fields under a watchful eye. I might never trust her, but she had a right to a place in this world, the same as the rest of us.

He nodded in the affirmative. I grasped the limb of an ice fruit tree and leaned over the edge of Dell'Aria to peer down into Lake Mavrovo. It was full of the selkie fae that had been spawned by Kit. The dwarves had rebuilt their strong mountain homes and the elves had moved back into the forest. Although things were tense, the elves realized they were outnumbered, and a truce had been struck even though their people had helped Pryn. It soon became obvious it was only a handful of the elves that had taken it upon themselves to make things worse for the rest.

"We got this message today." The birds were again being used to ferry messages between our world and theirs, and it didn't come as any surprise to me when I got the invitation for the wedding of Aric and Calliope. They had relocated to her island to make it their home. With Aric's help and the magic returning to the Realms, they worked to bring the once majestic kingdom back to its former glory.

"I'm happy for them. They truly belong together." A thickness formed in my throat, signaling the onset of tears I wouldn't let fall. I squeezed my lids tight and tried to shake off the memories always at the forefront of my mind. Dooley had spent weeks recovering. Today was the day we would speak about whether he was going to stay.

"What…" I raised my head to the sky. A bridge of light grew from a pinpoint, broadening from the center of the orange horizon "…is that?"

The gossamer span stretched down until it stopped at my feet. A woman floated down the stairs, and as she got closer I knew exactly who she was.

"Varuna!" I shielded my eyes as the Goddess, bathed in gold light, stepped from the last stair. The appearance of the Goddess garnered immediate attention. Soon Mane, Kit, and Dooley were standing beside me. "What are you doing here?"

"Your actions saved the Elysium from intrusion. You have lost so many defending us." Her glow was ethereal, and yet now I knew she was no real god, but just a very powerful being from a place altogether different from the Realms. "I wanted to give your people a gift."

The fae of Dell'Aria had been through a lot in the last several cycles, but nothing that had broken us. Nothing that had changed who we were. I wondered if that were the case with Dooley and I. Before I decided on this gift, I needed to know.

"Dooley." I took his hands and asked him the question. "Do you want to go back Earthside?"

His chocolate-brown eyes sparkled, his gaze weightless. His decision was made. I tried to ease the pain in my heart by telling myself he was alive, and that was all that mattered.

"It's your chance to get your life back. The life you were supposed to have." I ran my hand down his chest and traced the lines of muscle, the scars that etched his pain and marked his courage. Unable to stop myself from touching him one last time. In order to live here in the Realms, he would always have to be dependent on me. Without being half-fae or having any magic, he would be trapped. This was his one way out. He could be normal for the first time in his life.

"I have no intention of ever living a normal life, Valora."

Tears poured from my eyes. It was what I was hoping he would want, but dared not let myself truly desire. The Realms were his home, and I would do whatever in my power to keep him by my side, where he belonged.

"Then I wish for my friends, Mane and Kit, to live the life they have always wanted, as humans, Earthside."

"No selkie, no demon or elf. Normal. It's what I've always wanted," said Kit, bouncing up and down on her heels.

"We both have." Mane put his arm around Kit. "Of course, that doesn't mean we can't have visitors."

Varuna plucked a ball of golden light from the sky. "My gift to the both of you. Live your life with purpose and be happy."

As I observed the pulsating glow, a wonderful radiance flowed through me, my doubts and fears replaced with a tranquil stillness, a peace I wanted everyone to share. A great weight had been lifted from me.

The light disappeared, and I took a deep breath of shock. Mane caught me about the waist and helped keep me on my feet. "Dooley will probably crave you on the horizontal soon, but try and stay upright, queenie."

Mane could always make me smile. "You haven't changed a bit."

"Actually, I've changed a lot." I stared into his eyes, and the minute I did, I could tell the transformation had already been made. He was human, and so was Kit. "We are who we were supposed to be."

Varuna turned to leave, and as she did, she waved her arm and a portal opened before Kit and Mane.

"This is our door. I expect you two to visit soon." We exchanged embraces as they both stepped through the portal and it closed behind them.

"What do you say we tell Aric the good news?" said Dooley.

"Should we use the mirror? Maybe we can reach him and Calliope before the wedding begins."

"How about we go in person instead?" Dooley clasped my arm, and we dashed through the streets toward the airship docks. Quickly our ship ascended, and I waved goodbye to Orris down on the ground. Whatever happened from here on out, Dooley and I would be doing it side by side.

"Sounds like a great idea." We flew off up higher, and I let the wind catch my wings. Out over the skies. To anywhere and nowhere in particular. Black and white. Yin and yang. King and queen. Lovers for life. Fae Protectors.

Thank you for reading *Fae Warrior*.

If you enjoyed *Fae Warrior*, please consider helping others to enjoy this book as well.

- **Recommend it.** Please help other readers find this book by recommending it to friends, readers groups, and discussion boards.

- **Review it.** Please tell other readers why you liked this book by reviewing it at one of the following websites: Amazon, Barnes and Noble, or Goodreads.

ALSO AVAILABLE FROM NICOLETTE REED:

FAE HUNTER (*The Soulstealer Trilogy, Book #1*)

Valora Delos is a Hunter, charged with tracking the treacherous Soulstealers and bringing them to justice. Unlike the other fae of her kind, Valora was born with stunted wings that render her flightless, driving her to prove herself in the eyes of King Aric, with whom she has been infatuated since she first set eyes on him as a young prince.

She descends to Earth and finds herself trapped in suburban Seattle after the portal to her world closes. With the help of a sexy half-fae named Dooley, Valora must find her way back to save Dell'Aria. Dooley uses his own brand of magic to help Valora discover memories buried deep within her, which produce more questions than answers-questions about her growing attraction to Dooley and her devotion to her King. Uncovering who the Soulstealers are and who is behind the destruction of Dell'Aria brings Valora a truth she may not be able to handle.

MANE ATTRACTION
(A Soulstealer Novella, Book #1.5)

Being a demon trapped in an elf's body seemed a prison at first, but Mane has gotten used to his new home in the Riparian forest amongst the elves. When the waters of Lake Mavrovo start to run red it seems a sure sign that the demon king that cast him out may rise again. In order to investigate he will need to navigate the dominion of the selkie, and they aren't known for playing nice.

Going from an apartment in the suburbs of Seattle to living in a castle at the bottom of a lake in the Realms was one change that Kit had to get used to, being half-selkie was another. Now she has to get used to the changes she undergoes after the selkie sleep, one that involves bloodlust and lust of a whole different kind. A problem she is hoping Mane will help her with.

FAE GUARDIAN
(The Soulstealer Trilogy, Book #2)

Dealing with wedding day woes, naked elven rituals, a best friend with a biting problem, dragon battles, and a war brewing between the selkie and the fae are only the beginning for Valora, the Fae Guardian.

Valora needs to get Aric out of her mind if she's going to live happily ever after with Dooley. But nothing is ever easy with magic. Tying herself and Dooley to Aric becomes a matter of life and death, not just for them but for all of the Realms and even those beyond the portals to Earth.

But can Valora handle the affections of two half-fae brothers? She has to if she wants to save the Realms — a world filled with cloud cities, volcanic mountains mined by dwarves, deserts inhabited by dragons, and lakes teaming with ferocious selkie. And getting the two of them to get along may be her biggest battle yet.

MANE CHANCE
(A Soulstealer Novella, Book #2.5)

Mane, a demon trapped in an elf's body, has never been one to wait for the action to come to him. Sitting in the cloud city of Dell'Aria while he watches the red waters of Lake Mavrovo churn and boil is enough to get him moving. His old boss, the Demon King Ravanna, is on his way to the Realms and he may be the only one who can stop him.

Kit's selkie mother has done her best to ruin her life, but Kit's human side fears for her safety in Mavrovo. Her and Mane are the only two who can venture through the infected land unharmed. Unfortunately, they probably won't get too much alone time.

ABOUT THE AUTHOR

Photo by Phil Holden

Nicolette is a mother, wife, paralegal, writer, knitter, traveler, violinist and anything else she can get her hands on. She turned to writing stories at an early age, when filling out Mad Libs just wasn't enough.

She enjoys watching dark comedies, warped fairytales, and cheesy 80s comedies. Her interest in music spans from George Winston to Thrill Kill Cult to Bel Canto and U2. She loves to travel, and plans to do more as her son grows older. In her younger days she loved to go out dancing, and you may still, on occasion find her shaking her booty during 80s or goth rock nights at the few clubs they still exist at. She is constantly picking up new hobbies and interests. She knits socks, grows mini cucumbers in her garden, and played the violin for 5 years. She has a pug dog with a nervous temperament and speaks a little Spanish. She's eclectic.

Please come visit Nicolette Reed at: www.nicolettereed.com